The Songbird
of Sovereign

The Songbird of Sovereign

A NOVEL BY Jennifer Wixson

BOOK 3 IN
THE SOVEREIGN SERIES

For more information contact:
whitewavepublishing@gmail.com
or visit *www.TheSovereignSeries.com*

10 9 8 7 6 5 4 3 2 1

ISBN 978-0-9636689-9-8

eBook ISBN 978-0-9636689-4-3

THE SOVEREIGN SERIES

TRADE MARK

I went to Heaven—'Twas a small Town—Emily Dickinson

Published by

White Wave™

For more information on *The Sovereign Series* see p. 269
and visit our website *www.TheSovereignSeries.com*

*This book is dedicated to Elizabeth "Bess" Mae Klain
and to teachers everywhere
who inspire us.*

ACKNOWLEDGEMENTS

This is a book that was not meant to be. *The Sovereign Series* as I originally conceived it encompassed three novels—*Hens & Chickens*, *Peas, Beans & Corn* and *The Minister's Daughter*—however, after the publication of the first book some persistent fans begged me to add a story about their favorite character, Miss Hastings. When one doesn't have many fans, one listens to each of them. Hence *The Songbird of Sovereign* was born. So my initial thanks must go to those who encouraged me to stretch my literary limits and include this book about Miss Hastings.

I'd like to bestow my heartfelt gratitude upon my editorial team: my step-mother Marilyn Wixson, my lovely niece Laurel "Porcupine Head" McFarland, my Twitter friend @hobnob Rebecca Siegel, my Paris Hill compatriot "Aunt" Wini Mott, and my husband Stan the Cranberry Man. I'd also like to thank my Advance Readers for their kind and gracious words: Michelle Mogilevsky Harrison, Adeline Wixson, Carolyn Millar, Dorothy Fitzpatrick, Carrol Wixson Patterson, Carol Wong, Tanji Samson, Sue Simoneau, and Lucinda Hathaway. I'd like to recognize the valuable efforts of my creative design team from *Peter Harris Creative*, Peter Harris and Greg Elizondo. I want to thank Joyce Wixson Knight for her memories of the Central Maine Sanatorium and *The Maine Memory Network—Maine History Online* for their important information about the treatment of TB in Maine. Much of the historical information on World War II and Charles Lindbergh's fall from grace comes from the wonderful book, *The Borrowed Years*, by Richard M. Ketchum.

I'm very blessed to have been born into a family that encouraged and supported my writing career, notably my late grandmothers Hope Wixson and Winona Palmer, and my parents Rowena Palmer and Eldwin Wixson. Thanks Mom and Dad!

Kudos to Robert Conant for hooking me up with the family of Bess Klain (see, *The Inspiration Behind The Songbird of Sovereign*, p. 257) and special thanks to Joyce Klain Wilson for sharing her memories of her aunt (see, *A Niece Remembers*, p. 261) as well as the beautiful photograph of fifteen-year-old Bess that graces our cover. It's been said that a picture is worth a thousand words; however, in this case I think the picture is worth about eighty-seven thousand!

Finally, I hope you all enjoy reading *The Songbird of Sovereign* as much as I enjoyed writing it!

Jennifer Wixson
May 5, 2014
Troy, Maine

Gather ye rosebuds while ye may.

TABLE OF CONTENTS

CHAPTER I

DROUGHT

AUGUST 1941

Addie Russell steadied the hand-carved bread bowl against her ample breasts and deliberately tilted the wooden porringer until the risen dough rolled out onto her floured breadboard, filling the century-old farm kitchen with the sour scent of yeast. She set the bowl down on the counter and flipped the buxom dough over once or twice, sending a white cloud of flour up into the air. Despite the painful inflammation of arthritis in her fifty-five-year-old hands, the Maine grandmother dexterously tossed more dry flour into the mix and vigorously kneaded the dough until she was satisfied with its integrity. She pulled the elastic dough apart into five sections, rolling them into individual loaves, which she plopped into waiting buttered baking dishes. Addie set the tin pans onto the kitchen table in a warm slice of sunshine, lining them up like a small flotilla of ships at anchor awaiting further instructions from the Admiralty. She covered the bread with a kitchen towel and glanced at the clock, noting the time. One hour. She had one hour to make her morning call and return in time to bake the bread before the five little ships burst their brickles.

Addie stepped briskly to the black soapstone sink and washed the residual dough from her hands. She slipped on her watch and twisted her rings back over the knuckle of her swollen ring finger, and then untied her large, rose-figured apron with the big front pockets, pulling it carefully over her head so as not to mess up her short gray curls. She hung the apron back on its hook next to the door to the shed, brushed some flour from her printed cotton dress, and tucked a lace-edged handkerchief embroidered with her initials – *ALR* – into her matching

1

belt. She picked up her clutch purse from the oilcloth-covered table, retrieved her lipstick, and used Pappy's round shaving mirror next to the sink to apply a ceremonial coat of red. She daubed some lipstick off with a tissue, snapped the purse shut, and glanced back at the clock. Fifty-seven minutes.

The day was as dry as a paper birch, the fifty-second day without rain that summer of 1941. This was the longest drought since the proud but penniless Adelaide Libby had taken command of the old Russell homestead upon her marriage in 1904 to George "Pappy" Russell, one of the scions of the rural farming community of Sovereign, Maine. She exited the sprawling white farmhouse via the attached shed, and glanced around for her husband of thirty-seven years. As usual, there was no sign of Pappy or their hired hand Bud Suomela, a good-natured, round-faced Finn who had appeared like a stray cat on their doorstep in 1930 and who had been with them ever since helping with the egg business, which Addie had originated in 1923 to save the family farm. At ten o'clock in the morning, it was too early for "the boys" to be out drinking whiskey behind the barn. But Addie knew she didn't have time to seek out the elusive duo and explain where she was going, so she merely climbed into the old Ford and roared the pickup to life.

At the sound of the truck's engine, Pappy, fifty-seven, tall but slightly stooped, wearing the trademark fedora in which he presented himself year-round, ambled out from the back door to the hen pen. "Where ya agoin', Ma?" he called. His eyes widened slightly as he approached the vehicle and noted the bold strokes of lipstick and the familiar print of her Sunday dress. He stopped next to the driver's side, hesitated, and stuffed his hands into his pants pockets.

"I'm calling on Helen," she replied, in her matter-of-fact tone of voice. She grasped the stick shift with her bare right hand, pushed in the clutch and put the truck in reverse. She waited for his rejoinder, however, before releasing the clutch. The dark green pickup trembled in anticipation, making her breasts jiggle despite the confining squeeze of her bustier girdle.

Pappy lifted his stained and pinched fedora and scratched his balding white head. He liked to think that the brown felt fedora gentrified him, distinguishing him from all the other run-o-the-mill Maine farmers in their matching workpants, white tee-shirts, and suspenders. "Cain'tcha walk up, Ma? Bud and me is thinkin' o' goin' fer a load o' sawdust."

"I've got my dress pumps on. This is a formal call." She glanced down at her wristwatch. "I'll be back in fifty-five minutes. You could winch that hay up into the upper hay mow while you're waiting for the truck."

"Wal, you know …" But Addie had already released the clutch and was backing out of the dirt driveway, past the row of sentinel maples, before Pappy could finish his excuse.

The two families – the Hastings and the Russells – were good friends, as well as neighbors. The Hastings' two story cottage was situated a scant half-mile above the old Russell homestead on the Russell Hill Road. Typically when calling on Helen, Addie stepped up to the other house on foot. Today, however, wasn't a social visit or an egg delivery but a call of condolence. Country ways in Sovereign, Maine dictated that Addie should arrive unruffled, without perspiration, showing the proper consciousness of the situation.

The old Ford pickup with the high wooden sides chuffed up the hill. While she drove, Addie surveyed the short, sickly-looking grass in the fields on both sides of the road. Pappy and Bud had been able to take the first cut of hay in June per usual, but the lack of rain since then rendered a second cut improbable and a third cut impossible. Addie was already worried about the price of winter grain and corn for her laying hens and began to calculate in her mind how much she might have to go up on her egg prices if the drought continued. Helen's husband Andy was the supervisor of the local cornshop, Westcott's Canning Factory, and she knew that Helen also prayed daily for rain, albeit to a different God. "I'm sure the Good Lord doesn't care one whit which Testament we abide by," Addie said, aloud.

But the drought wasn't the reason for Addie's visit today. She glanced at her watch as the Hastings' two-story cottage hove into view. Fifty-three minutes.

The well-kept yellow cottage was an awkward affair, looking as though two very different houses had grappled for the same foundation, and, neither having won, had grudgingly agreed to share the same spot. The original house was built before the Hastings' arrival in Sovereign in 1929, and the addition, a music studio, had been added in the thirties by Anton "Andy" Hastings as a place for his wife to give piano and voice lessons. Helen Hastings had been a classically-trained pianist in Russia, from which country she and her husband had fled just before the Soviets had taken control of Petrograd in the October

Revolution of 1917. The émigrés had knocked about the eastern seaboard of the United States for a decade looking for work until Andy, an engineer in the Old Country, had finally secured a permanent job as supervisor of Sovereign's corn canning factory. The rural nature of her new home had precluded Helen from furthering her musical career, but rather than give up her art, she had chosen to share her gifts with the local community. Their only child, sixteen-year-old Jana Hastings, was also musically-inclined, and Addie's heart now swelled as she thought proudly of the national attention little Jana had brought to the farming community of Sovereign through her unparalleled voice. For the past five years Jana had been performing on the stages of New York, chaperoned by an old maid aunt, appearing nightly as *The Songbird of Sovereign*. However, a terrible illness, tuberculosis, had recently clipped Jana's wings, and this was the reason for Addie's visit.

"Adelaide! How good of you to call," said Helen Hastings graciously, receiving her visitor at the rarely-used front door as though it was the most natural thing in the world. In point of fact, Addie had never entered the Hastings' home that way. "Do come in." Helen spoke perfect English, with a slight Russian accent. She was a gracefully tall brunette, with shapely curves and womanly ways. Today Helen was wearing a gray silk dress that clung elegantly to her hips. Her cascading hair, still dark and lustrous, was swept up into a loose bun that perfectly framed the smooth alabaster skin of her face. Although she was nearer fifty than forty, Helen Hastings still exuded feminine fecundity, turning men's heads wherever she went. Today, she looked as though she had stepped out of the pages of *Life* magazine, although her fathomless dark eyes appeared tired and haunted.

"I came as soon as I heard the news," said Addie, reaching out and squeezing her friend's hand reassuringly.

The pressure was gratefully returned. "Thank you, dahrrrling!" Helen moved aside so that Addie could enter.

Addie stepped over the polished wooden stoop into the Hastings' well-appointed front hall and was greeted by a rush of cool air. The thick green shades were two-thirds drawn, keeping out the heat of the morning sun and yet allowing a mellow light to filter throughout the house. The scent of roses filled the formal hallway. Helen's music studio was to the left, and Addie glanced into that room and saw that the top of her friend's grand piano was closed.

Helen led her instead to the wainscoted and papered parlor, a re-
fined and comfortable sitting room that was as unlike most stiff New
England parlors as it could be, the use of that room in Maine being
reserved mostly for the laying out of the dead. By contrast, Helen's parlor was graceful and beautiful: two vivid Russian oil paintings decorated
the walls, colorful Asiatic lilies were grouped casually together in a cut-
glass vase, and a variety of enticing books beckoned from the shelves. A
French novel was lying open on a mahogany candle stand next to Helen's
rocking chair, and Addie knew that the other woman had been reading,
probably trying to distract herself.

The two ladies took opposing seats – Helen on the davenport sofa and
Addie in a matching upholstered wingback – and smoothed their skirts.
Helen Hastings was elegant, educated, and descended from an aristocratic
Russian line, the antithesis of her plebian American neighbor. Yet she and
Addie were good friends. They were seven years apart in age (Addie was
the elder) and worlds apart in experience, but were drawn together by the
mutual concerns of home, husbands, community, and children.

"How is she?" Addie inquired, settling back into the chair.

Tears filled Helen's eyes, and she searched in vain through the deco-
rative front pocket of her silk dress for a handkerchief. Addie retrieved
her own handkerchief from her belt, and held it out to Helen. It was one
of Addie's good handkerchiefs, yet even with the elegant purple embroi-
dery of her initials the white cotton hankie looked unsophisticated in
Helen's beautiful hands.

Helen daubed her eyes. "We took her to the sanatorium first thing
this morning."

"Oh, my dear! Is it as bad as that?"

Helen twisted the handkerchief between her long pianist fingers.
"The doctor at Windmere says she'll need six months for the lesion
in her right lung to heal. Her left lung is not yet affected. We are fortunate, hmm?"

"Why, six months will pass before you know it!"

"Her advance bookings will necessarily be cancelled," Helen continued. "Aunt Minnie, Andy's sister, will take care of that before she returns
home to Providence. Bless her!"

"You've left Jana alone at Windmere?" The question was out of
Addie's mouth before she could stop herself. Instantly, she regretted the
implied accusation.

For a moment, Helen's perfect posture sagged. "We had no choice. I wanted to bring her home with us, but they wouldn't let me."

"How stupid of me, my dear. I forgot she's contagious and must be segregated from the general population. Do forgive me. Windmere has an excellent reputation! I've heard nothing but good about it."

Helen's face brightened at the endorsement. "It does seem to be an exceptional facility, Adelaide. And such a beautiful old mansion! The supervisor, Mrs. Baker, showed us all around. Dr. Ketchum has his office and X-ray in the house, and there is a game room, a library, and two sleeping porches, one for the girls and one for the boys. They have plenty of books and games for the children, too."

"There, you see? What could be better!"

"Still, it's going to be a very difficult transition for our poor dahrrrling. Jana has always had her own way with everyone. Perhaps we've … overindulged her."

This was so true that Addie could not refute it. She recalled the time when Helen had asked her to give then ten-year-old Jana a cooking lesson. (The Hastings' family kept a housekeeper and Helen herself had never learned the culinary arts.) Little Jana had boldly rebelled. "I don't want to cook, and you can't make me!" she declared to Addie, right in Addie's kitchen. Had that been one of her own children Addie would have taken the child by the arm, and shown her that in fact she could make her. However, such strong-armed tactics couldn't be used on a friend's daughter. So Addie had simply bitten her tongue, and sent Jana home with a note saying that perhaps it was best for all involved if Jana stuck to her music. Helen had taken the hint, and the two women had mutually allowed the subject to drop. Yes, the child was spoiled, certainly nothing like Addie's three sons. But Addie knew that nobody was perfect, and she had come to love Jana despite her faults, and to appreciate the girl's musical gifts.

"You see, we tried—unsuccessfully—for children for so many years before Jana came along! After poor Alexei's death, we had given up hope. Eight years later, when we found I was with child again, it was like a gift from God. Small wonder we've spoiled her."

"And she has been a gift," Addie assured her friend. "For all of us. We're so proud of her in Sovereign! Don't you worry, Helen—Jana will be right as a trivet in no time."

"Ah, le temps nous dira! Time will tell. Her father thinks she hasn't fully grasped the gravity of her situation. Andy and I are familiar with tuberculosis; his uncle died of consumption and so did my older sister, Mariya. You remind me of Mariya sometimes, Adelaide."

"Your sister! I had no idea."

"It was terribly difficult watching Mariya fail. By contrast, Jana has hardly been ill a day in her life, except for the usual chicken pox and measles." A dark cloud passed over Helen's brow. "Perhaps we've done great wrong in exposing the child to the evils of the world at such a young age. When I think of all those public performances ... all those germs! I shudder to think what we have done to her. It was just that she loved to sing, and she has such a beautiful voice ..."

"My dear, I hate to see you waste a moment's thought on the choices you made in the past. You must marshal your thoughts and energies for choices you will need to make now and in the future."

"You're so practical, Adelaide; just like Mariya was. I wish I were more like you!"

Addie glanced at the smooth hands of her cultured friend—and then down at her own callused and knobby claws—and smiled. "And I wish I was more like you. But you know what they say about wishes: 'If wishes were horses then beggars would ride.'"

Helen laughed. To her friend's ears it was a beautiful, musical sound. "So practical and so cheerful! How do you do it?"

"I do it—and you do it—because we both know it needs to get done. There's no sense sticking our heads in the sand. Pappy says that's just asking to get whacked in the behind. Now, what can I do to help? Sheets?"

"Windmere provides the linens. They are washed once a week in bleach water."

"How awful! But necessary, I suppose. Eggs? Do they have enough eggs? We must keep her weight up; it's such a problem with consumption."

Helen nodded in agreement. "The children are weighed once a week, in order to make sure they are not failing. I'm sure your eggs are best, Adelaide, but at Windmere they have their own hens. Mrs. Baker remarked that they pride themselves on providing the children with fresh eggs and plenty of cream and butter. Those children who are well enough even help with some of the farm chores. Andy was especially glad to hear that; you know how our dahrrrling loves chickens."

Addie recollected only that Jana loved to chase her prize laying hens. Once again she held her tongue.

"They also grow their own vegetables and have their own milk cows."

"Well, well; but I'm sure they can't make lemon butter cookies as good as mine. When do you go again, Helen?"

"Next Saturday. Visiting hours at Windmere are from one o'clock to three o'clock every Saturday afternoon."

"Only two hours a week?"

"Sadly, yes. And only two visitors per child. They do not want to agitate the children, and I'm sure they're right about that. But it does place such a burden on the families!"

"I should think so."

"I shouldn't complain; we're very fortunate. We'll have the opportunity of seeing Jana more often than when she was in New York. Mrs. Baker informed us that many of the other parents live outside the state and can't afford to visit more than once or twice a year. I'm so grateful that Windmere is only twenty-five miles from Sovereign."

Addie glanced around the room—not a clock in sight. She looked at her watch. Fifteen minutes. "I'll bake a batch of my lemon butter cookies Friday night. I know how much Jana likes them. We don't want her to think that we've forgotten all about our little *Songbird of Sovereign*."

Helen draped Addie's handkerchief across the curved arm of the davenport sofa, and unconsciously attempted to smooth out the wrinkles. "I'm afraid we mustn't ... we mustn't encourage that anymore. We don't want to get Jana's hopes up." Her index finger absently traced Addie's embroidered initials.

"What do you mean?"

"The doctors say my poor dahrrrling will never sing again!"

"I'm so sorry to hear that, my dear. That's such a loss—for all of us."

Unable to contain herself any longer, Helen rose up from the sofa and began pacing the floor. "Oh, Adelaide! Ever since we received the wire from Aunt Minnie the day before yesterday—telling us that Jana had coughed up blood—I've been thinking the most horrible thoughts. What if she never recovers? What if my baby dies?" She buried her face in her hands and burst into tears.

Addie rose up and gathered the other woman to her motherly breast. "There, there," she comforted Helen. "This too shall pass, my dear. You'll see—little Jana will outlive all of us!"

CHAPTER 2

THE SUMMER IT WAS HARD TO MAKE DRY HAY

AUGUST 2013

For most of us, happiness is ever in the future—never reached but always hoped for. For some rare few, however, happiness is absolutely achieved in the past, transcending time like a triolet. Miss Jan Hastings, eighty-eight, beloved member of our rural farming community of Sovereign, Maine (population 1,048) was as a rare rose, ever blooming, and it was of this that I was thinking—or rather, the cause of this—as I motored home to Sovereign after a six-week summer sabbatical.

The church of which I am the pastor, the Sovereign Union Church, doesn't hold services in July and August, and therefore I had lately been travelling throughout the state, working on a cherished writing project, turning my Master's thesis on Maine's small churches into a book. After such an extended absence, I was now feeling like one of Leland Gorse's draft horses headed toward the barn, anxious to get home, and even more anxious to reconnect with my little flock, especially Miss Hastings.

Miss Hastings' health had taken a turn for the worse just before I left town, and I was now not only concerned with her wellbeing, but also worried that a story I had always wondered about might be left untold. Since I had arrived in Sovereign fifteen years ago, I'd marveled at the music teacher's ability to inspire others, especially children. Whence was the source of her Fountain of Youth? Where was that wellspring of unconditional love to which the good-hearted spinster returned again and again, replenishing her ageing spirit as the decades rushed past?

Selfishly, I was afraid that Miss Hastings, now approaching her tenth decade, might take this sacred mystery with her to the grave. Until now, my duties as pastor hadn't included detective work. But there's a first time for everything, I rationalized.

The freshest news in rural Maine is served up hot at the local watering hole, and so when I pulled into town I went directly to Gilpin's General Store. I noted with satisfaction that the parking lot was filled with the usual collection of rusty pickups. I had strategically planned my return to town around morning coffee break in Sovereign, the time of day when the Old Farts—those scions of the community generally imbued with the town's wit, wisdom, and gossip—could be found on the facing benches at the front of the century-old mercantile shop, swilling down coffee and gobbling up some of Maude Gilpin's homemade donuts.

I exited the car, feeling the moist warm breath of August against my face. It was already 78° and it was only ten o'clock. I caught a whiff of fresh cut grass, and heard the distinctive clickety-clack of a tedder's steel fingers hard at work turning hay. When an old-fashioned tedder is working properly it sounds like a bevy of old maid aunts furiously knitting on fat metal needles. No doubt Maynard Nutter, the farmer across the road, was trying to make up for lost time. The summer of 2013 would go down in the history books as being the summer it was hard to make dry hay. It takes at least four consecutive days without rain to make up dry hay, and to date all summer long we had only enjoyed two and a half dry days rubbed up against each other.

"Good to see ya, Minister!" bellowed Leland Gorse, as I pushed through the double glass doors into Gilpin's General Store. Sure enough, the men were all gathered at the front benches. I was met by the scent of peppermint intermingled with Murphy Oil Soap. "Hot enough to roast a goose, ain't it?" Leland continued, grinning. A local character now pushing eighty, Leland was Sovereign's firewood purveyor and raconteur extraordinaire. He was also the father of my good friend Trudy, whose nuptials I had performed earlier in the year. Trudy Gorse MacDonald was known far and wide throughout Maine for her fine organic butter, hand-made in small batches at her family's farm, Scotch Broom Acres.

"Maggie! We weren't expecting you just yet," said Ryan MacDonald, Trudy's handsome dark-haired husband. He rose up and gave me a kiss.

Formerly a big city lawyer, Ryan was now our town attorney, having traded in his Canali suits for L.L. Bean khaki shorts, a tee-shirt and barn boots.

"Thought you had 'nother couple of weeks off," added John Woods, the laconic and lanky First Selectman of Sovereign. Woods grouped his legs together and slid over on the wooden bench, allowing me space to sit down.

I couldn't help it—my eyes instinctively searched out another empty space, the seat directly across from John Woods, the seat next to Leland, where Clyde Crosby had always used to sit. Clyde's ninety-three-year-old heart had finally given out in June and one of the last sad duties I had performed in my professional capacity before I left town was officiating at Clyde's funeral service. Clyde – big-hearted and floppy-eared – had been on the benches longer than any of the rest of the Old Farts, and therefore his seat was left open in an unspoken reminder that, despite his physical absence, he was still present in spirit.

There was an awkward pause. The grief was palpable. Someone coughed, respectfully.

"It was a hard go," I said, seriously. I settled my ample frame down onto the cushioned bench next to John Woods and rearranged my rumpled cotton shorts. Immediately, the men's faces around me became even more graven.

"Thet bad, eh?" said Asa Palmer, the Road Commissioner, who occasionally drove his Cat-12 grader down to the general store when his truck wouldn't start. He nodded knowingly, as though he understood all about it.

"Yep, I couldn't find a damned decent donut anyplace else in the state!" I declared with a wink.

The men guffawed, and slapped their thighs. Ryan took the hint, and courteously passed me the plate of Maude's lard-laden donuts. After careful consideration, I selected a homemade chocolate donut rolled in fresh sugar.

"Take two, Minister; they're cheap," said Leland, whose hand hovered nearby as he waited to snatch what was probably a third donut for himself.

Ralph Gilpin, the seventy-seven-year-old proprietor of the store, sidled up to us, his sneakers squeaking on the heavily varnished wood floor. "Two sugars, right?" he asked, carefully holding out a cup of coffee. "'Tain't too hot for coffee, is it?"

"Never!" I said, taking the cup from his hands. I breathed in deeply, inhaling the delicious scent of freshly-ground, freshly-brewed coffee. "Ah, it's good to be home!"

Immediately, the men began talking at me all at once, like kids at a playground. "Didja hear about my new sawmill?" "Cain't hardly git the hay in!" "We had another calf at the farm, Maggie, another heifer."

I let them jabber for a minute or two, and then stuffed the balance of the donut in my mouth, washing it down with a swig of coffee. "For goodness sake, not all at once," I said, brushing a few crumbs of chocolate sugar off my lap. "Just tell me—what's the most important thing that's happened in Sovereign since I've been gone?"

Leland scratched his head. Ryan looked down at the floor. Finally, John Woods spoke up. "Miss Hastings has taken a turn for the worse," he announced. "Probably not what you were hopin' to hear, though."

The venerable selectman was correct. I'd been worried how Clyde Crosby's death would affect the town's beloved former music teacher. Last year, just after Thanksgiving, Miss Hastings' girlhood friend Mabel "Ma Jean" Edwards had unexpectedly passed away. Now, Clyde Crosby, with whom she used to play in the old corn canning factory while their respective parents worked—Clyde's mother operating the desilker and Miss Hastings' father overseeing the cornshop as supervisor—had also gone over the waterfall. I was afraid that even Miss Hastings' legendary optimistic spirit wouldn't be enough to outweigh the gross accumulation of her losses. And it appears that I was right; the bloom was beginning to fade from the rose. "How bad is she?" I asked, anxiously.

"Wal, you know, she ain't up to snuff but I seen a lot worse," offered the good-natured Wendell Russell, retired military and former chicken farmer. One of the things I admired most about Wendell was his optimism. Wendell said he inherited this positive outlook from his grandmother, Addie Russell.

"She's pale as dishwater, though," Leland added.

Ryan nodded. "I don't think she's been out of the house since you left, Maggie."

"Now, now, don't go scarin' her, boys," said John Woods. "Likely Maggie'll go visit Miss Hastings in short order and see for herself."

As usual, the sage selectman had hit the nail on the head. "I think I will just stop in and say 'hello'," I said, rising up. "Thanks for the welcome home." I started to leave, but stopped before I had gone two steps.

"By the way, any baby news to report?" I asked. Six sets of eyes suddenly turned toward Ryan.

The newlywed looked extremely self-conscious. "Trudy's due in late February," he allowed, beginning to puff up like a Bantam rooster. "But we haven't told anyone yet. Who told you?"

"You did," I said. "Just now."

Leland let out a choked cry, and clasped his calloused paws together. "By Gawd, I'm gonna be a Grandpa. Finally!"

As I left, I heard good-natured ribbing and back-slapping all around. I recalled the day nearly two years earlier when Ryan MacDonald had first come among us. I was grateful that God had given us this gift, apparently a gift that was going to keep on giving!

I had two stops to make before I visited Miss Hastings. The first was to check my email at the Sovereign Union Church, a traditional white New England church holding down the corner of Route 9 and the Russell Hill Road, where my office was located. I pulled up the hordes of messages onto the large outdated computer screen, and quickly scrolled down through the subject lines. Most of the messages were trash, which I deleted, but some were from friends and fellow classmates at Bangor Theological Seminary, and these I read. I was particularly grateful for these few old friends from seminary. Most of my classmates had shunned me when they discovered that I was pregnant with Nellie; however, a little group had stood by me. Probably not coincidentally these friends had gone into small church ministry, which was my own calling.

The remainder of my emails was from the local medical clinic, including several from Doctor Bart, our small town doctor and the son of one of my best friends, Jane Metcalf Lawson, from Albion. I hesitated, and then filed them away without reading them. There would be time enough for that later on.

My next stop was the old Russell homestead, Wendell Russell's family farm. If Gilpin's General Store was the gossip center of town, the old Russell homestead was the heart of Sovereign. Wendell's pretty new wife, Rebecca, had revived the family's role in the community, breathing new life into the old place and bringing the family forward once again. I hoped and expected she'd be at home to receive me, since this was Monday, and Ma Jean's Restaurant (which Rebecca and Maude Gilpin had operated since Ma Jean's untimely death last year) was closed on Mondays. Wendell had spent his youth here, helping "Grammie Addie" raise four hundred Rhode Island Red laying hens. "'Twas quite a real business, you know," Wendell drawled proudly, when speaking of his grandmother's egg operation. "'Twarn't no pin money thing."

When I pulled into the dirt driveway of the sprawling old white New England farmhouse, I discovered a shiny red late-model sedan with Massachusetts plates ahead of me in the dooryard. I debated whether or not I should intrude upon Rebecca and her company, but my debate was short-lived. I knew Rebecca wouldn't mind the interruption. I switched off my car's engine, and headed for the shed.

Sometimes when I enter the old place I almost expect to walk in on Grammie Addie bustling about the kitchen, wearing her large, rose-figured apron with the big front pockets. I'd heard so much about Addie over the years: her chickens, her business acumen, the deft way she handled both her husband and her hired hand, both of whom seemed to depend upon her for every decision. She was the lynchpin of Sovereign through the war years, too. I always thought if I could go back in time, I'd go back to the 1940s when the old Russell homestead was in its heyday, and Addie was in her prime...

CHAPTER 3

FEARS OF WAR

AUGUST 1941

Addie returned from her condolence call on Helen to discover that Fred Nutter, a local farmer and friend, had visited while she was out. She tracked Pappy and Bud to the sweet-smelling but dusty barn, where she found them regurgitating Nutter's news. As directed, the duo had been winching square bales from the first floor of the barn up to the top hay mow with the harpoon fork hay trolley, but had taken the opportunity offered by Nutter's appearance to abandon their work. As she stepped carefully inside the cool temple of the post-and-beam barn, Addie's eyes adjusted slowly to the dim light. She heard the squawking and fluttering of her laying hens from the attached hen pen, and saw the men sitting on a pile of bales in the middle of the wide floor.

"Fred's been here, Ma," Pappy said, as she approached. He lifted his hat and wiped the sweat from his brow with his forearm. Perhaps he wanted to make it appear as though he and Bud had just sat down. "His boy Errol's gone and joined the Navy." He replaced the fedora, and reached for a pitchfork to hoist himself up. "Fred says Maynard even wants to go; course, he's too young, jest thirteen."

This information was of such terrible significance that Addie temporarily forgot all about Helen and little Jana, as well as the hay and the small flotilla of ships awaiting their next command in the kitchen. An icy fear gripped her heart. She thought of her own three boys—Carroll, Wesley and George—aged twenty-two to thirty-five (George being the eldest). The prior year, in 1940, a peacetime conscription had been instated, requiring all men between the ages of twenty-one and forty-five to register for military service. The one-year term of service was selected by lottery, and—thank the Good Lord!—none of the Russell boys had yet been selected for service. At fifty-seven and forty-eight respectively, Pappy and Bud, of course, were too old to register. "Did Errol get called up?"

"Nope. He enlisted."

"Why? We're not at war."

"Fred says they been gearin' up, quiet like. Prepare yerself, Addie; war is comin'."

"Sartin as wintah," drawled Bud, spitting a long straw out from his near toothless mouth.

A swallow fluttered off its nest on a high beam above, and darted out the open aperture of the sliding barn doors, leaving a white calling card on Pappy's fedora on the way. Nonplussed, Pappy shook most of the bird turd off and replaced his hat on his head. "He says the army's been on maneuvers down south somewhere, Addie. They're playin' war games in the swamp. Fred's retired navy, Addie, so he knows all about it."

"I don't believe it," Addie stated flatly. "President Roosevelt promised we wouldn't get mixed up in any foreign wars. That's why we voted for him."

Pappy kicked a loose tuft of hay toward the cattle tie-up. His fealty to Roosevelt wasn't quite as strong as his wife's. Unbeknownst to her, he had voted for the Republican Presidential candidate, Wendell Willkie. Pappy believed that their three-term President, Franklin Roosevelt, was a warmonger at heart. "I'm jest tellin' ya what Fred says, is all."

Their tense conversation was interrupted by Charity, Pappy's favorite work horse, who, hearing the voice of her beloved master, stuck her head through the top of her stall's Dutch door. She snorted for his attention.

"Take 'er out, will ya, Bud?" Pappy directed the hired hand.

"Ayuh." Bud pushed himself up. He adjusted his red leather cap, and ambled across the hay-strewn barn floor toward the dappled white Percheron, liberating a black leather halter along the way. He slipped the halter over Charity's huge head. She stomped her front right foot, sounding a hollow thud of thanks to her master, who some said was the best horseman in Waldo County.

"But this isn't America's war," Addie protested. "This is a fight over Europe's boundaries."

Pappy shrugged. "Maybe. Maybe not. To the back pasture," he directed Bud. "There's still some clovah down there; but 'tain't 'nuff to hurt her." The horse whinnied and swished her ivory-colored tail at the happy thought of an afternoon in the clover.

He turned back to his wife. "Whaddaya think them ships is all fer, Ma," he continued, referring to the avalanche of new battleships that Congress and the President had commissioned in the prior few years. "They ain't jest fer looks."

"Why … we're leasing those to England," she replied. "Everybody knows that." Roosevelt, in selling to everyday Americans the idea of a lend-lease agreement between the U.S. and Great Britain, had utilized small-town imagery to explain the program. Addie herself had heard Roosevelt say on the radio that when your neighbor's house was on fire, you should lend him your garden hose, and this common sense platitude was something to which she could relate. The President had explained that the country was simply lending England some big hoses in the forms of ships, planes, and artillery. But Addie perfectly understood that the lend-lease program Roosevelt described didn't include her three boys.

"Wal, think thet if you like, Ma. What's fer dinner?"

Addie glanced down at her wristwatch. Two minutes. "Oh my heavens, my bread!" And she sprinted to the kitchen as fast as her dress pumps would allow, her grey curls bobbing.

Pappy watched her go. He rested the pitchfork back against the wall, and listened. He heard the distinctive thud of Charity's left rear hoof as she attempted to shake off a pesky horsefly, and knew that, as he had suspected, Bud was lingering in the cool shade of the north side of the barn. He joined his compatriot, running his hand affectionately over the still-strong back of his seventeen-year-old draft horse. Charity shuddered with pleasure.

"She doan believe it," suggested Bud, hand clutching the horse's halter.

"Thet's 'cause she don't want to believe it. We'll be at war afore the end of the year—you kin take thet to the bank."

"Gonna make 'er madder 'an a wet ket," Bud predicted. He spat over his shoulder.

"Jest don't go and remind Addie she voted fer Roosevelt," cautioned Pappy.

The hired hand's round face broke into a wide grin. "No way 'n hell I'd do thet, boss!"

"She don't know thet Roosevelt has extended the draft, neither. Them boys as get called up now has got to stay fer two years."

Bud whistled a long, sharp call. The juxtaposition of his remaining front teeth made him a particularly good whistler.

"And jest what do you think them Japs is up to?" Pappy continued, warming to his subject. "They're posturin' 'bout peace and reconciliation, but they warn't born yestiddy. Roosevelt had bettah watch his backsides, is all I kin say."

Bud nodded. He wasn't terribly interested in world affairs. While chatting, he had absent-mindedly relaxed his grip on the old Percheron. Charity swung her huge head around and stared at the two men as if to ask: "What's holding up the works?"

Pappy saw the impatient look in the horse's sentient black eyes, and translated it perfectly. "Bettah git goin', Bud, if ya want to git out to Charity's pasture and back in time fer dinner." The dappled gray horse shook her mane two or three times in agreement.

Bud reclaimed his grip on the halter. "C'mon ole gal," he said, patting her thick neck. "Let's see who gits there fust."

Back in the kitchen, Addie popped the five loaves of bread into the oven of her 1938 Westinghouse electric range and set the timer. She remembered only a few years ago when the Rural Electrification Project had brought electricity to the Russell Hill Road. Despite her very real fears about borrowing money, Pappy had taken out a mortgage on the place in order to install electricity in the house, shed, and barn. Addie, who remembered all too well the belt-tightening required during the first decade of the Depression, was willing to continue doing all the heavy lugging and lifting. But for once Pappy had put his foot down and she was glad he did. She was still amazed at how much easier their life had become with the advent of electricity. She no longer had to pump and carry water from the well to the chickens, nor trim and fill the oil lamps every morning, nor run the kitchen wood stove in summer, the heat from which forced them to seek the cool of the barn or cellar. "Cheapest hired hand I ever had," Addie said aloud, with satisfaction.

Once the bread was in the oven baking, she quickly changed out of her Sunday outfit, back into her everyday shift dress and shoes. Then she lifted her apron from its hook, pulled it over her head and went to work.

In rural Maine, the big meal of the day was served up at noontime. Tradition required meat, potatoes, vegetables, and plenty of fresh bread and butter served up hot at twelve o'clock, except on Sunday when it was set on the table at two o'clock, after Addie had returned from church. Every Saturday evening she planned her meals for the following week. Now, she had plenty of cold meat – leftovers from Sunday's roast – on hand to make up meals for the next two days. The day after that she'd roast two of her played out hens. While the potatoes were on the stovetop boiling, Addie slipped out to the garden to pick the last of the fresh peas. She had been watering a short row to keep them lingering despite the drought. It always seemed to her that when the peas were done she could feel the breath of fall on her cheek.

Addie's experienced hands quickly located the plump waxy pods hiding amongst the leathery, yellowing vines. While she picked, she thought about what she'd heard from her husband. Had she been wrong to place her trust in the President? Was Roosevelt going to send her boys overseas after all?

Addie's two brothers had served in the European War, which later became known as the Great War. They had gone overseas, and they had not returned. Her last recollection of the duo was of waving them goodbye from the front porch, when they had come to visit. She had been hanging out laundry when they arrived, with ten-month-old Wesley crawling around on the grass at her feet, giggling hysterically whenever he tipped over the laundry basket. Europe had swallowed up Charlie and Ralph, was it now going to take Wesley and his brothers, too?

Back in the kitchen, Addie drained the potatoes, and set them on the sideboard to cool. She drew two quarts of cold water from the sink's center faucet, the one that still brought the gravity-fed spring water directly from the hill up back. She stirred cider vinegar, brown sugar, molasses, and ground ginger into the water, mixing up old-time switchel, a favorite beverage in summer. She set the pitcher in the refrigerator to chill further.

Addie adeptly shelled and steamed the peas, singing one of the little ditties she sang often to help keep her spirits up:

"When all the world is dark and gray, keep on hoping!
When bad things sometimes come your way, no sense moping!" [1]

She put everything on the oak dining room table at noon sharp, just as the two men were pulling up their chairs. The shades were drawn on the south side to keep out the mid-day heat; however, Addie had released the east side shade, allowing some natural light to filter through the sheers.

"What's up at t'other place?" Pappy asked, filling his glass with switchel, releasing the refreshing aroma of the sweet 'n sour beverage. "Helen sick?"

"Jana has tuberculosis," Addie announced. She handed Bud, who was sitting on her right, the steaming bowl of buttered peas. The yellow chunk of butter was shrinking rapidly, coating the round green orbs with a shimmering jacket.

Pappy was parked in his oak armchair at the head of the table per usual, a stretch of six feet from Addie at the other end. "You don't say," he said. He picked up his fork, and helped himself to a hunk of cold meat from the white soapstone platter. He shook the meat off onto his plate, and turned to scout out the balance of his meal. "Hand me them peas, Bud."

"They took her to Windmere early this morning," Addie continued, lightly clutching the folded napkin in her lap. "They had to leave the poor girl by herself, in the special children's ward."

"Ain't thet the place they go to die?" Bud asked, masticating loudly. He reached for a hunk of bread, and slathered it with soft butter.

Addie gave him a sharp look. "What makes you say that?"

"Oh, I heared it somewheres. Windmere is fer the real sick chillens, and t'other places r' fer the chillens they thinks 'a'll pull through." At the time, there were three sanatoriums for the treatment of tuberculosis in Maine.

"Well, you wouldn't have Andy and Helen take Jana all the way to Hebron, would you?" Addie said, relieving the platter of a slice of meat. The Western Maine Sanatorium was situated in Hebron. "Windmere is only twenty-five miles away."

Bud shrugged. "'Tain't nuthin' to me," he said, smashing down his boiled potatoes. "She's a purty gal, though, 'n she sings powerful good. Cain't hardly believe sech a big voice comes from sech a leetle thing!"

Pappy chuckled. "She's got a powerful big temper to go with thet voice, too."

"Hush, Pappy. How can you say that?"

"I kin say it 'cause it's true."

Addie allowed herself a small serving of potatoes, and a spoonful of peas from the serving dish, which had come around the table again. "Well, if you haven't got anything nice to say, George Russell, you shouldn't say anything at all."

Bud snorted.

Addie turned to the hired hand. She could read him as perfectly as Pappy could read his horse. "Don't you be siding with him, either, Bud Suomela. Not if you know which side your bread is buttered on."

Bud looked contrite. "Oh, I surely do, ma'am. I surely do!"

CHAPTER 4

CATCHING UP

AUGUST 2013

A frequent visitor at the old Russell homestead, I entered the shed without knocking, rapping instead on the interior kitchen door. I heard an invitation to enter, and opened the door to discover Rebecca Russell, a pleasingly plump forty-something, sitting with a friend over half-empty teacups and a plate of hand-cut butter cookies. The other visitor, a well-dressed woman obviously from the city, seemed vaguely familiar. Rebecca's cheerful, eat-in kitchen was filled with the heart-warming scent of herbs, and I noted several bunches of fresh mint and thyme hanging from the ceiling to dry. The kitchen had an old black soapstone sink with the three nickel-plated faucets – including one that still brought water down from the spring up back – and was decorated with Rebecca's print curtains, photographs of her daughter Amber, and other household gods, one of which I knew was Grammie Addie's beloved cookbook, her "Bible," she had called it.

"Maggie!" Rebecca exclaimed, rising up from her accustomed seat at the head of the table. "I didn't know you were back in town."

"Don't get up—I had coffee down to the store." I pulled out the nearest antique pressed-back oak chair and joined them at the table.

"Do you remember Cora Batterswaith?" Rebecca reclaimed her seat and indicated her guest. "She's staying with us for a while."

Cora smiled an artificial smile, and bobbed her dark head. Her face was carefully made up, and her glossy red lipstick stood out like a stop light in Sovereign.

"I remember you from Lila's wedding," I replied. "You were Rebecca's boss at that insurance company in Boston, weren't you? Just think, if you hadn't fired her, we wouldn't be sitting here today!" (The story of how Rebecca and her best friend Lila arrived in Sovereign after being downsized from corporate America has been told in other chronicles, and therefore won't be repeated here.)

Cora offered up an embarrassed laugh. "It certainly seems to have turned out for the best, hasn't it? For Rebecca and Lila, anyway," she added, obtusely.

The pathos in her voice was unmistakable; I knew something was wrong. I examined her face more closely, searching for clues. I recalled that Cora had never married nor had children, but, rather, had settled instead for a twenty-year liaison with a married man. He was always going to leave his wife, but never did, of course. Probably the wife had finally put her foot down.

Rebecca pushed a soft brown curl back from her comely face. "That seems like such a long time ago, doesn't it?" she mused. "I can't imagine my life anyplace else! What would I do without Wendell and all of my wonderful new friends? How would Amber and Bruce ever have met?" (Amber was Rebecca's young daughter, who had recently been squired away to my hometown of Winslow by her new husband, Bruce Gilpin, Ralph and Maude's son. That tale, too, has been told in a prior chronicle.)

"Some things are just meant to be," I concluded, reaching for a cookie. "Are these Grammie Addie's?"

Rebecca nodded, pleased by the reference to Wendell's grandmother. "Lemon butter."

Cora, a consummate professional, made an attempt to get her chutzpah back. "Those cookies are absolutely divine," she said.

"They're one of Amber's favorite. Mine too," said Rebecca, taking another munch.

Cora turned to me. "Speaking of daughters—how is your daughter, Maggie? Nellie, isn't it?"

At the mention of Nellie, any animosity I'd felt toward Cora dispersed like the mist that rises up from Black Brook. I was gratified that the other woman had not only remembered my daughter, but also had recalled Nellie's name. I vowed to be nicer to her. "Nellie's fine, thanks," I said. "She's going into her final year at Columbia. She came home for about four hours when classes ended in the spring, and then took off for a backpacking trip across Canada with some of her friends. I haven't seen her since."

"Goodness, I had forgotten they were backpacking," said Rebecca. "I hope they've managed to stay dry with all this rain!"

Cora appeared concerned. "Backpacking? Across Canada?"

"Nellie's very capable. She's especially good at getting someone to do something for her if she doesn't want to do it herself, such as setting up a tent."

"Still, don't you fret about her?" worried Cora. "I know I would."

"I do worry about her," I admitted. "Like an old mother hen worries about her last chick. But there's not much I can do now that she's out of the nest. Until she comes back looking for my help, she's on her own, which is as it should be, I guess."

"She's such a lovely young woman," Rebecca chimed in. "So mature for her age."

"Stuck up, I think you mean," I added, with a dispirited sigh. When she was twelve, Nellie had begged me to send her to a private boarding school for her high school education. I'd relented only after Nellie, all on her own, had secured a full scholarship to an elite New Hampshire prep school. At the time, I didn't think I should refuse her such an opportunity. Now, I wished I had kept her here in Sovereign with me. Since her removal from Sovereign eight years ago, she hadn't come home much. She was always much happier trotting the globe with her school chums or in New York City, from where many of them hailed.

"That is *not* what I mean," said Rebecca. "I don't think Nellie is stuck up at all!"

"What's she studying?" Cora asked, smoothing over the choppy waters.

"Philosophy, with a minor in history, last I heard. I'm not sure what she's going to do with that education, but she does seem to enjoy having her head in the clouds, chasing epistemologies and first causes and such. I understand she's a star member of the debate team, too."

"Maybe she'll go into politics?" Cora suggested, taking a sip of tea.

"Just what the world needs—another politician."

"She's still young," Rebecca interjected. "She's got plenty of time to make up her mind."

"That's what I'm hanging my hat on," I agreed. I shifted in my chair, and shifted the conversation to the reason for my visit. "How's Miss Hastings?" I inquired of Rebecca. "I heard from them down at the store that she's taken a turn for the worse?"

"Oh, dear! I'm afraid so," said Rebecca, shaking her head, sadly. "Clyde's death has really affected her. Whenever I go up to visit, she seems to rally. But one time I came in quietly and found Miss Hastings in the parlor looking at some old black-and-white photographs. I think she'd been crying."

"What? Not that delightful little old lady?" Cora queried.

Rebecca nodded gravely. "I'm afraid so."

"Oh, no! She was the life of the party at Lila's wedding. Such an adorable thing, too. I love the way she dresses—that classic black suit and frilly white blouse. And her hair!" Cora put her hand up to her own carefully coiffed do. "That has a life of its own, like a wild animal."

"Miss Hastings is a true original," I remarked. "She's an inspiration to all of us. She taught music in the elementary school for more than fifty years, and even after she retired she used to take her pet chicken Matilda to school with her for special musical parades."

"Matilda died last year, too," Rebecca recalled, sadly. "It's just been one loss after another for her, the poor dear."

Cora's façade crumbled. "That figures! Everywhere I go, the world is going to hell," she pronounced. "Even here."

Rebecca gave her former boss a questioning look. "Cora … ?"

"Oh, I don't have any secrets," she continued, bitterly. "Not any-more, anyway." She slumped back in her chair, and looked at me with beseeching eyes. "Dennis dumped me. Would you believe it? We've been together twenty-two years. He always promised me that when the kids were grown he'd divorce his wife and marry me. Instead, out of the blue, Dennis and his wife decided to buy a place in the Bahamas. He dropped me like a bad date."

I made a sympathetic clucking noise, although secretly I believed this event was a good thing in her life. Perhaps now Cora might have a chance to get a real life instead of the shadow life she'd lived for twenty-two years. But I certainly couldn't say that to her now, when she was just beginning to grieve her loss. So I simply clucked again.

"She lost her job, too," Rebecca added. "Isn't that horrible? I told her she could stay with us as long as she needs to, until she gets back on her feet."

"He fired you?" I asked, almost not believing what I heard.

Cora hesitated. She examined her carefully manicured hands. "But he told Joe to give me a good severance," she said, trying to excuse Dennis. "I got a month's salary for every year. That's a lot of money!"

"But that's illegal," I protested. I knew that Dennis Zuckerman had been her boss' boss at the Boston insurance company, Perkins & Gleeful, where Cora—and also Rebecca and Lila—had worked. "Surely you're going to file a sexual harassment suit?"

Cora simpered. "Oh, I'd never do that to Dennis!"

I held my tongue. I saw at a glance that Cora Batterswaith had a long way to go before she could get over the long-term affair. But I knew from personal experience that Sovereign, Maine was the best place in the world to heal a broken heart and to get a new life. A few minutes later I made my goodbyes and exited, leaving the two women alone to plot Cora's rehabilitation strategy.

I heard the steady hum of a tractor as I motored the short distance up the hill to Miss Hastings' house. I saw that the grass was cut in the fields on both sides of the road, and noted where a tedder had recently passed on the right. The poufy rows of hay looked like the wake left by a mid-sized motorboat. I glanced at the sky. Dark, menacing-looking clouds were rolling in. Unfortunately, this hay too, like so much other hay this summer, was probably going to get wet.

Gray Gilpin's Ford Ranger was parked at the house when I pulled in to Miss Hastings' driveway. Seventeen-year-old Gray was the grandson of Ralph Gilpin, proprietor of the general store, and often worked for his grandfather after school and in the summer. Gray had remained in Sovereign with his grandparents when his father had moved to Winslow, and often did odd jobs for Miss Hastings – especially in summer – so I wasn't surprised to see his vehicle in the dooryard.

I let myself into the shed, pausing momentarily in the mudroom where Matilda-the-chicken's empty cage was a sad reminder that nothing lasts forever. I could hear a very faint murmur of voices through the interior door, and knew that Gray and Miss Hastings were in the parlor chatting. I didn't want to interrupt anything important, so I let myself into the kitchen without knocking and took a couple of quiet steps toward the parlor, listening carefully, trying to decide whether I should stay or go.

"I jest kinda feel like no one cares anymore," I overheard Gray lamenting. His voice broke as he reached the end of his sentence. The sentiment he expressed was so lachrymose that I stopped dead in my tracks. This was serious stuff, and I felt embarrassed eavesdropping on a conversation that was obviously not for my ears. "Dad 'n

Amber got a new life with Uncle Peter, 'n Grandma 'n Mrs. Russell got the restaurant."

"Oh, BLESS you, you poor dahrrrling!" expostulated Miss Hastings.

"Mom 'n Olivia even got a new home with Mr. Nutter," he added, in the same vein. His mother, who returned to Sovereign earlier in the year, homeless, with a new baby in tow, had recently been taken under the wing of the elderly farmer Maynard Nutter. "Nobody cares 'bout *me* anymore."

"OOoo, my GOODNESS, dahrrrling! Don't you know how much we ALL depend upon you?"

"Nope. OK, well, maybe you do," Gray admitted, grudgingly, his honest nature getting the better of him.

"Why, I wouldn't be able to live here in my very own home if it weren't for you! And I know for a fact that Ralph Gilpin couldn't run that store without you, not at his age. GOODNESS, your grandfather's nearly eighty now if he's a day! Why, we're nothing more than a bunch of Old Farts around here. We couldn't survive ONE DAY without you."

"Aw, yer jest sayin' that."

"I'm saying that because it's TRUE, Master Gilpin! BLESS you—you can't even see what's happening, can you, dahrrrling?"

"No…nope," replied Gray. I heard a sob escape, and could tell he was struggling not to cry.

"Why, you're growing up! You're separating from your family and creating your VERY OWN identity. I remember ALL ABOUT it. One day I felt like crawling under a rock so that nobody could see me and the next day I felt as though the world was my OYSTER."

"I'm gettin' my own identity?" Gray puzzled.

"Dahrrrling, I know you won't believe it, but what's going on in your life is PERFECTLY NORMAL. Someday you'll even look back on this time in your life and laugh."

"Ya think so?" he asked, tremulously.

"Dahrrrling, I KNOW so!"

There was more, but I didn't wait to hear it. I quietly retraced my steps to the shed. I'd known that this was a rough patch in young Gray Gilpin's life, but I'd had no idea that he was having such a difficult time adjusting to all the changes the past year had brought him. He was a spunky little pip (as my maternal grandmother would say), however, and I knew that Gray could have no better comforter and counsellor than Miss Hastings.

I exited the shed and returned to my car, pondering what to do next. The retired music teacher's voice had sounded surprisingly strong, stronger than I had expected. But then, sick people often psych themselves up for visitors, only to crash the moment the guests are gone.

For the thousandth time I wondered what it was that gave Miss Hastings such strength of character. Was she simply born with great spiritual reserves? Or had there been something—or *someone*—who had changed her life? I vowed to continue my detective work until I had the answer to those questions.

My reverie was interrupted by the appearance of Gray Gilpin leaning in the open passenger's window. "Hey," he said. "Are ya here to see Miss Hastings?"

I nodded. "How is she?"

"Pretty good, I'd say."

"Has she had her lunch yet?"

"Geez, is it lunchtime already? Creepers! I told Grandpa I'd help him with the noon rush. See ya!" Gray waved carelessly, and loped over to his Ford Ranger. I watched him peel out of the driveway, thinking fondly of the elasticity of youth.

Back inside the house, I found Miss Hastings struggling to get herself up off the couch. She was dressed in her summer nightgown with a matching figured robe. She spotted me before I could get a word out.

"Dahrrrling, you're JUST in time," she cried, weakly. "Can you help this old bag of bones back to bed?"

I put my arm around her, and half-carried, half-walked her into the downstairs bedroom, which was once the housekeeper's room. I pulled back the pretty print sheets, and then lifted her easily – too easily – into bed. She was a diminutive creature, never having reached five feet in height, even in her trademark high heels. I could tell she weighed much less than a hundred pounds. "Have you eaten anything today?" I asked.

"Tea and toast, dahrrrling."

"That's not enough to keep a flea alive."

She waved away my concerns. "DAHRRRLING, when you get to be my age it doesn't take much to keep a flea going!" She flashed me that cheeky smile for which she was known. "I'm so glad you're back," she continued. "But I told Rebecca you'd be home as soon as I saw the goldenrod in bloom—haaahaa!"

I chuckled at the reference to my annual goldenrod run. Every August, I shed my clothes and ran naked through the four-acre field of goldenrod next to my home on the Cross Road. I'd made the mistake of writing about this annual birthday suit skedaddle in my first book, and since then I'd been inundated with requests from people all across the country, who were seeking a similar experience for themselves and were willing to pay for it. Ryan MacDonald had helped me draw up a liability release form, and for the first time we were going to use the naked goldenrod run as a fundraiser. "The goldenrod run is next week," I said, pulling up a chair next to her bed. "We're raising money for the Cornshop Museum." The town of Sovereign's defunct corn canning factory was in the process of being renovated for a museum.

"Dahrrrling, what a WONDERFUL idea! My father would be so pleased."

Her shoulder-length hair, dark and threaded with gray, was in disarray and had probably not been brushed that day. I remembered the first time I met Miss Hastings; her unruly curls reminded me of a tangled mass of worms trying to wriggle free from the confines of a fishing container. I couldn't help my motherly instinct—I reached out and attempted to smooth the hair back from her face.

"Don't BOTHER with that, dahrrrling! I've been trying to get my hair under control for almost ninety years."

I smiled. My hand dropped to the crisp, rose-figured sheets. One of Miss Hastings' fetishes was clothesline-dried sheets. She paid Shirley Palmer, the road commissioner's wife, to hang the sheets out year-round, even in winter, when the sheets freeze-dried on the line. Shirley would wait for the sheets to freeze, and then bring them in to finish drying on a wooden rack next to the woodstove. This ritual had seemed extreme to me when I first met the retired music teacher, but over the years I had come to appreciate her many interesting quirks, and even take them for granted. Now, however, I wondered if there might be more to the story.

Was this my opportunity to segue into Miss Hastings' mysterious past?

Uncannily, she appeared to read my mind. "I ADORE the scent of clothesline-dried sheets, don't you?" she said, patting the crisp top sheet with her tiny blue-veined hand. "When I was released from the sanato-rium, I swore to myself that I'd ALWAYS have fresh sheets on my bed. By golly, I was going to sleep with the scent of MAINE on my cheeks, not that GOL DANGED yellow bleach!"

I was slightly shocked. "Sanatorium? What sanatorium?"

"Dahrrrling, it's a long story. Everything happened AGES ago. But maybe it's time I told SOMEONE my little tale…"

CHAPTER 5

WINDMERE

AUGUST 1941

Sixteen-year-old Jana Hastings stared glumly out the tall sitting room window onto the grassy expanse of Windmere's back lawn. Despite being urged to change by one of the nurses, she was still wearing her travelling outfit, a pleated black crepe skirt with a lime-green jacket, her favorite, the one with the ivory lace on the collar and onyx buttons. A delicate good-luck charm bracelet, a gift from her father when her parents had dropped her off, dangled from her wrist. Her mother had managed to brush her wiry black curls into obedience, except for a few unruly locks framing her pretty face, adorned now by a scowl. She could hardly fathom how much her little world—once so perfect!—had altered since Wednesday when she had coughed up a mouthful of blood at breakfast. A panicked Aunt Minnie had fetched to their hotel room the doctor who attended the travelling troupe of musical performers. Upon the doctor's advice, her aunt had placed a telephone call to her father, the end result of which was that Jana Hastings—once heralded far and wide on the stages of New York City as *The Songbird of Sovereign*—was imprisoned in this nasty place with no friends, no family, and worst of all, no music!

"Miss, you should change, you should," the persistent nurse repeated, laying her hand on Jana's shoulder to get her attention. The young nurse was dressed in Windmere's trademark crisp white uniform and matching pert cap. "You don't want to get blood on that pretty jacket, now do you?"

Jana pulled away. "Leave me alone," she said crossly.

The nurse, understanding something of the emotions that were passing through the girl's breast, obliged. She quietly withdrew from the green sitting room, leaving Jana alone with her thoughts. Mrs. Baker, the supervisor, had a strict protocol for the treatment of new arrivals, part of which was to allow them time to adjust to their new situation in life. After a few days, however, the new residents of the children's ward were expected to follow the sanatorium's regular rules and routines.

"It's not fair!" Jana wailed to herself. "How *could* they have left me here?"

She fought back hot tears, thinking of her parents, abandoning her to the care of strangers. If she had to be sick, she should at least be home, in her own rose-papered bedroom, being waited upon hand and foot by her mother and Mrs. Johnson, the housekeeper. Mrs. Russell would bring her up her favorite cookies to eat—like she always did when Jana was sick—and maybe her friend Mabel would come over and read the latest popular novel, *The Black Stallion*, to her.

And then Jana recollected that, no, Mabel wouldn't have been able to visit, because of her particular type of illness. She had been told that she had some sort of nasty communicable disease, and until she was cured, only a few people—such as her parents—would be allowed to visit her. Until then, she was stuck at this place with a bunch of stupid, sick children.

"Hell and tarnation," she swore feistily, utilizing some of the words she had picked up on the road with her travelling troupe. "Damnation!"

The nurse popped her head in the doorway again. "Did you call me, Miss?"

Jana ignored the nurse, for out of the corner of her eye she had spied a white chicken sprinting across the lush green lawn. It was soon followed by a dozen or more other birds, all running as fast as their little yellow legs could carry them. Jana leaned forward in the cushioned chair and spotted a tall, thin youth with several young children dangling at his heels slowly making his way toward the incoming wave of chickens. He held a small, galvanized pail in his left hand and, with his right, tossed cracked corn toward the hens.

"Who's that?" she condescended to ask the nurse.

The young woman approached the window. "That's Henry, and some of the younger children," she replied. "It's the same every day, as long as Henry feels up to it. He feeds the chickens and collects the eggs. The young ones love it, and him, too."

"Does he work here?"

"Lord, no. That's Henry Graham! He's been at Windmere off and on for ever so long. He's handsome, isn't he, Miss? He was here when I came five years ago. He left once, and we thought he was gone for good – some of the nurses were sad about that, for he's awfully nice – but then he came back last year."

"Good grief, five years! Why doesn't he get better?"

"Some of 'em gets better and some don't, Miss. And some gets better for a while and then takes a sudden turn for the worse. Those are the ones you've got to watch out for." Her voice ended on an ominous note.

For the first time, Jana began to have an inkling of the significance of her situation. Her skin began to crawl. The horror of it! "What happens if he never gets better?"

"Then, he'll die, Miss, of course. We had two of 'em go in January— that's a hard month—and one go in June. That was a surprise." The nurse spoke matter-of-factly, as though the children that had passed away were no more than dogs or cats … or chickens.

"Go away," said Jana. "You're a horrible person. How can you say that to me?"

Too late, the poor nurse realized what she had done. "I'm sorry, Miss," she apologized. She hurriedly exited the room.

Jana got up from her chair, and walked to the double French doors. Henry was still there, feeding the bevy of enthusiastic chickens. She pushed open the left-hand glass door, and walked out onto the spongy grass. The sun felt warm against her skin, but there was a stiff breeze on the hilltop and she was glad she hadn't removed her jacket. One of the chickens spotted her and came darting over. Despite her anger and anguish, Jana felt a slight rush of pleasure. She scooched down and petted the chicken on its soft head. The hen pecked at one of the shiny buttons on her jacket, and Jana laughed.

"She thinks your button is a June bug," explained Henry, approaching her. "Here, take some of this." He held out his hand, and poured some yellow cracked corn like flakes of gold into her willing palm.

Jana turned back to the hen, and the chicken quickly snapped up several pointed shards of golden corn. She laughed again. Mrs. Russell never let Jana feed her chickens, not anymore, anyway.

"C'mon, Henry, I want some!" cried one of the youngsters, a boy of about eight, sporting a blond Dutch-boy haircut and a sailor collar on his blouse. He tugged on Henry's shirt sleeve.

"Here," Henry said, passing the child the pail. "Be a good boy and share with the others, Arthur."

Jana tossed the rest of her handful of corn to the chickens, stood up, and brushed the powdery remains from her hands. With a flutter of wings, several birds made a mad dash for the treasure, clucking and cheeping. A white feather separated from one of the hens and floated past Jana's nose. She sneezed, and felt the now familiar rush of blood in her throat. Instantly, she regretted not changing out of her favorite jacket.

Henry recognized her predicament, and dug into his back pocket for a handkerchief. "I see they haven't outfitted you properly, yet," he said, in a friendly tone. "You'll learn soon enough to carry a stack of these with you; you never know when you're going to need one."

Jana gratefully accepted the hankie. She swallowed, and then used the absorbent cloth to wipe away the tell-tale remains of blood from the sides of her mouth.

"You'll get righted around soon enough, and be one of our little crew in no time!"

What the youth insinuated was in no way pleasurable to Jana. Part of their little crew! That would be a cold day in Hell. She, who used to be on stage, all by herself, now sharing the spotlight with that motley group?!

Jana drew herself up to her full four-foot, eight-inches. "I'm very famous," she announced, tossing her ebony ringlets. Her brown eyes flashed.

"You don't say? I'm going to be famous myself someday, too."

Despite herself, Jana's interest was piqued. "What for?"

"I'm going to discover the Northwest Passage," he said, confidently.

Jana regarded him closely, to see whether or not he was joking. His shoulder-length, dark hair was rather like an adventurer's, nothing like the sleek, sculptured cut of Errol Flynn or Cary Grant. One chestnut-colored lock slipped rakishly over his eye, and Jana watched as the youth absently pushed it back. But his hands were smooth, with fine tapered fingers, and his skin was pale, too pale for an adventurer who would naturally spend his days out-of-doors. "There's no such thing as the Northwest Passage," she stated flatly.

"That's because it hasn't been discovered yet," he pointed out. "Have you read the book?"

"What book?"

"*Northwest Passage*, by Kenneth Roberts. It's my favorite. Sometimes when I'm reading in bed, I close my eyes and pretend I'm with Rogers and his Rangers, slipping through the North Maine Woods."

"I've never even heard of it."

"Well, you'll have plenty of time for reading here. Reading is Mrs. Baker's number one preferred activity for us. I highly recommend *Northwest Passage*. There's a small bit about cannibalism that might make you squeamish, and a battle scene or two, but I think you'd like Phoebe. By the way, my name's Henry—Henry Graham. What's yours?"

Jana tilted her nose up in the air. "I'm Jana Hastings, *The Songbird of Sovereign*. You've probably heard of me—I'm a very popular singer. People come from all over the country to hear me sing on stage."

Henry had not heard of her, but he was too much of a gentleman to let on. "Well, we certainly need some musical talent added to our group. We're shamefully unmusical here. It's a crime, really. Welcome, little Songbird!"

Tears came to Jana's eyes, as—too late!—she remembered that the doctor had told her she would never sing again. To her, that meant that all meaningful life was over.

"Oh, go away!" she said. Her face fell. She crumpled up the blood-stained hankie, and handed it back to him. "I don't want to be part of your stupid group."

Arthur tugged on Henry's arm. "C'mon, let's go get the eggs, now, Henry," he urged. "The corn's all gone."

"You go ahead," Henry said, patting the boy on the head. "I'll be with you in a few minutes. Remember, don't run." Arthur walked off fast, but didn't run.

Jana turned her back on them. She didn't want Henry to see the tears in her eyes. To her further mortification, she felt her shoulders begin to shake with pent up grief and sadness. Why didn't he go away? She couldn't hold back her misery much longer! A muffled sob escaped her.

"Go ahead and cry," he said. "You'll feel a lot better. The first week is hard—I thought I'd never live through it. But life goes on, and here I am," he added cheerfully. "Of course I'm not famous yet, like you are, but I expect that unhappy circumstance to change any day now."

Jana smiled through her tears. She sniveled. Henry searched his pockets, secured a second, clean handkerchief and draped it over her shoulder. "Like I said, you'll need plenty of these. Don't blow hard, though, or she'll come gushing up red like a harpooned whale blowing her stack."

Jana took the new handkerchief and daubed the snot from her nose, checking anxiously to see whether it was bloody or clear. It was clear. Relieved, she turned back to face him.

"Excuse the graphic nautical imagery," he continued. "My great-great-great grandfather was a whaler, from Galilee."

"Galilee!"

He grinned. "Galilee, Rhode Island. Of course it wasn't named Galilee, then. Father says I get my adventurous spirit from Captain Stephen."

"Why are you here? Aren't there any sanatoriums in Rhode Island?"

"Not specifically for children."

"But you're not a child!"

"Good observation! And had I come to Windmere as a new patient, I would have gone to the old folk's home, that's what we call that ugly brick building across the way. But I first arrived here when I was ten, so you see this place is sort of my home. When I came back last year, they put me right back into my old cot, number six."

"How old are you now?"

"Twenty-one. I know a gentleman isn't supposed to ask a lady her age, but since you're famous ..." he broke off. She looked about twelve, but he could tell by the confident way she carried herself that she was much older.

"I'm sixteen," she said. "But I'll be seventeen in December." A bird swooped low, awakening Jana to her surroundings. The sweet scent of flowers filled the air. In the distance, she could see the soft blue outline of the western mountains. On the far side of a neat expanse of lawn stood a whitewashed hen house, attached by one wall to a large red post-and-beam barn. Something wasn't quite right, but Jana couldn't put her finger on it. "Why is the grass so green? Father told me we were having a drought; he was worried about the corn. He runs Westcott's Canning Factory in Sovereign."

"They water the grass here, and the shrubs and flowers. They want everything to look nice, for when our visitors come, you know. Mrs. Baker doesn't want the families to see dying foliage at Windmere. It would remind them that we might not come home again."

"What a horrible thought!"

"Death is only horrible because we never think about it; we hide it from ourselves. But when you bring it out and look at it in the light of day, it's not so bad. How old were you when you first learned about death?"

Jana thought a moment. An image of one of Mr. Russell's chicken running around with its head cut off, blood gushing everywhere, popped into her mind. "Five-years-old. I saw our neighbor kill a chicken. I went home and told my mother how fun it was, and she sat me down and lectured me about death."

"And how much time have you spent thinking about it since?"

"I never think about it, except when someone dies. Not many do, though, I expect."

"Now, there you are wrong. We're all going to die."

"I meant that not many die at once, of course."

"I know what you meant. I'll let you in on a little secret—we're the lucky ones, here, not them out there."

Despite herself, Jana was intrigued. "What do you mean?"

"Like I said, we're all going to die—most people don't know it, but we do. It's a reality that's been forced upon us at an unnatural age. I might not be famous, but I'm special because of it. And so are you."

"Special because we know we're going to die? How can that make a difference?"

"It makes a difference in how one chooses to live. You can see that, can't you?"

Jana felt an unnatural feeling in her head, as though her little world was expanding, not collapsing all around her. She carefully considered his words. "I suppose I do see that," she said, finally. "I've never thought about it, really."

"Exactly!" he said, triumphantly. "That's just what I mean. Most people never consciously think about their lives, about how they want to live. They just pass through life, half awake, oblivious to greater thoughts, ideas, visions, dreams. But here … here we're awake to all sorts of possibilities!"

Arthur poked his head out from the chicken house. "Hurry up, Henry, or you won't get any eggs!"

Henry took Jana's hand. He squeezed it reassuringly. His brown eyes looked deep into hers. For the first time in her life, a boy was looking at her—really looking at her! Jana's girlish heart leapt.

"I'm glad you're here," he said. "I feel like we're kindred spirits. The others are, well, they're children, as you can see. I can't talk to them, like I've been talking to you." He dropped her hand.

Jana's breath came tighter in her chest. She put her hand to her throat. Was she dying? Or was she now living, as he had said, with a heightened sense of awareness?

"See you later," he said. "At dinner. They feed us pretty regular, as you'll discover." He turned, and made his way slowly across the lawn to join the other children in the hen house.

Jana watched him go. She didn't know what was happening to her; she just knew that, all of a sudden, Windmere didn't seem like such a nasty place after all.

CHAPTER 6

CROSS ROADS

AUGUST 2013

"And that's how I met Henry Graham. Wasn't he just a DAHRRRLING boy?" Miss Hastings concluded her story to me with a question and a heart-felt sigh.

"He sounds like a sweetheart," I agreed. "So much compassion and understanding at such a young age! He must have been a very special person."

"OOoo, and Henry was HANDSOME, too! I've got a photograph of him in my trunk." She lifted one of her frail hands and gestured toward the leather-bound travelling trunk that was huddled like a sleeping dog at the foot of her bed. "In there, beneath the revue poster."

I knew that Miss Hastings wanted to see the photograph of Henry, and I was certainly curious myself, so I approached the trunk and carefully lifted the flat lid. The cloth-lined chest smelled of cedar and was filled with framed black-and-white photographs, mostly old family pictures. Lying on top was a colorful 1940s musical revue poster, proclaiming nightly performances by *The Songbird of Sovereign*. A saucy-looking girl in a lime-green travelling coat stared back at me from the poster. The coat's collar was decorated with a bit of ivory lace and had shiny round black buttons. "This is you, isn't it?" I asked, holding up the poster.

"That's me, dahrrrling! Back when I was young and foolish."

"You were beautiful," I said. "You still are." I set the poster atop her dresser, and then reached in for the next artifact. The black-and-white snapshot of Henry Graham was set in an antique five-by-seven filigreed wooden frame, an intimate-looking frame made especially for ladies boudoirs. Henry was seated casually on a set of wooden steps, which appeared to lead up into a white building, most likely Windmere

Sanatorium. Henry was smiling into the camera, and was wearing a light-colored, single-breasted suit with notched lapels, a white shirt, and a patterned tie. A lock of dark hair fell rakishly over his left eye. I handed the framed photo to Miss Hastings.

She didn't try to hide her tears. She stroked the filigreed frame fondly, as though she was stroking his hair. "His father gave this to me," she mused. "I remember the day of the photograph like it was yesterday! Henry had got all gussied up for the Judge's visit—his father was a judge in Rhode Island, a very important man. It was always a special day for Henry when the Judge came to see him!"

Her eyes glazed over, and her face altered. I instantly recognized the faraway expression, for I had seen it many times before while sitting at the bedsides of the terminally ill. It is the look on the face of a long-distance hiker who has caught a glimpse of the trail beyond the next bend. Miss Hastings had a caught a glimmer of the Other Side; there would be no turning back for her—it was only a matter of time.

She closed her eyes, and rested the framed photograph upon her chest. "I think I'll snooze a bit now, dahrrrling, if you don't mind," she croaked.

"Shall I put Henry away?"

"No, no, leave him here with me, a bit longer."

I returned the musical revue poster to the trunk, closed the lid and stood next to her bed. "Can I get you anything before I go?"

Eyes still closed, she weakly shook her head. "Shirley's coming later to give me a bit of supper." She groped for my hand, and gave me a fond squeeze with a cold, waxy hand.

Moved, I leaned over and dropped a kiss on her dry forehead. "Thanks for sharing Henry. He's a keeper," I whispered. She said nothing further, so I left.

I exited through the shed—and ran square into Doctor Bart.

"You've been avoiding me," he said, standing in my way and not letting me pass. He was six-foot-two, solidly made, and I knew I wasn't going to get around him. He folded his arms across his chest.

"Hello, Aunt Maggie," I chided him. "Nice to see you, too." Metcalf Bartholomew Lawson, M.D. was my friend Jane's son, and was my primary care physician as well as Miss Hastings' doctor. I used to change his diapers when he was a baby, so I took more liberties with him than I probably should have. He was a redhead, with a white freckled face that now looked extremely grave.

"You haven't answered my emails," he said, accusatorily.

"I've been away," I reminded him.

"Or my calls," he parried. "You can't outrun cancer, Aunt Maggie. Ignoring it is a surefire way to lose the race."

"I don't want to run any race," I said. "Well, except my goldenrod run."

"Be serious."

"I am serious. I'm perfectly serious. I had the lumpectomy like you wanted, but when they told me they found cancer in my lymph nodes I made up my mind to stop everything. I'm not gonna do the chemo and radiation and all the stuff you want me to do. There's a time to live and a time to die."

"I thought you hated *Ecclesiastes*?"

"Listen, Metcalf ..." He winced. I had forgotten how much he disliked his first name. "Sorry, Doctor Bart," I amended, hastily. "If your mother can't talk me into further treatment, believe me, you don't stand a chance."

"Do you understand what you're doing, Aunt Maggie?!"

"I understand what I'm *not* doing. I know that the cancer has metastasized and I know that I don't want to spend what little time I have left tossing up my cookies."

"Have you told Nellie? What does she say?"

The bristles on my backside relaxed, and my heart softened a bit. I had long suspected that Doctor Bart was in love with my daughter. He was a good man, one that would be sure to take care of Nellie when I was gone. Unfortunately, Nellie barely gave him the time of day. Since Doctor Bart was older than Nellie (he had been a teenager and Nellie only eight when we moved to Sovereign), Nellie seemed to regard him as in an altogether different generation. In point of fact, I hadn't told Nellie about my cancer yet, but I certainly didn't want *him* to know that I hadn't told her. "Look, I know you mean well, but ..."

"There's always a 'but' with you, Aunt Maggie." He stepped aside. "Just think about what I said. This isn't all about you. Think of Nellie, too."

Nellie! How could I do anything but think of my daughter? I'd been thinking of my daughter for the last twenty-two years. Every move I'd ever made, every job I'd ever taken, everything I'd ever done since I'd discovered that fateful day in seminary that I'd missed my period, had mostly been for or about Nellie.

"Right," I replied. "Thanks."

He rested his black doctor's bag on the shed freezer. "By the way, how is Miss Hastings?"

"She's sleeping at the moment."

"OK, no problem. I've got a few other calls to make so I'll stop by later when she's awake."

He turned to go, but I caught his arm. It was a solid, well-muscled arm, just right for a young woman like Nellie to lean on, if she would only open her eyes. "Thanks for caring about me, dear," I said. "I do appreciate it, although I might not always show it."

Doctor Bart tried to shrug the compliment off, but I could tell he was pleased. "Hey, we're family," he explained, unnecessarily.

"Second cousins once removed," I reminded him.

"Close enough."

Ten minutes later I was pulling into the driveway of my sweet little home on the Cross Road. Six weeks was a long time to be away from my herbs, perennials, and apple trees. I was certainly glad to be back, although my book project had become almost an obsession with me since I'd found out I probably had less than a year to live, especially without further treatment.

I discovered a familiar-looking pickup parked in the dooryard, and the shed door was unlocked. I let myself in to find a fresh wildflower bouquet on my kitchen table, infusing the stuffy kitchen that had been shut up during my absence with the astringent scent of Queen Anne's lace and sweet goldenrod. My childhood chum from Winslow, Peter Hodges, was sitting in my favorite chair, the rocker next to the south-facing window, where I often sat and watched the world go by. Peter and I had been best friends since Kindergarten at Halifax School. Mutual friends have asked me over the years if I didn't think that Peter was handsome. I never know how to answer them, because I never see Peter as he is, I always see him as the elf-eared kid who stepped onto the school bus three minutes after I did with that same terrified expression in his eyes. Today, there was hearty good humor in those familiar brown orbs.

"It's about time, Maggie—I'm starved!" he announced, grinning. He stood up, and pushed back the brim of his Boston Red Sox cap.

"Did you bring any milk?" I replied, dumping a sheaf of papers, some books and my purse onto the table with a muffled thud.

He nodded. "Natch. And some fresh cheese. We're selling that at the farm, along with the milk and eggs now. That's Amber's doing." Amber was Rebecca's daughter, she who had recently married Peter's nephew Bruce Gilpin and lived on the farm with them.

"Thanks for bringing in the mail," I said, spotting a neat pile stacked on the secretary in the corner. I had asked the Postmistress to deliver my held mail to my mailbox today. "How did you know I was back?"

"Maude called me after Ralph told her you were in the store. I didn't have anything better to do—they won't let me drive tractors yet—so I thought I'd ride over and bring you some supplies. I brought a loaf of fresh bread, and some peanut butter cookies, too."

"My hero," I said. I moved across the room and gave him a quick hug. When I tried to pull away, his right hand clung stubbornly to my hip. For once, I yielded. Peter had suffered a terrible accident in the spring, when his bulldozer had flipped over on him. I hadn't realized until then how much I cared about this man who had always stood by me despite my failure to return his love and devotion via a formal commitment. "Should you be driving already?" I asked. He had broken an arm and leg in the accident, and crushed a few ribs. Peter had spent the entire summer recuperating at Oaknole, and this was the first time I had seen him away from the family farm, which was situated about a half hour away.

He nodded. "It's OK, but automatic transmissions only. No clutches and no bulldozers."

I smiled, and attempted to extricate myself; however, he held me tight with his left arm, the one he hadn't broken. "Not so fast," he said. "I want a word with you."

I knew what was coming. "Et tu, Brute?"

"Well, you can't expect me to stand aside and let Jane and Doctor Bart fight the battle themselves. Honestly, Maggie, I didn't know you had a death wish!"

"I don't. I've just seen too many cancer victims try all sorts of crazy stuff to give themselves a few extra days and the end result is that those extra days are filled with unnecessary pain and suffering."

"So, you're the medical expert, now?"

"When it comes to me and my body, yes!"

His hazel eyes glinted knowingly. "Still think you're Queen for a Day, don't you?"

"King," I reminded him. "You said I could be King, if I reached the lily in the frog pond first."

He chuckled. "No, I said 'queen' but you weren't satisfied with that, were you?"

While we were talking, his hand had slipped from my hip. Sensing my opportunity to escape, I stepped away from his iron grasp. "Let's not argue about it, Peter."

"Translated: 'Let me do what I want, like you usually do, Peter,'" he said, mimicking me, "'and everything in our relationship will be hunky-dory.'" There was no mistaking the bitterness in his voice.

"I'm sorry," I said, stubbornly. "I just feel like it's got to be my decision." I picked up the tea kettle, filled it with fresh water and set it onto the gas range to boil. I had gone through the usual period of "Get it out! Get the cancer out of me!" But the desperate longing to do anything to prolong my life had been replaced by an even stronger desire to spend my last days doing as *I* wanted, in living, not dying.

Peter sat down heavily. He took off his baseball cap, and turned it round and round in his calloused hands. I knew just how gentle those weathered hands could be, however. Immediately, I felt contrite. Peter had done so much for us over the years! When I was pregnant with Nellie, he was one of the few friends who stuck by me. When I had lost my first church and needed money to pay the electric bill and put food on the table, Peter had provided. Was I to shut him out now?

"I *am* sorry," I said, resting my back against the counter. "I know you want …"

"Aw, I'm the one who should apologize, Maggie," he interrupted. "Of course it's your decision—I wouldn't take that from you. You know I'll support you one hundred percent, whatever you decide. I just wish … well, I wish you'd let me take care of you."

I made a vain attempt at a laugh. "I've got a feeling you'll be taking care of me a lot more than either of us realizes over the next year."

He looked up. "Is that how long you've got?" he asked, anxiously. The cap twirled faster and faster.

I nodded. "According to Metcalf, anyway. A year. Probably less."

"It's that bad?"

"It's metastasized. At best, chemo and radiation would probably only give me an extra three to six months."

"Then we haven't got a moment to lose."

"What do you propose?"

He placed his ball cap on the table, and then rather gingerly went down on one arthritic knee. He held out his hands to me. "Maggie Walker, will you marry me?"

CHAPTER 7

SETTLING IN

SEPTEMBER 1941

Life at Windmere was very different from Jana's former life in New York, but then her life in New York had been a far cry from her life in Sovereign. She was nothing if not adaptable.

Windmere was a stately nineteenth century mansion that had once been the hilltop home of Leona Buckminster, the millionaire daughter of a central Maine lumber baron. It was so named by the heiress because, reportedly, one day she spied the ocean from the windy ridgetop. Upon her death in 1908, Mrs. Buckminster willed her estate to Dr. Edwin Parkhurst (Dr. Ketchum's predecessor) for the establishment of a privately operated tuberculosis treatment center. The sprawling white home featured a large front portico and two matching side porches, on which the children slept in dormitory-style cots year round, even in winter, when they were bundled up in fur coats, their feet kept warm by pre-heated soap stones. Windmere opened for the treatment of adults only in 1909. In 1915 the state of Maine passed a law providing for the care and treatment of tubercular persons, and in 1921 a larger, institutional brick building was constructed next door, to which the adults were moved, freeing up the original home at Windmere solely for the treatment of children. Dr. Parkhurst retired in 1932 and Dr. Ketchum had been at the facility ever since.

Dr. Ketchum preferred the grand old house to the ugly brick building and so he utilized the library there for his office and the study for his surgery. Mrs. Baker had appropriated a smaller space for her office, and a walk-in closet was lined with lead and turned into the X-ray room. The live-in staff (including Mrs. Baker) slept upstairs, and the laundry was all shuttled over to the new building where a well-trained staff ensured the annihilation of the *Tubercle bacillus* bacteria by the excessive use of bleach.

The goal of TB treatment centers in Maine was twofold: to segregate afflicted people and their infectious sputum from the rest of the general population, and to attempt to cure them. The Western Maine Sanatorium in Hebron accepted only patients whose outcomes looked promising; however, Windmere accepted even the worst-case scenarios and, thus, the central Maine facility had the reputation as being the place where the sick went to die. Patients regularly underwent sputum testing to check for the presence of the TB bacteria. In order to be discharged, one needed two "clean" tests in a row. Jana had tested positive, and would be retested in a month.

Over the course of the next two weeks, while she settled into a new daily routine at Windmere, Jana found that her world wasn't going to end after all, even without her music. She discovered that Mrs. Baker was a firm but fair supervisor, who truly cared about the children. Dr. Ketchum was kind and generous in allowing access to the hard candy he kept in one of the glass cotton ball jars in his surgery. And the other children were especially eager to learn about the world beyond Windmere. Why, she was as much of a celebrity at Windmere as she was in New York and Sovereign! Henry constantly sought her out for illuminating conversation, and Arthur and the other younger children always clamored for her to tell them a story. In addition, it was at Windmere where Jana finally realized one of her life-long dreams: a sister, a bosom buddy of her own age, with whom she could share all of her inner most thoughts and secrets. This dream was actualized in the person of Eleanor Luce, a girl of fifteen, whose cot, number nine, was next to Jana's on the open air sleeping porch.

The two girls carried on interesting (although strictly forbidden) whispered conversations at night, under the cover of darkness and the soughing of the wind in the pine trees, their beds being the furthest from the attending nurse. Eleanor, whose condition was much worse than Jana's, was currently on complete bed rest after Dr. Ketchum had manually collapsed one side of her lungs. Like Henry, she had been at Windmere off and on for more than a decade. It was Eleanor who explained the disease of tuberculosis to Jana, who, until the morning she coughed up blood, had been completely ignorant of what the general populace called "consumption," the wasting disease.

"Did it hurt?" Jana asked, referring to the procedure AP (artificial pneumothorax), which Eleanor had received shortly before Jana's arrival.

"Not at first, because of the anesthesia, you know." The AP consisted of repeated injections of an absorbable gas into the pleural cavity of Eleanor's lung in order to maintain the collapsed lung for an indefinite period of time. This procedure was done by Dr. Ketchum in his surgery with the use of a local anesthetic. "When I woke up, it was hard to get comfortable, though."

"Why did they do it?"

"To give my lung time to rest, like a broken leg or arm. So the lesions will heal."

"Does it hurt now?" Jana queried her new friend, anxiously.

"I had a refill on Tuesday and Thursday and I didn't even notice. Today, I had an X-ray, …"

"I had one of those. That doesn't hurt."

"It's a good thing, too, because we get a lot of X-rays around here. Anyway, during yesterday's X-ray – it was a screening, where they do an X-ray but they don't take a plate; you just stand there in your shift while they look at the machine. Anyway, I heard Dr. Ketchum say to the nurse: 'Good general collapse,' so I'm hoping for the best."

Unfortunately, Eleanor in divulging this last bit of information had attempted to mimic Dr. Ketchum's baritone voice: "Good general collapse," the result of which was that Jana burst into fits of giggles. The six-foot tall, stocky doctor was nothing like her slightly framed, blonde-haired friend. "Good general collapse!" Ha, ha, ha! The attending nurse heard Jana's muffled giggles and walked over and scolded the two girls. "Shhh! No talking, now. Your need your sleep. Do we need to switch your beds around?" Instantly, the girls were quieted for fear of being separated.

On Sunday afternoon, when Jana had taken a break from reading aloud to her new friend, she asked Eleanor why some children were treated differently than others. "Why is Arthur allowed to feed the chickens and collect the eggs, but some of the others aren't? That doesn't seem very fair."

"Because Mrs. Baker separates us into three groups, like the disciples—Matthew, Mark and John—according to how sick we are," Eleanor explained, from her prone position in bed where she was forced mostly to examine the white painted ceiling. "That's so the nurses know how to treat us. Arthur is a disciple of Matthew; he's one of the healthiest, like you. I saw it on your chart—it's that blue star next to your name."

Jana wondered about Henry, and felt a little thrill of fear. "What's Henry?"

"Henry's in the middle group—he's a disciple of Mark—the ones with the green stars. They're not supposed to overexert themselves, but of course the nurses let Henry do what he wants because most of them are in love with him. Don't you think he's handsome?"

Jana, who not only thought Henry was handsome but also one of the nicest boys she had ever met, blushed when she heard this question. "I suppose so," she demurred, glad that her new friend was watching a spider devour a house fly caught in its web and couldn't see the ruby flush that stained her cheeks. She wasn't ready to share this special secret, yet.

"That poor fly will never get away. See how hard he struggles! I think the spider is just toying with him." Eleanor was equally fond of all living creatures, but in this instance she gave her sympathies to the loud buzzing cluster fly.

Jana cared for neither spiders nor flies, and was more particularly interested in learning about Henry. "Have you ever met Henry's father?"

"Oh, yes. He's very important—he's a judge in Rhode Island. But you wouldn't know it when he comes here. He's so nice and cheerful. We all like it when Judge Graham comes to visit because every time he comes he brings us lots of presents. Last visit I got the card game *Flinch*. It's ever so fun." She abandoned the arthropod and its prisoner, and turned her neck to look at Jana. "Have you ever played *Flinch*?"

Jana shook her head. Her childhood so far had consisted of countless hours of voice and piano lessons; there was little time or inclination for games. She almost began to envy her friend her childhood spent with Henry and the others at the sanatorium playing *Flinch*, *Rook*, *Rummy* and *Bingo*. "Why aren't there any disciples of Luke?" she asked, only now realizing that Mrs. Baker had named the three groups after the authors of the Christian Gospels. Although she had never read the Bible, she knew, thanks to her friend Mabel in Sovereign, that there were four Gospels, not three. Once, when she had spent the night at Mabel's house, her friend's mother had taught her to say a bedtime prayer: "Matthew, Mark, Luke and John, bless the bed that I lie on." Mrs. Edwards had also taken the opportunity to expound on the New Testament and Jesus Christ.

"Mrs. Baker doesn't think Luke actually knew the Lord; she thinks he took most of his Gospel from Matthew and Mark. So we've only got Matthew, Mark and John."

"And whose disciple are you?"

"I'm one of John's—we're the ones with the gold stars."

"Why do *you* get the gold star?" Jana asked, enviously.

"Because we're the ones closest to Heaven."

By this time, Jana had become somewhat inured to talking about death. She examined her friend's pale but serene face closely. "Do you think about it a lot?"

"I'm not afraid of dying, if that's what you mean. I'm happy here, now, but I know when I die I'll be happy there, too. I'll get to see my mother again." Jana had discovered earlier that Eleanor's mother had died of tuberculosis when Eleanor was seven.

"Do you miss her very much?" Jana asked, her heart constricting in sympathy, as she thought of her own lovely and passionate mother, who had recently visited Windmere, bringing with her a big batch of Mrs. Russell's lemon butter cookies.

"Sometimes. But sometimes it feels like Mother's still with me. Sometimes I hear her laugh at something Father says at dinner or see her peeling potatoes at the kitchen sink when I come home from school, and then I wake up and find it was only a dream. Strange, it seems so real at the time. She turns to me, and asks me how school was, and what I learned today. And I tell her all about the artificial pneumothorax just like I told you. She used to brush my hair at night—long, hard strokes—and I miss that most, I think. I'd sit on the little cushioned stool at her dressing table and close my eyes, and it was like we were one person, not mother and daughter. I think that's how it will be in Heaven, when I get there, like we're all one person and there's no more pain or sorrow. Here on earth, you see, everyone has some kind of burden to bear, like a big splinter that's never pulled out as long as we're alive. Some children never have enough to eat and others are cold at night. Some don't even have any parents at all. Our splinter is this sickness. But when we get to Heaven we'll wake up and find out that the splinter is gone."

"But ... don't we ever get rid of our splinters in this life?" worried Jana, who privately was planning on being cured at the end of six months or a year at the very most as Dr. Ketchum had promised.

"We'll always have some sort of cross to bear, I think. If you get one splinter pulled out, there will be another one waiting for you just around the corner. Thank goodness there are people in the world like Dr. Ketchum and Mrs. Baker or we'd all be walking around with a lot more splinters. Why, we'd look just like porcupines!"

Jana smiled, but didn't laugh. There were so many different things to think about at Windmere! She marveled at how she could have lived so long without thinking of them, and wondered if she would ever be as smart and knowledgeable as Eleanor and Henry.

"Tell me about Lady Hamilton," Eleanor asked wistfully, referring to the recently released motion picture, *That Hamilton Woman*, starring the dream couple Vivian Leigh and Laurence Olivier. "How lucky you were that you got to see it in New York before you came here. Is she very beautiful?"

"She's the most beautiful thing ever! But not in the beginning of the picture, Eleanor. She's an old hag on the street then, stealing a bottle of alcohol from the store. She leaves her husband and runs off with Lord Nelson. After he dies she becomes very poor and starts drinking."

"How tragic!"

"Some people say she got what she deserved."

"Oh, no!"

"Father says that it's Winston Churchill's favorite motion picture. He says the Prime Minister cried when he first saw it."

"The poor Prime Minister! Men do cry sometimes, I suppose. Do you think we'll go to war? Like England?"

Jana made a face. "I should think not. Why should we care what happens over there? Our neighbor, Mrs. Russell—she's the one who bakes me cookies—she has three sons, and Mother says she's worried that if we go to war to help England they'll be sent overseas and get killed."

"I remember those cookies," Eleanor whispered. She shut her eyes. "They were very good."

Jana realized that her best friend was becoming overtired. Eleanor was taxing herself and her afflicted lung by talking so much. What would Jana do if something happened to Eleanor? Where would she be at Windmere without her new friend?! Suddenly, she felt very protective and motherly. "Let's read some more," she suggested, reaching for the thick, hard-cover book she had laid next to the sputum test cups on the metal hospital stand that separated their hospital cots.

"Alright," Eleanor agreed. She opened her eyes, and gazed fondly at Jana. "It's awfully nice having you here." She reached for Jana with her small white hand, and squeezed reassuringly. "Don't worry. I think you'll live a long time—you have so much life in you! I wish I could have heard you on stage. I bet you were brilliant."

"I'll never sing again, you know." It was the first time Jana had admitted this out loud, and, as she said it, she felt a weight drop from her shoulders.

"Then I suppose you'll have to help others make beautiful music," Eleanor mused.

The two girls fell silent. From her restful seat on the porch at Windmere Jana spotted two robins hopping along the side lawn looking for worms. A songbird fluttered to the low-hanging limb of a nearby blue spruce, opened its throat and poured out a glorious refrain.

"Listen!" cried Eleanor. "It's a warbler. He's singing us a song!"

Jana cocked her ear and listened. "Sounds more like he's practicing his scales," she said. "He needs to take lessons from Mother."

Eleanor laughed. "Poor bird! You're very hard on him." Affronted, the warbler flew away. "Do tell me, Jana—what was your favorite song to sing?"

Jana paused for consideration. "I liked to sing *God Bless America*, because that's new and everyone likes it. Aunt Minnie said I did that one as well as Kate Smith. But I think I liked *After the Ball* best because it's so sad. When I got to the end of that most of the ladies would be crying and even some of the men would pull out their handkerchiefs and blow their noses." She absently smoothed a wrinkle from her plaid wool skirt. "I always did at least one encore, too. And then the audience would throw flowers up on stage for me—roses, mostly, because those are my favorite."

Eleanor sighed. "Sounds heavenly."

"Let's read now, Eleanor. Don't talk." Jana opened Henry's prized copy of *Northwest Passage* and searched until she found their place. "Now, where were we? Oh, yes. Phoebe has just gone through Langdon's knapsack and tossed out all the things he doesn't need for his trip in the woods."

"I like Phoebe so much, don't you?"

"I do like her," Jana admitted. "Henry said I would."

"And what Henry says is generally right," Eleanor conceded. She shut her eyes again, and folded her hands back on her chest. Jana began reading aloud, her exquisitely-trained musical voice rising and falling with the fluctuating tide of the novel's drama.

Later, after supper, when Henry and Jana were sitting together companionably sipping cocoa at the great mahogany dining table, Henry asked her what she thought of the book. "It's very realistic," she replied, thinking privately that some of the battle scenes were perhaps *too* realistic for her taste. "He's a very descriptive writer. I feel like I'm sloshing through the swamp with Rogers and his Rangers, and I keep looking over my shoulders for Indians. I think Eleanor likes it, too."

"You'll find that Eleanor likes whatever you like," Henry replied, drily. "She wants to see people happy. It's her one failing in life."

Instantly, Jana's back was up. She thought that her new friend was perfect, and said so.

"Nobody's perfect, Songbird. Not even you, although I have to admit, you're giving me a run for my money."

Jana blushed. Unfortunately, this time there was no way for her to hide her embarrassment.

"What? Blushing like a schoolgirl? I thought you were used to praise, being famous as you are, and all."

"Oh, don't remind me of that!" she protested, covering her hot cheeks with her hands. "That's not me anymore."

"And what are you now, Songbird?"

Jana's hands returned to the highly polished tabletop. "I'm not sure, but I certainly have learned how to think in here."

"And do you like thinking?"

"Almost as much as I like singing. And it's certainly a lot easier!"

Henry laughed. "Touché!" At the sound of his laugh, the attending nurse lifted her head and surveyed the two of them from the opposite end of Windmere's elegant dining room. Henry waved at the nurse and winked, and the young woman quickly looked back down at her handiwork.

"You're shameless," Jana scolded him. "You're flirting with her, just so she won't come over here and tell us to keep it down."

"Flirting! Me? You must be mistaken. At least, mistaken in that I'm flirting with the nurse. There is a girl here I'd like to flirt with, though."

"Go away. You're teasing me. I don't like to be teased."

He reached out and tugged one of her dark curls. "Oh, I think you do like to be teased, Songbird. But I won't do it anymore, if it bothers you. I'm sorry; truly I am. Father says I'm incorrigible, and he's probably right. Come to think of it, he's always right."

"When is your father coming to visit again?"

"Sometime around Christmas."

"Not until Christmas! Why, that's ages away. My mother comes every week."

Henry's face fell. He nodded sadly. "That's the soonest Father says he can get away. I got a letter from the Judge yesterday. He told me all about his newest cases. There's a big murder trial that's supposed to start in October, but he thinks he'll have that all wrapped up by the first of December."

Jana shuddered. "A murder? How horrible!"

"The details are particularly gruesome, too. But don't worry, little Songbird. I'll keep those to myself. I wouldn't want to give you nightmares. Now, why don't we find Arthur and some of the others and have ourselves a rousing game of *Flinch*?"

"Not too rousing, or this time the nurse really will shut us down." And for once with Henry, Jana had the last word.

Chapter 8

Harvest Dinner

September 2013

Rebecca Russell cornered her husband in their kitchen the Saturday afternoon before the harvest dinner they were hosting later that evening. A little group of friends (including yours truly) was celebrating the autumnal equinox. "Do you think we should seat Leland next to Cora?" she asked in a lowered voice so that their guest, who was reading a magazine in the next room, wouldn't overhear.

"Don't know why not," the good-natured Wendell drawled. Leland Gorse was one of his particular friends, and so it might not have been as evident to the old chicken farmer why there would be any difficulty placing the uncultured woodsman next to the couture escapee from the city. "She won't hurt him none."

"That's not exactly what I was worried about," Rebecca said, smiling despite herself. "Don't you think he talks a little too much? And sometimes he makes the funniest noises when he eats."

Wendell attempted to picture his friend's table manners. "He do like to eat," he conceded.

Rebecca sighed. It was at times like this when she really missed the companionship of her best friend, Lila Woodsum (now Lila Hobart), with whom she had arrived in Sovereign after being downsized from her job in Boston. Lila would have understood what she was trying to say without her having to spell it out in so many words. But Lila was so far away, living up north in Aroostook County. On top of that, Lila was terribly busy. Her young friend was not only the marketing manager of her husband's family farm but also a new mother. No, she couldn't even send Lila a tweet without worrying she was interrupting something.

"Leland tells awful good stories, too," Wendell added.

"Well, he is very funny," Rebecca conceded. "And there doesn't seem to be any other good place to put him. You're at the head of the table, in your usual spot, of course, and I put Ryan at the other end, with Trudy on his left. I'm so happy she's pregnant! And Peter and Maggie will go on Ryan's right, with Doctor Bart between Maggie and me. That leaves Leland next to Cora, who'll be at your right. You will keep a close eye on her though, won't you?"

Wendell, who hadn't followed the seating assignments much beyond his own, nevertheless wanted to support his pretty young wife. "What am I lookin' for?"

Rebecca patted her husband's arm fondly. "Just make sure Cora has everything she needs. You know perfectly well how to charm a woman, Wendell Russell, for all your country boy ways. Just don't forget at the end of the night whose bedroom to go to!"

Wendell flashed his signature gold-toothed grin. "'Tain't likely," he said. He winked.

By six o'clock the food was served up steaming hot and we were all seated comfortably at the old oak table in the great room, a combination living-dining room just off the kitchen. There was still some lingering daylight, but not enough to eat by, so Rebecca had lit a few candles and turned on the hanging hurricane lamp that was overhead. The old oil lamp had been converted to electricity during Grammie Addie's day, and the light filtering through its hand-painted floral shade cast a warm rosy glow over the table. As I surveyed our little group of friends, I felt the happiest I'd been in many a day.

Rebecca, a newly minted locavore (converted by her daughter Amber, a proponent of the Slow Food/Slow Money movements) had acquired a leg of lamb from a local farmer, and accompanying the deliciously roasted meat was a fall cornucopia from Wendell's garden: boiled onions, mashed potatoes, broccoli, Brussels sprouts, and two types of winter squash—all of which were smothered in Trudy's sweet butter. Also making an appearance at the table were Rebecca's tangy rhubarb sauce, a variety of homemade pickles, and a dish of sweet spearmint jelly that she had put up only the day before. Rebecca asked me to say grace, which I did, obliging everyone by keeping the thanks-giving short.

"Now, please let me know if you need anything," Rebecca said, spreading her napkin on her lap. We all followed suit (except for Leland, of course) and the food was passed around amid some hearty chatter and laughter.

"Shore looks good 'nuff fer a last suppah," said Leland, smacking his lips loudly in anticipation. I saw Rebecca cast a quick glance at her friend, but Cora appeared not to notice the noises of her neighbor. "Don't hog thet mashed potato down theah, now, son," he said loudly to Ryan, his son-in-law.

Ryan smiled. "Don't worry, Leland. Looks to me like there's enough potato here to go around the table three times."

"We're passing to the right, Father," Trudy said, quietly. "The potato will come around in a minute. Be patient."

Leland thrummed his fingers against the table. I saw him turn and give Cora Battelswaith the once over. She was dressed neatly in a plaid wool skirt and yellow silk blouse, and seemed much more serene than when I'd seen her last.

"You been heah long?" Leland inquired pleasantly.

"Almost a month," Cora replied. "I can't believe it's gone by so fast."

"She's been helping us down at the restaurant," Rebecca said, passing a bowl of creamed onions. "It's been wonderful to have the extra help."

Cora glanced down at her hands, which weren't perhaps as finely manicured as when she arrived in Sovereign. "It's been a long time since I washed dishes, but I find that I'm actually enjoying it."

Conversation flagged as the company piled their plates high with mouth-watering delectables and began to eat. I leaned out in front of Doctor Bart so that I could speak to Rebecca directly. She always sat at Wendell's left hand, not only because she liked to sit next to her husband but also because it was the seat closest to the kitchen. "Thanks for inviting us," I said, including Peter with a little nod of my head. I felt his rough hand grope for mine under the cover of the tablecloth. He gave my hand a warm squeeze. My heart swelled with love and gratitude. After Peter had proposed marriage last month, to the astonishment of both of us I had said—"Yes." I'd always loved my childhood chum, but I never realized how much until we nearly lost him in that bulldozer accident. Peter and I had decided to keep our engagement a secret, however, at least until I had told my daughter Nellie.

Rebecca, her pretty face flushed from her labors, gave us both a fond look. "We're happy to have you here, aren't we, Wendell?"

Wendell looked up from his plate. "Ayuh."

"And we're glad you're back on your feet again, Peter," she continued. "You scared us all, especially your sister. It's too bad Maude and Ralph couldn't join us tonight."

"They've gone to Ralph's sisters' for the weekend. Gray is minding the store."

"What would we do without Grayden? Especially Miss Hastings!"

I popped a bread-and-butter pickle into my mouth and was in the process of swallowing it when Rebecca added: "Did any of you know she had tuberculosis as a child?" I nearly choked, and some clove juice went up my nose. What Miss Hastings had told me about her time in the sanatorium I had kept in confidence of course. I hadn't known that she had shared the information with anyone else. Not knowing what to say, I decided to say nothing, and daubed my nose with my napkin.

"Miss Hastings had tuberculosis?!" Trudy exclaimed, obviously surprised.

"How awful!" expostulated Cora. "No—no more potato for me, thank you, Wendell. I've got to watch my figure."

Leland scratched his head. "I nevah heared nuthin' 'bout thet."

"Did *you* know, Wendell?" Ryan asked, curiously.

Wendell set the bowl of mashed potatoes back onto the table. "Wal, I guess I do recollect Grammie Addie tellin' me once thet Miss Hastings was awful sick as a girl. Come to think of it, thet might be how come she had to give up her singin' on the stage."

"She was one of the lucky ones to survive TB as a child, then," said Ryan, helping himself to more lamb from the platter. "Tuberculosis was the cancer of the nineteenth and early twentieth centuries. Antibiotics used to treat TB didn't come around until, well … when did antibiotics arrive on the scene, Doctor Bart?"

Doctor Bart was in the process of reaching for a second moist and fragrant yeast roll, but his freckled arm paused mid-air. As Miss Hastings' doctor he was familiar with her medical history, but, conscious of HIPPA, he had kept silent. With all eyes on him, he quickly withdrew his hand from the napkin-covered basket. "Streptomycin was developed in 1946," he said, gravely.

"That's about when I thought," continued Ryan. He regarded the table at large. "Did you know that in the early part of the nineteenth century in England one in four deaths was from TB? Twenty-five percent! Can you imagine today if twenty-five percent of our population died from one infectious disease? They called it consumption back then, because the disease seemed literally to consume the person who had it." Ryan was an aficionado of the nineteenth century, particularly its literature.

Cora opened her eyes wide. "How shocking!"

Rebecca did a quick calculation in her head. "Miss Hastings told me she was sixteen when she was diagnosed with TB. That would have been in 1941, before the use of antibiotics." She turned to her neighbor. "How was she treated, then, Doctor Bart?"

Doctor Bart cleared his throat, and steadied his water glass with his left hand. He carefully considered his words, mindful of confidentiality issues. "Before the advent of antibiotics, sanatoriums were utilized to segregate the infected population," he said. "Some patients underwent a pneumothorax technique, a practice that involved collapsing an infected lung, giving it time to rest, which allowed the tuberculosis lesions to heal. Maine had three sanatoriums, including Windmere, where Miss Hastings was treated, I believe. Fortunately for her, the disease was caught in its early stages. Many others weren't so lucky, particularly the poor, who had little access to healthcare."

"They still don't," I added, sadly.

"Unfortunately, that's true," said Doctor Bart. "It's also unfortunate that TB, which was almost stamped out in the twentieth century thanks to the use of the BCG vaccine, is making a comeback."

"Why is that?" Rebecca asked, curiously.

"Because of the rise of drug-resistant strains of the bacteria. The World Health Organization actually declared the resurgence of TB a global health emergency in 1993."

"I can't believe Miss Hastings never mentioned this," Trudy said. She looked toward the head of the table. "What else did your grandmother tell you about her, Wendell?"

"Wal, you know, 'tain't nuthin' folks used to talk 'bout, I suppose. Least not in the old days. All's I recall was thet Miss Hastings had to give up the stage, and thet she come back heah to live. Course, I warn't born then. She taught music for a livin' 'n helped Grammie Addie in her last years—thet was when I was in the Navy, you know. She 'n Addie had a special affection for each other. I never see two ladies so different who got 'long so good as those two did."

"That's so sweet," said Cora. "I'm sorry Miss Hastings couldn't be here tonight."

"She isn't well enough to go out," Doctor Bart said. "Anyone else would need to be in a managed care facility, but Miss Hastings is fortunate enough to have friends and neighbors who can help keep her at home while …" He faltered, and looked down at his plate.

I knew that Doctor Bart had been about to say, "While she dies," and I thought perhaps it was time to steer the conversation in a more positive direction. "Tell us more about your grandmother, Wendell. I always like to hear stories about Grammie Addie."

Wendell looked bashful, but the others chimed in with additional encouragement, and so he took a moment to think. "Wal, there was always somethin' 'bout the way the house smelt in the fall," he said. "I don't know whether 'twas what Grammie Addie was cookin' or cannin' or what. This place jest smelt like a place you'd want to be when you'd come in from the barn or wherever you was. 'Twas always real warm and cozy like. She used to can pumpkin bread 'n mincemeat 'bout this time of year, and maybe thet was it. When I was in the Navy, on board ship, you know, I used to think of home and Grammie Addie a lot." He glanced around the great room with obvious affection. "Sometimes I kin hear her voice, in my head. Seems like she's still with us, 'specially tonight."

Silence pervaded the table, as we all wallowed in this memorable moment in time. Truly, there are occasions in our lives when we step off the merry-go-round of life and look on in restful amazement as the world goes swirling by. In the distance I heard the distinctive hoot of a barred owl: *"Who? Who? Who cooks for you?"* I hadn't even realized until hearing the owl's provocative call that the autumnal dusk had enveloped us all in her thick dusky cloak. Peter reached for my hand again, this time in plain sight. I knew he was feeling the same as I: warm, safe and cherished.

Rebecca sighed. "I wish I had known her."

"I wish you hed, too," Wendell said. He grasped his wife's hand. "I would've liked Grammie Addie to see what a keeper I got," he added gallantly.

Rebecca blushed, but did not contradict her husband nor withdraw her hand. Likewise, Ryan reached for his wife, feeling the peculiar intimacy of the moment.

For some reason, I glanced across the table, and saw tears in Cora's eyes. I suspected she was thinking about Dennis, and how differently her own life had turned out from that of her friend. Rebecca was in the midst of a community of caring people, with a safe and secure future to look forward to accompanied by a steadfast partner who loved her, while Cora … well, when Cora left Sovereign she would be on her own with no one by her side for support. Once again, I felt grateful for Peter's unconditional love. I knew he would do anything for me, and suddenly the health obstacles I was facing seemed small and insignificant.

Rebecca had baked two apple pies and a lemon sponge cake for dessert, and soon had the dinner dishes cleared from the table and was plating up our sweets selections. Complementing dessert was a full-bodied herbal tea she had created from her own bee balm, mint, and licorice-flavored anise hyssop, which naturally required the use of Wendell's honey.

"By the way, Maggie," Rebecca said, passing me a cup of hot tea, "how much money did you raise in your goldenrod run? I never heard."

I set the antique teacup into its saucer. "Twenty-two hundred dollars. Right, Ryan?" Ryan was on the board of directors of the Cornshop Museum, and had handled the money collected during the fund-raising event.

"Twenty-two hundred and fifty, to be exact. I wouldn't have believed so many people would line up to run naked through the goldenrod unless I'd seen them with my own eyes."

"Leastways, not with all them honeybees on the goldenrod," Wendell added, chuckling. "I put up a lot of goldenrod honey this year."

"Bees? I wouldn't take my clothes off around any bees!" Cora exclaimed.

"That's the charm of it," I said. "At least for me. I love the harmonic buzz of thousands of honeybees at work. It's such a joyful noise! I can actually feel their happiness through the vibrations in my skin."

Cora held up her hands in mock horror.

"Wal, you know, they won't hurt you none," Wendell assured her. "Them bees is so busy gettin' to the hive 'n back they ain't gonna bother you none."

"Not unless you accidentally step on one," I added. "That's why I made sure everyone had their sneakers on."

"I never heard how you got started with your goldenrod run, Maggie," Ryan said. "There must be a good story behind that?"

"It all began with the Harmonic Convergence," I said. "You probably don't remember the Harmonic Convergence."

"Sorry, that was before my time."

"Tell us about it," Trudy begged.

Peter smiled at me. "Careful, you're dating yourself."

"If I'm dating me than I'm dating you, too, since we're the same age!"

"I remember the Harmonic Convergence," Cora added, thoughtfully. "That was when the planets were all going to line up and bring us something like world peace."

"That obviously didn't happen," said Trudy.

"No, it certainly didn't," I said. I fell silent again, thinking not only about our current wars, but also about the world conflagration that had been building while Miss Hastings was in the sanatorium. For the first time I wondered how many of Addie's sons had gone off to fight in World War II. How many of them had come home?

"OK, now I've really got to hear it," Ryan declared, leaning forward in his chair. "C'mon, Maggie, tell us the story."

Ryan's words brought me back to the present. "The Harmonic Convergence was a synchronized global meditation that was planned for a couple of days in August of 1987," I recalled. "It was supposed to be a time when something like eight or nine planets were going to line up and usher in, as Cora said, a new era of world love and peace. It had something to do with the Mayan calendar, I think."

"Seems like lots of things are related to the Mayan calendar," Rebecca mused.

"Well, I didn't really believe in any of that New Age stuff at the time, but I figured, 'What the heck!' So I went out to the big hill behind my grandmother's house where I was living—the hill was in the middle of a hayfield—and the day was so perfect that all of a sudden I found myself taking off my clothes. I spread my arms and ran naked down the hill. The sun on my skin felt so good that I just kept on running. There was an old woods road through the property, about half a mile long, and I ran buff as a baby down that road. Then I turned around and ran all the way back, up the hill. When I got to the top, I found a soft bed of clover and laid down and looked up at the sky. The world was spinning and I felt like I was flying. I don't think I'd been naked outdoors since I was a kid and I couldn't believe how wonderful it was. I began to think of Adam and Eve, and the Garden of Eden, and wondered if maybe there wasn't something to the Harmonic Convergence after all." I paused a moment. "That's when I heard my first call to the ministry, too. On top of that hill. The next day I contacted Bangor Theological Seminary, and the rest is history."

"You don't say!" said Ryan, obviously impressed.

Cora's eyes were wide. "How very interesting."

"When I moved to Sovereign, the hill out in back of my house reminded me of my grandmother's big hill. The only difference was that this was a hayfield gone wild. It was overrun by tall, glorious goldenrod. I mowed paths up through the goldenrod with my lawnmower, and every August after that I had my own private Harmonic Convergence. Last year folks began asking me if they could run through the goldenrod, too, and this year I opened it up to the public as a fundraiser."

"The fundraiser is such a wonderful idea," said Rebecca. "Maybe next year I'll try your goldenrod run."

"What about you, Wendell?" Ryan asked.

"I'druther keep my shots on." Everyone laughed.

"Your run does sound like fun," Cora added, wistfully. "But I wouldn't want anyone to see me naked, especially people I don't know."

"Oh, it's all very discreet," I replied. "The back hill is screened by some trees and shrubs, and there's a tent in which you change. Everyone draws a number, and while you're waiting for your number to be called I serve tea and cookies in my herb garden. This year Peter and his great-nephew Gray helped me with that, thank goodness."

I became conscious that Leland was fidgeting in his chair, most likely awaiting an opportunity to share one of his tall tales. He had pushed away his empty dessert plate, and laid his forearm on the table. I could tell he was winding himself up. "It was a fun day," I concluded, "but I'm glad it's over." I picked up my dessert plate and proffered it to Rebecca. "Do you think I could I have another helping of that sponge cake? That was delicious."

Rebecca obliged, and a lag in the conversation ensued. Leland took advantage of his opening, and entertained us with some of his tall tales and tarradiddles for the next forty-five minutes.

The little party broke up shortly after ten o'clock, and I thought it was one of the most agreeable evenings I'd spent in a long time. As Peter and I drove by Miss Hastings' house, we noticed a light on downstairs. I almost asked Peter to stop, but I decided it was too late for the both of us to drop in on her unannounced. I made a mental note to visit her in the morning. I only hoped that morning wouldn't be too late.

Chapter 9

"When You See a Rattlesnake Poised to Strike"

September 1941

"That will be all, thank you, Mrs. Emerson," said Helen, gently dismissing their housekeeper. She could tell by the agitated, abstracted way her husband was acting at lunch that something was bothering him. She wanted to give Andy the opportunity of sharing his thoughts privately before he returned to work. Currently, Westcott's Canning Factory, where he was supervisor, was in the process of canning butterbeans, and it was possible he wouldn't make it home for dinner.

"Yes, yes, another fine lunch, thank you," Andy added. He tossed his crumpled cloth napkin onto the dining room table and stood up. Hands in his pants pockets, he turned away from the polished maple table and stared out the water-splotched dining room window. The fall rains had commenced, mercifully bringing an end to the drought. As a result, however, the September afternoon was dismal.

Mrs. Emerson, equally as observant as her mistress, picked up a handful of dirty dishes and quietly withdrew. Helen arose, and moved gracefully to her husband's side. She placed her hand on his arm. "What's wrong, Antonsha?" The couple still used their pet names for each other, the same ones they had used when they were married in Petrograd a quarter of a century ago.

"I had a visitor at the factory this morning," Andy replied, now observing as a gray squirrel scampered across the leaf-strewn yard toward one of the old oak trees lining the property. "A Chief Petty Officer Steele."

"Yes?"

The squirrel selected its nut, and sat back on its haunches examining the brown-capped acorn. "He's visiting all the canning factories in Maine, assessing our ability to supply canned corn and beans to the Navy. He arrived on the nine o'clock train from Boston and left on the twelve o'clock, for the factory in Brooks."

"Did you make a large sale?"

"Not yet. I gave Chief Petty Officer Steele the information about our production capabilities. I'll need to talk with Westcott and some of the farmers about prices, of course. But that's not what I want to speak with you about."

"No?" Helen's voice faltered. "What is it, dahrrrling?"

The squirrel shook the rain from its furry back, and scooted back across the lawn, apparently satisfied with the quality of its new treasure. Andy watched the squirrel disappear into the dripping woods, and turned to his wife. He took her by the hands. "When was the last time you heard from your aunts in Kiev, Alyona?" he asked, quietly.

"My aunts?! Why, not since the spring, Antonsha. Nonna wrote to me in March, but I have heard nothing since. Why?"

"Are they still in Kiev?"

"Certainly. Where else would Nonna and Olga be? They have lived in the same home for more than seventy years."

"Brace yourself—you must be strong. The Chief Petty Officer says the Germans have invaded Kiev."

Helen tried to break away. *"Nyet!"*

He drew her into his arms, and held her fast. "Do not upset yourself unnecessarily; it may even yet be alright," Andy reassured his wife. He did not believe this himself, but he did not want to alarm her. Wherever the Nazis went, they left behind a wide swath of death and destruction. "He says the Navy is itching for an opportunity to fire at one of their subs or surface raiders. You remember what Roosevelt said in his speech the other night after the torpedo attack on the *USS Greer?*" He waited for the briefest nod of her head. The two of them had listened together to the President's fireside radio chat on September 11th. "We will fire first. When you see a rattlesnake poised to strike, you do not wait until he has struck before you crush him." This last line was a direct quote from Roosevelt. "The Nazis are so arrogant it's only a matter of time – weeks or even days – before the United States is officially at war with Germany."

"But that might be too late for Olga and Nonna!" Helen protested. "Why, oh, why did they not come to America with us, like your sister?" This was a rhetorical question, one that had been asked many times before.

"I'm sorry, Alyona. We must hope and pray for the best." Andy gave her a warm hug, and stepped away. His duty done, he was preparing to return to the factory when he recalled an important caveat. "By the way, the Chief Petty Officer asked me to keep the news about the Kiev invasion secret, at least until it hits the papers. It hasn't been made public yet."

"Who would I tell? It is too late to warn Olga and Nonna," she added, sadly.

Even as she said this, Helen knew that she would defy her husband. She would tell someone, one person, who ought to know. It might make a difference. It should make a difference. She hovered over Andy until he departed for work, waving 'goodbye' from the dining room window as was her custom. Then Helen passed quickly into her parlor, where she liberated a handful of bills from a small drawer in her secretary and stuffed them into her purse. She drew on her ankle boots, slipped into a raincoat and pulled a thick scarf over her dark head. "I'll be back soon," she informed Mrs. Emerson. "We will have the chicken for dinner, hmm?"

She briskly walked the half mile down the road to her friend's house. Soon, Helen was knocking at the interior shed door of the old Russell homestead. She heard Pappy call for her to enter, and pushed open the door to discover him and Bud kibitzing at the kitchen table, huddled in close proximity to the roaring heat from the woodstove. Addie was no place in sight.

"Where is your wife, George?" she asked him. After all these years, she still could not bring herself to call her neighbor by the impertinent-sounding name of "Pappy."

Upon her entrance, both men scrambled to their feet. Bud respectfully slipped off his red cap and stuck it under his arm. Pappy doffed his fedora.

"She's down in the hen pen, Helen. Want Bud to go 'n git 'er?" Bud shuffled his feet bashfully and gave an amenable nod.

"No, no; I wouldn't ask Mr. Suomela to go to so much trouble."

"'Tain't no trouble at-tall, ma'am," assured Bud, standing up taller. "I'd be right glad to fetch 'er."

But Helen preferred to carry out her mission in secret, not in front of a larger audience. She smiled graciously. "I will just go myself, I think. I know where to go—down those clever circular stairs you built, George, hmm?"

"Yep. Them's the ones. She's down at the bottom."

"Thet's whar Addie cleans 'n sorts 'er eggs," Bud added, anxious to prolong the conversation.

Helen rewarded them both with another bright smile, and exited the kitchen. After the overpowering heat of the kitchen, the shed felt damp and raw. She shivered, and pulled her coat tighter. She passed through another interior door into the entryway of the hen pen, the two-story shed that connected the house to the barn and the center of the egg operation. She noted several wooden grain and sawdust bins strategically placed, she supposed, so that their contents could be shoveled down to the chickens below. Helen knew that her friend's work area, as well as the nest boxes and chicken coop, were situated on the ground floor beneath. She spotted the iron railing to Pappy's circular stairwell and, holding carefully onto the moist wrought-iron, wound her way down the battle-scarred wooden steps. She heard the cacophonous squawking of Addie's four hundred laying hens and smelled the unmistakable stench of ammonia. The odor was strong but not unbearable, and she recollected Addie explaining to her once that Pappy had designed and built a unique ventilation system that – by way of natural convection – replaced the ammonia-laden air of the chicken coop with fresh air from the outside. At the bottom of the stairwell she stepped onto a sawdust-strewn concrete floor, and was relieved to note that she was separated from the chickens by a barrier constructed of two-inch chicken wire, with a door in the middle. Several chickens tumbled over each other to line up at the wire, cackling for her attention. Feathers and dust floated freely like snow. She turned in the opposite direction and followed shards of light around a corner, where she spied her friend, back to her, bent over a waist-high work station where Addie was busy cleaning, sorting, and grading eggs. A palm-sized strip of sandpaper dangled from Addie's wrist on a rubber band. Every few seconds she'd clasp the sandpaper and rub some dried manure from an egg.

Helen approached her friend and tapped her on the shoulder. Addie gave a little jump. "Goodness, you startled me!"

"Pardon me for interrupting, dahrrrling," Helen apologized. "But I have something I must tell you."

Addie wiped her hands on her work apron, and smiled. "To see you here, my dear! What a sight!"

Helen surveyed her friend's dominion, which was illuminated by a large, bright incandescent bulb hanging overhead. The work area was lined with well-ordered wooden shelving, upon which crates of big brown eggs were awaiting delivery. The watermelon-shaped basket in which Addie collected the eggs was resting upon a three-foot wide work bench, next to a metal egg-sizing scale. "I wonder that I have never been down here before," Helen marveled, almost forgetting herself. "You have a very orderly operation, Adelaide."

"I try to run a tight ship," Addie replied, with satisfaction. "But this is hardly the place to talk, my dear." She slipped the sandpaper from her wrist. "Shall we go upstairs and move the boys off the kitchen table?"

Recalling her mission, Helen shook her head. "I would much rather stay here with you, please. This will not take long."

Addie raised her eyebrows, but said nothing.

Helen felt a constriction in her throat. "The Russians have invaded Kiev," she croaked. "Anton … Andy heard this news from a man in the Navy today."

"Kiev? Isn't that a city in the Soviet Union?"

Helen felt her skin crawl. Even today, she could hardly bear to hear her native homeland denoted as the USSR. "Ukraine," she elucidated. "Some of my mother's family still lives in Kiev, her sisters. I fear for their lives. And … and I fear for your sons."

Addie sagged down onto a tall, three-legged stool. She leaned an elbow against the counter for support. "So, it's come, then?"

"Andy says it is only a matter of weeks – perhaps days, before America joins Europe's war. Is there not some place your sons can go where there is no conscription? Canada, perhaps? Or to Australia?"

Addie shook her head tiredly. "Even if I could convince my boys to leave, they couldn't afford to start a new life someplace else. We couldn't help them, either. Everything we have in the world is tied up here. We're what you call 'land poor,' my dear. Like everyone else around here."

Helen clicked open her purse, and drew out the wad of bills. "Not everyone." She held the cash out to her friend. "Please, I want you to take this."

Addie eyed the money somewhat suspiciously. The first thought that popped into her head was that Helen had somehow gotten the money from the canning factory. "Where did you get all that?"

"It is not what you think—it is perfectly legal. Andy gives me money every week to run the household, but I do not spend it all. For years, I have been putting money aside for emergencies. This is an emergency." She gently pushed the money into her friend's palm, and closed Addie's fingers around it. "Please, take it. If for nothing else, take if for young Carroll's sake."

Addie hesitated. The idea of her youngest son, Carroll, fleeing to western Canada where thousands of acres of rich farm land were available appealed to her. He was still young, only twenty-two, and unencumbered. Or George! Perhaps her eldest son, George, could flee with his family, so that his child – her four-year-old granddaughter, Evelyn – wouldn't have to grow up without a father.

Helen saw her friend's hesitation, and redoubled her petition. "When you see a rattlesnake poised to strike, you do not wait until he has struck before you crush him," she quoted the President. "War is a rattlesnake. Your sons must remove themselves before it crushes them."

"My dear, you do not understand! You simply do not understand."

"I understand that you have already lost your brothers in Europe's wars—our wars—and now you are in danger of losing your sons. Is that fair? How much is a woman expected to give! Must she give everything? For what?!" Helen heard the hysterical, high-pitched timbre of her voice, but couldn't stop herself. She trembled in passionate anger. "They never think of us—never! They move us around the world like pawns in their adolescent war games. And if we do not go, they kill us. And when we do go, they kill our sons. And for what? Pour quoi?!"

"Calm yourself, my dear," urged Addie. "You're becoming over-excited." She reached out and squeezed her friend's hand. Helen didn't pull away, and Addie took the opportunity to snag Helen's purse, replacing the wad of bills. She snapped the purse shut. "Some things in life we can change. Some things we can't. War is something we must learn to accept." She held the purse out to her friend.

Helen brushed it aside impatiently. "*Nyet!* I will never accept it. Nor should you, Adelaide. There is a chimerical culture built up around war, a golden calf with which they continue to trick men into fighting. Women are not so foolish. We know what is in the calf—death and destruction.

But they glorify battle and give out colorful ribbons and pin medals on our men like prizes at the livestock shows at the county fair. Bah!" She shuddered. "Whenever I hear the words 'honor' or 'glory' I know that more young men are going to die!"

"My dear, to hear you talk like this! Would you have us *not* help the English? Or your own people, in Kiev?" Ironically, Addie suddenly found herself taking the other side of the argument. "Would you have us abandon them all to Hitler's war machine?"

"Yes! I would have us not fight. Hitler will burn himself out soon enough. He is an evil man, and will come to an evil end. In the meantime, how many more boys like your sons will march off to fight him and not return, hmm?"

"But how many more, like your aunts, will die if my sons don't go?" Addie asked, sorrowfully. "The problem with war is that there is no way to win without losing."

"Then we must refuse to participate, like the Quakers. Your son's ancestors were Quakers. They must claim the right of conscientious objectors. There are enough others who will go to fight."

"My sons are not religious; they are Americans, and they will do what the President and the country asks them to do."

"Then they are fools for their pains," announced Helen. "Although I am sorry to say so."

"My dear, I'm deeply touched by your concern, and your offer of money. But you must know we can't accept it. Besides, you might need the money to help with Jana's medical bills."

Helen had not considered this possibility. Might they need the money for Jana's treatment? She had not even asked Andy how much Windmere cost.

"War is a horrible thing," Addie continued, feeling the need to further clarify her position to her friend. "And you're right: there is something about war that men can't resist. I saw this in my brothers; I see it in my sons." She picked up the purse from where she had laid it on the workbench, and gently pressed it into her friend's hands. "Until men learn other ways to solve their differences, we women must accept it."

Helen shivered. She became aware that there was no heat in the hen pen, except what little bit was thrown off by the incandescent bulb and the nearby chickens.

"Won't you come up for a cup of hot tea now, my dear?" asked Addie, taking Helen by the arm, and steering her in the direction of the wrought-iron stairwell.

Helen laughed bitterly, but allowed herself to be propelled along. "Tea and cookies, Adelaide? Is that your remedy for war?"

"Until I find a better remedy, my dear, that one will have to do. Now, let us go prepare ourselves for the worst."

CHAPTER 10

MUSHROOM HUNTING

OCTOBER 2013

The morning after our harvest dinner at the Russells, I dropped in on Miss Hastings. I was relieved to discover that the light I had spotted on the way home the prior evening was no more than the parlor light she had forgotten to switch off. Although obviously failing, Miss Hastings was still feisty. As Doctor Bart had mentioned, the retired music teacher was fortunate to have caring friends around her who enabled her to remain in her home. Anyone else would have been consigned to a managed care facility or a nursing home long before this. After my visit, I contacted Shirley Palmer, the retired Postmistress in Sovereign, who was in charge of arranging Miss Hastings' meals and caregivers, and I signed up to cook her lunches on Tuesdays and Thursdays, as well as to provide overnight care on Sundays when that should become necessary. I would utilize our time together to plumb the mysteries of Miss Hastings' past. Today, I wanted to follow up on something Wendell had said during the harvest dinner, that she and his grandmother had had a "special affection" for each other. "I never see two ladies so different who got 'long so good as those two did," Wendell had said. This remark had piqued my curiosity.

"Did you know Wendell's grandmother well?" I asked, propping two pillows behind Miss Hastings' fragile back so that she could eat the chicken soup and grilled cheese and tomato sandwich I had prepared. I wasn't much of a cook, but Miss Hastings was always grateful for whatever food her friends fixed, even me. Generally, she ate her meals at the kitchen table. Today, however, she hadn't felt well enough to get up, and so I had brought her lunch in bed.

"OOoo, I knew Addie Russell like my favorite book, dahrrrling! I could find my way around her in the dark." She spoke affectionately, like a child speaks of her mother.

I unfolded the napkin across her lap. "What was she like?"

"She was a grand Maine dame of the best kind! No matter what happened, she'd seen worse. They don't make 'em like Addie anymore. Young people today don't know what some of the old timers around here like Addie suffered, and yet, no matter the set-back, she still got up each and every morning with a smile on her face, and went out to do her chores. Right into her eighties." Miss Hastings surveyed the tray I placed in front of her. "What a LOVELY lunch, dahrrrling! Thank you so much."

"It's just grilled cheese and tomato. But Peter likes it," I demurred. We had been keeping our engagement a secret, but suddenly I felt the urge to share. I sat down in my accustomed chair next to her bed, and watched her nibble away at the sandwich. "He's always asking me to marry him, you know," I continued. She nodded, and winked. "Well, the other day, I finally said, 'Yes.'"

Too late, I regretted my words. Not because I'd let the cat out of the bag, but because instantly she stopped eating. Miss Hastings set the sandwich down on the salad plate. "Dahrrrling, how WONDERFUL! I was hoping you'd wake up—thank the GOOD LORD."

I wasn't quite ready to give God all the credit, but, if the truth be told, I don't know what had come over me. Love, I guess.

She leaned over and patted my hand. "When is the big day? Soon, I hope! I don't want to miss it. Haaahaa!"

"We haven't set a date. Actually, you're the first to know. I've been waiting for Nellie to come home so I could tell her in person."

Miss Hastings put her finger to her lips. "Shhh! Mum's the word, then. Your secret is safe with me, dahrrrling!"

At the mention of the word "secret," I recollected that somehow I'd gotten turned around in my mission. Instead of plumbing Miss Hastings' secrets, I was spilling my own. But this was what happened when one was in the presence of such a caring individual as Miss Hastings. She had a way of pulling the humanity out of us like splinters from a barn board. But how did she get this way? Was she born an exceptionally understanding person? Or had something in Miss Hastings' past changed her?

"Did you make the chicken soup, dahrrrling?"

I nodded. "Rebecca gave me the recipe; it's from Grammie Addie's cookbook. Was she as good a cook as they say?"

"Better than that! She could make a chicken pot pie that would stick to your ribs for THREE DAYS. And her cookies, mmm, mmm, good! She used to bake me lemon butter cookies; they were my favorite. And Addie sewed, knitted and quilted, too. One time I remember, after she found out we slept outside on open-air porches in winter at Windmere, Addie had the Ladies Auxiliary knit stockings, mittens, and scarves for all of us at the sanatorium. Didn't the children LOVE that!"

"I'd love it, too. Have some more soup," I encouraged her. "You've hardly eaten a thing."

Her eyes became misty, and had a far-away look to them. I could tell she was no longer present, but was somewhere in the past. Was she back at the sanatorium with Henry, Eleanor, and Arthur?

"She was full of aphorisms, too. Well worth paying attention to, mind you!"

No, she was still with Addie. "Did you listen to her?" I asked, calculating that a young woman like Miss Hastings probably wouldn't be inclined to take an older woman's advice.

"You'd better believe it, dahrrrling! She told me once, when she had something very difficult to say to me—something that nobody else dared to say—that it's best to meet your troubles straight on, full speed ahead, like a sailing ship on the ocean. Nothing makes for fewer headwinds in the long run than facing the truth at the start. There might be a bit of choppiness in the beginning, but you'll avoid those storms that will eventually sink you if you put the bad news off for another day."

I had some difficulty picturing Grammie Addie sailing on the open ocean, and smiled to myself. It was most likely that the closest Addie had ever come to salt water was a Stonington lobster. I'd learned from Wendell that his grandmother's one annual outing away from the farm was a picnic to the nearby Millett Rock. Still, I understood Addie's metaphor for tackling trouble. Better to ride the waves up on top than to let the ocean suck you under.

This seemed like a natural segue, and I was going to proceed with my questioning; however, when I turned my attention back to Miss Hastings, I discovered that the retired music teacher had drifted off to sleep. Her frail, blue-veined hands were folded peacefully across her chest. I quietly removed the tray and gently rearranged the bedcovers. In the kitchen, I cleaned up my mess. I checked on her once before leaving, and discovered that she was still sleeping. How much time did I have before she departed this world for the next, taking her secrets with her?

I needed a few groceries, so I stopped at Gilpin's General Store on my way home. As I entered through the double glass doors, Leland Gorse exited. "Hallo, Minister," he said cordially, holding the door for me. But he didn't pause to chat like usual. He snuggled a brown paper bag against his chest, and hustled off to his truck. I thought I heard the distinctive clink of glass bottles coming from the bag when he moved.

I knew that Leland didn't drink alcohol, and so I was naturally curious to know what was in his brown paper bag, and why he was in such a hurry. I tried to shrug it off—it was probably nothing.

But when I entered the glassed-in foyer, I was overpowered by the scent of men's aftershave lingering in the trapped air. Leland? Leland Gorse wearing aftershave?!

This was too much! I turned around, and quickly noted which way Leland drove out of the parking lot. He headed north, toward the Russell Hill Road.

I'm not a stalker, by any means. I'm just curious. Normally, I wouldn't give in to the base human urge to know what Leland was up to; however, when a person discovers she has only a year (maybe less) to live, well, that sort of colors how she proceeds in life. Why not? Why not follow him?

I kept my distance, of course, so Leland wouldn't know I was behind him. I saw him pull into the dirt driveway of the old Russell homestead. That in itself wasn't odd; Leland and Wendell were best friends. Maybe he was simply bringing Wendell something from the store. Wendell was always tinkering on some project or other, like the Mouse Motel he'd built to capture (and later release) all the mice at the old place. But … maybe something else was going on.

I motored up to Miss Hastings' house, and parked in the yard where I knew I wouldn't be suspected of anything nefarious. I decided to wait a few minutes, and, sure enough, in less than ten minutes Leland drove past looking smug. Beside him in the pickup's passenger seat was … Cora Batterswaith!

"Well, I'll be hornswoggled," I said aloud, slapping my palm against the steering wheel. "Who'd a thunk it?"

I had suspected during the evening of our harvest dinner that Leland had taken a shine to Cora, but I certainly didn't think that there was any reciprocity. Cora was a big city girl, who probably considered Leland as a friendly grandfather type (although I suspected they were only about ten or fifteen years apart in age). I couldn't imagine where they were going or what they were doing and so, naturally, I decided to follow them.

Leland pulled into the parking area of one of the town's public woodlots. I tamped my brakes, and nosed my car into a turnaround about a hundred yards south of the same entrance. I popped open the car door, grateful that I was wearing my sturdy hiking boots and jeans, and my brown L.L. Bean fleece.

I hopped over the ditch and landed in the squishy woods, still wet from a recent rain. I wound my way carefully around slippery, moss-covered logs and through the thick underbrush, taking care not to snap off a dry pine branch and alert Leland and Cora to my presence. I hunched over, keeping myself as low to the ground as possible. Perhaps if he spotted me from a distance he might think I was a deer. I only hoped he wouldn't shoot me. Deer season didn't open for another couple of weeks; however, hunters like Leland had been known to bag many a trophy out of season.

The southerly breeze carried the sound of the couple's voices on the air. I closed my eyes and tried to make out what they were saying. I heard Cora's high-pitched laugh, but her words were indistinguishable. I crept closer, and closer. Finally, I spied the two of them in a clearing where the wood had been harvested a year or two earlier. I concealed myself behind the fragrant branches of a balsam fir and watched as Leland dropped onto his haunches, then popped back up again and handed something to Cora. She squealed with delight, turning the orange-yellow object over in her hands. They were mushroom hunting!

"Why, this looks just like something I'd buy from the mushroom man at Union Square! His prices are crazy expensive, though. How much do you charge, Leland?" Cora giggled.

"'Tain't no charge at-tall fer you," he replied, gallantly.

"What kind is it?"

"Thet's a chanterelle."

"I thought so!"

"Thet's jest the beginnin', de-ah," Leland promised. "You ain't seen nuthin' yet." He drew a cloth napkin out of a medium-sized potato basket and carefully wrapped up the chanterelle. He placed the mushroom into the woven basket and held the basket out to Cora by the curved ash handle. "Now, let's git us some mo-ah, de-ah."

The Maine woods in October are crawling with musty-smelling mushrooms, and I hunkered down where I was and watched as Leland and Cora harvested more chanterelles, several reddish-brown honey caps, and a patch of pink bottoms. Leland, the old-time woodchopper, had spent more time in the woods than anyone else in Sovereign. He had known exactly where to go to make the best mushroom score. He was like that with fiddleheads, too. While everyone else spent hours scouring the stream bottoms of Black Brook, Leland would disappear into the woods and come out thirty minutes later with a pail-full of fiddleheads.

When their basket was filled with mushrooms, Leland retrieved his brown paper bag and pulled up a log. He patted the seat beside him. Cora hesitated, glanced around, and then gingerly lowered herself down next to him. He reached into the bag, and pulled out two bottles: a bottle of white wine and a bottle of Moxie. He flipped open the corkscrew on his jackknife and dexterously removed the cork from the neck of the wine bottle. He handed the bottle to Cora. She giggled again, but accepted the wine and took a modest sip. Likewise, Leland flipped off the Moxie cap, and swigged down some of the refreshing Maine beverage. "Ah," he said, wiping his mouth with the back of his hand. "Ain't nuthin' so good as Moxie. Evah tried it?" He proffered the Moxie bottle to Cora.

Cora eyed the dark bottle with its distinctive orange label with skepticism. "Isn't that the stuff that tastes like medicine?"

"Nope. Tastes real good."

Cora accepted the glass bottle from his rough paw, and took the smallest sip. She made a face, but managed to swallow the bitter beverage. "How can you like that?"

"Wal, how kin you like thet, de-ah?" Leland replied, indicating her wine. He had a good point there, I thought.

I began to worry how long they were going to stay in the clearing. If they didn't move further into the woods I might not be able to get away unnoticed. I'd been lucky so far, but I knew that the only reason Leland hadn't spotted me was because he was focused on impressing his female companion. He was acting like a silly old gander in a gaggle of geese.

"I gots somethin' else I want ter show ya," he announced, resting his Moxie bottle against the log. He bravely pulled himself up—I could tell he was trying hard not to make the usual exclamation all old folks make when we try to unfurl our arthritic limbs. "Ovah heah, de-ah."

I should have taken the opportunity to escape, but I couldn't leave without knowing what Leland was going to reveal next. Once I met a forester who told me he always liked to look under the roots of blow downs, because he never knew what he might find there, such as the axe he had found, which had been laid in the woods a hundred years earlier and disappeared from sight when the pine tree grew right up over it. After that story, I'd never been able to get through a patch of woods without peering under uprooted trees.

Leland led Cora into a copse of hardwoods. I crept a bit closer over the cold, wet ground, soaking and staining the knees of my jeans. "Whaddaya think o' this?" he asked, proudly. He reached around the side of a maple tree, and broke something off. He handed the prize to Cora. From a distance the mushroom looked like something from the underground, like the skull of a poor creature that had been long dead. I suspected it was bear's head, *Hericium caputursi*.

"Gross!" she exclaimed, quickly passing the mushroom back to Leland. "You don't eat that?!"

Leland grinned. "Does the Pope shat in the woods? Is a bear Catholic?"

The strangest things go through your mind when you are in the Maine woods and you have an incurable disease. I suddenly found myself feeling sad thinking that the Pope, the new Pope, Francis, who seemed like such a nice guy, probably never did have the opportunity to relieve himself in the woods, thereby missing out on a very fine experience. When I was a kid growing up on the banks of the Sebasticook River in Winslow, my childhood chum Peter and I had been as free as wood nymphs. If nature called, we were generally too far away (and too busy playing) to go home and use the indoor plumbing. Instead, we'd pull up a piece of ground, and squat there listening contentedly to the birds sing while we did our business.

When was the last time? I wondered.

Leland and Cora had drifted further into the woods, but my eyes refused to focus on them. Instead, a blur of moving images came to mind. Peter, calling for me to follow him through the woods. My parents, waving me off to college. My daughter, wobbling her first step away from me.

There are so many last times, one can't remember them all. Last kiss. Last hug. Last time you make love...

When I came back to the present, Cora and Leland had disappeared from sight. I was able to retrieve my car and return home with no one – but myself – the wiser. Like Miss Hastings, my grieving process had begun. We were both wrapping up our lives here on earth, even as we were preparing to move on.

CHAPTER II

"I AM THE *THEY*"

OCTOBER 1941

"Where's Henry, Jana?" Arthur piped up in his distinctive falsetto voice, interrupting Jana in the middle of a sentence. She was reading aloud to Eleanor a chapter from *The Black Stallion*, a novel which both girls much preferred to *Northwest Passage*. "It's time for us to collect the eggs and I can't find him anywhere." The eight-year-old shifted slightly from foot to foot, betraying his anxiety.

Jana glanced around the outdoor sleeping porch, where several girls were reclining in various stages of undress. "He's certainly not here," she replied. "How did you get past the nurses?" The boys and girls sleeping quarters were supposed to be carefully segregated.

"Oh, the nurses don't care about me; I'm too young. Do you know where Henry is?"

Jana had last seen Henry at lunch, where he had received a letter from the Judge. At the conclusion of the meal, Henry had slipped away to read his father's missive in private. Jana suspected that he had gone to Dr. Ketchum's study, a sanctuary the use of which was offered to him by the kindly doctor for whenever Henry was overpowered by Arthur and the other children. There were not a lot of places to escape Arthur at Windmere, and Jana knew that Dr. Ketchum was out making his rounds at the brick building.

"No," Jana replied, not actually lying. "I'll help you get the eggs today, Arthur." She marked her place and set the book down on the metal hospital stand, noticing as she did so the clean sputum cup. "You haven't done your sputum test yet, Eleanor," she reminded her friend. She picked up the collector cup and held it out. Eleanor was propped up in bed, her condition having been upgraded slightly although her star had not been changed from gold to green.

"What's the use? I know it's going to come back positive." Eleanor started to cough, and reached for a handkerchief to cover her mouth.

Jana glanced quickly at Arthur. It wasn't like Eleanor to be so despondent, especially around the younger children. She set the cup back on the table. "We'll do it later, then," she said, cheerily. "And don't peek while I'm gone. Once you start reading you know you won't be able to stop."

Eleanor clutched the handkerchief between her hands. She smiled faintly. "I won't read ahead," she promised. "Don't be gone long."

Jana allowed Arthur to lead her out to the chicken coop. She and the younger children gathered the eggs and fed the chickens. She often participated in this activity, not only because it afforded her an opportunity to spend time with Henry, but also because she loved to watch the hens and their funny antics. Today, one of the birds flew down off its perch and attempted to land on the rim of the galvanized scratch corn pail. The fat chicken failed to get a grip on the thin rim, however, and batted its wings madly against Arthur's chest and face, knocking the pail out of his hands and sending the corn and him sprawling.

Arthur immediately blamed the chicken. "He made me spill the corn!" he wailed. He picked himself up off the thick sawdust that covered the floor of the coop.

"It's not a HE, it's a SHE, stupid," pronounced Suzanne, a bold-faced little girl of six or seven who sometimes reminded Jana of her younger self. "Chickens are GIRLS, Arthur."

"Not all of 'em," Arthur protested, hotly. "Roosters ain't girls!"

Suzanne stuck her tongue out at him. "Silly, roosters aren't chickens."

"They is too! Ain't roosters chickens, Jana?"

Jana—who thought that the question was akin to: "Which came first, the chicken or the egg?"—was fortunately able to avoid the conundrum when the youngest member of their little group attempted to grasp three eggs from a nest box at once. "Don't drop those, Julia," she cautioned, leaping forward in the nick of time. Jana added the eggs safely to the wicker collecting basket, and, stepping back, surveyed the situation with amusement. She smiled to herself, picturing what the members of her old travelling troupe of musicians would think if they could see her now. Big John Kauffman the baritone, with whom she occasionally sang duets, would probably say: "Hell and tarnation! You're wasting your life, Songbird!" But then, Big John wasn't a teenage girl in the throes of an identity crisis.

The past two months had been a restful period for Jana, as had been intended by the doctors. But her time at Windmere had also triggered a strange transmogrification of spirit. It seemed as though when she had removed her favorite travelling coat (the lime-green jacket with the lace collar and shiny black buttons), she had removed her *Songbird of Sovereign* persona. She had moved out of the spotlight and into a state of "being" not "doing." She felt a new vulnerability, much like a shedder lobster must feel when it shucks its protective green shell. Jana knew that she was in a period of growth and maturation. She hadn't realized how fatigued she had become continuing to pretend that she was still a precocious child entertainer until Windmere had given her the time to think about what she wanted to be instead. And here, at Windmere, Henry and Eleanor had taught her *how* to think. She knew she was evolving, but she didn't know into whom or what she was evolving. Sometimes she felt like that molting lobster must be feeling, hiding its vulnerability and its strange new shape in the depths and darkness of the ocean, waiting for something or someone to come along and tell her that her new shell was beautiful.

She began to wonder what would happen next spring or summer, when two clean sputum tests in a row would release her from the safety and security of Windmere. Would she return to New York and continue a career in music of some kind? Or would she return home to Sovereign? Would she marry, as most other girls did?

Jana thought of Henry, and her teenage heart skipped a beat. Where would Henry go when *he* left Windmere? Would he return to Rhode Island, to live in Providence with the Judge? Would he continue his college education? (Jana had learned that, before returning to Windmere in the spring, Henry had been a student at Brown University.) She thought of her Aunt Minnie, now back in her cozy little home in Providence, and wondered how far away from the college her aunt's home was situated.

Thinking of Henry refocused Jana's thoughts to the present. She wondered what was so important in the Judge's letter that it had kept Henry from his favorite daily activity.

When the chickens were fed, the eggs collected, and Arthur shaken loose, Jana was finally free to seek Henry out. Shortly before three o'clock, she knocked softly on the door to Dr. Ketchum's study. "Henry?" she whispered. "Are you in there?" Hearing no reply from within, she placed her ear to the smooth wooden door. She thought she could hear the mantle clock ticking, and carefully turned the brass doorknob. With just the lightest touch, the door swung inward to reveal Henry sprawled in a striped George III chair near the open cavity of the painted brick fireplace. He stared obliviously out the south-facing window, the letter from his father lying unfolded in his lap. His arm rested on the side of the chair, and in his hand he held a newspaper clipping.

The radiator under the window hissed loudly and released a burp of steam, startling Jana and alerting Henry to her presence. "Songbird! You tracked me down," Henry cried, rising up. He stuffed the letter and clipping back into the envelope and glanced at the mantelpiece clock. "Don't tell me—little Arthur is nagging to collect the eggs."

"The chickens are done, Henry. I helped the children today. Is everything alright?"

He took three steps toward her. "What would be wrong, Songbird? I had a letter from the Judge, and it wasn't even his time for writing."

"Did your father have good news?"

Henry hesitated, and then abruptly turned on his heel. "It's no use," he said, dejectedly. He slumped back down into his chair. "I can't lie to you."

Jana clicked the door shut, and stepped quickly over to his side. She felt a thrill of excitement at being alone with Henry. "I don't want you to lie to me," she said, touching the back of his chair. She wanted to touch him, but didn't dare. "I like it that you tell me the truth."

"Even about the bad things?"

"Especially about the bad things."

Their eyes met. Because Henry was seated, their heads were at about the same level. Jana felt the room begin to spin. He reached out, as though he was going to tug on one of her curls as usual. Instead, his hand dropped back into his lap. "Take a chair. I'll let you read it."

Jana tucked her full skirt and sat down in the matching George III chair opposite him. Henry held out the fat white envelope from his father. She hesitated. What if she couldn't understand what the Judge had written? She might not be able to focus on the meaning of the words with Henry watching her. Better for him to tell her what the letter contained. "Can't you tell me what he says?"

Henry slapped the thick envelope against his thigh. "He says that my idol has feet of clay."

"Oh, is that all? I thought your father was sick or dying."

He laughed. "You've been in here too long, Songbird. You're start-ing to think that everyone is dying." The good-humored expression in his brown eyes quickly faded. "There are some things worse than death."

"Like what?"

"Like the loss of a dream. A fall from grace for someone you thought was better than everybody else. Someone who gave you hope that the world was actually better than it appeared to be."

Jana struggled to follow Henry's rhetoric. "I don't understand," she said, embarrassed to admit her ignorance. Probably Eleanor would know what he was talking about. She vowed to spend more time thinking, and less time reading novels. "Do you mean … your father?"

"Good heavens, no. The Judge is a good man, and I'm grateful to have him and all. But he's not a game-changer."

"Then who, Henry?"

"Lindbergh," he replied, angrily. As he said the name, Henry chucked the letter and its contents into the fireplace, where kindling and paper had been laid carefully on a pair of brass andirons in preparation for Dr. Ketchum's evening fire.

"*Charles* Lindbergh? The aviator?"

"The one and only. Lucky Lindy. The Lone Eagle! He was my hero and role model. At least he was until today."

Jana wanted to ask what had happened to change Henry's opinion of the great man, but she didn't want to reveal any more of her igno-rance. A noteworthy event must have occurred of which she was in the dark. They never did hear much of the outside world at Windmere. She remained silent, knowing full well that Henry would soon fill in the gaps.

"They're calling him un-American, and I'm not so sure but what they're right." Henry thrummed his fingers against the side of the chair.

"Lindbergh?! But … he's one of the great heroes of our times."

"That's what I thought; that's what millions of us thought."

"Who dares to say he's un-American, Henry?"

"*The New York Times*, for one. Lindbergh gave a speech the other day, in Des Moines. He often does speak out against the war, you know, for the American First Committee. But this time he went too far. His remarks targeted the Roosevelt administration, the British, and the Jews." Henry ticked off the three groups as he talked. "Lindbergh specifically accuses them of pushing America into this war simply to serve their own ends, their own selfish purposes. The Judge says in his letter that many newspapers, not just *The New York Times*, are calling him a Jew-baiter as well as un-American."

At Henry's first use of the word "Jew," Jana had unconsciously sat up a little straighter in her chair. At the second reference, she felt her face flush. Fortunately, Henry appeared not to notice.

"Let me read you what Lindbergh said, and you tell me what you think." Henry retrieved the envelope from the fireplace, and liberated one of the pages from inside, scanning down through the piece until he found the section for which he was looking. "Here ... listen to this—this is the most damnable part: '*I am not attacking either the Jewish or the British people. Both races, I admire. But I am saying that the leaders of both the British and the Jewish races, for reasons which are as understandable from their viewpoint as they are inadvisable from ours, for reasons which are not American, wish to involve us in war. We cannot blame them for looking out for what they believe to be their own interests, but we also must look out for ours. We cannot allow the natural passions and prejudices of other peoples to lead our country to destruction.*' Well, that says it all, doesn't it?" Henry's hand dropped to his lap. He glanced over at her, expecting ready confirmation, yet none came.

He leaned towards her. "Don't you see?" Henry continued, passionately. "To even name the Jews as a group separate from Americans—to denote them as the 'other'—seems to suggest that Lindbergh thinks that *they*, the Jews, even American Jews, are different from *us*. I read the entire speech three times; the Judge thought I should see it, as well as the *Times* opinion piece. Father knows how much I admire Lindbergh, and he wanted me to know what everyone was saying about him. The Judge didn't tell me his opinion. He's too good a man for that. He brought me up to think for myself. But I can read between the lines of the Judge's letter. He agrees with *The New York Times* and I'll be damned if I don't agree with the paper, too. How could I ever have idolized him?! It just goes to show that you never really know someone, even someone as famous as the Lone Eagle."

Jana remained silent.

"Well, Songbird? Don't you have any thoughts at all?"

Jana nervously moistened her lips. She had listened carefully to Henry as he read Charles Lindbergh's words, and she thought that she understood them. Hearing what the aviator had written made her feel slightly sick to her stomach. "I think … I think that I am the *they*, and you are the *us*."

Henry started up in surprise. "What?! You—Jewish?"

Mortified, Jana felt her face become hot and sticky. She nodded.

"I didn't see that! I can't believe it—I must be slipping."

Henry's words, and the callous, careless way in which he had said them, angered Jana. "To hear you talk, you'd think there should be some sort of a black mark on my forehead," she replied, crossly. "You sound just like Lindbergh and you don't even know it!"

Instantly, Henry was down on one knee in front of her. He clasped her slim hands, cradling them between his own much larger ones. "I'm sorry, Songbird! You're absolutely right—I'm an infernal ass. I go around pretending I'm smarter than everyone else, and all that does is to prove I'm an idiot."

At his touch, Jana's heart fluttered wildly. "Oh, get up," she said. "You *look* like an idiot." Nevertheless, she didn't pull away from him. A lock of his dark hair had fallen across one of his eyes. She longed to reach out and push the hair back from his forehead, but he was gazing at her with such an intent look that she felt paralyzed. She heard a loud buzzing in her ears and felt a strange sensation in her head.

Her breathing became shallow. Was she even breathing?

Jana closed her eyes, willing herself not to faint. There was a slight movement of air against her left cheek, and she sensed that he was close to her. Was he going to … to kiss her?!

Who knows what might have occurred if Dr. Ketchum hadn't returned. But at the sound of his heavy footsteps in the hallway outside the study, Henry and Jana broke guiltily apart. The two scrambled to their feet just as the door was flung open.

"What, you here, Miss Hastings?" asked the good-natured doctor, tossing his old-fashioned bowler hat upon the three-pronged oak coatrack. He perched his leather doctor's bag on his desk and turned to face them. "Little Arthur too much for you, as well, eh?"

"I … I," Jana stuttered, unwilling to lie to the doctor but unsure how to explain her presence in his study alone with Henry.

"Jana and I were discussing Lindbergh's Des Moines speech, sir," Henry interjected, hastily. "I received a letter from my father today, with a copy of his speech. Have you read it?" Henry held up his envelope.

"Not very likely. I've got rather too much on my plate here to worry about what's happening out there. Some dust up, I suppose?"

"Lindbergh's blamed the Roosevelt administration, the British, and the Jewish people for dragging us into the war in Europe."

"What? Not giving any credit to Hitler, is he? Now, there's my main suspect. No sense getting ourselves worked up over it, Henry. There's not much we can do about the war from here, is there?"

Henry straightened his back. "Sir, I registered for selective service in June, when I turned twenty-one."

"Now, now, you know you're ineligible at present, Henry. The bar is low, I admit; they'll take almost anyone these days. But they're not yet taking men with communicable diseases."

The youth relaxed. "At least I weigh more than a hundred and five pounds. Not much more, though," he admitted, wryly. The minimum weight for military service was one hundred and five pounds. His comment broke the ice, and the three of them laughed.

"Get along, you two, and let me have my study to myself." Dr. Ketchum sat himself down at his desk, and picked up the receiver of the black telephone. "Etta, get me Pilgrim 3-2882, please. Yes, that's Dr. Barrow's number. I want to consult with him about a case." He looked over at them and made a little shooing motion with his hand.

Henry obligingly held the door open for Jana. The youth indicated with a discreet nod of his head that she should follow him down the hall toward the green room.

Jana hesitated. She wanted to be with Henry, but she was worried about Eleanor. She had been gone from her friend a long time. She made a garbled excuse to him, which sounded lame even to her own ears, and returned to the girls sleeping porch where she discovered that supper for the invalids had already been served. Eleanor was sitting up in bed, toying with – but not eating – her food. At the sight of her friend, Eleanor set her fork down on the edge of the ivory-colored plate with the blue Windmere insignia. "Did you get a lot of eggs? You were gone an awfully long time."

Jana felt her face turn red. "Less than yesterday, actually. Mr. Dunkirk says the hens are beginning to notice the lack of daylight." Mr. Dunkirk was the farmer who managed Windmere's agricultural resources.

"I suppose Arthur wanted you to play *Rook*, then," said Eleanor, regarding her friend's face closely.

Jana perched on the edge of her chair. "Please try and eat, Eleanor," she begged, side-stepping the implied question about what had kept her away so long. "You've got to eat something or you won't get better."

"Not tonight. I don't think I'll eat tonight. You can tell the nurse to take the tray away." Eleanor rolled over onto her side, presenting her back to her friend, and shut her eyes.

Jana sighed. At the moment, the world outside the sanatorium— even the war in Europe and Charles Lindbergh's fall from grace—seemed much less complicated than the world inside Windmere.

Chapter 12

Visitors

November 2013

The ethnic mix of Sovereign is not quite as white bread as one might think, given our rural nature. True, the town was first settled by descendants of those who sailed from England in the seventeenth century, and thus the old Anglo Saxon names of Nutter, Peabody, Edwards, and Russell are predominant in the our cemeteries. Over the centuries, however, a smattering of other ethnic groups seeking economic opportunity also settled in Sovereign, people such as the Finnish Bud Suomela and the Scottish MacAlpines (whose name along the way became Anglicized to Gilpin), and even an occasional Jewish family, such as Miss Hastings' (although now that I found myself thinking about it I realized that I had never seen her parents' graves in my many trips to the Russell Hill Cemetery).

I had suspected Miss Hastings was Jewish without ever having spoken a word to her on the subject. There are some things you just garner by osmosis. She was a member of our church, the Troy Union Church, mostly, I suspect, because we were Universalist in theology. I never prescribed one particular religion over another and we often celebrated Jewish holidays and holy days. I had noted on my many forays into her family library that in addition to several shelves of French and Russian literature there was one shelf dedicated to books written in Hebrew.

Today was the first time we had spoken about her family's heritage, and I found myself wondering why. Most likely it was because she herself had never brought the subject up, having been taught that it was more socially acceptable (and probably much safer) not to draw attention to her Jewishness.

"What happened to Olga and Nonna?" I asked. Miss Hastings had just shared with me the story of her great aunts.

"The poor dahrrrlings were killed in the pogrom at Kiev!"

This piece of information was disconcerting, but not unexpected. "They didn't make it out before the Nazis got there, then?"

The fire in Miss Hastings' eyes blazed up. "How could they? They were old and weak, and couldn't run away. Hitler's *Einsatzgruppe* herded Olga and Nonna up with some of their neighbors and drove them like sheep into a ravine. They shot them—the DAMNED BEASTS."

I had never heard Miss Hastings swear before, although Wendell had once mentioned she had learned some salty language during her youthful days with the travelling troupe of musical performers.

"Thirty thousand were murdered at Babi Yar," she added. "THIRTY THOUSAND."

"Your poor mother!" I sympathized, thinking to myself how much those of us who are born in this country take for granted. Ironically, the city of Kiev had recently been in the news following an attack by police on some peaceful anti-government protestors there. The situation was becoming increasingly heated as tens of thousands Ukrainians were taking to the streets to protest against their President's decision not to sign a key trade agreement with the European Union but instead to throw the country's economic lot in with Russia. The descendants of Olga and Nonna – assuming they had descendants – could be some of the protestors whose lives were imperiled. How differently their lives would have been had the two sisters decided to immigrate to the United States with Helen and Andy!

Suddenly, from out of the blue, an image popped into my mind of two marble tombstones in the Russell Hill Cemetery. I had always wondered about these mysterious matched gravestones, because the surname etched on them was unusual, especially for New England. "Your father's last name wasn't 'Hastings', was it?" I asked, as the light dawned.

"Good heavens, no! There's not even an 'h' in the Russian language. Our name was 'Yaroslavsky'." She pronounced the name with a delightful foreign trill. "Well, at least father and mother's name was—I hadn't come along yet. One bright young government clerk at Ellis Island heard the name and thought that 'Hastings' was close enough, although goodness knows how he got from 'Yaroslavsky' to 'Hastings!'" She cackled loudly.

I smiled. "It is kind of a leap."

"My mother's name was 'Alyona,'" she continued, musically elucidating, 'A-lyo-na.' "That means 'light.' Isn't that LOVELY?"

I nodded.

"She was a light, too—a light in the wilderness. Everyone loved her."

"Helen," I suggested. "They changed her name to Helen."

"Yes, and father's name – 'Anton' – was changed to 'Andy.' That wasn't much of a stretch for him."

"But how did your mother find out what had happened to her aunts at Babi Yar?"

"One of Olga and Nonna's other neighbors, who wasn't Jewish, was brave enough to write to Mother—bless her! Poor Mother was grateful to know the truth, hard as it was on her." Miss Hastings slapped her frail hand against the kitchen table. "We must face the truth if it kills us—and by God, sometimes it nearly does!" Her sentence ended in her familiar crackle of laughter, and I was relieved to hear it. I was beginning to worry that Miss Hastings was becoming depressed. We were expecting important guests – Lila and Mike Hobart – and I knew she wanted to be cheerful for their visit.

We were sitting at her kitchen table, where a fire in the wood cookstove chased away the chill and gloom of the November day. The copper tea kettle steamed on the hot stovetop, sending a fine warm mist throughout the room. A plate of cookies that Rebecca had sent up from the restaurant sat expectantly in the middle of the table, next to a pile of antique linen hors d'oeuvres napkins. Miss Hastings was dressed in her best nightgown and matching robe, in preparation for the afternoon tea with Lila and Mike. The young couple, both former Sovereign residents, was driving down from Hobart's family farm in Maple Grove, bringing with them their eight-month-old daughter, Claire. Miss Hastings hadn't seen the child since she was about a month old and I had never met Claire, who was named after Lila's deceased mother. We all suspected that this would be the last time the retired music teacher would be together with her young friends.

The conversation flagged. I suspected that Miss Hastings was recollecting her parents. Or perhaps she was thinking that it wouldn't be long now before she herself was with them in the cemetery. Idly, I wondered how long it would be before I, too, was pushing up daisies.

We both heard the noise at the same time—the sound of rubber tires turning onto the paved driveway. Our visitors from the north had arrived! Miss Hastings started up in her chair like a small child. "Is that them?" she asked, excitedly.

I got up and peered out the window. "Yep! They're here."

In two minutes, twenty-eight-year-old Lila rushed into the house, through the kitchen's front door, leaving her husband to deal with extricating Claire from the car seat. She threw herself into Miss Hastings' outstretched arms. "Here I am!"

"Oh, my DAHRRRLING!"

They hugged each other, and the tears flowed freely. I found myself wiping tears from my own eyes as I watched their embrace.

"You look absolutely SPLENDID, doesn't she, Maggie?" Miss Hastings declared, including me in the welcome.

"Top notch," I said. Lila did indeed look happy and healthy. She was heavier than when I'd seen her last, but the extra flesh looked good on her tall frame. Her eyes were shining gloriously, highlighted by the dark lights from her signature black bob, which always reminded me of a chickadee's cap.

"Omigod, I'm so happy to be back!" Lila cried. Her eyes moved quickly around the familiar kitchen, seeking reassurance that nothing had changed in the mustard-colored room. The kitchen still sported brightly-figured red and yellow curtains that matched the tablecloth, and every hen and chicken tchotchke was in its appointed place.

I busied myself with the tea things, discreetly removing myself from the limelight. I was only there to facilitate the tea, so that Lila and Miss Hastings could spend this time together in unalloyed happiness. We all have special people in our lives, and I knew that Lila was one of Miss Hastings' favorites. In truth, Lila was here to say 'goodbye.'

Lila's handsome blond husband shortly entered through the shed, carrying Claire on his hip like a small sack of potatoes. Mike Hobart set the child onto floor on her bottom and knelt down to remove her coat. He rose up, the epitome of a proud, first-time father. "She's just learning to motivate on two legs, so watch out," he warned. He leaned back against the refrigerator. In less than a minute, Claire had hooked onto a kitchen chair, and hauled herself up on her sturdy feet. "Mmmama!" she cried, with outstretched hands.

"Oh, isn't she just DAHRRRLING!" Miss Hastings squealed.

Lila scooped up her daughter, and triumphantly set Claire on the kitchen table for the retired music teacher to inspect. The child immediately put out a small hand and grasped hold of a wiry gray-black curl. Miss Hastings broke up with laughter. "Go ahead, give it a good tug, you DAHRRRLING!"

While the two women were ogling the baby, Mike and I exchanged amused glances. "This is just how I thought it would be," he said, smiling. "Lucky for me I spotted a few loose shingles on the back of the shed when we drove in."

"Did you bring your hammer?" I joked. Mike Hobart had once made a living doing odd jobs and carpentry work in Sovereign.

"I never go anyplace without my tools, Maggie, even on the tractor," he replied. After their marriage in 2012, Mike and Lila had returned to the Hobart family's potato farm in Aroostook County.

"How was the harvest this year?"

"Wet and muddy. But we got 'em dug."

"Dahrrrling, let me give you YOUR hug!" Miss Hastings interrupted us. "I don't want you to think I'm ignoring you." Hobart good-naturedly obliged her with a hug and a kiss. He winked at me, and quickly made his escape from the kitchen.

"What a DARHHHLING, boy!" Miss Hastings pronounced, after he had exited into the shed. "I'm SO happy you two got together ... even though he wasn't what I'd planned for you."

"What?!" said Lila, jokingly. "You mean you didn't plan for Mike and me to meet and fall in love when you sent me that tweet?" As readers of earlier chronicles know, Miss Hastings had invited Lila and Rebecca via Twitter to come to Maine for a weekend visit after hearing that Rebecca had been fired from her job in Boston.

"Haaahaa! No, no—not HIM, dahrrrling."

"Well, who did you have planned for me?" she asked lightly.

Miss Hastings looked guilty. "Wendell."

"Wendell?!"

"But you see," the retired music teacher continued hastily, "everything's turned out for the best, dahrrrlings! I have a DELIGHTFUL new neighbor in Rebecca, and you have a BEAUTIFUL new baby. Now, tell me, how is your father-in-law?"

But Lila refused to let the topic go. "I thought you just wanted me to take Wendell's house. I didn't know, like, you wanted me to take him, too!"

"Oh, it was silly of me! But then I'm a silly old coot. I just wanted to do one last thing for Addie."

I was busy refilling the tea kettle, but at the mention of Addie's name I stopped what I was doing to listen. I had fathomed that there was *more* to the story about the relationship between Miss Hastings and Grammie Addie, although I'd yet to learn what that "more" was.

"Grammie Addie? Wendell's grandmother?"

"The very same! Adelaide Libby Russell. There was an old debt I wanted to repay—not money, mind you. This was a personal debt. That used to mean something, in my day."

Lila pulled out a chair and sat down. She snuggled her baby onto her lap. "OK, now you've got to talk."

I set the hot teapot on the table, and likewise appropriated a chair for myself. It appeared that Lila was going to help me with my detective work this afternoon.

"People were so unique in my day," Miss Hastings mused. "SO much different from today."

"You mean, Grammie Addie?"

"Addie... Mother, and Henry—you remember, Henry, don't you, dahrrrling?"

Lila nodded. Miss Hastings had obviously shared some of her history with the younger woman. How much did she know?

"Henry. Addie and Pappy. They were real CHARACTERS. They prided themselves on being different, not like some store-bought shirt on a shirt rack. Young people today trip over themselves to look alike, and talk alike, and if they don't wear the right kind of jeans, why they're OUSTED from the herd—just like that!" Miss Hastings snapped her fingers. "When I got to know you on Twitter, DAHRRRLING, I fell in love with you. I knew that you were an original, and I thought you belonged here with us in Sovereign."

"Now you're flattering me," Lila said, smiling. "But I love it—keep going. What's all this originality got to do with Wendell's grandmother?"

"It was the old place—I didn't want to watch it fall down. Addie thought more of that old pile of sticks than anything else in the world! The homestead had been in George's family for almost a hundred years when she came there in 1904. That was WAY before my time, of course! Pappy never cared two hoots and a holler for the place—just about his GOL DANGED horses. But Addie never had two nickels to rub together until she came to town, and she saw that place as a future lifeline for her children and grandchildren and great-grandchildren. She had a

THE SONGBIRD OF SOVEREIGN

grand dream of keeping the old place going forever, and God knows that dream was just about the only thing that kept her going sometimes, especially through the war years."

"But what's that got to do with me?"

"Addie's dream had petered out—excuse the pun, dahrrrlings, because Wendell was the last of his line and the old fogey was determined to be a bachelor. I thought if I could dangle some original bait in front of him I might be able to reel him in before it was too late."

"Omigod, I was *bait*?"

Miss Hastings looked guilty. "I was just trying to keep Addie's dream alive, dahrrrling! To pay back an old debt."

"But … me and *Wendell*?!" Lila repeated, incredulously.

Miss Hastings nodded, shame-faced.

Lila laughed so merrily that the baby started to giggle, too. Next thing I knew, we were all laughing.

"That is too funny!" Lila exclaimed, wiping the tears from her eyes. "Why, he's old enough to be my grandfather!"

"Not quite, dahrrrling."

"Well, my father, anyway."

"But I didn't know how old you were until I saw you, dahrrrling. That's one of the WONDERFUL things about Twitter—age is irrelevant. How old did you think *I* was?"

Lila thought a moment. "Sixty or so."

"Haaahaa! Guess I had YOU fooled." Miss Hastings had been eighty-seven at the time to which they were referring. "But you see, everything's turned out for the best."

"Except that I don't think Grammie Addie is gonna get her dynasty with Rebecca and Wendell. I think you waited a little too long to bait your hook."

"Don't think I hadn't been keeping an eye out for him! But you don't know how HARD it is to tempt original young women to move to Maine."

"No kidding. Seriously, I wonder what *will* happen to the old place?" Lila surreptitiously glanced around Miss Hastings' kitchen again. I could see her thinking: "I wonder what will happen to *this* place?" but she was too much of a lady to ask. None of us, except perhaps Ryan MacDonald who had recently drawn up Miss Hastings' will, knew the disposition of Miss Hastings' worldly assets. We all fell silent, each lost in our own thoughts.

Seeing my opportunity, I got up to excuse myself. Having served tea – and liberally availed myself of the cookies – I thought it was only right that I should leave, allowing Lila and Miss Hastings some private time together. "I'll see you later," I said to Miss Hastings, one hand on the kitchen doorknob. "And I'll see *you* again before you go back up north," I said to Lila. "Are you staying at the cabin?" Mike Hobart had built a post-and-beam cabin when he was a student at Unity College, and naturally I expected them to stay there.

"We can't—he's just rented that out to Doctor Bart. We're staying with Rebecca and Wendell. Do you believe it? Queen Cora's there, too!" 'Queen Cora' was Lila's derogatory nickname for their former supervisor at Perkins & Gleeful, where she and Rebecca had been co-managers of the insurance company's marketing department.

"Are you OK with that?"

Lila shrugged. "Sure. There's plenty of room. You know, I almost feel sorry for Cora, now."

"Because Dennis dumped her? I think that was a good thing," I said.

"Dahrrrling, maybe now she'll find somebody to make her an honest woman!"

"Well, she won't be able to find somebody as wonderful as Mike, that's for sure. Or even Wendell," Lila added.

We all laughed.

"But I suppose there's somebody out there for Queen Cora, too," she admitted.

How could I help myself? What I knew was too good *not* to be shared. Besides, there is something about a covey of women that is irresistible, unless you're not part of the covey, of course. "I think maybe Cora already has a beau here in Sovereign," I said. My hand dropped from the doorknob.

Lila eyed me askance. "No way!" she protested.

"Yep."

"Do tell, dahrrrling," urged Miss Hastings.

Needing no further encouragement, I reclaimed my seat at the kitchen table. I leaned toward them conspiratorially. "I think Leland Gorse is sweet on her."

Lila nearly choked. "Omigod, Leland?!"

Miss Hastings beamed. "WONDERFUL."

And so I proceeded to share with Lila and Miss Hastings the story of the mushrooms, and the bottles of wine and Moxie. After all, I reasoned with myself, what one sees when one is in the Maine woods mushroom hunting isn't exactly covered by the sacred confessional bond!

CHAPTER 13

MOTHERS

NOVEMBER 1941

While waiting for Jana's mother to arrive Saturday afternoon, Jana, Eleanor, and Henry chatted lightheartedly in one of the sunny south-facing window nooks situated in the grand foyer. They were grouped together in a matched set of black Windsor chairs, rotated so that the young people faced looking out the large, arched window, which offered a view of the winding uphill approach to the sanatorium. No longer having mothers of their own, both Eleanor and Henry regularly availed themselves of this weekly opportunity to live vicariously through Jana's mother, and Jana was just as eager to show off and share her beautiful maternal parent.

Today was the first time Eleanor had been pronounced well enough to sit up for a prolonged period, and her promotion lent an additional air of festivity to the occasion. Eleanor's thin frame was wrapped in a paisley shawl, and she was wearing one of Jana's necklaces and a pair of matching earrings, which captured and reflected the afternoon sun. Jana was bedecked in her favorite lime-green travelling jacket, which she discovered to her chagrin she could no longer button. Thanks to plenty of fresh eggs, milk, cream, and butter, her small breasts had blossomed over the past few months. Henry had adorned a tie and vest for the afternoon, although privately he had debated whether or not he should add the matching suit coat that he usually donned for the Judge. In the end, he had decided against the formal jacket. The little group claimed the window seats just after lunch, thus ensuring not only the earliest possible glimpse of Helen's vehicle but also the luxury of an hour or more of conversation uninterrupted by the younger children.

"There's no more unfettered freedom than sailing on the open ocean," Henry blithely informed the girls, throwing his arm across the curved back of his chair. "On the ocean, one has no cares, no worries, no tomorrow, no yesterday—only the sun and salt spray on your face. When I'm in Narragansett in summer I take my catboat out almost every day. Ah, now, that is the life! Have you even been sailing?" This question he addressed to Jana first, before he generously turned to include Eleanor.

"I've taken the Queen Mary to Paris," Jana admitted, not entirely sure whether this trip would count as the type of sailing to which Henry referred.

"Oh, Jana!" Eleanor gushed. "The Queen Mary? How romantic! The Duke and Duchess of Windsor and all the movie stars sail on the Queen Mary."

Henry felt some of the wind go out of his sails. "The Queen Mary isn't a sailing ship. She's an ocean liner propelled by steam."

"That's still a boat, which sails on the ocean," Eleanor pointed out. "I think that counts as sailing, Henry."

"And the Queen Mary isn't even taking passengers at the moment because of the war in Europe," he continued, expanding his argument. "I was going to tell you about my great-great-great grandfather Captain Joshua, the sea captain, and his private zoo at Narragansett Bay; however, if you'd rather speak about movie stars and romance, then of course, I'll yield the floor."

Eleanor responded with a coughing fit. She reached down into her lap for her absorbent handkerchief.

"Don't talk like that, Henry," Jana pleaded. "I want to hear about Captain Joshua and his zoo."

Eleanor recovered herself and discretely returned the handkerchief to her lap. "You shouldn't give way to him, Jana. I don't see why Henry always has to direct the conversation."

"That's because I'm older and have more worldly experienced than you and Songbird, here." Henry paused a moment, and, hearing no further objections, launched with satisfaction into his tale. "Captain Joshua had his own sailing vessel, the Emma Mae, a splendid two-masted schooner, which he sailed 'round the world. Some sea captains brought home spices and silk and beautiful things, but Captain Joshua's particular penchant was collecting exotic animals. He brought a Bengal tiger home from India, an elephant from Africa, and half a dozen monkeys from South America. He had a private zoo built for all his creatures on his estate on the shores of Narragansett Bay."

"Did he bring home a koala bear?" Jana asked, wistfully. "I've always wanted to see a koala bear."

"No, I'm sorry to report, Captain Joshua failed to secure a koala."

"Why didn't you go to the zoo when you lived in New York?" Eleanor asked curiously. "I bet they had a koala bear there."

"I wanted to go to the zoo—and we always talked about going, Aunt Minnie and I. But somehow we never had time to go. We had rehearsals every day, you know, and performances every night, except Sunday, when we had a matinee in the afternoon."

"There—you see, Henry! Some girls have just as much experience in the outside world as you do!"

"I hardly think that's a reasonable inference, Eleanor."

Their conversation was interrupted by another of Eleanor's coughing fits. These fits were becoming more and more frequent. Jana watched anxiously to see if her friend would cough up blood, and was relieved to note that once again the white handkerchief was returned to her lap unstained.

Mrs. Baker appeared around the corner of the nook, and smiled at the little group. The final resting spot of her eyes, however, singled out Eleanor. "Could you come with me, dear? There's a telephone call for you."

Eleanor, still weak from coughing, looked frightened. She wobbled to her feet. Jana sprang up to help her friend but Henry was quicker. He caught hold of the invalid's arm and steadied her.

"It's nothing to be worried about, Eleanor," said the supervisor. "Your aunt in Brattleboro has simply telephoned to speak with you. You can take the call in Dr. Ketchum's office." Mrs. Baker gently clasped Eleanor's other arm. "You won't be away from your friends very long. One of the nurses will bring you back."

Henry and Jana followed Eleanor's shaky progress with their eyes as she carefully negotiated the hallway with Mrs. Baker. Henry reclaimed his seat, but Jana remained standing for several seconds after her friend had disappeared. "Eleanor is going to die, isn't she?"

Henry picked some light-colored lint off his dark pants. "Yes," he said, frankly, dropping the fuzz onto the polished marble floor. His usual devil-may-care attitude was replaced by a watchful expression. "You told me you wanted me to be honest with you, and so I am. I don't know when Eleanor might die—next week or perhaps next month. But the TB has broken through the scar tissue in her lungs and is spreading. Most likely her kidneys and bones have already been damaged. Her heart is under incredible stress, and her lungs are compromised. She'll probably die from pneumonia."

As she listened to Henry clinically detail Eleanor's condition, Jana felt the ground beneath her feet give way. She sank down into her chair, a thousand thoughts jumbled together inside her head. Was Henry's assessment correct? Why had she even asked the question in the first place? Did she really want to know the truth about Eleanor? Wasn't it better *not* to see the shadow of death lurking around every corner? Or was it truly a gift to know when the clock was going to run out, as Henry believed?

"Is that what you wanted to hear?" Henry asked, in a gentler tone of voice.

"I wonder whether the Robert Moses Zoo *does* have a koala bear?" she mused in reply.

Henry regarded her with thoughtful dark eyes. "*Carpe diem*, Songbird?"

"Carp—what?"

"*Carpe diem*. It's Latin for 'Seize the day.' That what you were thinking, isn't it? One had better go see the koala bears while one can?"

Jana toyed with the delicate charm bracelet that dangled from her wrist. "I suppose I was thinking something like that, only I hadn't gotten it into words yet."

He leaned forward in his chair. A lock of hair fell over his left eye and he pushed the hair back automatically. "There's a famous poem by Robert Herrick about *carpe diem*. I won't tell you the title because it would make you blush, but it occurs to me that the poem is perfect for the moment. Would you like to hear it?"

"You know the poem by heart?" asked Jana, impressed.

"We'll find out. I'm fairly sure that once I'm off to a good start I can muddle through."

"Shouldn't we wait for Eleanor?"

"What? And give her another opportunity to sink my ship?" Henry stood up and paced several steps away from Jana. He ran the opening stanza through his mind once or twice until he felt certain he could recite the entire poem. He composed himself, and then he turned around, and, facing his small audience, began to quote:

"GATHER ye rosebuds while ye may,
Old Time is still a-flying:
And this same flower that smiles to-day
To-morrow will be dying.

The glorious lamp of heaven, the sun,
The higher he's a-getting,
The sooner will his race be run,
And nearer he's to setting.

That age is best which is the first,
When youth and blood are warmer;
But being spent, the worse, and worst
Times still succeed the former.

Then be not coy, but use your time,
And while ye may, go marry:
For having lost but once your prime,
You may forever tarry." [2]

He bowed. Jana clapped enthusiastically. "Oh, I wish Eleanor had been here to hear that!"

Henry dropped back down into his chair. He pushed the wayward lock of hair away from his eyes. "You really liked it?" he asked, boyishly.

"Oh, yes! The poem reminds me of some of the ballads I used to sing. You did it beautifully, too."

Henry puffed up, pleased by her praise. "It seems the Judge's money spent on my education wasn't entirely wasted, then."

"I'm so glad the poet wrote about roses—roses are my favorite flower. Mother grows roses, and our house is filled with them in summer. My bedroom wallpaper has roses on it, too. It's the most beautiful room in the world!"

Suddenly, Henry's face became very serious. "My mother loved roses, too."

They both fell silent, each thinking of their respective mother: Jana, appreciating her mother more with each passing day that she matured into young womanhood; Henry, regretting more his loss with every sunset. Perhaps because it was visiting day or perhaps because of the melancholy he always felt with the diminishing daylight of November, his eyes

111

filled with tears. He searched through his pants pockets for his handkerchief, daubed his eyes and blew his nose.

Jana's heart constricted. "Did you love your mother very much?"

He nodded. "There are no words that can describe how much we *all* loved her," he said, his voice thick with emotion. "My father, my brother and me. She was like the sun and the moon and the stars all rolled into one. Something that you loved beyond belief, yet took for granted at the same time."

"I think I know what you mean."

"Those early years—before we all became sick—seem so real to me still. Compared to back then, this is almost a shadow life. Even the snowmelt from our boots in winter had more substance than I have now. I keep reliving over and over this one perfect day. I think God gave me that day so I'd have the strength to go on without her."

"Can you tell me about the day?" Jana asked, shyly. "I'd like to hear about your mother."

Henry looked up at the light pouring through the half-moon transom window situated near the top of the cathedral ceiling, and there, in the floating dust motes, he summoned up the memory. "My younger brother Nate and I were out sliding on the hill behind our house—not the house in Providence where the Judge lives now, but Captain Joshua's old cape in Narragansett where we were living then. It's February or March. We come bursting in through the back door. Our cheeks are flushed with cold and excitement. We both try to talk at once, to tell Mother what it feels like flying down the hill on the toboggan. We race into the kitchen, forgetting to take our boots off, like we always did. And I remember looking down while Nate is talking and seeing the puddles of snowmelt on her clean kitchen floor. I look up, and there is such unconditional love and joy in her eyes, that … that…that I have to turn my eyes away because it's like looking into the face of God." Henry covered his face with his hands. His shoulders shook with silent sobs.

Jana moved quickly to his side. She placed her small hand on his shoulder, and caressed him like she'd often seen her mother comfort her father. She didn't feel the least embarrassed; instead, she felt as though she'd earned the privilege to comfort Henry since he'd trusted her with his special memory.

In the blink of an eye, Jana matured from girlhood to womanhood. She felt as though a magician's cape was whisked away, revealing to her unsuspecting heart all the wonderful and yet terrifying secrets of femininity. She became aware of a deep ache in her solar plexus, and suddenly she understood the love that her mother felt for her father. She knew now why her mother stood by the window and waved her father off to work every day and how it was that he always had his favorite foods waiting for him every evening. She sensed a new vulnerability in herself, not for herself but for Henry. She was terrified that something awful might happen to him, something that would be beyond her control. What if his tuberculosis were to take a turn for the worse like Eleanor's?

Henry straightened up, and wiped his eyes with his handkerchief. "Thanks," he said. "I needed that."

Confused by her new sensibility, Jana allowed her hand to drop from his shoulder. What should she do or say next? She tried to imagine what her mother would do, and that thought precipitated a quick glance out the window. She spied a black 1939 Nash snaking up the long, curved gravel driveway. "Oh, look!" she cried. "There's Mother!"

Eager to see her parent, Jana rushed out the door, down the granite steps. She greeted her mother as the elegant woman stepped out of the parked car.

"DAHRRRLING!" Helen Hastings exclaimed, scooping Jana into her arms. She hugged her daughter tightly, and dropped several kisses on top of her head. "I'm so sorry I'm late. There was ice on the roads today. You know what a careful driver I am!"

"That's alright, Mother. Henry and I have been talking." The two women hooked arms, and Jana proudly led her mother up the stone steps, back inside the stately mansion.

Henry awaited them in the foyer, hands clasped behind his back. "Hallo, Mrs. Hastings."

Helen pulled off her black cotton gloves, one finger at a time, revealing her beautiful hands. "Hello Henry. You look very thoughtful today. Jana tells me you two were having a nice chat?"

He nodded. "We were discussing carpe diem—seize the day."

"You don't need to translate for her, Henry," Jana whispered. "Mother speaks five languages."

"But not Latin, dahrrrling. Latin is a dead language. So, you two were seizing the day, hmm? That is a philosophy Jana's father espouses." She smiled, winsomely. "Me? I'm for saving up a little of that joy for a rainy day."

"Very prudent, Mrs. Hastings. May I take your coat?" Henry held out his hand.

At that moment, Jana realized that her mother was dressed all in black: black hat, black gloves, black coat, black wool dress, black heels and black silk stockings. "Mother, why are you all in black?"

Mrs. Hastings slipped out of her coat. "Thank you, Henry." She gracefully appropriated one of the Windsor chairs in the nook, while Henry hung her coat upon the hall tree. "I am in mourning dahrrrling. I've had a letter from Kiev—sit down, next to me, here." She patted the seat of the nearest chair. Henry made a motion to leave mother and daughter in private, but she stopped him. "No, no, Henry, don't go."

Pleased to be included, Henry stood his ground. Jana settled herself into the chair next to her mother. "What did your letter say, Mother?"

"You remember me telling you about my aunts in Kiev? Nonna and Olga?"

Jana nodded.

"The letter was from a neighbor who said Olga and Nonna were murdered by the Nazis. It was a terrible thing, and I do not want to go into details today, for it would spoil our visit. But I wanted you to know I am wearing black for your great-aunts. Your father says that nobody in this country goes into mourning anymore but I don't care about that. When your heart weeps, you cannot wear bright clothes, hmm?"

"I suppose not," Jana murmured, realizing how much more there was in the world to think about.

"Poor Mrs. Russell is worried that her sons will be called up to go off to fight Hitler or the Japanese or somebody somewhere. I feel for her—I do!"

Henry leaned in to the conversation. "I'm very sorry for your loss, Mrs. Hastings."

"Thank you, Henry. That reminds me—would you be good enough to bring me the packages that are in the back seat of the car? Mrs. Russell sent over some hats, scarves, and mittens that the Ladies Auxiliary has knitted. I think there is something in there for everyone." She turned to Jana. "I've brought you my fur coat, dahrrrling, for the sleeping porch."

"Did Mrs. Russell bake us more cookies, too?" Jana asked, anxiously.

Helen laughed. Henry, who had turned to retrieve the packages, was momentarily transfixed by the musical beauty of Helen's laugh.

"Certainly she did! Adelaide is nothing if not industrious. She puts me to shame, she does."

"But you're so beautiful, Mother!"

"Dahrrrling, the beauty to which you are referring is only skin deep. The beauty that Mrs. Russell possesses is of a more permanent nature, like granite."

"I deny it!" Jana protested, hotly. "She's not like granite, she's fat. You're ten times more beautiful than Mrs. Russell, inside and out."

"Someday, I hope you will have the opportunity to see Mrs. Russell for the gem she truly is. Now, Henry, about those packages ... ?"

Henry obediently disappeared out the front door. Helen swiveled back to inspect her daughter. She noted the expanding breasts, and the pensive expression in Jana's eyes. Her baby was growing up! "What would you like for your seventeenth birthday, dahrrrling? I didn't want to ask you in front of Henry, because I wouldn't want to embarrass you. But I see right away you need some new brassieres. My little girl is bursting at the seams."

Jana blushed.

"Don't be ashamed, dahrrrling! Don't ever be ashamed of your womanhood. Being a woman is a marvelous thing. Would you like a pair of high heel shoes for your birthday, hmm?"

"May I?!"

"Dahrrrling, you may have two pair, if you like. Just don't use them as an excuse to stop growing! And a new dress, too? I will stop at the shops in Waterville on my way home and see what I can find for you. Quickly, now, before Henry returns—is there anything you would like to discuss with me, one woman to another?"

Jana felt her face become even hotter. "Oh, Mother! Is it so obvious?"

"Mothers have a way of seeing these things. Now, out with it!"

"Well ... how did you know when you were in love with Father?"

"Ah, I had a feeling this was about love! *On ne voit bien qu'avec le cœur.* I wonder if Henry is familiar with that one? I knew I was in love with your father when I saw a spot on his tie. He had taken me out to dinner in Petrograd—it was still St. Petersburg, then. We were dining at a very nice restaurant, and some gravy dribbled down his tie. He did not see it; your father never does notice things like that. But I saw it and before I could stop myself I was standing next to him wiping the gravy off with my napkin. *Voilà!* Just like that, I knew I would be wiping spots off your father's ties for the rest of his life."

Jana laughed. "So, that's what love feels like?"

"Dahrrrling, that is what devotion feels like! There is a difference between what your romantic novels call love and true devotion. The first—so selfish!—is centered on the physical gratification of the senses. The other, true love, is self-denying, and centers on the welfare of the person you love. When you love someone—truly love someone—I promise you, dahrrrling, you will know it without having to ask your mother!"

Chapter 14

Daughters

December 2013

"*On ne voit bien qu'avec le cœur*—We see well only with the heart,"[3] I said, aloud. "There! I finally got it." I glanced up victoriously from where I was sitting cross-legged on my living room couch, a thick, hardcover French-English dictionary open in my lap and a yellow legal pad and pen resting on a pillow beside me. Tonight, an early December snowstorm was piling up more of the white stuff outside the windows. We had been pounded with snow and cold for two days, and it looked as though we were on track for a real Maine winter. But Peter and I were warm and snug inside my little cottage.

My home was formerly one of those one-room schoolhouses that you see holding down the corners of country roads in Maine, often half-tumbled-down, their gray shingles helping them fade into the woods that has grown up around them. My particular schoolhouse, which was built upon the dirt road that connected the early nineteenth century settlements of Sovereign Center and South Sovereign, had been rescued from obscurity by several previous owners. What began its career as a one-room schoolhouse had morphed over the past century and a half into a rambling seven-room cottage. When I had first seen it, I had immediately fallen in love with the place. I'd purchased the old schoolhouse even though at the time it had been a serious stretch financially. But I'd never regretted my decision.

Peter was sprawled in the recliner by the cast-iron woodstove, toasting his stocking feet. He yawned. It was nearly nine o'clock, his bedtime. "Finally got what?" he replied.

"The translation of the phrase Miss Hastings' mother said to her one Saturday afternoon at the sanatorium. She was telling me about the visit the other day, and I was too embarrassed to ask her what it meant."

"I doubt that," Peter said drily. "I don't think there's much that embarrasses you these days, Maggie." Unfortunately, I had also shared with Peter my mushroom hunting-cum-stalking experience. Not being a member of the female covey, he couldn't quite understand what had prompted me to follow Leland and Cora into the woods.

"Is that a backhanded way of asking me to put my underwear in the laundry hamper? Because if it is, I'll kindly remind you whose house we're living in."

"No, no, I've waited more than forty years to pick your panties up off the bathroom floor. Please don't rob me of that."

"Quite the comedian, aren't you?"

"You think that's funny? How about this?" Peter reached down the side of the recliner and tugged on the handle. The chair snapped shut. "I've been thinking a lot lately, and I think you're using Miss Hastings' death to avoid thinking about your own."

"Ouch!" I exclaimed, loudly. I slammed the heavy dictionary shut. "I thought you were a farmer, not a butcher? That cuts pretty close to the bone."

"If the shoe fits ..." He leaned forward in the chair, his serious brown eyes searching mine.

I was about to toss out another flippant remark, but I bit my tongue. "Oh, you're probably right. When did you suspect me?"

"When you stopped working on your small church book and started working on Miss Hastings like she was one of your special projects."

"Miss Hastings has an important story to tell," I protested, "despite what you might think."

"I'm sure she does. She's a delightful little old lady with an unusual life history. But is her story really important enough to dedicate the last year of your life to?"

I sighed. "Maybe. Maybe not. It's always easier to pay attention to someone else's life than it is to your own."

"My point exactly. I think you could make better use of your time. *Our* time." Peter leaned back in his chair, and began to rock steadily.

"OK, I see where you're going with this—this is your latest tactic to get me into radiation and chemotherapy. Ugh!"

"Nope. I just don't want all the sand to run out of your hourglass and have you turn to me on the last day and ask: 'Where did all my time go, honey?'"

I picked up my cup. The cinnamon-laced hot cider was long since cold, but the mug gave me something to hide behind. "What if I promise not to do that?"

"And then there's another thing…" he continued.

"Oh, my God! What else?"

"I'm not sure how to put this—I'm not the wordsmith you are—but you're not quite the same old Maggie I've known and loved since we were five."

"People do grow and change, I suppose," I replied, somewhat sarcastically.

"You're not as honest as you used to be. Not just with yourself, but with the rest of us. You haven't even told Nellie about the cancer yet, and that scares me most of all."

"At the risk of repeating myself, I'm waiting for her to come home so I can tell her in person. Stop rocking, please. It's driving me crazy."

Peter obliged, and the rocking chair ground to a halt. "If you picked up that phone and told Nellie the truth, she'd come home fast enough."

"I don't want my daughter's love under duress."

"Sweetheart, if I were you, I'd take Nellie's love any way I could get it. Beggars can't be choosers."

"I didn't know you could be so mean, Peter Hodges!"

"Too late now—we're hooked." He grinned.

It was true. My childhood chum and I had indeed tied the knot only last week. One of my minister friends from seminary had performed a very simple wedding ceremony with Rebecca and Wendell acting as witnesses. Our honeymoon was a daytrip to Schoodic Point, a lesser-known part of Acadia National Park in downeast Maine, one of my favorite places. Now, for better for worse—in sickness and in health—Peter and I were united as one.

"Maggie? You're not regretting it already, are you?"

"What? Oh, no. Sorry, I just spaced out for a minute there. I was thinking of Miss Hastings—she was so genuinely happy when I told her we were married—it made me wonder if she regretted not getting married herself."

"Already back to Miss Hastings? Seriously, Maggie—haven't you heard a word I've said?"

"Apparently not." I set the cup down and rose up. "See you in bed, dear husband. You can lecture me up there all you want."

"But you're always asleep before I even turn out the light!"

"Eggs-actly."

He made a lunge for me. "Come back here, you!"

But it was too late; I'd already skedaddled up the narrow winding stairs to our bedroom. Peter stopped to load the stove with firewood, and then followed me post-haste.

Our bed was tucked beneath slanted eaves, which often gave my six-foot husband an unexpected bump on the head if he forgot where he was in the morning. Peter disrobed quickly, shivering in the chilly room. He slid into bed and reached for me, pulling me willingly into the crook of his well-muscled arm. I snuggled closer, listening to his heart beat with one ear and to the howl of the wind in the pines outside with the other. I felt safe, warm and loved. "Mmm, this is nice. Almost makes me wonder why I didn't take you earlier."

"Because you're pig-headed and stubborn, just like Nellie," he replied, dropping a kiss on my forehead.

"Well, at least I have something in common with my daughter!"

To my surprise, Nellie called me the next day while Peter was out plowing the driveway. I hadn't heard from her that fall, much beyond a text message saying she survived the Canadian camping trip and was back at Columbia. I'd sent her a hundred dollar check for her birthday and a funny card, and she emailed me to say 'thanks' and to let me know she wouldn't be home for Thanksgiving. The timing of the phone call and Peter's and my conversation about Nellie seemed overly coincidental and at first I suspected my new husband of something underhanded; however, as the conversation progressed, those fears evaporated and I was just glad to hear from Nellie.

"I finished my last final," she said, "and I thought I'd come for a visit."

"That's wonderful, honey! Can you stay through 'til Christmas?"

"I'm taking the bus into Bangor," she replied, either not hearing my question about Christmas or more likely ignoring it. "Can you pick me up Thursday afternoon?"

"Just tell me what time to be there!"

"We're supposed to come in at four o'clock, but I'll call you from Augusta and let you know if we're on time."

"Do you need any money?"

"No thanks. See you Thursday."

Thursday was my day to fix lunch for Miss Hastings, and while we were sitting over our customary hot tea and grilled sandwich, I shared with her the news of Nellie's intended visit.

"That's WONDERFUL, dahrrrling! You tell Nellie she'd better roll out her best duds for my party!" Miss Hastings was turning eighty-nine on Sunday, and the Ladies Auxiliary was hosting a birthday open house for the beloved retired music teacher.

I hesitated. I knew my daughter, and the likelihood that Nellie would attend the party was very slim. She never enjoyed mixing much with Sovereign folks. I wasn't sure whether this was because she didn't like to be shown off by her mother or whether it was because she was shy. Maybe it was a little bit of both. I nodded glumly, and picked up the teapot. "I'll tell her," I said. "More tea?"

"What's wrong, dahrrrling? Is something the matter with Nellie?"

I set the teapot back on the hot mat. "No, no. I was just thinking how much you and Henry and Eleanor all adored your mothers. Nellie and I don't seem to have that same kind of special relationship." I fought back tears. "What's wrong with me?" I hadn't actually meant to say that last out loud, but I did.

Miss Hastings reached out and covered my hand with her own crooked member. "You poor dahrrrling—you mustn't compare us! Remember, you're hearing my stories with seventy-five years of hindsight. If Mother were here, let me tell you she'd be singing a different tune altogether!"

"Really?"

She bobbed her head energetically. "Why, I rarely wrote to her the WHOLE TIME I was in New York and yet Mother was as faithful as the tide. She wrote to me twice a week, telling me the juicy news in Sovereign and sending me photographs and newspaper clippings and all sorts of goodies. And when I was at Windmere, she came just like clockwork every Saturday afternoon—she was more regular than the Post Office!" Miss Hastings patted my hand. "Don't you worry, dahrrrling, what you're feeling is perfectly normal. Nellie might not see it now, but someday she'll realize what a WONDERFUL mother she has."

Who wouldn't be cheered by such words of encouragement? Feeling better, I poured myself a second cup of tea.

When Nellie stepped off the bus later that afternoon, backpack slung over her tall, squared shoulders, hair pulled back in a long blonde ponytail, I was amazed, as always, to think that something so lovely had come out of my body. The bus driver gave her a hand down, and several men turned to stare at her. She's a beautiful creature, and when

Nellie smiles, it's as though the sun comes out after a long rainy spell. Unfortunately, Nellie rarely smiles. My daughter is serious about everything: serious about saving the environment, serious about her studies, serious about relations between the sexes, serious about world peace—you get the drift.

"Nellie!" I cried, rushing up, eager to enfold her in a motherly embrace. It was so good to have my daughter back in my arms again!

She set her backpack on the ground, and endured my caress for a few seconds before pulling away. "I need to get my suitcase, Maggie."

I bit my tongue. I hated the new vernacular where kids called their parents—especially their mothers—by their given names. It was all I could do not to shout: "Mother! I am your mother!" Whatever happened to 'Mom'? I wondered. What was wrong with that appellation? I'd even settle for the stilted 'Mother', which Nellie had called me from age ten to fourteen; however, once Nellie had gone away to that private college-prep school in New Hampshire she had seemed to want to mark the change in our relationship by demoting me from 'Mother' to 'Maggie'. I sighed, and picked up her backpack. "OK, I'll be waiting in the car. It's parked out front."

Peter and I had discussed how Nellie should be told about our marriage. I didn't think she'd be shocked or upset to hear of our nuptials, since Peter had always been a big part of our lives. Also, it certainly wasn't as though Nellie might feel threatened that my love for Peter would replace my love for her. On the contrary, she'd probably be relieved to hear that I had someone other than her to focus on. I tried to explain all this to Peter, however, he still thought it would be better for the two of us to have some mother-daughter alone time, and so he packed up his toothbrush and returned to Oaknole.

The plan was that I was to tell Nellie about our marriage, and then in a few days, if everything went well, Peter would come back so that she could get used to seeing the two of us living together. We both knew that Peter was going to be the one taking care of me during my last year, and he wanted Nellie to know that I had the support I needed so that—once I told her about the cancer—she wouldn't feel compelled to drop out of her final year at Columbia.

"She's not gonna drop out," I had protested to Peter.

"You don't know that, Maggie."

"You don't know Nellie. She'll work her butt off to save the whales, save the earth, and save the natural pollinators—but not her mother."

It's about a forty-five minute drive from the bus station in Bangor to our home in Sovereign. I planned to launch into my marital confession first thing, but I found myself wasting the first thirty minutes on a vain attempt at small talk that went nowhere, and we fell silent. Finally, when we turned onto the Russell Hill Road, I just decided to blurt it out.

"Uncle Peter and I got married two weeks ago."

"It's about time," was the careless reply from my daughter.

"You really think so? You think I did the right thing?"

"It's about time you put the poor guy out of his misery. You've been leading him on for, like, fifty years."

I gritted my teeth. "Thanks for the congratulations."

She shrugged. "Hey, I like Uncle Peter. I think you'll be happy. Does that mean you'll be moving to Oaknole?"

"No, Bruce and Amber have taken over the farm. Peter is living here with me now."

"Great. Maybe I can finally beat him at *Scrabble*."

When we reached the house, Nellie automatically began ferrying her stuff inside. I slipped my cell out of my winter jacket and speed-dialed Peter's number. "Come on home," I told him. "It's not gonna make any difference to Nellie whether you're here or not. And frankly, I'd just as soon you were here."

"You're sure?"

"I'm sure I need you, Peter."

"Those are the nicest words you've ever said to me, Maggie Hodges!"

CHAPTER 15

THE JUDGE

DECEMBER 1941

Helen Hastings departed Windmere on Saturday well after three o'clock, pushing the boundaries of the sanatorium's visiting hours by nearly thirty minutes. Dr. Ketchum and Mrs. Baker, like everyone else who knew Helen, were enchanted by her warmth and vivacity. The good doctor was even half in love with her, and it was entirely possible that if Helen had asked to move permanently into his study, he would have packed up his books and bottles and retired to the brick building.

Helen departed with a long list of things to do and goods to purchase in preparation for the party planned for Jana's seventeenth birthday on December 8th. Not wanting her daughter's special day to be marred by negative memories of the sanatorium, Helen had suggested to Mrs. Baker a celebration that would suit the important occasion, and yet not overtax the children. There would be sedentary games and contests, with prizes for everyone, even the most invalid. And Helen was going to ask Adelaide to bake a birthday cake that would feed all twenty children, as well as the nurses and the staff. Mrs. Baker had made large allowances for the party, which was scheduled to be held a week from Monday from two o'clock to four o'clock, normally the rest period at the sanatorium.

From Windmere, Helen's immediate destination was downtown Waterville, a manufacturing city in central Maine that had sprung up in the nineteenth century along the mighty Kennebec River, enticing immigrants from around the world to come and work in its factories. Waterville was located only eight miles from the sanatorium and in less than twenty minutes Helen was stepping cheerfully along the bustling Main Street, her high heels clacking confidently, as she considered what shops to visit. In addition to English she overheard a smattering of French, German, and Yiddish, and was even able to distinguish between the peculiar native Franco-American French and the Arabic French spoken by the Lebanese immigrants.

Helen's eye was caught by a pretty necklace displayed in the window of Russakoff's Jewelers, and she paused briefly to admire it, knowing how much Jana loved necklaces. But jewelry was Andy's provenance, and she quickly moved on to her list. In Stern's Department Store, Helen went first to Ladies Lingerie to pick out brasseries and other undergarments for Jana. A salesgirl offered her assistance, but Helen politely declined. The Franco-American shop girl fell back into conversation with another clerk, and Helen listened with a smile as the two chatted in French about their upcoming dates for that evening, not suspecting that Helen could understand every word they said.

Before she left the city, Helen stopped into several other department stores: Stern's, Butler's, Dunham's and even Levine's, the store for men and boys, where she picked up some socks for Andy. The winter sun had long since set when she returned to her automobile. She hadn't realized how time had flown. The city lights had obscured the gathering dusk. She would be late for dinner! But Helen was a careful driver, and she was prudent enough to know that while Andy might worry about her because she was late, he would much rather that she arrive home late for dinner than not at all.

The road between Waterville and Sovereign was winding and narrow, with thick-set maple and fir trees skulking along the edges as though seeking an opportunity to leap out in front of motor vehicles. In addition, there was a particularly nasty curve near the bridge in Burnham. Helen had navigated the road many times, but never at night. She had only learned to operate a car last year, at Andy's insistence, and was still wary of the darkness. Until learning to drive, she had been perfectly content to stay at home with her music and her roses, and her piano and voice lessons. Since first negotiating the back roads of Sovereign, however, she had eagerly stretched her boundaries into Bangor and Waterville, where some of the best shops were located. The Hastings family owned only one automobile, and so Helen's forays into the cities occurred on the days that the canning factory wasn't running. Andy occasionally accompanied her, although most often she went by herself. In the last few months, much to Helen's delight, she had convinced Adelaide on several occasions to join the expedition. Addie was a much better and certainly more experienced driver, and her friend had given her some helpful pointers about driving in snow and ice. The two women had even dined out at a restaurant, something Addie rarely did, and Helen was gratified to see her friend's face light up in laughter.

Helen arrived home a few minutes after the household's seven o'clock dinner hour. At the sight of the car's lights turning into the driveway, Mrs. Emerson began putting the meal on the table.

Andy greeted his wife at the door. "I was just about to call Windmere and find out where the devil you were." He relieved her of a pile of packages.

She leaned forward to accept a kiss on the cheek. "What a day I have had!" She pulled off her black hat and set it on the kitchen table.

Her husband stood in the middle of the kitchen floor, helplessly considering what to do with his armful of packages. "Where should I put these, Alyona?"

"Just set them on the table for now, dahrrrling." She slipped out of her coat, and pulled off her gloves. "How much Jana has grown, Antonsha! Why, she's looking so much better than when we took her to Windmere in August."

"Dinner is served, ma'am," interjected Mrs. Emerson. "I put the covers on."

"Thank you, Mrs. Emerson. Antonsha, please, take your seat, I'll just wash my hands." Since the advent of Jana's diagnosis, hand washing had become an important everyday ritual at the Hastings house.

Shortly, Andy was helping his wife into the chair at his elbow. Upon Jana's departure for the sanatorium, Helen had chosen to move her seat around the corner from her husband instead of at the opposite end of the table. This somewhat lessened the loss of the third person at table by creating a more intimate dining experience. Tonight, the candles flickered softly and the heavy drapes were drawn to keep out the damp December breezes.

She lifted one of the covers, and peeped at the broiled fish. "Mmm, smells divine!"

"Wine, Alyona?" asked Andy, splashing some Sauvignon blanc liberally into her glass without waiting for an answer.

"Yes, please. Do you know, Antonsha, I do believe our Jana has a sweetheart."

Andy plunked the bottle down onto the table. "What?!"

"Be careful, dahrrrling—you spilled on the tablecloth." Helen sopped up the spreading beige stain with her napkin.

"She's just a child!"

Helen returned the napkin to her lap, and gazed at her husband with adoring eyes. "Not really, dahrrrling. Remember how old I was when we first met, hmm?" She had been just fourteen when Andy had seen her at a coming out party for her older sister, Mariya, in St. Petersburg.

"That is different."

"True," Helen mused, mischievously. "Jana is nearly three years older than I was back then." She helped herself to a small piece of the herb-buttered haddock.

Andy chuckled. "You know that is not what I meant. It is different because she is my daughter and you were, well, you were a girl I wanted to get to know better."

Helen's musical laughter filled the room. "So, it is all about you? Dahrrrling, he's a very nice boy. His name is Henry. His father is a judge in Rhode Island. He is educated, intelligent, and thoughtful and kind. That should make a difference, hmm?"

"Only because now I won't drive over there tomorrow and kill him. With a father for a judge, I would be too afraid. The judge would lock me in jail and throw away the key."

"As well he should." She affectionately rested her left hand on her husband's arm. "Now, listen, Antonsha, you must promise me that you will attend Jana's birthday party."

"When is it to be?"

"A week from Monday, on her birthday."

"But I'll be work…"

"No, no more excuses," she interrupted. "Not even work. I know you do not like to go to the sanatorium, dahrrrling, but you must put in an appearance for this. Jana will be heartbroken if you do not attend on her special day. She is looking forward to showing her father off to all her new friends."

"Oh, very well," Andy said, grudgingly. "We haven't begun canning the winter squash yet, and maybe I'll have an opportunity to cross-examine this Henry."

"Let us hope that the judge is not there, hmm? Or you might find that you are the one who is cross-questioned."

The Judge finally made his long-hoped-for appearance at Windmere on Saturday afternoon. His murder case had come to its conclusion—the culprit was found guilty and sent off to the penitentiary for life—but another important case had landed almost immediately on the Judge's docket. In order to ensure he didn't break his promise to visit Henry before Christmas, Judge Graham shuttered his Providence office and hopped the train for Waterville. He was met at the train station by Farmer Dunkirk, who often doubled as an errand boy, and was hauled to Windmere rather unceremoniously in the facility's 1933 International Harvester pickup.

Henry, who had been keeping watch for his father, spied Dunkirk's pickup chugging up the gravel driveway and went down the steps to greet him. The Judge was a hale-looking, barrel-chested man about five-foot nine-inches tall, who still boasted a full black beard despite his fifty-odd years. He was proud of his beard, which grew up one side of his face and down the other, everywhere, in fact, except for the shiny bald pate on top. Judge Graham was dressed in a three-quarter length black wool coat, a black Homburg hat and black gloves. When he engulfed his son in a prolonged hug, Jana, who was peering out the window, thought that Henry looked like he'd been swallowed up by a bear.

The Judge was certainly not what she had expected!

She watched as Judge Graham swept his son up the steps, quickly pulling away from the window so that they wouldn't see her. "He's awfully furry, isn't he?" she said, turning her attention to Eleanor, who was lying on the couch. The two girls had been playing *Flinch* in the green room with Henry until he had gone to meet his father. "Henry doesn't look anything like him!"

Jana reclaimed the chair in which she had been sitting. The blue cards were scattered on the low coffee table that was situated between the couch and the chair, but she didn't make any attempt to gather them up.

"I think he takes after his mother," Eleanor replied, folding her hands across her chest.

"He must!"

Jana hardly knew what to do with herself next. Would Henry bring the Judge back to the green room? Or would they duck into Dr. Ketchum's office? She smoothed out an imaginary wrinkle in her skirt, and regretted that the Judge had come for his much-heralded visit before her mother was able to return on Monday with the promised gifts of a new dress and high heels. She was anxious to make a good impression on Henry's father, who was, after all, the most important person in Henry's life. She had already learned that, after having lost his wife and Henry's brother to tuberculosis more than a decade ago, the Judge had remarried, and had two young daughters. Henry had told her that his stepmother was a good woman, but nothing at all like his mother. "I'm just glad he's got someone to keep him company," Henry had said good-naturedly about his father's second family.

"I think I'll rest now," said Eleanor, drawing Jana's attention back to the invalid.

Jana quickly rose up, and placed a blanket over her friend. She had been so busy thinking about Henry and his father she had forgotten all about poor Eleanor! "Can I get you anything?"

"Only wake me when the Judge comes 'round, please."

Jana picked up a book, and returned to her chair. She tried not to think about Henry and his father; however, she soon found this to be impossible. She set the book down and succumbed to the more gratifying experience of daydreaming. She wondered what Henry and the Judge were talking about. Was Henry speaking of her? If so, what was he saying? Was he telling his father about the many interesting conversations they shared? Or perhaps Henry had already written everything about that in his weekly letters to the Judge?

She ran several pleasing scenarios through her head, all of them ending with Judge Graham inviting her down to visit them in Rhode Island, not to the home in Providence, where Henry's stepmother and sisters would be, but to that more romantic locale on the seaside. Jana pictured Captain Joshua's farm on Narragansett Bay and thought she could taste the salty ocean breezes on her tongue as she and Henry held hands and gazed out over the bay.

A light knock at the door woke her from her reverie just as two white seagulls were gliding over the bay and … and Henry had turned to kiss her! Jana glanced guiltily over at Eleanor, but her friend was slumbering soundly. Mrs. Baker stuck her head inside and Jana put her finger to her lips and motioned toward the sleeping girl. The supervisor beckoned, and Jana quietly slipped out into the hallway.

"My dear girl, the Judge has asked to meet you!"

So, her daydream was already coming true—the Judge specially asked to be introduced to her!

Henry must have told his father *something* about her. An exquisite thrill pulsed through her being. Jana took a deep breath and willed herself to remain calm employing the deep-breathing techniques she had learned on stage. She eagerly followed Mrs. Baker down the hall, practically gliding over the highly polished floor.

Mrs. Baker paused at the door to Dr. Ketchum's study. "Just go right in, dear. The Judge is expecting you."

Jana stepped gracefully into the room, which was bright with sunlight from the south-facing window. She blinked to adjust her vision. Suddenly, a dark shadow loomed large.

"Ah, there's the little lady—come in, come in!" a man's voice boomed. It was Henry's father!

Judge Graham clasped her right hand with two moist paws. "I'm very happy to make your acquaintance," he continued, looking down at her. His small round mouth, which was very nearly swallowed up by facial hair, revealed itself only when he spoke.

Henry, who had been standing by the fire, now approached and started to make the introduction.

"Why, there's no need to introduce her to me, Henry! I've seen this little lady many times on the stage. She's *The Songbird of Sovereign*."

Startled, Jana stared up at his furry-faced visage. His eyebrows swam like eels. They were dark and expressive. Why didn't they stop moving?

"I asked Mrs. Baker to send for you as soon as I heard you were here. I hope you don't mind?"

Jana's heart sank. She hadn't been sent for because she was Henry's special friend. Judge Graham had simply wanted to meet her because she was 'somebody'. He had seen her on stage, not once, but apparently several times. She almost didn't know what to make of it and of him.

"The first time I saw you, little lady, they had you stand up on a chair to sing so we could see you in the back. What a sweetheart you were!"

Jana withdrew her hands from his earnest clutch, and bobbed a cool curtsy. "I'm very pleased to make your acquaintance," she said, in her most quelling voice. Surely, if he had seen her on stage so many times, he could see how much she had grown and matured?

"Look at that, Henry! That's just how she carries herself on stage. Isn't she the cutest little thing?" The Judge turned first to Henry and then back to Jana. "Oh, I wish you'd had the opportunity to hear her sing, son. You'd never believe such a big voice could come from such a small package!"

Henry shifted uncomfortably. "Maybe Jana doesn't like to be reminded of those days?"

Jana tossed her head. Her black curls bounced. "I don't mind. I'm not ashamed of what I did as a child."

"Ashamed? I should think not! Why, one of my clerks went to see you five or six times, just in one summer. Shall we sit down?"

The Judge moved abruptly toward the pair of striped George III chairs poised on either side of the crackling fire, startling Jana with his swiftness. She hadn't expected something so bulky to move so fast!

"Pull up Ketchum's desk chair, will you, Henry?"

Jana selected the seat across from the Judge, and waited for Henry to join them with the rolling desk chair before she perched herself on the striped cushion. When she was seated, Henry's father lowered himself down, and threw one stout leg over the other, revealing a glimpse of black gaiters. Good heavens, what kind of a man was this?!

Under lowered eyelids, Jana surreptitious examined Henry's father, trying to figure out whether she liked him or not. Compared to her own father, Judge Graham was certainly uncouth. He was loud and voluble, but he also seemed warm-hearted and sincere. Plus he was Henry's father! She thought at first that he wasn't anywhere near as intelligent as his son; however, after ten minutes of conversation she realized that the Judge was much more discerning than he had initially appeared.

"So, there's to be a big birthday bash Monday—and I'm to miss it! I always miss out on all the good parties."

"Perhaps you could stay a couple of extra days, Father?" Henry suggested, hopefully.

"Perhaps, perhaps. But … perhaps Mrs. Hastings wouldn't like me crashing her bash, eh?"

Poor Jana didn't know whether she should address him as 'Judge Graham' or as 'Mr. Graham.' So she said neither. "My mother would be very happy to make your acquaintance," she demurred. "I'm sorry she's not here to meet you today, but she's coming Monday instead." She idly wondered what her elegant and cultured mother would think of such an overgrown beast. Her mother would probably like him. But then, her mother liked everyone.

"Well, well, maybe on your next birthday, eh?"

"I hope not!"

The Judge burst out laughing. He slapped his thick thigh. "She hopes not!"

Too late, Jana realized her mistake. She blushed. "I mean, I hope I'm not still at Windmere next year," she corrected, hastily.

"I know what you meant, little lady!"

"Are you staying in Waterville, Father?" Henry asked, smoothly changing the subject.

"No, no. Ketchum is putting me up at his place. Now, there's a smart man—killing two birds with one stone by hosting me."

"How so, sir?"

"He gets to polish his halo *and* he gets to share my good Cuban cigars!" The Judge laughed heartily.

Jana felt her pulse leap. "Dr. Ketchum's halo doesn't need polishing!" she declared, hotly.

"There, Henry—what do you think of that?" said the Judge. He patted his breast pocket absently, searching for his cigar. "She's only just met me and already she's putting me in my place!"

"It's no more than you deserve, Father."

"Rightly so, rightly so. Well, do you make lots of beautiful music here at Windmere, Miss Hastings?"

Jana recognized a slight shift in the tone of the Judge's baritone voice and sensed he was finally treating her as an adult. "I'm not allowed to sing anymore," she replied, coolly.

"No, no. Certainly not. But if I remember correctly, you were an old hand on the piano, eh?"

"They won't let me have a piano, either."

The Judge liberated the cigar from his pocket, and now pulled it lovingly through his hands. "Why not, Miss Hastings?"

"Because once I start playing the piano I can't stop."

Judge Graham pointed the cigar at her like a conductor's baton. "Don't you think that's a bit obsessive?"

"Yes, but I still can't stop," Jana said, truthfully.

The Judge laughed, and slapped his thigh again. Henry chuckled. Jana giggled. It was difficult to stay mad at the Judge!

"Do you think Ketchum would mind if I smoked?"

"You know you shouldn't, Father," Henry chastised.

"No doubt, no doubt." The Judge pocketed the cigar and patted the pocket reassuringly. "Well, well, I'll save them for later. Ketchum is an old hand at overlooking vice."

Jana sat with Henry and his father for nearly an hour, warming quickly to the Judge. She marveled at this strange and wonderful creature that could almost have been something Captain Joshua brought back from one of his seafaring adventures. The Judge did most of the talking, bringing Henry up to date with the latest on Henry's stepmother and sisters. When the clock chimed four-thirty, Jana saw her opportunity, and excused herself. She calculated that she had been on display long enough and also that Henry would want some time alone with his father.

She had hoped to slip away unremarked, but the Judge popped up as soon as she regained her legs. "Do forgive my impertinences, Miss Hastings," he begged. This time he held out his hands, and waited for her to take them, which Jana did. He squeezed reassuringly. "I feel as though we're already acquainted—Henry's written so highly of you."

So, Henry *had* told his father about her!

"And I hope you won't hold it against Henry that his father is such a bore, eh?"

Jana looked up into Judge Graham's expressive eyes. His black eyebrows were on the move again. He seemed so anxious! And so truly sincere. Surely, he must be a very good man?

Jana decided that she liked the Judge. "I'm not at all bothered by you. Although, I was at first," she admitted.

The Judge burst into belly-shaking laughter. "She sees right through me, Henry! You'd better watch out."

"Oh, I think she's already sounded my depth, sir."

Jana moved away from the fireplace. The Judge lunged ahead of her to the opposite side of the room in order to reach the door first. He swung the polished wooden door open and stepped around to the other side. Jana followed him out into the hall.

"Thank you for keeping my boy company, my dear," he added, conspiratorially. "I've been worried about his fine mind mildewing away, but it seems as though you're keeping him shipshape."

Pleased at the compliment, Jana smiled at up him. "I like to talk with Henry. He makes me think about things."

"Things like love and babies, eh? Well, just keep on doing what you're doing, Miss Hastings, and I've got a feeling that everything in that department will come out straight!" He winked.

And so, this was the Judge!

Chapter 16

The Birthday Bash

December 2013

Since early fall, the Ladies Cornshop Auxiliary of Sovereign, formerly known as the Ladies Fire Auxiliary, had been planning a birthday celebration for Miss Hastings' eighty-ninth birthday. The local service organization was originally planning to host this gala event at the meetinghouse annex to our church; however, given the retired music teacher's failing health, the party had been downgraded to an afternoon tea at her home. Maude Gilpin, President of the Auxiliary and Rebecca's partner at the local restaurant, was baking an enormous cake, and although the party was to be an open house, the ladies had allocated specific time periods to attendees so that Miss Hastings wouldn't be overwhelmed by hundreds of well-wishers all at once.

Around the first of December there had been some talk of cancelling the birthday bash altogether, but Miss Hastings had immediately put her foot down. "Don't you dare cancel my party, DAHRRRLINGS, or I'll come back and haunt you when I'm gone!" She had cackled with boisterous laughter as she laid down this edict, but there were enough present having had Miss Hastings as a teacher to remember that she always made good on her threats. And so the party was to go on as scheduled, after church on Sunday afternoon.

I was especially anxious for Nellie to attend the birthday bash, not only because Miss Hastings had asked specifically to see her, but also because I thought it would be a good opportunity for Nellie to reconnect with old friends in Sovereign. We can't have too many friends in this world, and I'd discovered in the past few days that my daughter didn't appear to have many. Oh, I had seen her checking her messages now and then, and I'd spotted her sending and receiving a few texts, but not with the same fervor that I had witnessed other young people texting their every move to their buddies and boyfriends or posting "selfies" on Facebook, Twitter and Instagram. Nellie had always been a loner, and this worried me now more than ever. Not for the first time I regretted not having married Peter earlier and given Nellie younger brothers and sisters. When I left this earth to claim my Great Reward, Nellie would have no other family in the world except Peter.

"You're coming to the party?" I anxiously asked Nellie on Saturday, taking a break from putting the finishing touches on my sermon. I tossed another stick of wood into the woodstove, stood up and dusted off my hands. "It's right after church tomorrow. We'll stop on our way home— that's our time slot."

She put down her electronic tablet, on which she had been reading something esoteric like Immanuel Kant's categorical imperative. "Probably not. You can drop me at the house first."

I stifled the urge to tell her she could walk the two and a half miles from Miss Hastings' house to our home by reminding myself that at least she was coming to church. That was something. "Miss Hastings will be so disappointed not to see you," I allowed, instead. I had already passed on to Nellie Miss Hastings' particular invitation.

"She won't miss me. Anyway, I don't know her that well."

"How can you say that? You've known her since you were seven. You used to love it when she came to school and did her musical parade."

"I did like Matilda—she was cute, hopping along in the parade with us." Nellie paused, as if for reflection. "But that was a long time ago." She picked up her tablet and began reading again.

I sighed, and returned to my study. An hour later, Gray Gilpin arrived on our doorstep, long-handled shovel at the ready. I had hired him to shovel off some snow that had clogged up the north side of the metal roof. There was a section, where two roofs had been cobbled together out back that the snow never slid off. As a result, when the January thaw came—assuming that the thaw was going to come this winter—ice dams would form and melt water would come streaming down the back wall into the living room. Peter had threatened to climb up and shovel off the roof, but I had forestalled this catastrophe by a timely phone call to his great-nephew.

"Looks like I'm gonna make a bunch of money for college this wintah," Gray said, when I answered the doorbell, which Nellie had ignored. "Good thing I got this!" He hoisted his shovel like a knight's lance. Gray had just been accepted at Thomas College in Waterville, a widely regarded business school. He was eventually going to take over the running of Gilpin's General Store if ever his grandfather Ralph decided to retire, and Thomas College would allow him to live at home, commute to school, and still work part-time at the general store.

"That's great for you but not so great for the rest of us," I joked. I showed Gray the problem area, and returned to my study. I cracked the back window slightly, in order to keep an ear on him. Although Gray wasn't getting up onto the roof, it was still possible for an avalanche of snow to come crashing down on his skinny frame. I didn't want to be the one to tell Maude and Ralph Gilpin that their grandson wasn't going to college after all.

The draft of cold air brought in the pleasing scent of wood smoke and, reinvigorated, I redoubled my efforts on my sermon. I was hard at work slashing unnecessary passages in an effort to keep my message brief, when a murmur of voices out back caught my attention. I cocked my ear; my desk being close enough to the window so I could overhear what was being said without getting up.

"Ya comin' to the party tomorrow?" I heard Gray ask someone, although I couldn't imagine at first to whom he was speaking, Peter having gone over to the farm for the day to help Bruce push back the snowbanks with their heavy equipment.

"Maybe. Maybe not."

It was Nellie! My daughter must have donned her winter gear and wandered out back. Most likely she was bored and looking for younger companionship. Gray was about four years her junior but he and Nellie had known each other since they were kids.

"Ya should go. She's a really nice lady."

"She won't miss me. There will be a lot of other people."

"Yeah, I guess. She knows everybody in town. She's like, a hundred years old. She's pretty cool, though."

I could picture Nellie smiling smugly, at hearing Miss Hastings pronounced "pretty cool."

"What makes her so special?"

"She knows lots of stuff—stuff ya don't think about much. I was pretty bummed out a while ago, but aftah talkin' ta Miss Hastings everythin' made sense."

"Really? What did she say to you?"

"Oh, jest stuff 'bout growin' up—separatin' from yer parents. Ya must know all about that."

"I don't have parents, just a mother."

"Yeah, right. What happened to yer dad, anyway? Did he die or what?"

This was dangerous territory. I leaned toward the window, anxious to hear how my daughter answered this pointed question.

"I'm not sure. I don't think I have a father. I think my mother used a sperm donor."

"Cool! Didja evah think 'bout who 'twas?"

There was a slight pause before Nellie answered. "Growing up I used to think he was either a theoretical physicist like Stephen Hawking—someone who wanted to spread his genes around, you know—or a California beach bum trying to pay for his surfing habit."

"Ha, ha! Ya sure don't look like Stephen Hawking, so must be the surfer dude."

"Most likely."

"Hey, I guess we're, like, some kinda cousins now that Uncle Peter and yer Mom are hitched. Pretty cool, huh?"

"That's right—I forgot Peter is your uncle."

"Actually, he's Dad's uncle. I guess that would make yer mom, like, my great-aunt or somethin'."

"Right. Well, it's been nice chatting, Gray."

"Yeah, I guess I bettah git back ta work or yer mom will disown me already. Ya should come to the party tomorrow, though, Nellie."

"Maybe I will."

The sound of snow being scraped off the roof replaced their voices. I sank back in my chair, perplexed by what I had overheard. My daughter thought her father was some unnamed sperm donor? Was this how she answered all questions about him? Should I sit her down and have a talk with her?

But if I did speak with Nellie, what could I say? The truth was so painful that I had never been able to share it with her. Nellie's father was a very real sperm donor, not a scientist or a surfer, but a jerk who had abandoned us as soon as he'd learned I was pregnant. I had elected to go it alone as a single parent, and although our life had been difficult, I'd never regretted my decision, even during the hardest of times.

I wrestled with what I should do, but in the end I decided to let sleeping dogs lie. I wanted to talk the situation over with Peter first before I said anything to Nellie about her father, or lack thereof.

140

On Sunday, I brought the church service to a close shortly before noon, and, without saying anything to Nellie about her preferences, I drove straight to Miss Hastings' house. Nellie didn't put up any argument and I was relieved to discover that her conversation with Gray appeared to have changed her mind about attending the party.

Rebecca greeted us in Miss Hastings' bright red and yellow kitchen, wearing the traditional Ladies Auxiliary apron and a colorful paper party hat. "Nellie! I'm so glad to see you, dear!" She gave Nellie a fond squeeze, and turned abruptly to me. "Your husband is outside someplace with Wendell—how I love saying that!" Peter, not used to attending church on a regular basis, had soon fallen into the way of many recalcitrant husbands in Sovereign, and had arrived at Miss Hastings' early to "help out" but, in truth, using the party preparations as a good excuse to skip church.

"Thanks. Anything I can do?"

"No, no, just pick out a hat and go." Rebecca pointed to a stack of pink, yellow, and blue party hats on the counter. "The cake is on the dining room table, and there's coffee and tea in the urns."

I popped on a party hat and secured the elastic band under my chin, looking as ridiculous as all the other guests wandering around the house. I passed through the dining room and peeked into the parlor, where instinct told me Miss Hastings might be holding court. I saw her diminutive figure gaily entertaining a throng around her chair. I decided to wait to congratulate her until the crowd thinned out, and turned back to the cake table. I'd left Nellie in the kitchen talking with Rebecca, who I knew was eager to fill my daughter in on everything that was going on in her own daughter's life. Amber and Nellie had met each other a few times over the years, and a weak friendship had been established. Again, I thought it would be a good opportunity for Nellie to strengthen her Sovereign ties.

I joined some of the others at the cake table, including Ryan, who was helping his very pregnant wife, Trudy, to a cup of tea. Doctor Bart hovered awkwardly over the sugar bowl. Seeing Doctor Bart reminded me of his feelings for my daughter. "Nellie's in the kitchen," I informed him. "Why don't you go say 'hello'?" Immediately, his face brightened and he straightened up.

Without further ado, Doctor Bart hastily departed for the other room. I helped myself to a slice of cake, feeling I had done my good deed for the day.

"He's got such a crush on Nellie, doesn't he?" said Trudy. "I'm so glad she came with you today, Maggie."

"Me too. How are you feeling?" I poured myself a cup of hot spicy tea, and liberally availed myself of Wendell's honey. The silver spoon tinkled against the fine china tea cup as I stirred.

"Fat! I'll be glad to get him out of me."

"Oh, wonderful! You found out the baby is a boy?"

"Nope," Ryan interjected, with a smile. "She just thinks it's a boy because she thinks that's what *I* want. But I hope the baby is a girl for her sake. We'll find out in two months, I guess."

"Let's just hope it's not twins," Trudy said, fondly patting her protruding belly.

I spotted an unusually swank-looking Leland sidling up to the cake table, one hand on Cora's back as he ushered her up. "Hallo, Minister!" he said.

I cordially returned the greeting, noting as I did that Cora was the only one in the room not wearing a silly party hat. Ryan and Trudy were silent when Leland joined us, Trudy frowning slightly as she regarded this strange duo together. I sensed she was concerned about her father's budding relationship with Cora, probably afraid that his feelings would get hurt.

Leland turned to his sidekick and attempted to convince Cora to accept a large slice of the moist chocolate cake. "'Twill be jest the thing for ya—put some flesh on them bones," he assured her.

Cora made a face. "Too much butter cream frosting! Do you want me to look like *her*?" With a little nod of her carefully coiffed head she indicated Maude Gilpin, Peter's older sister, who was gathering up dirty tea cups on the other side of the room.

Now, Maude Gilpin was nearly sacred in Sovereign, being not only the President of the Ladies Cornshop Auxiliary but also the woman who supplied the Old Farts at her husband's general store with free donuts and goodies every day. Ryan, Trudy and I were shocked by Cora's careless crassness, and I could see that even Leland was a bit taken aback. The old woodsman was rarely at a loss for words, however, and soon recovered himself. "Maude's got sech a big heart she needs all thet space ter put it in," Leland declared, cheerfully.

"Well said, Leland," asserted Ryan.

"Oh, I didn't mean anything, I'm sure," said Cora. She smoothly changed the subject. "Do you always get so much snow up here in winter?"

"'Tain't what we've hed in the last coupla years," Leland replied. He looked around the table, as if seeking general confirmation from the rest of us.

"That's for sure," I said, helping myself to the slice of cake that Cora had passed up. "We've had it pretty easy lately. I think we've forgotten what a real Maine winter is."

"Don't you get tired of it?" Cora asked, wearily.

"Not me!" Ryan replied. "I'm really enjoying being my own boss this year because I've actually had time to slap on the snowshoes and hike out to where Leland's working."

"Yep, he's helped us yard out a tree o' two. Yer not a bad hand at the reins, son."

"Thanks. That means a lot, coming from you, Leland."

Cora appeared confused. "He's helping you … what?"

"Yard out firewood."

"I thought you people chopped firewood?"

"Ya gots ta cut the tree down fust, de-ah, and git it out o' the woods." Leland chuckled. "Yer a real city gal, ain'tcha? Ya oughtta come out with me sometime when I harness up Cain 'n Abel. Ya'd like it."

Trudy frowned. I took a bite of cake, thinking to myself how unlikely it was that Cora would enjoy yarding wood with Leland. But much to my amazement she seemed predisposed to his proposition. "Do you think I could? I'd love to go with you sometime only… only I don't have anything to wear."

Leland considered this handicap. "Rebecca don't got nuthin' ya kin borrer?"

This was dangerous territory again, because Rebecca, while not as big a woman as Maude Gilpin, was pleasingly plump. Cora, on the other hand, looked to me to be about a size two.

"No, no, we're not the same size at all."

"Wal, I gots jest the thing, then. We got a whole closetful of wintah clothes thet Trudy's Ma wore, some good Pendleton wool 'n stuff. She was a leetle gal like yerself so there'll be somethin' ya kin borrer fer sure."

"Father!" Trudy exclaimed. Trudy's mother had died when she was a young girl, and I suspected that it would be difficult for her to see another woman wearing her mother's clothes.

"Oh, I couldn't," Cora demurred.

Leland ignored his daughter's outburst. "Them rags ain't doin' nobody no good jest hangin' up theah, is they? Now, ya come ovah tomorrow mornin' 'n we'll gits ya fitted up right."

"That's awfully kind of you Leland," Cora said, simpering.

"'Tain't kindness, 'tis a pleasure. Then, if ya likes, we'll plan ourselves a wintah picnic during January thaw. How's thet sound?" Leland glanced around the table, including the entire party in his picnic invitation. "Ain't thet a good ider?"

"Hey, a winter picnic does sound like fun," Ryan agreed. Quickly remembering that his wife would be eight months pregnant in January, he turned and put his hand on her shoulder affectionately. "Would you mind if I go, honey?"

"I won't mind, because I'm going, too!" Trudy pronounced. I could see that she was still hot under the collar. Ryan started to protest but his wife stopped him. "I'll be just fine—I'll ride on the sled."

"Ayuh, we gots ta take the sled—the Portland Cutter don't hold but two, 'n we'll have lots o' gear ta take out, too. I knows jest the place ta go. A cuttin' I did 'bout five years ago is growin' up real purty ta fir. We'll have ourselfs a bonfire 'n some good eats 'n I'll be danged if ya won't think yer'd died 'n gone ta heaven, sittin' out thar in the Maine woods in the middle o' wintah!"

Before we departed, I was able to find Miss Hastings alone and wish her happy birthday. She appeared fatigued, but obviously thrilled to greet everyone. "Do go see my pictures, dahrrrling, before you leave," she encouraged me, squeezing my hand. "They're in the studio." She lowered her voice. "Henry is there, and my parents and Addie. I knew you'd want to see them."

In the attached studio, I found her grand piano shut and covered with a beautiful silk Russian shawl. On top of the shawl dozens of framed photographs from the trunk in Miss Hastings' bedroom had been set up on display. There were baby pictures of Miss Hastings, and photographs of her on stage, including the musical revue poster that I'd already seen. Some later color pictures of her teaching in the local schools rounded out this selection. I found Henry's picture set to one side, next to a photograph of a teenage Miss Hastings with a group of children, obviously taken at the sanatorium. I turned the picture over and saw on the back scribbled in pencil: *Me and the Petite Troupe: Arthur, Suzanne, Bobby & Billy.*

What interested me most were the black-and-white photographs of Miss Hastings' parents, Anton and Alyona Yaroslavsky, including their wedding picture. I picked up a walnut framed photo and studied Helen Hastings, who was rapidly becoming a real person to me. She was lovely—her face and figure were perfect. But it was the life sparkling from her eyes that struck me most. Here was a woman passionate about the people she loved, and the life she lived! One of the photographs of Helen was an image of her standing next to a stiff, matronly Mainer in front of a black 1939 Nash. The two women were dressed in winter jackets, hats and gloves, and both held clutch purses. It was Helen and Addie Russell, getting ready to go out "kalooping," as Miss Hastings had once described their adventures together. The two couldn't have been more different in appearance; however, the love and respect they shared for one another was perfectly captured in this one black-and-white still.

Peter, who finally came in from outside, touched me on the elbow, alerting me to his presence. "Did you see this?" I asked, holding up the photo of Helen and Addie in front of the Nash. "The one on the right is Wendell's Grammie Addie."

"It's good to put a face to her, isn't it?" Peter said, examining the photograph closely.

I nodded. "The other one is Miss Hastings' mother, Helen."

He handed me back the photograph and I returned the black-and-white to the appropriate spot on the piano. "I feel as though I know them, like we're friends, almost."

Peter slipped his arm around my waist. "Forget what I said the other night, Maggie. It's a good story you're working on—I think you should stick with it."

"Really? You're not just saying that?" I anxiously searched my husband's handsome, weathered face. Already I had memorized every wrinkle around his smiling blue eyes, and lovingly examined every salt and pepper strand of hair on his head. I recollected what Helen Hastings had told her daughter about the difference between 'love' and 'devotion' and felt a new urgency to love this man completely and to be loved by him.

"It's obvious that Miss Hastings has a story she wants to tell, and I think you're just the person to do it," he said.

I gave him a big hug. I didn't need any more encouragement than that to pursue what was fast becoming an obsession with Helen and Addie, Henry, Eleanor, and *The Songbird of Sovereign*.

CHAPTER 17

THE BIRTHDAY GIFT

DECEMBER 7, 1941

Sunday morning around seven o'clock Addie Russell began whipping up the butter cream frosting for Jana's birthday cake. She had let the fire burn down overnight so that the kitchen would be cool enough to frost the triple-layer chocolate cake. She planned to put the cake together and decorate it before church so she could rest and enjoy her radio program in the afternoon per usual. Two hours later, as she was putting the finishing touches to the cake, Pappy and Bud entered the kitchen from the hen pen, allowing a draft of cold air to follow their footsteps. "Close the door," she said, quickly. "Do you live in a barn?"

Bud shut the door, and doffed his red leather cap. Pappy pulled up one of the pressed-back oak chairs at the kitchen table, keeping his pinched fedora stubbornly on his head even though he knew this act of defiance would irritate his wife. Occasionally he liked to remind her whose family farm it was.

The hired hand shuffled up to the counter in his stocking feet. "Thet's 'n awful purty cake ya got thar, ma'am," Bud said, impressed.

"It's Jana's birthday cake, for tomorrow."

Bud glanced hopefully at the remaining frosting in the bowl and licked his lips. Addie scooped a generous spoonful out of the glass mixing bowl and handed it to him. He accepted the pointed spoon eagerly and slurped down the frosting. He closed his eyes and his fat, round face issued a look of delight. "She'll like thet, ma'am—she surely will."

"You goin' ovah to Windmere with Helen tomorrow to deliver the cake?" Pappy interjected. He casually removed his hat and laid it on the leather-padded seat of the chair next to him, hoping that act of contrition might net him a taste of frosting.

"I'm not invited. Andy is going with Helen—he'll help her with the cake."

"Helen best be drivin', then—ya know what a lead foot ole Andy is." His wife rewarded him with a measured smile and a spoonful of the sweet stuff. Pappy took the peace offering, and licked the frosting slowly, savoring the buttery flavor.

"Ayuh, 'at cake 'a'll end up 'n the woods fore sartin," Bud predicted.

"The cake will be fine. Helen won't let anything happen to it. Now, Bud, do you think you can get that woodbox filled before we go to church?"

"I surely kin, ma'am."

Addie turned to her husband. She untied her rose-figured apron and pulled it over her head, revealing her Sunday dress. "And you're not even changed yet, George!"

Pappy hesitated. This was the crucial moment. But life was so much more comfortable when he didn't try and defy her. He set down the cleaned spoon. "I'll be ready direck-ly," he said, heaving himself obediently to his feet.

When the dinner dishes were done up after church, Addie was finally ready to claim her weekly reward, *The New York Philharmonic Society* Sunday broadcast. She retreated to the living room portion of the great room, which was demarcated from the dining room by various furniture groupings upon a room-sized red braided rug. Carroll, the youngest son who lived with them at the farm, was sprawled on the couch reading a magazine. Pappy was snoozing in his chair next to the radiant heat from the nickel-plated pot-bellied stove. Bud had departed immediately after dinner for his modest cabin in the woods, which he had built out behind the barn and where he spent his off-hours. Addie suspected that Bud kept a bottle or two in his cabin, but what she didn't know wouldn't hurt her and Bud had certainly earned his reward.

Addie paused at the occasional table that stood behind the couch to switch on the 1931 Philco radio. She fiddled with the dial until she locked into CBS, and swiveled the tabletop radio to face her chair. She moved around the front of the couch and coffee table and eased her tired body down into her old oak rocker with the overstuffed pillows. She propped her thick ankles up onto the cushioned footstool and adjusted her neck pillow. She had finished her dishes a little early today, so they were hearing the end of the radio news program, *The World Today*. Addie gave her full attention to the radio, but couldn't quite make out what the announcer was saying.

"Turn it up, will you please, Carroll?"

Without removing his eyes from his magazine, her son reached up and adjusted the volume. "Good 'nuff?"

"Yes, thank you, dear." Addie pulled her hand-knit sweater tighter and closed her eyes. She listened to what the announcer was speaking in a crisp, business-like voice:

"We just have a bulletin from London that President Roosevelt's announcement of Japanese air attacks on United States Pacific bases staggered London, which awaited fulfillment of Prime Minister Churchill's promise to declare war on Japan within the hour if she attacked the United States. Well, of course, the United States and Japan are not formally at war; however, it seems probable that, in view of the Japanese attacks, this is only a question for the reassembling of Congress tomorrow since if you've actually been attacked by the enemy you can do but little else than declare war. Here are more details from the front ..."

Carroll sat up. "What the hell—did he just say we were attacked by the Japs?"

"Shush!" exclaimed his mother, frantically motioning at him. "Keep quiet! I can't hear it."

Pappy opened his eyes, not sure whether or not it was worth his while to wake up. Carroll gave a vicious twist to the volume dial until the program boomed throughout the great room. The three Russells listened in disbelief as the announcer matter-of-factly continued to report that fifty to one hundred Japanese planes had attacked—were still attacking—the United States naval base at Pearl Harbor in Honolulu, Hawaii. They listened in stunned silence for several minutes, until *The New York Philharmonic* broadcast came on a few minutes after three o'clock.

Hearing the music, Carroll switched off the radio. "I don't believe it—it's a hoax," he declared. He tossed his magazine onto the coffee table. "They got me once; they ain't gonna git me agin." Carroll was one of the many who, while listening to *War of the Worlds*, believed that aliens were actually attacking the earth.

"Goddamm," said Pappy, clutching the arms of his chair with his gnarled hands. "I'll be goddammed! Whaddaya think, Ma?"

Before she could reply, the telephone jangled, startling them all. Addie, who had been sitting on the edge of her chair, felt her heart leap from her chest. She collapsed against the back of the rocker. The flounce on the overstuffed pillow gave a little flop.

Carroll jumped up.

"No, no—I'll git it," said Pappy. He heaved to his stocking feet. "Might be George."

Addie remained transfixed, watching as if in slow motion while her husband shuffled toward the kitchen where the telephone hung on the wall.

"I tell ya, it's a hoax," Carroll repeated, stubbornly.

"Shush," she said, straining to hear the muffled conversation from the other room.

Pappy returned in three or four minutes. Trembling, Addie pushed herself back up. "Who was it, George?"

"'Twas Andy. He wants to buy all the squash we got. Ain't no joke, Ma—we're agoin' ta war."

Carroll leaped up exultantly. "Yes-suh!" He flashed his mother a triumphant grin. "Looks like I'm gonna go shoot me some Japs."

His words stuck in Addie's craw. She shook a hard, knobby fist at her youngest son. "You stupid fool," she said, blazing up. "Go ahead and get yourself killed!" She slumped back into her chair, threw her apron over her face, and burst into tears.

The news of the Japanese attack on Pearl Harbor burned up the telephone lines, quickly making its way into every American home. Up the road from the Russells, Helen was humming a cheerful little ditty as she finalized things for Jana's birthday party on the morrow. The prizes and gifts were wrapped, and Jana's new dress was washed and pressed. Helen was reviewing her 'to-do' list when Andy burst into the parlor. His tie was askew and his face was red with energy. "We've been attacked by Japan," he said. "They've destroyed our fleet at Pearl Harbor!"

Helen dropped her list; the paper fluttered to the floor. She heard the thin sheet touch the hard wood and slip under the chair with a slight *whoosh*. "My dahrrrling! What does it mean?"

"It means we're at war with Japan, or very soon will be. I'm headed down to the factory, now."

"Today? Surely, that can't be necessary?"

"Chief Petty Officer Steele called me with the news. He gave me the go-ahead on the winter squash. They'll take everything we've got: corn, squash, peas and beans. I've already contacted Pappy Russell and Henry Gorse. We'll be working 'round the clock for the next few weeks."

Helen put her hand to her throat. "But what of Jana's party tomorrow?" she asked, with a slight hysterical timbre to her voice.

"Don't be ridiculous, Alyona. That must be all off now. This is war—*war*. Surely you understand what that means?"

Tears filled Helen's lovely brown eyes. "It means that my daughter will not have her seventeenth birthday party—and that many, many men will die." She shuddered at the grotesque uselessness of it all.

That evening at Windmere, just before bedtime, Dr. Ketchum made the unusual request for all the children to be gathered once more into the dining room. The good doctor stood at the head of the long table and, with hands clasped behind his back, gravely informed the children and the staff what had occurred at Pearl Harbor earlier in the day. He didn't know much more than the fact that the fleet in the harbor had been destroyed by the Japanese, he said, and that there were many deaths, perhaps thousands. Some sailors were still trapped alive in burning ships. Some had already gone to the bottom of the sea. President Roosevelt was to make a speech to Congress on Monday, which would be broadcast live over the radio. When the broadcast began, he and Mrs. Baker would gather them all up again to listen together as one family to what the President had to say. In the meantime, they were to stay close together, to comfort and cheer one another. He would not leave them—he would sleep in his study—until the world around them was once again on a safe and secure footing.

When Dr. Ketchum stopped speaking, the dining room was at first completely silent. The two attending nurses slipped out of the room, anxious to touch base with their families. Jana, who had been only half listening to the doctor, her head filled with excitement about her upcoming birthday, spoke up first. "What if the President's speech is the same time as my party?" she worried.

Dr. Ketchum frowned. "Young lady, there will be no party," he admonished sternly. "Men have died—they are dying still."

"But ... what of Mother?"

"Your mother telephoned earlier to say they will not be here. There will be no celebrating, now. We are at war."

Jana fought back tears. Frustrated, she slapped her small hand against the table. "That's not fair!" she cried.

All eyes in the room turned to stare at her. "It's not!" she repeated, but her voice wavered, quelled by the unexpected and unfriendly attention. Her hand and her heart throbbed in unison.

Eleanor reached for Jana under the table. "Hush," her friend whispered. "We'll talk later."

But it was with Henry, not Eleanor, that Jana spoke her first words about her disappointment. He arrested her, as she stalked off down the hall by herself, fuming with indignation. How dare they cancel her celebration! And her own mother ... allowing such a thing to happen!

"Oh, Henry—how could they put off my party?!" she wailed, when she perceived in the dim light of the long hallway that it was he who had pulled her aside. Henry would be able to provide her the comfort she sought.

But Henry wasn't comforting at all. His thin, handsome face appeared wan and old. "I didn't realize you were so selfish and self-centered," he uttered, hoarsely. He gazed at her with a look in his eyes she'd never seen before. Surely that wasn't ... disgust?

"What do you mean?" she asked, toying nervously with her necklace. "What are you talking about? I don't understand you."

"I'm speaking of your spiritual poverty. I've never seen it before, until tonight."

"You know I'm Jewish, Henry," she replied.

"That has nothing to do with it, Jana. This evening you revealed an amazing lack of sensitivity, and ... and downright spiritual shallowness." With a little shock, Jana realized that it was the first time Henry had called her by her given name.

"Men are being burned alive and all you care about is your stupid party! I can hardly believe it. I thought you were different. You fooled me, I guess."

"I didn't fool you, Henry. I am what you want me to be, truly," she pleaded.

"That's just it. You are as I want you to be, conveniently, at that moment. But I don't want you to be anything for me. I want you to be something for yourself. You've been given a gift from God, the ability to rise above all the pettiness in this world and love for the sake of love alone. I've seen you with Eleanor, and Arthur, and some of the other children, and I know you have this gift. But it comes and goes, like the hummingbird moth in summer. It's in you, I know, because I *have* seen it." He let go of her elbow. "But not tonight."

Jana groped for the security of the wall. Her head felt disoriented, disjointed. She stared down at the polished floor, concentrating, carefully considering his words. He had seen something in her that was special, that gave her the ability to rise above—what?

He turned on his heel to leave. She reached out to stop him. "Wait—I don't understand!"

He brushed her hand away. "Leave me be."

"Henry! Please, don't go."

Unheeding, and with bowed head, he strode off down the hall.

What had she done? What had he meant? What was happening to them all?!

Jana felt sick to her stomach. The life drained from her limbs, and she sank down to the hard floor, feeling as though she might retch at any moment.

She relived Henry's words, and for the first time began to apprehend the horror of the day's events. The Japanese had bombed Pearl Harbor. Thousands had been killed. Sailors had been burned alive or had gone to their graves with their ships. Even now, German submarines could be skulking off the coast of Maine, awaiting an opportunity to attack.

And she—she had been worried about her birthday party! Mortified, she put her face in her hands and wept silently.

Ten minutes later, feeling emotionally bruised and seeking a place to hide and lick her wounds, Jana crept into the green room, where in the past she'd occasionally found solitary refuge. But upon entering the small back room she found Arthur and two of the younger boys huddled by themselves on the couch, holding each other and shivering. She glanced around for an attending nurse, but there was none in sight.

"I want my Mummy," Arthur whimpered, his fat lower lip trembling.

Jana's heart was touched by the pathos in his eyes and voice. "I'll be your Mummy tonight," she said tiredly. She searched out a blanket, and pulled it over the three children. "Everything is going to be alright," she assured them, although she didn't believe it herself.

"Don't leave us," Arthur begged. His little white face examined hers anxiously.

"I won't," she promised. "Now, go to sleep."

"Do you think they'll find us here? Are we going to get bombed, too?"

"I think there are better targets than Windmere, Arthur." She dropped a kiss on the top of his head, and pushed his little Dutch-boy hair back behind his ears. "Don't worry—I'll be right here. Now, go to sleep." Satisfied, Arthur stuck his thumb in his mouth and rolled over into the couch. The other two children stared up at her, open-mouthed. Jana had dubbed these five-year-old twins, Billy and Bobby, the 'Snow Babies' because after the first winter storm she had glanced out the dining room window and spied them playing in their snow in their underwear. The Snow Babies were still wide-awake. "You, too," she scolded. "Go to sleep." The twins quickly shut their eyes.

Jana was casting about for a suitable chair in which to sleep her-self, when, from the other side of the room, she heard a sob. She searched and, under the tall occasional table, she discovered Suzanne, the bold-faced little girl who often reminded Jana of her younger self. The girl was crouched alone, tears running down her cheeks. Without stopping to think, she lifted the child out and settled her onto her lap in a chair.

"Shhh, don't cry—everything's fine," she whispered into Suzanne's ear. She felt the soft wet fuzz of the girl's cheek as Suzanne pressed against her, and pulled the child closer. Responding to the encouragement, the child burrowed her face fervently into Jana's shoulder. Suzanne slurped in a wet lungful of air, and then exhaled an ecstatic sigh of relief. Jana, who had just drawn a deep breath herself, inhaled Suzanne's ardent sigh into her lungs like a living creature. She became aware that the child's spirit had entered her own—their heartbeats had become synchronized—and she experi-enced a profound feeling of love. She tenderly brushed a stray hair from the little girl's face, and as she did she felt a curious uplifting sensation such as she had never felt before. Her being was expand-ing joyfully, soaring above its earth-bound limitations like a songbird liberated from its gilded cage. The dim, wallpapered room rapidly retreated as Jana felt herself rising up and up through dark clouds of mystery and wonder. Suddenly, she burst through the darkness into a warm white light, which quickly enveloped her in a sensation of pure, liquid love.

This, *this!* This was what Henry was talking about! She had risen above the smallness and meanness of earth to catch a glimpse of Heaven.

CHAPTER 18

COLD-HEARTED COMFORT

DECEMBER 2013

"I've had a LOT of birthdays since then, but never one quite like that!" Miss Hastings recalled. "I still remember holding that PRECIOUS Suzanne in my arms. That was the most WONDERFUL birthday gift I ever got, by golly!"

I almost didn't know what to say. I was floored to hear that her seventeenth birthday bash had been obliterated on December 7, 1941, along with Pearl Harbor. I had known that her birthday was December 8th, of course; I had just never connected the dots.

Miss Hastings' revelation helped explain so many things: her love for children, her compassionate nature, her understanding. She had not only been given a gift from God, she herself was a gift from God.

I picked up my pen. "Do you mind if I just jot that down?" After Peter's encouragement, I had asked Miss Hastings if I could write a book based on her life. She had agreed, with one caveat—that I would wait until after her death to publish the book. We were sitting at her kitchen table, lingering over our lunch. The plates had just been pushed aside, and my yellow legal pad was at the ready.

"Do, dahrrrling! I want young people to know that STUFF isn't as important as how we care for one another. No amount of charity endowments when you're seventy can make up for being a tight-fisted twit the rest of your life—doggone it! When we get to the end of the road, it's not God's judgment we need to worry about, it's our own." She cackled with laughter.

I jotted down some key words, glanced up, and glimpsed a halo of golden dust motes around her head. What a woman! What a story. I scribbled faster.

"Life was never the same after Pearl Harbor," she continued. "That was OUR 9-11. Suddenly, there was an evil bugaboo behind every tree. Poor Arthur was scared to go out and gather eggs for weeks because he was afraid he'd get bombed on the way to the chicken coop."

"What about the others at Windmere?"

"Eleanor had been recovering nicely, but after Pearl Harbor she began slipping away—poor dahrrrling! She stopped eating, saying she didn't want to live in such a HORRIBLE world. And she was tired, and ready to join her mother. I was frantic, trying to figure out what I could say or do to keep her alive as long as possible. But I was seventeen. I had no special powers—except love." She paused for reflection. "But sometimes even love isn't enough."

"And Henry?" I asked, daringly.

"My dahrrrling Henry found me the next morning with Suzanne in my lap. I never said a word to him, not ONE WORD, about my selfish outburst. I didn't have to—he could see the transformation in my eyes. He took Suzanne out of my arms and helped me with the other children. But he became an old man overnight."

"Surely Henry didn't think that evil lurked behind every tree?"

"No, no—not that. But after listening to Roosevelt's speech to Congress the next day—we all gathered 'round the radio to listen— Henry told me that he felt as though he had lived the life of a well-fed moth in a cocoon, barely registering what was going on in the world outside Windmere. The attack on Pearl Harbor did more than sink our ships; it sunk our psyche, our *élan vital*, as Mother would say. Suddenly, Henry's world—our world—became all topsy-turvy."

I wrote furiously, trying to keep up with her. Dozens of follow-up questions floated through my head. What about her mother? How had Helen Hastings handled the war years? And Addie? Did Carroll go off to fight? What about young George and Wesley?

Miss Hastings shut her eyes. Her shoulders drooped. I recognized that she was becoming fatigued. The pale skin covering her blue-veined hands and arms had become almost translucent. It wouldn't do to tax her unnecessarily. Hopefully, there would still be plenty of opportunities to talk, but now it appeared as though she needed some rest. And I was actually feeling tired myself. My back ached. Suddenly, I was mindful of my own mortality. I set my pen down. "Why don't I help you back into bed," I suggested. "I've got to go down to the church for a while, and then I think I'll go home and take a nap myself."

"A good idea, dahrrrling—you look all in. Is your sermon for Sunday so scintillating? Or is your handsome new husband keeping you up at night?"

"Let's go with the husband," I said, smiling.

Prior to my cancer diagnosis, I had kept open office hours at church both Wednesday and Thursday afternoons, just in case anyone wanted to drop by and talk. You'd be surprised how many people like to stop in and chat—I myself had been surprised over the years. But since I'd realized how fast the sand was running out of my hourglass, I'd dropped the Wednesday hours, satisfying my conscience with Thursdays and with a note on the door the rest of the time giving out my contact information.

The Sovereign Union Church is a very traditional-looking New England church, boasting the requisite white steeple and pointed spire that could be seen for miles. The steeple was a beacon in the old days, a signal to many a weary traveler on foot or horseback that their destination was almost reached. I had fallen in love with Maine's small churches while at Bangor Theological Seminary, spending more than a year of my life on my master's thesis about the valuable role these institutions played not only in the past but also in the present day. Back then, I jokingly called them "white dinosaurs," because, while their congregations were nearly extinct, their white carcasses were still extant and ubiquitous throughout the state.

The church was unlocked—a sanctuary isn't a sanctuary unless it's available, after all—and I lifted the wrought-iron latch and let myself in, stomping the snow off my boots onto the rug in the unheated entryway. I stepped quickly into the nave and paused, enjoying the peaceful scene before me. The afternoon sun streamed in from the elongated, leaded-glass windows casting a warm glow over the white polished pews with their plush new velvet seat coverings. The brass candlesticks sparkled on the altar, and the overall effect was one of uplifting brightness. There's nothing more mystical than natural light in winter and when I saw the phosphorescent light flowing into the chancel, I had the impression that God was being beamed aboard our little church like Captain Kirk.

For the first time I began to consider whether it might not be worthwhile to try and prolong my life. Why had I refused treatment for the cancer? Why was I giving up without a fight? In such reflective mood, I went into my office and began working on my sermon for Sunday.

Because we're a Universalist-Unitarian Church, we don't follow the common Christian Lectionary, which gives me lots of leeway for topics on which to preach. I thought this week I might spin a sermon out of Miss Hastings' story of transformation, with Suzanne and the animating sigh, changing the names, of course. I was deep in the middle of my pastoral message when I heard the shrill sound of a woman's voice calling out my name. I rose from my desk, opened my office door, and spied Cora Batterswaith.

"There you are, Maggie!" she said, approaching with quick steps. "I wondered where you were hiding yourself. Rebecca told me you were here on Thursdays."

"Cora! How nice to see you," I lied. Sometimes we do lie. I'm sorry, but that's the truth of it.

I could see that Cora had already taken Leland up on his offer of his deceased wife's clothing. She was dressed in stylish-but-dated black knit ski pants, a cream-colored turtleneck, and a lovely Nordic wool cardigan, which looked as though it could have come right off the shelf at L.L. Bean. The unplumbed area of our church isn't heated during the week, however, and despite the warmth added by the sun and the new clothes, she shivered. "Brrr, it's cold in here!"

I took the hint. "Let's go into my office where it's warm." I held open the heavy, double-crossed wooden door and she advanced. "Take a seat," I said, closing the door behind us. I motioned toward the gothic-looking chair situated in front of my mahogany desk.

As my guest settled herself regally onto the red velvet cushion I could see why Lila had dubbed her "Queen Cora." I reclaimed my matching desk chair.

"So, this is where you hide out?" she began.

"Well, I'm not sure if I'm hiding. Everyone knows I'm here Thursday afternoon. I also see folks by appointment and after church on Sunday. But otherwise I'm not in my office much in winter—I try to save on the oil bill, you know."

"Must cost a fortune to keep this mausoleum going!"

There is always a certain amount of small talk necessary to make visitors comfortable. So I smiled, but said nothing. I would let Cora dictate the course of the conversation until I could figure out in which direction we were headed. Then I could help her along.

"Is your daughter still with you? What a lovely girl!"

"Thanks. Nellie's gone to spend Christmas with some friends. She doesn't hang around Sovereign much—there's not much happening here for young people."

"That's for sure!" Cora glanced around, taking note of the three walls of books in my little office. "My, you must read a lot."

"Those are just for looks," I said. She laughed, and relaxed. That joke worked every time.

Cora crossed her legs neatly, at the ankles. "What do you think of Leland, Maggie? He's rather a silly old goose, isn't he?"

Now, I myself had thought that Leland's courting of Cora was reminiscent of an old gander with a new goose let loose on the farm; however, to hear such words spoken aloud seemed slightly sacrilegious. Leland Gorse, for all his faults, was a warm and wonderful human being. He was cheerful, good-natured, and considerate. Whenever anyone in town needed firewood Leland was always at the shed with a delivery, whether that person could pay for the wood or not. "Ketch me when ya kin," he'd assured many a recipient of some of the town's best rock maple, knowing full well that if he ever did get paid it would be in canned string beans and venison, something of which he had plenty at home.

"I think Leland is enjoying having you here," I replied, side-stepping the question. "It's been a long time since he's had female companionship, except for Trudy, of course. His wife's been gone for many years."

"What was she like?"

"I never knew her, but I've heard Miss Hastings and some of the other old timers speak of Rowena with great reverence and respect."

"Oh, well. Everyone always says good things about the dead. Do you think he owns that farm by himself?" she hurried on. "Or do you think Trudy and Ryan's names are on the deed?"

My skin began to crawl. I couldn't help thinking she sounded like a gold digger, but I forced myself to give Cora the benefit of the doubt. Who knows what was going on inside that carefully made-up head of hers? Judge not that thee be not judged, I chastised myself.

"I don't have the least idea. But Scotch Broom Acres has been in Leland's family for nearly two hundred years and it seems likely he'll make sure it stays that way." I straightened up some papers on my desk, and adjusted a book or two.

"Yes, yes, probably so." She paused, and pursed her lips thoughtfully.

I decided to take the bull by the horns otherwise we might be there all afternoon. I still had my eye on that nap. "What do you want in life, Cora? A wise person once told me that all we have on this earth is our time. How do you want to spend what's left of your time?"

Those words had the effect of untying her emotional corset. Strange how we bind ourselves up! She sagged back into the comfort of the padded armchair, suddenly looking haggard and tired. For the first time since I'd met Cora Batterswaith in 2012 she appeared real, vulnerable and entirely human.

"I just don't want to end up a bag lady, Maggie!" she proclaimed, miserably. "I'm almost sixty-five years old. I'll never work again—who will hire me? I know better than anyone that companies want kids right out of college. God knows I've hired enough of those kids myself, including my own replacement, although I didn't know it at the time. I haven't saved anywhere near enough money for retirement and I'll probably live to be ninety. What's to become of me?"

"Social Security?" I suggested.

"Oh, please! Don't be ridiculous. I couldn't live on that!"

Unfortunately, a lot of people do live on their Social Security – especially in Sovereign – and with a lot smaller monthly benefit than Cora, who had worked all her adult life, was likely to receive. I myself even got by on less than what that would be; however, I wisely held my tongue. I knew that if Cora truly wanted to stay in Sovereign, money wouldn't be an issue. She could grow her own food like the rest of us and even continue to work at Ma Jean's restaurant. She would have plenty of friends here, and never want for anything, even if the Social Security system went bankrupt. Would she live high on the hog? No. But would Cora have that security for which she apparently yearned? You bet.

"Dennis always promised to take care of me, and I believed him. He said he'd marry me when his kids graduated from high school, but then that turned into when they graduated from college, and then after his wife got over that silly little episode with breast cancer. *And* do you know how much money it cost me sneaking around all those years?!" she added, in a shrill voice. "We never stayed close to home because he was always afraid someone would see us—like everyone in the office didn't know what was going on! No, no—we always had to go to some pricy, out-of-the way B&B in upstate New York or the White Mountains or even here on the coast of Maine. I usually paid for everything because Dennis convinced me I could afford it better than he could." Cora laughed bitterly. "The kids in college, you know. What a sucker I was!"

"Well, at least you've finally seen the truth of it," I said. "That must be a comfort."

"It would have been a lot more comfortable if he'd kept his word!"

"People like that usually don't," I replied, thinking of the cheap, easy promises Nellie's father had made to me. I glanced at the mantle clock, suddenly eager to see Peter's reassuring face.

"I kept myself crammed into a one-bedroom apartment for twenty years because I couldn't afford to buy a place of my own," Cora continued. "Now, I just want a secure home, for me and Esmeralda."

"Esmeralda?"

"My cat. My sister's been taking care of her since I gave up my apartment and put my things in storage."

"You gave up your apartment!"

"Of course. To save money. Rebecca said I could stay with them as long as I want. But what I really want is my own home, with a big kitchen and pretty country curtains—something like Leland's place. Is that too much to ask? There's a sunny spot in the dining room at Scotch Broom Acres where I could set up my sewing machine, and we could easily turn the upstairs guest room into a second bath."

"I think that room's spoken for," I said. I knew that Trudy and Ryan were planning to use the guest room as a nursery.

"Oh, they won't be there long," Cora predicted, confidently. "Ryan and Trudy will want a home of their own."

"I think that *is* their home."

Cora shrugged. She examined her ruby-painted nails. While speaking during the last few minutes she had excogitated herself back into Queen Cora. I could see that she was smitten by the pleasant idea of living at Scotch Broom Acres, but not necessarily smitten by Leland himself.

"You'll have to take the farmer with the farm," I pointed out. "Do you love Leland?"

"Oh, I could get used to him. And after all … he is almost eighty."

Oh, Lord!

I thought of Miss Hastings' story of little Suzanne, and calculated that it would take a lot more than a child's sigh to release Cora Batterswaith from her grip on the material world.

CHAPTER 19

A TEA PARTY

DECEMBER 1941

Eleanor was failing fast. As the snow fell softly outside, Jana sat alone by her sick friend's bedside. She had finally shaken off her young entourage for an afternoon, for Arthur, Suzanne, and the Snow Babies had attached themselves to her since the night of Pearl Harbor. Eleanor had been transferred to a small back room, formerly a maid's room, where she could receive more individual care and where Jana discovered that the sickest children were consigned until their deaths. Eleanor lay in bed listless, eyes closed, with her fine blonde hair in disarray on the pillow, looking like a tangled mass of threads. Her breathing was loud and labored.

Jana regarded the threads and recollected how Eleanor had spoken lovingly of her mother brushing her hair. She had a sudden longing to perform the same sacred duty. Quietly, she searched through the drawer in the bed stand until she located Eleanor's brush. She gently brushed the hair away from Eleanor's face.

"That feels nice," her friend whispered.

Jana could see the muscles in Eleanor's taut face relax. She lifted her head, and pulled the tangled hair forward. She separated the hair with her hands, and then brushed it against the pillow until the flax-colored strands were beautifully displayed and crackled with electricity. Satisfied with her work, Jana set the brush down on the side table. There were no sputum cups on the table now, only a small metal basin and a pile of starched white towels.

Eleanor broke into another violent coughing fit, which sounded to Jana's ears as though a bucket of marbles was rolling loose inside her friend's lungs. She supported Eleanor's back so that she could cough more easily, and was surprised by how little flesh was covering her bones.

Eleanor managed to press a towel against her lips while she coughed, and this time when the fit was finished Jana could see that the towel was stained bright red with blood.

Gently, Jana returned Eleanor to a prone position. She removed the bloody towel and rearranged the blankets. "Do you want me to read to you?" she asked, picking up her book.

"No, no, I'll sleep now."

Jana examined her friend's face, attempting to memorize every line, every detail, every mole. She would never forget Eleanor! Her first best friend. Would there ever be anyone else with whom she could speak so freely about all her hopes and dreams?

Henry's handsome face popped into her head. Henry! Of course, she would still have Henry.

A cardinal whistled loudly from a nearby fir tree. Jana, lost in her thoughts, was oblivious to the noise. But Eleanor heard the bird's call. The piercing whistle seemed to reinvigorate the sick girl. "Why, it's just like he's speaking to me," she said, struggling to sit up. "Did you hear him, Jana?"

The cardinal whistled again, and Jana nodded. "He sounds as though he's right outside the window."

"I used to dream that when spring came we'd have a tea party on the lawn," Eleanor continued, wistfully. "We'd get dressed up in long gowns and pretty straw hats and spread a blanket on the grass and feed the birds out of our hands. I know now that will never happen. But when I hear him talking to me, why, it's just as though the walls weren't there and it was the middle of May."

"Don't say that, Eleanor. Don't say it will never happen."

Eleanor sank back onto the starched white sheets. "Why not? We both know I'm dying."

"But you're not dead yet."

"No, no, not yet." She closed her eyes.

Immediately, Jana began to calculate how her friend's dying wish for a tea party with the wild birds could be granted. But she would need help for that, with resources far beyond her own slim means. If only she could see her mother!

Nearly two weeks passed before Helen Hastings was able to make her way to Windmere, however. Andy was racking up long hours at the canning factory preparing and shipping canned goods to the war front, and the family automobile was necessarily dedicated to his every need. He never knew when he might, at a moment's notice, be required to run to Bangor to purchase bulk sugar or corn starch, or drive out to a farmer's house to discuss the minutia of the upcoming season's corn planting, which was going to be the largest harvest the town of Sovereign had ever seen. Helen, who had been physically aching to hold her daughter in her arms since the advent of Pearl Harbor, almost thought she might go out of her mind.

"Oh, Adelaide, what shall I do?" Helen beseeched her neighbor on Wednesday afternoon. Despite the snow and cold, she had walked down to take tea with Addie. "Surely he can't mean for me never to use the car again? The war could go on for years!"

"Don't think that way, my dear." Addie set down the teapot and she squeezed her friend's hand reassuringly. "Why don't I drive you to Windmere on Saturday?"

"But what about your chickens? Who will clean all those eggs?"

"The boys can take care of things for one day, I hope. I've wanted to go and visit Jana myself for some time now, but I've always felt I'd be in the way. This seems like the perfect opportunity."

"Bless you, dahrrrling—you've an answer to everything!"

"Well, well. There are no problems in life, Helen, only solutions we haven't discovered yet."

"Then you are the solution to a mother's prayer!"

Saturday dawned with clear skies and bright sunlight. Just before one o'clock, Jana spied the Russells' pickup wending its way up the gravel drive. She gathered her retinue and went out to greet her mother and Mrs. Russell on Windmere's front steps. Arthur was holding her right hand and Suzanne was clinging to the left, and the two Snow Babies were grouped together at the end of the line next to Arthur. "What's this?" Helen said, climbing gracefully down from the passenger seat in the old Ford pickup. "A welcoming committee, hmm?"

At the sight of her mother's loving smile, Jana dropped the hands of her charges and flung herself into her mother's arms. "Mother!"

"My dahrrrling! I've missed you so much."

As mother and daughter exchanged mutual hugs and kisses, Addie stepped around the front of the truck and waited patiently to be noticed. Her gray curls were neatly in place—she had slept on her curlers overnight—and she was wearing her best Sunday dress. Still, next to Helen, she felt old and dowdy looking. Dissatisfied with herself, she frowned, and brushed a few stray flakes of sawdust from her winter coat.

Helen broke away first. She reached out and drew her friend forward. "Look who's here! Mrs. Russell has been so kind as to drive me over, otherwise, who knows when I might have been able to visit. Your father is being so stingy with the car."

Jana smiled at the older woman. "Thank you for bringing Mother," she said, sincerely. "And thank you for all your cookies, Mrs. Russell."

Addie felt herself relax. "It was nothing, my dear. I'm only glad to see you looking so well."

"Did you bring more cookies today?" Arthur piped up.

The three women laughed.

"Not today, I'm afraid." Addie opened her large pocketbook and pulled out a three-inch square of something wrapped tin foil. "But I did bring Jana her birthday cake—well, what's left of it." She handed the parcel to Jana. "This is the biggest slice I could fit into my ice box."

Jana eagerly accepted the cake. She peeled back the cold tin foil to discover the number '17' decorated with red roses on the buttercream frosting. Tears came to her eyes. "Oh, thank you!" she cried.

"You're very welcome, my dear," Addie replied, pleased. "Bud and Pappy said your cake was very good." She returned to her purse. "Pappy sent you some Wint-O-Green lifesavers and Bud made you this." She drew out a hand-carved songbird perched on a small branch.

Jana accepted the gifts. She put the lifesavers in her pocket, and turned the small piece of wood over in her hand so that she could admire the intricacies of Bud's carving. "It's beautiful!"

"Bud likes to whittle in winter, you know."

"I can't wait to show it to Eleanor—she loves birds."

"Bud is very fond of birds, too. He has the chickadees eating out of his hand at home."

"Please, give Mr. Suomela my thanks."

"I hope you'll be home soon to tell him yourself."

Helen took her daughter by the elbow, and turned to encompass the younger children. "Now, remind me—who are your little friends, dahrrrling?"

Jana made the introductions. Arthur shifted his feet, and the Snow Babies, who had condescended to wear clothing today, gaped at Helen with open mouths.

"And where is Henry, hmm?"

"He's writing a letter to his father."

"And how is Eleanor?"

Jana hesitated. "She's ... she's not good. Mrs. Baker says she shouldn't have any visitors."

"Ah, so sad. Shall we go inside? You can tell us all about it, dahrrrling."

Once settled into the front parlor, Jana laid bare her idea for Eleanor's tea party. To her gratification, both her mother and Mrs. Russell immediately proffered their assistance. Detailed plans were made for the event, which, after they had secured Mrs. Baker's blessing, was to be held on the girls sleeping porch on the following weekend. "We can't put it off too long," Jana allowed, sadly.

"Dahrrrling, you can count on us!" Helen declared. "I'll have Mrs. Emerson polish up the silver tea service."

"And I have my list," added Addie, patting her pocketbook reassuringly. "I've been wanting to use my mother's good tea cups for years. This is the perfect opportunity."

"What do you think, Eleanor?" Jana said to her friend, after the two ladies had departed. "We're going to have a tea party!"

Eleanor smiled faintly. "How nice for you."

"How nice for *you*," corrected Jana. "We're going to turn the sleeping porch into a picnic ground and Mother is going to buy us long dresses and fancy hats."

Eleanor struggled to rise up on her elbow. "Can we feed the birds?"

"Don't you worry about the birds! Bud is taking care of that. Mrs. Russell says he has the birds eating out of his hand at home."

"Oh, Jana—I can hardly wait!"

On the following Saturday, the old Ford pickup once again descended upon the sanatorium. This time Bud was squeezed into the middle of the bench seat. He bravely straddled the stick shift the entire trip. The bed of the Russells' truck contained a half dozen wooden packing crates and a travelling trunk.

"Thank you for my bird," Jana said, when Bud extricated himself from the truck. She leaned close and gave him a kiss on his scruffy cheek.

Bud lit up like a cherubim, his face becoming nearly as red as his leather cap. "Aw, 'twarn't nuthin' special," he said, bashfully. "Now, whar shall I put yore boxes, young ma'am?"

Jana led the way to the staging area on the girls sleeping porch. Some of the cots had been pushed together, and several green linen tablecloths were thrown over them in an attempt to give the area the appearance of a grassy knoll. Two of the large porch window screens had been removed, opening the porch up to the peaceful winter vista. The afternoon sun was shining, and several chickadees fluttered happily from one low bush to another. A fresh scent filled the air.

Bud set down the first wooden crate and surveyed the scene. A chickadee landed on the flat windowsill for a closer look. "I'll git 'em eatin' outta my hand in no time," he assured Jana.

Bud drew a small sack of seed from under his jacket and scattered the mix of coarsely ground corn and sunflower seeds on the wide sill. Then he returned to the truck and carted several crates into the kitchen. The trunk with the hats and clothing he placed in the green room. He returned to the porch, and in short order, the gentle Finn had the chickadees and a chipmunk eating out of his hand. The cardinal was much more wary; however, having expected this Bud had made a platform feeder that he set up on a pole in the snow about eight feet away. He drew some white safflower seeds from his pants pocket, placed them on top of the feeder with some of the other seed mix, and retreated to the porch. "Doan be shy, now," he cajoled the brilliant red bird. He whistled sharply, and the cardinal whistled back.

On the prior Saturday, when returning from Windmere, Helen and Addie had stopped in Waterville and purchased the long-sleeved gowns for Jana, Eleanor, and even little Suzanne. In addition, Helen had purchased a dozen hats. Half of these hats Addie decorated with colorful bows and ribbons for the girls, and around the bellies of the other half she had wrapped plain blue bands for the boys. Helen had charged Henry with dressing the younger boys, and she now helped the girls into their hats and gowns.

While the children were dressing, Addie took command of the kitchen. She put the water on to boil, and carefully unpacked her heirloom tea cups and saucers. She hummed to herself as she adeptly prepared the feast. This time, little Arthur was not going to be disappointed. Addie had outdone herself baking cookies and tea cakes. There were jelly tots and angel cupcakes, gumdrop squares, butterscotch brownies, and chocolate walnut wafers. Jana's favorite lemon butter cookies were included, as well. In addition, Mrs. Emerson had contributed raspberry tartlets, apricot almond bread, and an orange poppy seed tea cake, another of Jana's favorites, the recipe having come from her Aunt Minnie.

At two o'clock, Eleanor, dressed in a long pink gown, was carried onto the porch, where the tea things had been laid. Arthur, Suzanne, Bobby and Billy were already there, wearing their hats and eagerly consuming cookies from the silver tray. Henry was wearing his best suit, but instead of a tie he wore a dashing blue scarf that matched the blue band of his hat and which he had tied like an old-fashioned cravat.

"Everything is so beautiful!" Eleanor exclaimed. "Just the way I imagined it." She glanced around the porch happily. She spotted Bud and the birds at the windowsill. "Oh, let me feed them, please!" she cried.

The nurses had been in the process of settling Eleanor onto the green bedspread, but now transferred her to a chair next to the open window where Bud was supplying seeds to the chipmunks and chickadees. Wordlessly, he handed her the bag, and motioned for the sick girl to scatter a few seeds on the sill. Eleanor followed his direction, and a chickadee hopped over, looked at her sideways, and snapped up the seed. The little black-capped bird immediately took flight, landing in one of the bushes about three feet from the side of the building.

Eleanor clapped her hands. "Why, he's got the shell open already. And he's eating the seed inside. What a smart little fellow!"

"He'll be back for sartin, ma'am," Bud assured her. "No more will 'at fella, thar." He pointed to a striped chipmunk that was now clinging to the side of the wall, hoping to appear invisible. The other chipmunk approached boldly, running up the windowsill a few paces and then stopping to assess the situation.

Eleanor reached into the sack and pulled out a small amount of seed. She held out her hand. "Come here little one. I won't hurt you!" The chipmunk wouldn't budge, however, and Eleanor was forced to toss seeds to him from a distance.

The cardinal, who had been watching the proceedings from the safety of a pine tree about thirty feet away, condescended to approach. He glided into the limb of a tall fir tree situated next to the porch. The bird hopped down the limb and whistled sharply, as if to call the others away from their smorgasbord. But none of his feathered friends obeyed and he was forced to fly closer. He landed on the platform feeder, and Eleanor caught her hand to her breast.

Surely, this was her special friend? The one who talked to her through the walls!

The cardinal released another biting whistle. Eleanor held out her hand. The brilliant red bird cocked his head and regarded her thoughtfully. Unfortunately, Eleanor broke out into a coughing fit, startling the bird, which lifted its wings and careened off in flight. Eleanor recovered herself quickly, and watched the cardinal disappear into the afternoon sun. She shaded her eyes. "He wants me to follow," she said, dreamily. "He's showing me the way home!"

When Eleanor turned around, Jana, who was sitting near her chair, saw a beatific expression on her friend's face. Moved to tears, Jana took Eleanor's hand, kissed it, and pressed it against her heart.

Five days later Eleanor died. Jana was sitting alone with her friend at the end. Jana had nodded off to sleep, but when Eleanor exhaled her last rattle of breath she started up. She strained her ears waiting to hear the next labored inhale, but the breath was never taken. Instead, there was a strange change of air pressure and the outlines of objects in the dim room became blurred. Jana felt a mysterious new liberty, a freedom of being, as though time had been rent and the laws of gravity suspended. A spiritual mist descended, falling like luminous dew over Jana and the forlorn little figure in the sick bed. The hair on the back of Jana's neck stood up. She felt the softest of kisses upon her face and realized that Eleanor's spirit was passing by. She held out her hands to stop her friend, but there was nothing upon which she could catch hold. Eleanor's spirit had become one with the mist, now rising up out of her reach.

Poor Eleanor had finally gone home to be with her mother.

Chapter 20

January Thaw

January 2014

"I'm going to plant daffodils this spring—hundred and hundreds of daffodils!" Rebecca vowed, crunching along over the crusty snow tamped down by her husband's snowshoes. Wendell's legs were much longer than hers and she had to take two quick sliding steps with her snowshoes for every one of his to keep up. "My heart aches for the sight of green things! It's been such a hard winter and it's only January."

The January thaw had finally arrived, and our little group of friends was heading out on the winter picnic that Leland had proposed during Miss Hastings' birthday bash. Wendell paused to consider the best way around a large blow down, the trunk of which was blocking the deer trail we had been following through the woods. The pine's exposed roots dangled around its maw like tangled hair and smelled of earth and fungus. "This wintah ain't no hardah 'n it used to be," he said with a grin. He was wearing an antique set of ash and rawhide beavertails and Rebecca sported traditional bearpaws, both manufactured in my grandmother's hometown of Norway, Maine, which was once the snowshoe capital of the world. I knew that the two pair of snowshoes had been in the Russell family for generations—they'd been hanging in the shed since before I'd come to town—and I pictured Pappy and Bud using the snowshoes to rabbit hunt or to survey the woodlot making their firewood selections for the following season.

I caught up to Wendell and Rebecca and pulled off my gray woolen mittens. "We've just forgotten how winters used to be," I said, puffing heavily. "The winters we've had in the last few years have been so easy." I leaned down to adjust the leather binding on my right snowshoe, glad that Wendell was the one breaking trail through the woods to the clearing that Leland had selected for our outing. Wendell was in better shape than I was, plus he wasn't battling a terminal illness.

We had all met at Scotch Broom Acres at eleven o'clock: Peter and I; Wendell, Rebecca and Cora; and of course Leland, Ryan and Trudy. Wendell had reported that his honeybees were taking their cleansing flights on this sunny winter morning and I could see why. The polar vortex that had gripped two-thirds of the nation had ended and it was nearly 50°, which seemed like a heat wave compared to our prior chill. There was a light southerly breeze and the woods had a fresh astringent scent to them, a mixture of pine and balsam. We paused, as Wendell reconnoitered the best way around the blow down. The cheerful sun filtered down through the sweet-smelling canopy, highlighting the grains on the bark of the evergreens. You never realize how many different shades of brown, black, and gray there are in this world until you venture into the Maine woods in winter.

Two days of warm rain prior to today had shrunk our snowpack to a manageable amount and gave us good crust over which to make our way. I could hear the crunching of Peter's and Ryan's snowshoes in the distance. They had fallen behind when they stopped to examine the lime-colored new growth shooting out from the tips of a nice stand of young firs, Peter explaining to Ryan how to properly harvest the tips in order to promote healthy tree growth. Tipping is a big industry in Maine; thousands and thousands of balsam wreathes, which are made from tips, are sold during Christmas time, making their way to almost every state in the nation, including to our nation's capital where they are laid upon the graves of the fallen soldiers buried at Arlington National Cemetery.

I heard the jingle of sleigh bells that signaled Leland and his team weren't far away. Leland had harnessed Cain and Abel to the barn-door-sized wooden sled with which, prior to the advent of electricity, the family had used to haul blocks of ice from the pond in winter. The sled was ferrying not only our picnic supplies and accoutrements but also Cora and Trudy. Leland and the horses had taken the direct route to the picnic spot via the old woods road, but the rest of us had selected the more circuitous and scenic route through this cathedral of white pine and balsam fir. I was glad we did. Forty-five minutes of traipsing through the woods had cleansed and restored my spirit. I realized how much, without being aware of it, I'd been worn down by anxiety, worrying about stuff over which I had no control, such as what would happen to Nellie after my death. *Carpe diem*, I reminded myself, taking Henry's advice. If ever there was a day for seizing, today was that day.

Leland reached the designated spot first, a pretty little ten acre clearing in the midst of his three hundred acre working woodlot. He'd harvested this area six or seven years earlier so it was mostly open, except for a few towering seed pines, a smattering of immature hardwoods, and a cluster of balsams whose varying heights were reminiscent of eager students in a one-room schoolhouse. Leland released his draft horses from their harnesses and liberated his chain saw from the sled. In short order he had a healthy campfire going. Once we broke out of the woods we followed the smoke to the picnic spot, discovering with delight that Leland already had the banquet table unloaded and the folding chairs set up around a snapping fire.

One of the pleasures of winter picnicking is the style of the thing. Mainers might slack off around the house, but when we're in the woods half of the fun is "doing it up right." Leland had tramped down the picnic area to make it comfortable, so we were able to remove our snowshoes and stick them on edge into the snow. Rebecca quickly located the floral linen tablecloth she had packed away in a large wicker basket, draped it over the table, and proceeded to unpack the rest of the goodies.

"What can I do?" I asked, hovering over her shoulder.

Rebecca pointed to a five-gallon plastic pail with various accoutrements that was still strapped to the sled. "See if you can find a place for that."

"That" was a Luggable Loo, a portable toilet kit comprised of a plastic pail, a doodie bag, and snap-on lid. I figured Rebecca had added the loo as a concession to Cora. Most of the rest of us would be satisfied dropping drawers behind a bushy balsam; however, the makeshift potty with its comfortable height and standard plastic seat would no doubt be welcomed by the very pregnant Trudy.

I strung a clothesline from two small hardwoods about eighteen feet away from the campfire, and draped a red blanket over the line for privacy. After fitting the liner inside the bucket and attaching the seat, I thought I might as well check to see that the thing was working properly. Rebecca had certainly thought of everything because, when I resurfaced from behind the blanket, she wordlessly handed me a container of baby wipes. "Where are the flowers?" I joked. She rummaged through one of the wooden packing crates and with a flourish held up a glass vase containing dried pink hydrangea blossoms. Like I said, we do our winter picnicking up in style.

While Trudy and I helped Rebecca unpack the dishes and the victuals, Peter, Ryan and Wendell cut and gathered a big pile of firewood. Leland set up his cast-iron tripod, and hung a pot of water over the fire to boil, adjusting the chain until the pot was at just the right height. Rebecca handed him Trudy's leek and potato soup to warm, and then some of Wendell's baked beans. She had prepared a batch of skillet corn bread in advance, and next passed the pan to Leland to preheat. He set the cast-iron pan into some early coals, and, after about a minute, Rebecca added some sunflower oil and sprinkled in two tablespoons of freshly ground cornmeal. When the cornmeal was browned slightly she spooned in the corn bread mixture. Soon the sweet scent of baking cornbread wafted deliciously throughout the clearing and I half expected the woods creatures to creep out and join our little party at any moment.

Other additions found their way to the fire including buttercup squash halves wrapped in foil and venison backstrap. The venison was fresh and obviously shot out of season but our little crew was too politic to say anything and Cora was happily ignorant of the meat's identity.

Cora had parked herself in one of Leland's canvas-and-wood lawn chairs and was surveying the scene appreciatively. "It's really very nice here," she said, to no one in particular. She rearranged her wool scarf. "Much warmer than I expected."

Leland placed a second cast-iron skillet on some coals to preheat for the backstrap. "Thought you'd like it heah, Cor-ree," he said affectionately. He tossed some butter into the pan.

Cora rewarded him with a sweet smile. One of the horses snorted and she glanced over to where the untethered Cain and Abel were munching on a square bale of hay. "I hope your horses don't run away, Leland."

"Don't worry, de-ah; they ain't goin' nowheres. If'n they do skedaddle, I got me a back-up plan." Leland hoisted a pail of oats and shook it. Both horses immediately lifted their heads.

The coffee began to perk, and Leland's attention was drawn back to the fire. He moved the pot back from the hottest coals so that the coffee could perk in a leisurely fashion.

I inhaled the delicious scent of the perked coffee. "This is the life, isn't it?" I said, appropriating the chair across from Cora's. I stuck my legs out to warm my feet by the fire. "Need a hand?" I asked Trudy, as she carefully lowered herself into one of the other vacant seats.

"No, thanks. I've got it. As long as the chair holds up."

"No one back at Perkins & Gleeful would believe it if they could see me now!" Cora exclaimed.

I glanced at the older woman. She was unusually animated. The sled ride had brought roses to Cora's cheeks and she looked much younger than her sixty-five years. She was once again adorned in some of Trudy's mother's winter clothes: black ski pants, a turtleneck, and a lovely hand-knit wool sweater.

"I love that sweater—it's such an unusual pattern," I remarked.

"Thank you," said Cora preening herself.

"My mother designed that," said Trudy, quietly. "She knit the sweater as a gift for her sister, but when my aunt died my uncle thought we'd like to have it back."

"Oh, well. I'm sure I had no idea," said Cora.

"Rowena was real clevah like thet," added Leland. He fiddled with the frying pan, and tossed in the back strap. The deer steak immediately started to sizzle. "Member all them rabbits we used to shoot in heah, Wendell?"

"Shore 'nuff do," replied Wendell, lowering himself down into the chair next to mine.

"When Wendell was jest a leetle fellah, he used to tag 'long with me 'n his cousin Harold," Leland added, for our edification.

Wendell chuckled. "Didn't I hate rabbit huntin'! 'Twas always so dang cold."

"Why did you go with them, then?" Rebecca asked, smiling. She pulled up a chair on the other side of her husband, and tucked her hand inside his arm.

"Wal, you know, 'twarn't much else to do in wintah."

Rebecca laughed. She tossed a fat dry pine cone into the fire. The pitch-covered cone crackled and burnt up aromatically.

"I 'member one March when we shot so many rabbits we dinn't know what to do with 'em all," Leland continued. "On the way home we stopped in to see ole Two-Toe Tozier—'member him, Wendell?—'n Harold asked ole Two-Toe if'n he wanted a rabbit. Wal, when Two-Toe said he guessed maybe he wouldn't mind one or two, we stuffed his fridge so full o' them rabbits we could hardly shut the door!" Leland chuckled at the pleasant reminiscence. "Ole Two-Toe musta been mighty surprised the next time he opened thet fridge!"

We all laughed. "Likely he et rabbit clean through 'til July," Wendell added, with a gold-toothed grin.

"Doan seem possible now, do it? Ain't seen one rabbit all day," Leland lamented.

Wendell shook his head, commiserating with his friend. "Thet's 'cause o' all them kai-yotes."

"Yessuh, by Gawd—we niver used to have kai-yotes like we do now."

Cora straightened her slim legs, stretching them closer to the fire. "Why not?" she inquired.

Leland scratched his head. "I doan rightly know."

Peter, who had been sitting quieting in the chair next to mine, spoke up. "Habitat change?" he suggested. "Maybe Maine is more hospitable to coyotes these days."

"Mebe."

Cora shivered. "I heard them yipping and howling the other night," she said. "They sounded like they were having a party."

"Chasin' deer, probbly."

"Coyotes are a natural and important part of the ecosystem," Trudy interjected. A research librarian, she was particularly interested in our little pocket of natural history. She shifted in her chair, trying to get comfortable. She was carrying the baby in front like a big beach ball. The midwives of old would have taken one look at her and sworn she was carrying a girl. "I'm glad the coyotes are back—just as long as they stay away from my cows and chickens, that is."

Cora made a little face. "I don't care if they're important—they still give me the creeps!"

In half an hour, dinner was officially announced. One thing about snowshoeing, you work up an appetite. A serving line quickly formed at the banquet table, and I helped Rebecca plate up the hot food. "This is your only meal for the day," I warned Peter, as he came through the line. "Eat up."

"You don't have to tell me twice," my husband replied, piling a second piece of steaming corn bread onto his full plate. He glanced around the heavily laden table. "What's for dessert?"

"Mincemeat tarts with cream cheese, cranberry-apple pie, and a chocolate torte with raspberry sauce."

"That's it?"

"Oh, and Leland made two kinds of fudge: chocolate and peanut butter."
Peter returned the second piece of corn bread to the warm basket.
"Guess I better save room for dessert."

After dinner, while we were digesting our food and enjoying the fire,
Ryan entertained us by reading aloud several poems penned by Holman
Day, the celebrated nineteenth century author from Vassalboro. Ryan
had discovered a cache of leather-bound books by Day in the library
at the old farmhouse and had begun dipping into them. Rowena Gorse
had been a lover of Maine literature and had often read aloud to Trudy
when she was a little girl. I saw Trudy's eyes sparkle as she listened to her
husband read *Ha'nts of the Kingdom of Spruce*:

> *"The sheeted ghosts of moated grange*
> *And misty wraiths are passing strange;*
> *The gibbering spooks and elfin freaks*
> *And cackling witches' maudlin squeaks—*
> *—They have terrified the nations, and have laid the bravest low,*
> *But intimidate a woodsman up in Maine? Why, bless you, no!*
> *Merely misty apparitions or some sad ancestral spook*
> *Serve to terrify a maiden or to warn a death-marked duke.*
> *But the woodsman scoffs their terrors, though he'll never venture loose*
> *'Mongst the ha'nts that roam the woodlands in the weird domains of Spruce.*
> *—He'll mock the fears of mystic and he'll scorn the bookish tales*
> *Of the fearsome apparitions of the past, but courage fails*
> *In the night when he awakens, all a-shiver in his bunk,*
> *And with ear against the logging hears the steady, muffled thunk*
> *Of the hairy fists of monsters, beating there in grisly play,*
> *—Horrid things that stroll o' night-times, never, never seen by day.*
> *For he knows that though the spectres of the storied past are vain,*
> *There is true and ghostly ravage in the forest depths of Maine."* [4]

"Hey, you read pretty good," Peter commented, when the lawyer
finished. "Practicing for court?"

Ryan shook his head. "Not anymore. But I read to Trudy almost
every night. She's having trouble sleeping these days—for obvious reasons." He dropped his arm across his wife's shoulder and caressed her
neck. Trudy smiled lovingly up at him.

"Lucky woman," I said, without thinking.

Peter turned his accusing eyes on me. "Hey—you never said you wanted Captain Benwick!"

I nearly fell out of my chair. "Captain Benwick?!" I repeated. "That's pretty impressive, husband dear."

Peter preened himself. "Thanks, wife dear."

"Who's Captain Bennett?" Cora asked, curiously.

"Benwick," I corrected her. "He's the lovelorn admirer of the Romantic poets in Jane Austen's novel *Persuasion*."

Cora shrugged. "Oh, no wonder I never heard of him."

"I'm surprised *you* know about him," I said to Peter.

"Like Wendell says—'twarn't much else to do in wintah. 'Twas rabbit hunting or reading Jane Austen."

We all laughed, and then fell silent. A comfortable hush descended upon the clearing. Between the mesmerizing fire, the sweet scent of wood smoke, and the calories from dinner I nearly dozed off.

"Did I evah tell ya 'bout the time me 'n Phil Fernald pushed ovah the outhouses?" Leland spoke up. He had addressed Wendell, but I knew his question merely served as opening for one of his tall tales.

"Don't think you evah did," said Wendell, obliging his friend.

Leland grinned, and glanced around the little group expectantly.

"Let's hear it, Leland," Ryan urged. He set his book down on the table. "We all know you want to tell us the story."

That was all the encouragement Leland needed. "Wal, ole Phil was all-ways lookin' fer somethin' highfalutin to do. 'Twarn't 'nuff for him to go fishin' 'n huntin' like the rest o' us boys. One night Phil come knockin' at my door, wantin' me to go out with 'im. I warn't much bigger 'n thet grandson o' Ralph's, Grayden theah, but my Ma thought we was goin' coon huntin' so she let me go." Leland paused, and took a gulp of coffee. "Course Ma dinn't notice Phil dinn't hev no hound with him, but I did, so I says to him: 'Where's Fannie Farkle?' 'We doan need no dog tonight,' he says. 'We're gonna help folks git inna the twennieth century.'"

Leland paused again, and Ryan gave his father-in-law a skeptical look. "The two of you were going to move people in Sovereign into the twentieth century?"

"Yep," replied Leland, looking innocent.

"How?" Ryan asked, swallowing the bait.

"We was goin' to git rid o' all them de-tached outhouses 'round town."

Rebecca glanced over at our makeshift toilet. "But what would everyone use for a bathroom, then?" she worried.

"Oh, by thet time we all hed indoor plumbin'—'twas jest thet some o' them ole timers still preferred to go out 'n sit." He turned to Cora. "I doan 'spect you knows much 'bout outhouses, Cor-ree."

Cora gave a little laugh. "No, I'm afraid not."

"'Tis a real pleasurable experience sittin' out theah in the dark, listenin' to the hoot owls 'n the night crickets 'n sech." Leland paused, and as if on cue I heard the peculiar advertising song of the saw whet owl, which sounds like the back-up warning signal on a dump truck—*beep, beep, beep.*

"Phil thought 'twas time for them folks to git inna the futchah," Leland continued, "'n I thought 'twarn't a bad ideah myself. So we crept 'round town real quiet like 'n pushed ovah two o' three o' them outhouses—they ain't real heavy, once you git 'em stahted. We gits to Fred Nutter's place, 'n prepares to tip his outhouse ovah. We give it a good shove, 'n all o' a sudden we hears a high-pitched scream that was like to curl yer hair. By Jesus, if ole Fred's wife Arnhilda warn't in theah! Ho-ly cow! She come flyin' outta theah like a pissed-off hound outta a doghouse. I nearly wet myself, 'n Phil stumbled a bit, 'n I'll be demmed if'n he dinn't tumble head fust into thet turd hole. Ha, ha, ha!"

We all burst out laughing. "I'd say old Phil got his just desserts," Ryan declared.

Leland wiped tears of laughter from his eyes with the sleeve of his plaid wool jacket. "Phil warn't sure which would be wurst," he continued. "Stayin' in thet shit hole or ..."

"Father!" Trudy exclaimed.

"... or haulin' himself out 'n facin' Mrs. Nutter!"

"What did he decide to do?" asked Rebecca.

"By Jesus, I dunno—I was long gone by then!"

We stayed around the campfire telling stories and singing songs until just before sunset. The purple shadows had begun to creep in like wolves and the horses had long been stomping their feet before we packed up to leave. I hated to say goodbye to our winter picnic, but I knew that when the sun went down the temperature would drop by twenty or thirty degrees plus we'd have a hard time negotiating our way back through the woods in the gloaming.

"What a wonderful day!" Rebecca exclaimed, as she and I were packing up the remnants of the feast. "We should make this an annual outing. What do you think, Maggie?"

"Count me in!" I replied, enthusiastically. Too late, I realized—with a sick, sinking feeling in the pit of my stomach—that in all likelihood I wouldn't be around for next year's January thaw.

Chapter 21

"I Know What I Want To Do!"

February 1942

Andy Hastings, having just boorishly slurped down a spoonful of chicken soup, looked guiltily up at his wife. "Sorry!" he apologized. "I'm very hungry this afternoon, and Mrs. Emerson's soup is excellent."

Helen regarded her husband lovingly. "No need to apologize, dahrrrling. If I was going to chastise you for slurping soup I would have started ages ago. I certainly wouldn't begin today, when you so rarely join me for lunch anymore."

"Still, I know how fastidious you are, Alyona—my mother warned me about it when I told her I wanted to marry you."

Helen smiled. "Did she also warn you that I like to have my own way?"

"She might have mentioned something about that."

"Good, because I have made my mind up about something, Atonsha. I want the car for Saturday, and I will not take 'no' for an answer, this time. We can't continue to trespass on the good will of our neighbors."

Andy placed his soup spoon onto the under plate. He sighed. "No, no. I suppose not. Your friend must be complaining—rightly so—about running a taxi service to Windmere every week."

"*Our* friend would never say a word about it. Adelaide Russell would continue to drive me to the sanatorium every week until Jana came home, but I do not think it fair to expect her to do so."

"Nor do I, when I stop to think about it."

"But you haven't stopped to think of it, hmm? And that's why I'm bringing it to your attention."

Andy reached for a second yeast roll. "I tell you what, Alyona; I need to go to Portland to see Westcott. I was going to drive down on Saturday but I'll take the train instead. That will free up the Nash for you to use. Satisfied?" He tore the warm, sinewy roll in half and buttered it liberally.

Helen noted the generous application of butter but elected not to mention the transgression. This was not the time to remind Andy that his waist was thickening and that he was no longer a young man. That battle could be fought later. Now, she had other fish to fry. "I'm delighted to have the car, but disappointed you won't be accompanying me to see your daughter."

"Well, why didn't you say that in the first place, if that's what you wanted?" He nestled the roll onto the bread plate, and took his wife by the hand.

"Because I wanted you to *want* to visit the sanatorium, Antonsha. Jana has been there for six months now and you've yet to go over to see her. One would almost think you were afraid of the place!" Helen carefully removed her hand from his, and readjusted the napkin in her lap.

"One would be wrong. I simply have too much to do these days, Alyona, to take time off. The war has changed everything—can't you understand that?"

"It should not have changed a father's devotion."

"Nor has it! Jana is still the apple of my eye, next to you, my darling. But I must keep the canning factory running smoothly in order to feed our troops. Let us not argue about this. I'll go visit Jana before spring planting commences."

"Promise?"

He recaptured his wife's hand, and held it fast. "I promise. Now, what do you think happened today? When I got back to the office from Henry Gorse's place, I discovered that young scamp Leland hiding in the back seat of the Nash."

"But little Leland is only six or seven years old!"

"Apparently, he's old enough to try and run away. He had his bindle with him—tied up with a blue bandana—with a half-loaf of bread and a set of underwear in it."

"Just like a little hobo! But why was Leland running away?"

"He said his mother wouldn't let him go to work in the woods with his father."

"He's just a child!"

"And a troublesome child, at that, like his father. I remember—not so long ago—when Henry put a mud turtle on the conveyor belt during the sweet corn harvest just to see how the women would react." Andy chuckled. "I came running from my office when I heard their screams. I couldn't imagine what had happened on the line. I should have known it was Henry; he was always pulling some prank or other."

"That was before Henry's marriage, dahrrrling. Margaret has settled him down nicely."

"That's true. Henry is one of my best sweet corn producers, now. Well, there's hope for Leland, I guess." Andy paused. He gazed beseechingly at his wife. "Alyona, you must remember how much we owe to the Westcott family. They placed an enormous amount of trust in me at a time when no one else would give us the smallest opportunity. We would not be able to afford to send Jana to Windmere if it weren't for my very generous salary. I have never told you, but our share of the cost of Jana's care is considerable. Most families pay only a few dollars a week, but we pay more because we can afford more."

Helen rewarded her husband with a brilliant smile. "Do not say another word, Antonsha. I have your promise of a visit, and that is good enough for me. Would you care for more soup, dahrrrling?"

"Yes, thank you." Andy obediently held up his soup dish. "Be sure and give Jana my love on Saturday. Tell her I haven't forgotten her."

"I always do, dahrrrling. I always do."

On Saturday before her mother's arrival, Jana burst into Dr. Ketchum's study where she knew Henry to be hiding out. "What do you think, Henry—I know what I want to do with my life!"

Henry, who had been reading a Russian novel by the fire, set the book down upon her entrance. "You gave me a start—I was deep into Dostoyevsky. Now, there's a troubled soul. Imagine writing about a murder to prove one has free moral will! Now, what was it you said?"

"I'm going to become a music teacher," Jana announced triumphantly. She appropriated the chair opposite his. "What do you think of that?"

"A music teacher? What a splendid idea! Now, why didn't I see that? It makes perfect sense for you."

Henry seemed genuinely pleased, and Jana felt validated. "I've been giving music lessons to the Petite Troupe." (The Petite Troupe was the name Henry had dubbed her little band of admirers.) "We're going to have a parade next month."

"And what, Madame Teacher, are you using for musical instruments?"

"Arthur is on the stock pot—that's our snare drum. Suzanne is on the cake tins, and Bobby and Billy are on the lids."

"Sounds noisy."

"Oh, but so much fun! We're working up our costumes, now."

He raised an eyebrow. "Costumes?"

"Mrs. Baker has donated some old sheets and pillowcases to the cause. The children are going to dress up as historical figures, although I'm not sure their costumes will be very accurate. Bobby and Billy have decided to paint their breeches orange. One of the nurses has promised to help us sew the costumes. You will be part of our parade, won't you, Henry?" she pleaded.

"But who'll be in the audience if I'm to participate in the parade?"

"Why, everyone else!"

"I think you might find the crowd rather thin. No, I'll sit on the sidelines and make sure the Petite Troupe is properly rewarded for their efforts."

"Oh, very well. I suppose we do need an audience. Perhaps we can hold the parade on a Saturday, and invite all the parents, as well as the nurses and staff?"

"That sounds like a good plan. I admire your energy and enthusiasm, dear. I wish I had some of it myself. I can barely get out of my own way this winter." Henry had taken to substituting "dear" for his familiar sobriquet of "Songbird" since Pearl Harbor. There had been an unspoken understanding between them since that day. They had become closer, more intimate, almost like an old married couple.

Jana quickly moved over and perched on the wooden arm of his chair. "Don't worry, Henry," she said, encouragingly. "When spring comes, you'll be yourself again in no time!"

He slipped his arm around her waist. "I wish I could believe that. Tell me more about your dream, Madame Teacher. I need to hear something that will cheer me up."

"You really should stop reading the Russians," Jana reprimanded him. "Mother says too much of them is bad for one's mental health."

Henry laughed, and gave her a fond squeeze. "She'd be right about that. I do get depressed reading Tolstoy and Dostoyevsky, but then, their understanding of human nature is remarkable. So, distract me please, dear."

"Well, we were in the middle of a rehearsal, marching around the kitchen …"

"I bet Mrs. LePage loved that!" Mrs. LePage was the sanatorium's head cook.

"... and I glanced back and saw how happy all the children were. Arthur had a big grin on his face, and even Suzanne was smiling. I felt such a rush of joy, Henry! All of a sudden it came to me that this was what I wanted to do with my life. You know how it is, sometimes? When you catch a glimpse of yourself in twenty or thirty years? I saw myself as clearly as though someone had parted a curtain and I could see into the future. Unfortunately, I wasn't any taller ..."

"Imagine that!"

"... and my hair was very wild. I was wearing high heels and a terribly short skirt. You would blush if you could have seen it!"

"I doubt that! Tell me more—it's sounding better and better." He patted her leg through the folds of her thick wool skirt.

"Stop that, Henry! You're distracting me. Anyway, I was marching along with my knees very high, a line of children following me around a classroom. We were having the GRANDEST time."

"Sounds wonderful, dearest—I'm so happy for you. So very, very happy! To have a vocation, a calling, such as yours is the highest good to which a person can aspire. I admire you, and I'm envious of you at the same time."

"What will you do, Henry, when you leave Windmere?" She looked anxiously into his eyes. "Please tell me you'll be a teacher, too! Then we can find a school where we'll teach together."

"Ah, I wish someone would part the curtain for me so I could see into the future, dear. I truly do."

The mantelpiece clock chimed one, and Jana started up. She slid off the arm of his chair. "I didn't realize it was so late. Mother will be here, soon. Hopefully Father will be with her this time. Won't you come and wait with me today, darling?"

"Not today, dear." He picked up his book. "I must find out whether Rodoin will be able to rid the world of an unscrupulous pawnbroker. But let me know when your mother arrives so I can be sure to hide my book. And don't rat on me, either."

Jana made the requisite promise, and quietly let herself out of Dr. Ketchum's study. Mrs. Baker spotted her closing the door. She smiled at the matron, and turned to go. But the supervisor stopped her.

"I'd like a word with you, dear. I won't be long—I know you're expecting your Mother any minute."

"Yes, Mrs. Baker?"

"I feel that I must caution you about spending so much time with Henry."

This was unexpected. Jana found the supervisor's warning offensive. Immediately, her back was up. She calculated that Mrs. Baker had assumed the worst after seeing her exit the doctor's study. "And why is that, Mrs. Baker?" she challenged, eyes flashing dangerously.

Mrs. Baker gently took her by the arm. "Please don't be angry with me, dear. I'm trying to protect you. I don't want to see you hurt."

Jana shook off the supervisor's touch, and drew herself up to her full four-foot, eight-inches. "Do you think Henry would hurt *me*?"

Mrs. Baker hesitated. "Certainly he wouldn't hurt you on purpose. Henry isn't that kind of a boy. But things ... things will happen."

Jana felt a flicker of fear. She noticed that Mrs. Baker, while answering that last question, had avoided looking directly into her eyes. Something was up! "What kind of things?" she asked, anxiously.

"Things over which we have no control. By the way, dear," Mrs. Baker rushed on, "let me be the first to congratulate you. Your last sputum test came back negative. We'll be sorry to see you leave us—the younger children especially—but soon it will be time for you to reenter the world. I hope you've given some thought to your future?"

Jana nodded automatically, her head spinning. She said nothing about her plans to become a music teacher. Instead, her mind was given over to wondering about the veiled warning. What had Mrs. Baker meant by the cryptic "Things over which we have no control"? The warning obviously related to Henry. What was going on with him? Was Henry ... worse?

Jana excused herself, and quickly made her way to the green room, where she had left Arthur and the Snow Babies earlier. She easily persuaded Arthur to fetch Henry's medical chart from the back wall of the boys sleeping porch. The charts were hung on the wall for easy access by the nurses, who recorded the children's weight and daily habits. With trembling hands, Jana reviewed the top page of the chart. A quick glance revealed the awful truth: Henry had lost ten pounds in the last month—and his star had been changed from green to gold!

Her mind flew back to the early conversation with Eleanor, in which her friend had explained Mrs. Baker's system of categorizing the health of the children by the assignment of colored stars. "Why do *you* get the gold star?" "Because we're the ones closest to heaven," Eleanor had replied.

We're the ones closest to heaven!

Oh, dear God—Henry was dying!

Chapter 22

A New Arrival

February 2014

On Saturday morning, Ryan telephoned to invite Peter and me over to play board games with him and Trudy that afternoon. The day was cold and gray, with intermittent snow, continuing a pattern that had been in place all winter. I suspected that the couple was getting a little anxious while waiting for Baby MacDonald to put in his or her appearance. But Baby was in no hurry, obviously. Trudy's due date was Valentine's Day, and that was eight days ago.

Having finished writing my sermon for the following day, and pretty sure that my husband had no other plans for us, I agreed to the date. Ryan suggested one o'clock, which gave me just enough time to bake a raspberry pie, something for which I'd been pining and which I knew would be a welcome hostess gift.

The Gorse homestead, Scotch Broom Acres, is an unpretentious but pretty antique Cape situated on the Ridge Road, only a few miles from our house. It's one of those traditional white New Englanders, a story-and-a-half high, with a brick center chimney and a long shed that connects the house to the requisite red barn. Since our winter picnic, the surrounding area had been blanketed with yet another round of heavy snowfall, and when Peter and I pulled into the circular driveway at the old homestead I noted that the snowbanks half covered the first floor windows. What a winter! Would it never end? I could only imagine how Trudy must be feeling, now more than nine months pregnant.

"Thanks for coming," said Ryan, greeting us at the shed door. "We're going a bit stir crazy here."

"No problem," Peter replied good-naturedly. "Maggie always likes the opportunity to show she's the *Monopoly* queen."

I made a little face at my husband. "King," I corrected him.

"Excuse me—*Monopoly* king."

Ryan ushered us into the shed, where we doffed our snow-covered boots and winter jackets. "I'm sorry, I can't concede that," he said, gravely.

We entered the warm, pleasantly scented kitchen, heated by a wood-burning Atlantic End Heater, a white porcelain rig about three-feet tall and two-feet wide. Peter set the pie down on the table and turned around to face Ryan. "No?"

"In all fairness, I must warn you—I rarely lose a game of *Monopoly*," Ryan explained.

Peter held up his hands in mock horror. "Hey! Watch your back, friend. Stay away from the railroads and the utilities and you'll probably survive, though."

Ryan turned to me. "Ah, so that's your strategy, Maggie? You're a railway mogul? Funny, I would have pegged you for the Baltic Avenue type. Myself, I prefer to sink my money into houses and hotels on Boardwalk and Park Place. You can't build a hotel on a railroad, and you can't win *Monopoly* without hotels."

"Hmm," I replied, thoughtfully. I glanced around the neat country kitchen, appreciating as always the charm of the place. "We'll just see about that, buddy."

Scotch Broom Acres is one of my favorite homes. It's not the biggest house in town or even the oldest. It's simply the most fetching. The house was designed for comfortable living, with the kitchen opening up to the dining room and the dining room opening up to the living room. The center stairway is situated in the front entry, to the left of which is Ryan's law office. There's a pantry off the kitchen, containing the most eclectic collection of earthen glassware and jugs you've ever seen, including four sizes of baked-bean pots. A sweet country bathroom is conveniently situated off the shed end of the kitchen and comes complete with a monstrous claw-foot bathtub. Leland's grandfather had been exceptionally tall and so the porcelain tub stretched nearly from one floral papered wall to the other.

The Gorse-MacDonald home was filled with an interesting assortment of antiques, oil paintings, hunting and fishing gear, books and magazines, braided rugs, and embroidered throw pillows. I knew that the throw pillows and other finely embroidered linens in use had been hand-wrought by Rowena Gorse. I peered into the dining room, spying the *Monopoly* board already set up on the polished maple table. An open door off the dining room revealed a small bedroom, which Ryan and Trudy had appropriated during the last trimester of her pregnancy. I noted with relief that Cora had not as yet installed her sewing machine in that sunny spot in front of the south dining room window, which she had wistfully mentioned during her visit to my office. "Where's Trudy?" I asked, turning back to Ryan.

"She's in the barn."

I stared at my host. "Seriously?"

Ryan nodded. "Yep, checking the cows. You know how she is, Maggie."

I started to protest, but Ryan stopped me. "I know what you're thinking—and, no, she's not doing the milking anymore. Even if she wanted to, while she could probably lower herself down onto the stool to milk Rosebud, she'd never be able to get herself back up again. Rest assured, Leland does the milking at night and I do it in the morning. By the way, we're taking a hiatus from the butter business for two months, too."

"That's good to hear. Although Peter and I will miss the butter and yogurt, of course."

"Trudy's been having a back ache all day, and the plug came out yesterday morning, so we figure it's only a matter of time before she goes into labor."

Peter leaned into the conversation. "TMI," he said.

"He's kidding. He's delivered more babies than any of us, even Doctor Bart."

"Calves," Peter corrected me. "Not quite the same thing as a baby."

"Hey, when you've seen one placenta, you've seen 'em all," I said, shrugging him off. "Is Leland out in the barn with Trudy?"

"No, he and Cora have gone into Waterville for dinner and a movie."

"Seriously?!"

"C'mon, Maggie …" Peter began.

"It's OK," Ryan said, sighing. "I totally get it. I wish I could tell you that I paid Leland five bucks to get Cora out from underfoot, since Trudy doesn't exactly enjoy having her around the place all the time. But unfortunately Leland came up with the idea on his own." The attorney dispiritedly ran his fingers though his dark hair. "Don't ask me where that relationship is going! I couldn't tell you in a million years. But no matter how I look at it, I can't see a happy ending."

"Me either," I agreed, sadly.

"I've known Cora for many years—she was on the hiring commit-tee at Perkins & Gleeful when they brought me on board. And while I admire her tremendously, for the life of me I don't know what she and Leland can possibly have in common."

"Copy me that," said Peter.

A pile of snow slid off the roof, landing on the snowbank under the kitchen window with a muffled thunk, startling Ryan, who knocked into a kitchen chair. Embarrassed, he straightened the chair and laughed. "I guess my nerves are pretty strung out."

"I can't imagine why," said Peter.

Trudy joined us in a few moments, her face rosy from the cold barn. I gave her an awkward hug, and got kicked for my efforts. "Hey, I felt that!" I cried.

The baby kicked again. Trudy put her hand over her belly and rubbed soothingly, attempting to quiet the baby down. "You can come anytime, little one! We're ready for you."

"Sooo ready for you!" added Ryan.

We played *Monopoly* for several hours, and just when it appeared as though Ryan was indeed going to crush me—I never quit until every dol-lar has left my pocket, even when all my property is mortgaged—Trudy's water broke. Suddenly, the house was a mass of confusion. Ryan anx-iously helped Trudy to the bathroom to clean up; I found myself scrub-bing the chair and floor; and Peter telephoned the midwife to alert her to the situation. All of the Gorse babies over the past hundred and eighty years had been born at Scotch Broom Acres, and Trudy and Ryan had decided that their baby would be delivered at home, as well. Doctor Bart had suggested a local midwife, and for the past few months Anita had been preparing the couple for home delivery. Unfortunately, Anita lived off-the-grid in a remote cabin in Freedom and she now informed Peter that she wasn't sure she could make it out of her long driveway because of the recent heavy snow.

"What should we do?" Peter said worriedly, closing his phone.

"Call Doctor Bart," I replied, without hesitating.

Doctor Bart, who rented Mike Hobart's log cabin on the North Troy Road, arrived in less than twenty minutes. He examined Trudy in the little downstairs bedroom, pronounced her five centimeters di-lated, and packed his stethoscope back in his black doctor's bag. He assured Ryan that everything was normal, and encouraged Trudy to get up and walk around or take a bath if she felt like it. Since the baby's arrival wasn't imminent, Doctor Bart decided to run over and check on Miss Hastings.

"I'll be back soon, though," he promised. "Just in case Anita doesn't make it over."

I accompanied Metcalf out into the shed. "Before you go, there's something I want to talk with you about," I said, somewhat anxiously.

"Don't worry, Aunt Maggie. Everything's fine. She's just beginning to go into active labor." Doctor Bart popped his tweed driving cap over his unruly red curls. "And Anita will probably be here any minute." He gripped his doctor's bag in two hands and stepped down onto the top step, facing me on the stoop like a kid with a lunch box off to his first day of school.

"That's not it. It's, well, it's about me. The treatment options you talked about a few months ago—are they still open to me?"

Doctor Bart was so surprised he nearly lost his footing on the slippery granite step. "Aunt Maggie!"

"Watch it!"

He recovered his balance on the bottom step and readjusted his cap. "You're having second thoughts?"

"Second thoughts, as well as third and fourth thoughts," I admitted.

"Thank God! I thought you were throwing away a good chance to live to a reasonable age. Well, reasonable given your weight and family history," he added. "The Walkers aren't known for being particularly long-lived and you could stand to lose twenty pounds."

"The prognosis, Metcalf!" I prodded him. "Do you think it's too late? I mean, after all, it's been six months. I bet those little cancer cells have just been having a field day multiplying inside me."

"Maybe. Maybe not," he said, thoughtfully. "Just because we detected some cancer cells in your lymph nodes doesn't mean that they've taken up housekeeping anyplace else, although it's a good bet. Have you been having symptoms?"

I nodded. "My back aches. And I'm tired all the time. Sometimes I have trouble catching my breath, too."

"That's not good. Why don't you come into my office Monday? I'll check you over and then I'll give you a referral to see Dr. Grimson. He's the best oncologist in our area."

I made a wry face. "Not exactly a reassuring name—Grimson. But thank you, dear."

"By the way, does Mom know you've changed your mind?"

"Nobody knows. I haven't even told Peter yet. I wanted to talk to you first. To see if there was hope, you know."

"There's always hope, Aunt Maggie." He stepped back up to the top step and gave me a big hug. "I'm glad you changed your mind—I can't tell you how relieved I am!" He pulled away, and I saw tears in his sincere hazel eyes. "I felt like a complete failure as a doctor, not being able to convince you to follow a treatment plan that I was pretty sure would save your life."

"It's not your fault. I'm just so damn pig-headed, as Peter would say."

"What made you change your mind? Don't tell me, if you'd rather not, though."

I pondered his question a moment. I myself had been giving it a lot of thought. "I guess it's all the deaths we've been having lately," I replied, finally. "They've made me realize just how incredibly precious life is, and that if I have any chance at all I shouldn't throw it away."

"Especially at your age," Metcalf added. "You're still a young woman, Maggie. Well, considering all the parameters."

"First Ma Jean died," I continued, unheeding of his remark. "And then Clyde Crosby." I ticked the deaths off on my fingers. "And then poor Eleanor, and now maybe Henry!"

"Henry? Who's Henry?"

I realized I had conflated the two worlds—the present day and the forties. "Nobody you know," I replied, hastily. "A friend of a friend. A *good* friend of a friend."

"OK, well, I'll be back in a couple of hours. And I'll see you Monday down at my office. Come in around lunch time, and they'll fit you in."

"Right. Thanks."

When I reentered the shed a vision flashed before my eyes. It was Addie Russell, in her everyday dress and rose-figured apron. Stout, dependable Addie. In the vision she appeared to be reaching out through the years to tell me something. Tell me … what? That I had made the right decision? That life was worth fighting for every week, every day, every minute, every second? With each breath becoming more and more precious and poignant as the hourglass runs out?

My eyes filled with hot tears, and I sank down onto a straight-back chair conveniently placed outside the kitchen door. I sobbed violently for several minutes, grateful for the distraction offered up by the imminent arrival of the baby. I wiped my eyes with the tail of my flannel shirt, and searched through my pockets for a tissue to blow my nose. I came up empty handed. I smiled though my tears, remembering Addie and her white embroidered handkerchief always at the ready. I felt as though a load of fear, doubt and confusion had been lifted from my shoulders.

I laughed aloud, luxuriating in a new sensation of grit and resolve. I wasn't going down without a fight! No-suh, by Gawd! I wasn't going to let this cancer quash *me*.

Ryan and Trudy's baby was born three hours later, delivered into the capable hands of Doctor Bart. The midwife had gotten stuck while attempting to back out of her driveway—the irony of which wasn't lost on me. She called later, apologizing profusely.

"No worries," I assured Anita. "Don't bother to drive over, now. Everyone is doing fine."

The baby was an adorable, and I do mean *adorable* little girl, with a rather pointed skull thanks to the child's travails in the birth canal, and a full head of dark hair that stuck straight up. After mother and child were cleaned up, Ryan attempted to smooth the baby's hair down several times—even slathering the hair with baby oil on the final attempt—but the stubborn black fronds sprang back up like a porcupine's quills.

"Porcupine Head," I said, artlessly. I always give all my 'kids' nicknames.

"Seriously, Maggie?" Peter said. "That's the best you can do?"

Ryan laughed, and settled the baby into his wife's eager outstretched arms. "It certainly fits her."

Trudy cuddled the baby close. "Don't you worry, Momma's little sweetheart," she crooned in a baby voice. "We won't let those silly big people name you, no matter how helpful they've been!"

"What *are* you going to name her?"

"We haven't chosen a name yet," Ryan admitted. "We wanted to see the baby first. But we certainly were considering something more cerebral and much less descriptive than Porcupine Head, something like Emily or Joanna."

"What was your mother's name, Ryan?" I already knew that Trudy wouldn't be naming her child after her mother, Rowena having been her own middle name.

"Alice. Alice Rose."

"That's lovely!"

Ryan stole a glance at his wife. Trudy was studying the baby's scrunched up red face, touching it with light eager fingers as though she couldn't believe that the beautiful creature in her arms only hours before had been inside her womb. "She does look like a rose, doesn't she?" Trudy mused. "A floribunda, just coming into bloom. What do you think, darling?"

Ryan cleared his throat. I could see he was manfully trying to hold back his tears. Peter put his hand on the lawyer's shoulder, and the waterworks let loose.

"I'll take that as a 'yes'," said Trudy, smiling. "Alice Rose it is!" She christened the cherub with a kiss on the cheek. As if on cue, the baby started to wail.

"That's our cue to leave," said Peter, taking me by the hand.

We gathered up our things, and let ourselves out. The sun had set, but a rosy glow was reflected in the thin cumulous clouds, staining the western horizon with hope for a better day tomorrow. "Red sky at night, sailor's delight," I recited.

"Alice Rose," Peter whispered, staring into the sunset. "This is *your* day!"

I paused, reveling in the wonder of the moment. If ever there was a time when new life was welcome in the world, this was it. There is something about experiencing a child's birth—the beginning of the circle of life—that is so comforting and reassuring. Babies are God's way of saying: "Hope is here, don't give up the ship just yet!"

I might be pig-headed, but every now and then I do listen to what God has to say. Sometimes I even act on it.

CHAPTER 23

THE EDGE OF THE CLIFF

APRIL 1942

The parade had been delayed until Patriot's Day—April 19th—per order of Dr. Ketchum. That edict hadn't stopped the Petite Troupe from practicing every day, however. Mrs. Baker quickly relocated the little group from the kitchen to the well-insulated basement, much to the relief of the staff. In addition, Helen rescued Mrs. LePage's kitchen utensils, replacing them with actual instruments. A child's marching snare drum with shoulder straps was substituted for Arthur's stock pot, which was returned to its hook in the kitchen. Suzanne was given a tambourine in lieu of the cake tins. Bobby was rewarded with a kazoo and Billy with maracas. Word spread about the parade and several of the other young children joined the Petite Troupe, Helen securing instruments for them, as well. Altogether, everyone at Windmere thought that the changes and additions were definitely for the better.

In the meantime, while the Petite Troupe practiced and waited for the unique state holiday to arrive, Henry was failing. There was no doubt now in anybody's mind—except possibly Jana's—that the most popular resident of Windmere was dying. Jana refused to give up hope altogether, dividing her time equally between instructing her charges and reading to and talking with Henry.

As the days passed, Jana began to suspect that her mother and Mrs. Baker were conspiring between them to wean her from Henry. The two matrons spoke repeatedly to her of her future, of what she might do when she left Windmere. She noted that their spate of possibilities never included Henry. But Jana was resolved not to be separated from her beloved.

When the time for her next sputum test rolled around, Jana enticed Arthur to spit into her cup. "Why?" queried the boy looking up at her innocently. "Don't ask me why—just do it, please, Arthur?" she begged. Of course, Arthur acquiesced.

Not surprisingly, Jana's test results came back positive. Helen, who like everyone else had expected the second result to be negative, releasing Jana from Windmere, was shocked and disappointed when Dr. Ketchum telephoned with the news. "Oh, my poor dahrrrling!" she exclaimed.

"It's very unusual," Dr. Ketchum allowed. "I'm afraid your daughter will be with us a bit longer Mrs. Hastings."

"Does that mean Jana has regressed?"

"No, no. Most likely last month's test was nothing more than a false negative. I'm sorry this has caused you additional grief. It's not what we were expecting certainly. There's no doubt but what Jana is much better than when she arrived. I feel quite sure she'll be going home soon, perhaps even this summer. We'll test her again in another month."

Jana had never kept anything from her mother, but now she found herself keeping her own counsel. When alone with Henry, the two plotted her future, Jana still holding out hope that he might yet get well so they could become teachers together. "I've applied to Plymouth Teachers College, as you suggested," she informed him, not long after her fake sputum test came back positive. By this time, Henry had been told of the rigged test.

"Good work, Songbird! Did I tell you Robert Frost taught there, back when it was Plymouth Normal School? You'll like the place, dearest; it's nestled in a perfectly sweet valley near the White Mountains."

"*We'll* like it, Henry," she corrected lightly. "Still, they might not take me. I'm afraid I wasn't a very good student. I've got to write to my tutor and ask him to send my grades off to New Hampshire."

"I don't know how you managed to study at all—you seemed to have spent all your time working when you were on stage."

"I read my lessons between practice sessions and took the exams on holidays."

"Some holiday!"

"But I thought everybody worked as hard as I did," Jana protested. "Harder than me, even. I didn't have much to compare it to, Henry."

"I adore your mother, dear, but sometimes I have to wonder what she was thinking!"

"You mustn't blame Mother. She only wanted the best for me. I was the one who begged her to let me sing—she never made me. Still, I see now that I did miss out on a good deal of fun. Imagine coming to a sanatorium to learn how to play games!"

"I can't imagine," he said, drily.

"And what do you think, Henry? I've been training one of Farmer Dunkirk's chickens to be our mascot in the parade! I toss a little cracked corn to her as we go, and she marches along just as though she's one of the children. I've been trying to figure out what to name her. I thought at first I'd name her after Captain Joshua, but that wouldn't be right, would it, because as Suzanne keeps reminding us all—'Chickens are girls!'"

"Why don't you name your mascot 'Matilda'," Henry suggested. "That was Captain Joshua's wife's name. Considering Matilda's situation in life—helping care for a zoo full of strange creatures while her husband sailed off around the world—I'd say she earned the compliment."

"That's perfect!" Jana cried, clapping her hands. "Matilda it is."

Henry was resting on the couch in the green room, where he spent most of his days now. He still slept on the sleeping porch, not yet having been relegated to the small back room in which Eleanor had died. He began to cough, a sickening, bone-shaking cough. Jana leaped to her feet and with practiced care supported his back and shoulders. When the coughing fit subsided, she helped settle him back onto the couch pillows. "You mustn't talk so much," she scolded, wiping the sweat from his face and the sputum from his lips. "Look what it does to you!"

Henry inhaled deeply, attempting to refill his lungs, which were raw with lesions. "But I have so much to say, and so little time left to say it," he croaked. He placed his hand over Jana's and squeezed affectionately. "I'm so glad you've discovered what you want to do with your life, dear. It makes me happy—so very, very happy—to think of you in the future."

Jana reclaimed her seat, still holding his hand. "I feel as though I was meant from the very beginning to be a music teacher. I just didn't see it."

"God is always calling us to our highest and best purpose. Sometimes we don't always hear Him, but fortunately, God never gives up—He just keeps on calling us."

"Even on our death beds?" Jana asked.

"Then God is calling us home."

A week after this exchange, Jana was reading to Henry, when suddenly he interrupted her. "Listen! Do you hear that?"

Jana strained her ears, but could distinguish nothing out of the ordinary. She shook her head.

"Open the window, please," he begged.

Jana did as he bid her. Immediately, the room was filled with the musty scent of the evening air and the sounds of spring peepers. "Why, I didn't know the peepers were out yet!" she exclaimed. "They sound just like sleigh bells in the distance, don't they?" The cold damp air sank to the floor, chilling her legs. She closed the window and returned to her chair.

"The ice must have gone out of Dunkirk's pond," Henry mused. He paused a moment for reflection. "It's funny the things you think about while waiting to die."

Jana felt conflicted. She didn't want to encourage Henry to talk, because she knew that talking was bad for him. But at the same time she wanted him to share his memories. In the end, that might be all she had left of Henry. Beautiful memories!

"What are you thinking about?" she finally asked. She absently toyed with her newest necklace, a birthday gift from her father, whom she still hadn't seen since he'd delivered her to Windmere last August.

"I'm thinking of all the afternoons my brother and I spent trying to catch frogs in the pond next to our house in Narragansett. Frogs are hard to catch, a lot harder than you think. Did you know—bullfrogs give a little 'woof' when they're startled? To alert the other frogs, I suppose. Then they plop back into the pond with a big belly flop before you can get anywhere near close enough to catch 'em. I wonder if I'll ever hear that peculiar 'woof' again? Probably not," he added, sadly.

"Rest now, darling," she entreated him. "You're wearing yourself out. The nurse will be coming to take you to the porch soon."

"She's not the only one coming for me," he joked. "I wonder if Heaven has frogs? The other place is certainly too hot to hold 'em."

The next afternoon, Jana rounded up Arthur and the Snow Babies and set out for the pond. It was a beautiful day, 50° with a bold, beguiling sun. Jana inhaled the vigorous scent of spring deep into her lungs, guiltily conscious of her own good health. She noted the shrinking patches of snow clinging to the bedraggled back lawn. The grass was just beginning to turn green. She and the children slipped under Farmer Dunkirk's fence, skirted fresh cow patties, and paused on the rise above the vernal pool to plot their strategy. Arthur crawled down to the pond on all fours to reconnoiter the situation, and came back five minutes later with muddy hands and knees.

He stood up, and saluted Jana as though she were his commanding officer. "I seen hunnerds of frogs! They was settin' on some logs."

"Hundreds, Arthur?" Jana questioned, suspiciously. "Surely not."

Arthur stuck his thumbs in his belt loops. "Well, I seen five frogs at least." He grinned wickedly. "I think we should go arter 'em."

Jana decided that "going arter 'em" was probably the best course of action, given the composition of her crew. So on the count of three, the children rushed the pond. Immediately, a handful of turtles plopped into the water and a half-dozen or more frogs leaped spasmodically in all directions. Billy and Bobby screamed joyfully in unison, and splashed into the shallows chasing after the fat amphibians, oblivious to the cold and wet. Jana spotted one small frog just as it was hopping off a downed tree limb. "There!" she shouted to Arthur. She pointed to an expanding pool of ripples on the surface of the black water. The boy obliged her by dashing into the pond, immediately becoming mired in thick mud. "Oh, oh. I lost my shoe!" Arthur cried. He began fishing around for his footwear.

The next thing Jana knew she was in the pond herself, splashing and laughing, and tossing handfuls of slimy mud at Arthur and Billy, who had splattered her with mud first, ruining her dress. Fortunately, Bobby remained focused, and after a few minutes of intent searching he cried out: "Gotcha!" He gleefully held up his prize to show the rest of them— a fat squirming bullfrog.

Mission accomplished, Jana and company crept back to the sanatorium. She tried to sneak her disheveled crew into the house via a side door that served as the supply entrance. Unfortunately Mrs. Baker, who was just exiting the kitchen, spotted them. "Dear God, what has happened?" she asked, approaching Jana. The matron eyed Jana's dress and the three wet, dirty boys, who were hiding behind their captain. "Really, Jana! I must say I'm surprised at you."

"I'm sorry," Jana apologized, hanging her head. "We were just trying to get Henry a bullfrog." She looked like a shipwreck survivor. Her tangled black hair clung to her face and neck like seaweed. A puddle of water was forming on the floor under her dress, and in her right hand she clutched Arthur's ruined shoes.

Bobby held up the shoebox for Mrs. Baker's inspection. "Wanna see Sammy?" he asked, triumphantly.

"No, thank you very much, Bobby." Mrs. Baker quickly relieved him of the shoebox and secured the cover. "But I will keep an eye on, ah, Sammy while you all go clean up. My goodness, look at your clothes!"

Vanquished by the firm matron, Bobby's lower lip wobbled. He stuck his dirty thumb in his mouth. Billy timidly reached out and took his twin by the hand.

Arthur drew himself up defiantly. "What's gonna happen to Sammy?" he challenged.

"You may take your frog to Henry once you're washed up—I'll have one of the nurses bring you some clean clothes. Go now, please, children."

In half an hour, the four regrouped in the green room where Henry was resting on the couch. His eyes were closed, but he opened them and smiled when he saw Jana and her entourage enter. Bobby thrust the shoebox into Henry's hands. "What's this?" Henry asked, peeking beneath the lid.

"Sammy," said Bobby. "I caught 'im."

"Be care…" Jana began. But it was too late. Henry had already removed the cover, allowing the frog a taste of freedom.

"*Woof!*" went the bullfrog. Sammy gave a giant leap and landed on the floor near the door. In a second, the black spotted amphibian hopped again, this time gaining access to the rest of the stately mansion.

The three boys immediately hooted and hollered, then rushed out the door after the bullfrog. Jana sank into an easy chair, giggling hysterically. Henry laughed so hard he could barely catch his breath. "Did you … hear it?" he cried, exultantly. "Did you hear … the 'woof'?!"

Jana wiped the tears from her eyes. "I did! Oh, dear—Mrs. Baker will never forgive me, now. I hope she doesn't cancel our parade!"

"The parade will go on," Henry vowed. "Don't worry, dearest, I'll talk to Dr. Ketchum. He won't refuse me anything. Not now."

Henry was correct—the parade was held as scheduled on Sunday, Patriot's Day. The Judge had arrived from Providence the Friday before, and on Sunday afternoon he carried Henry to the front steps where a chair and warm blanket awaited him. The rest of the children, a few parents, nurses, and staff gathered on the granite steps to watch and cheer as the red, white, and blue parade marched around the corner from the back of mansion. Jana had lined the eight children up by twos, and this combined with their colorful colonial costumes gave them the appearance of patriotic salt and pepper shakers. Fortunately, Jana had been able to convince Bobby and Billy to change the color of their pantaloons from orange to navy. The children's legs lifted up and down in time to the regular rat-a-tat-tatting of Arthur's snare drum. The parade passed twice by the little knot of spectators on the steps, then marched off down the hill, as though they were headed from Concord to Lexington, instruments crashing, banging, whistling, ringing and blaring in a spectacular assault on the senses. Matilda the chicken hopped proudly beside Jana like a miniature Band Meister.

"Marvelous!" applauded Helen Hastings, clapping her black-gloved hands enthusiastically. "Such wonderful costumes—très magnifique."

The Judge nodded vigorously in agreement, batting his thick mitts together like slices of ham. He leaned sideways to speak to Helen. "Your daughter is going to make a wonderful teacher," he shouted. "She's very good with children. Henry says she's going to Plymouth, eh?"

Helen gave a little start. She put her hand to her ear. "Plymouth—what did you say?"

Judge Graham waited until the band had pulled far enough down the driveway so that he could speak in his regular tone of voice. "Plymouth Teachers College," he repeated. "Henry says she's been accepted to study there. It's a very good school. Congratulations!"

Henry anxiously glanced up at Jana's mother. "I hope you don't mind, Mrs. Hastings. I've told Father all about Jana becoming a music teacher."

Helen caught her hands to her bosom. "Vraiment! My dahrrrling, you've surprised me. This is the first I've heard of her decision."

Too late, Henry recognized his blunder. "We thought … well, that is, she thought it was time for her to consider her future," he said, awkwardly.

"But her last sputum test—it was …"

Henry hesitated.

"Henry, if you know something, speak up," the Judge ordered. His eyebrows wriggled ferociously.

Henry felt trapped. He wrestled with whether or not he should reveal more, but finally felt as though he had no choice. "Faked. She got Arthur to spit in her cup last month," he admitted. "To give her a false positive. She didn't tell me what she'd done until afterwards or I would have discouraged her. Of course, she's staying here for me."

Tears of relief came to Helen's eyes. "Dieu merci!" she exclaimed. She leaned over and kissed Henry on the cheek. "Of course she is staying here for you, dahrrrling!" Helen dropped her voice. "I promise you, we will not take her away, but perhaps we should keep this little secret to ourselves, hmm?"

The Judge turned away, unable to hide his emotion. He pulled a crisp white handkerchief from his breast pocket, and blew his nose. "I heard that—that's very kind of you, Mrs. Hastings. I'm sure you must miss your daughter very much."

Helen stood up and rewarded the Judge with one of her brilliant smiles. "Helen," she corrected him. "Please call me Helen. After all, we're almost family now, hmm?"

Helen departed the sanatorium without mentioning the incident to her daughter. Wisely, she had decided to let Henry to explain his gaffe to Jana. The Judge, however, felt compelled to relieve his emotions. He tracked Jana to the green room, where she was helping the children out of their costumes. Jana had become used to the Judge's furry face, wandering eyebrows, and rough-cut manners; however, she was somewhat startled when Henry's father stuck his head in the door and rather abruptly called her out into the hall. "Miss Hastings—a word, please!"

Jana placed Arthur's velvet tricorn hat on a chair. "I'll be right there, sir. Don't tear that, Bobby," she entreated the twin. "You might want to wear your costume again."

In the hall, Jana was further surprised when she was swept up into a bear hug by the Judge. "I know what you've done, my dear. Thank you, thank you!" Judge Graham released her, and daubed a few giant tears with his handkerchief. "Henry has told us all about it. The sputum cup switch, you know. You're a brave young woman to stay here and wait out death with my son! Braver than me, and that's about it."

"I love him," she said, simply.

"I understand completely, and I honor your decision to remain by his side. But I'm not sure Ketchum and Mrs. Baker will appreciate your devotion."

Jana tossed her head defiantly. "No one can make me leave Henry!"

"No, no. Who would dare? Certainly not I, Miss Hastings! Perhaps those, ah, auspicious authorities need not know about the sputum switch, eh?"

Since this was obviously her intention, Jana remained silent. She clasped her hands in front of her, waiting to see if he had anything further to say.

Judge Graham glanced restlessly up and down the long hallway. He absently trolled four fingers through his beard as though he was fishing. Jana watched fascinated to see what kind of strange creatures might be hiding in that black bush. "Is there someplace we can speak privately?" he continued. "All these closed doors make me nervous."

She led him to the small back room in which Eleanor had died. The white painted room had been recently sanitized and smelled of cleaning fluids. The room was not in use at the present moment, but Jana suspected it was only a matter of days before Henry would be installed there. The room, situated on the north side of the house, was illuminated by the weak daylight offered up by one casement window. She perched on the straight back chair that was stationed at the foot of the narrow cot, and waited patiently for the Judge to settle himself. The Judge grasped the arms of a wicker rocker and placed it close to her. Jana could see beads of perspiration on his shiny pate.

Judge Graham lowered himself gingerly into the chair, and began rocking. "I love my wife," he said, mopping his forehead with his handkerchief. "She's a good woman and a good mother to our girls." He inhaled deeply, taking some time to gather his thoughts. The rocker scraped back and forth. "But she's not the woman Henry's mother was."

Jana felt herself relax. The Judge was not going to lecture her, then. "Henry's told me about his mother," she said, softly. "He loved her very much."

"Ah, we all loved her! Madeline was everything a woman should be." The Judge stuffed his handkerchief back into his pocket. "Your mother reminds me of her. So lovely and so vivacious! And you're just as precious as your mother, my dear. I'd be proud to squire you around Providence— introduce you to my friends and associates as my daughter-in-law."

"Thank you."

"But I think we both know that is not going to happen. God is not going to grant me this one last opportunity to save Madeline!" The Judge's nervous energy was too much for him and he bounded to his feet. The rocking chair bobbed back and forth as he paced the floor in the small room, wringing his hands. "No! God takes delight in crushing my hopes. I don't know what I've done to warrant such affliction.

Certainly, I've tried to lead a good, honest life. Be fair on the bench, be kind to my neighbors, and cherish the poor. But maybe there is nothing I've done. Maybe divinity is blind. Maybe that's just the way the chips fall, and we must leave them where they lay." He suddenly recollected Jana and now glanced over to see if she was following him.

Jana only half understood his rant. "I'm sorry, I ..."

"The seeds of my wife will die with my son, and that's about it," he said, throwing up his hands. "Forgive my impertinence, Miss Hastings, but I had cherished a vision of bringing Madeline back to life in the form of Henry's offspring. Your children—my grandchildren."

Jana was too astonished to blush. Why, the Judge had daydreamed about the future just like she did! He had planned not only for her to marry Henry, but also for them to have a family! Who knew that old people had dreams?

"When Henry passes I will lose not only the best son a father could wish for, but also future little Madelines running around the house, comforting me in my old age." He smacked his fist against the palm of his hand. "God has teased me with a glimpse of Heaven, only to slam the door in my face once again. What have I done to deserve such cruelty?"

Jana was slightly shocked by the Judge's irreverence. "But you have Henry's sisters," she pointed out.

"Bah, that is not the same! They are good girls, but they can never smile up at me like Madeline did, like Henry does. Watching him die is killing me twice over. Can't you understand? I've been holding onto the hem of Madeline's skirt all these years, determined not to let her go over the edge of the cliff. And now ... now I must stand back and watch them both go over! There's nothing left for me to live for," he sobbed. "I might as well have Dunkirk drop me in Waterville tomorrow and jump off the Two Penny Bridge!"

Unable to bear any more of the Judge's suffering, Jana jumped up and threw her arms around his thick neck. "Oh, let *me* be a comfort to you in your old age, Father!" she cried. "I promise I'll never leave you. Why, Mrs. Russell says I'm going to outlive everyone!"

CHAPTER 24

"NEVER UNDERESTIMATE THE POWER OF A HANDKERCHIEF"

APRIL 2014

"I think I was a comfort to the Judge in his old age," Miss Hastings recalled mistily. "Lord knows I tried! Every summer we both took a week off—I gave piano lessons in the summer, you know—and we went together down to Captain Joshua's saltwater farm in Narragansett. We'd stroll along the beach, arm in arm, with our pants rolled up and our shoes dangling. We'd kick up our heels in the surf just like two old horses let loose from the barn. In the evenings we'd sit and rock on the porch, telling each other stories about Henry and Madeline. That's how we kept them alive. There were times when I half expected to hear the screen door creak and see Henry come out and join us." Miss Hastings paused, lost in fond reflections.

So, Henry had died, then. I had suspected it, of course. But I had yet to ask Miss Hastings point blank what had happened to him—the love of her life. I'd clung to the faint hope that somehow he had survived the sanatorium. I think there was a part of me that had fallen in love with Henry Graham and I was loath to say 'goodbye' to him. I smiled to myself as I recognized how successful Miss Hastings had been in keeping Henry alive to this day.

I wanted to know about Henry's final moments, but I couldn't bring myself to ask about his death on such a beautiful spring afternoon. Hopefully, there would be time in the future, although I knew that Miss Hastings' hourglass was fast running out of sand. "What happened to Captain Joshua's salt water farm?" I asked, instead. I tucked the bedclothes around her fragile frame as I helped settle her back into bed. We had just finished our Thursday luncheon. Once again she had barely eaten enough to keep a flea alive.

"The Judge left me the place in his will. He said it would have been mine—ours—if Henry had lived. Didn't I ADORE Judge Graham! He was like a father to me." She snuggled into the soft mattress, her wild, wiry hair splashed across the pillow. The look of contentment on her face made her seem so alive and youthful, much younger than her eighty-nine years.

"Do you still own the place?"

Miss Hastings shook her head. "A few years ago I donated the farm to the *Stop TB Partnership*, a non-profit trying to put the kibosh on TB. It's what Henry would have wanted. Who knew that dreadful scourge we thought we'd wiped out in the fifties and sixties would make such a comeback? Makes me HOPPING MAD when I think about it."

"I had no idea until recently that TB had even made a comeback," I said.

"TB is like the Lernaean Hydra. Every time you cut off one of its heads two more grow back in its place!"

"Thank God we have vaccines and antibiotics to fight it, at least. You had nothing, back in your day." I moved her glass of water from the top of the dresser to the nightstand in preparation for my departure.

"Nothing but plenty of fresh air and lots and lots of love! Just think if we'd had antibiotics, Henry might still be alive."

I tried to imagine what Henry Graham would look like today. What kind of teacher would he have been? How many young lives would he have touched along the way? How many of those children would have grown up to become better people because of Henry?

So sad, I thought. What a tragic waste of a young life!

"A few years can make a big difference in medicine," I agreed. "Especially these days when technology is moving so fast." I had just begun my second cycle of a four-month course of chemotherapy and I could only hope for the sake of future cancer victims that that nasty treatment would soon be outdated. Maybe one of today's ten-year-olds would grow up to discover a cure for this scourge of the twentieth and twenty-first centuries. Unfortunately, I probably wouldn't live long enough to avail myself of the cure. Like Eleanor and Henry, I would probably go over the cliff just before the next monumental breakthrough occurred.

Miss Hastings touched me on the arm. Her hand was cold, and the icy sensation woke me from my reverie. "I'm sorry—did you say something?"

"Dahrrrling, forgive me, but you aren't looking well. Is anything the matter? This old bag of bones might not be good for much, but I can still listen."

I hesitated. Should I share my tale of woe? Or should I keep it to myself? Didn't Miss Hastings have enough on her plate already? But then, what would I tell her when I started shedding hair like a dog in summer?

"Out with it, Maggie!" she ordered, in her teacher tone of voice. I could see why she was so effective with children. Obediently, I told her about the cancer.

"Now, what are you doing for treatment?" she demanded.

"I did a short-course of radiation first—they think they got all the cancer in my right breast with my surgery, so I didn't need a long-course. And I just started chemotherapy. Thank goodness my insurance covers oral chemotherapy so I can take the pills at home and don't have to go into the hospital for intravenous treatment."

"You poor dahrrrling! All this time you've been coming over here to help me out you've been carrying that awful weight on your shoulders?"

"Peter's with me, and I told Nellie when she was home just before Christmas. Doctor Bart's been trying to get me into treatment since last August. I just wish I'd listened to him sooner."

"You know what Addie would say to that! If wishes were horses then beggars would ride," she said. "Don't you waste ANOTHER MINUTE on regret. There's no point to it."

I sighed. "You're right."

"Of course I'm right! I'm eighty-nine years old." She cackled loudly. "As though age had anything to do with wisdom. Speaking of wisdom—thank God for Doctor Bart! I don't know what we'd do without him."

"Yeah, he's a pretty special guy. His mother, Jane, is one of my best friends, you know. He's always wanted to be a doctor, ever since he was a little kid. One time his cat got run over by a car and he turned Jane's kitchen into an operating room. He sewed the cat's guts back up on the kitchen table using Jane's good sewing kit for his instruments. He was only eleven or twelve at the time. Wasn't Jane angry when she came home and found that bloody mess in her kitchen!"

"Did the poor creature live?"

"Metcalf? Or the cat?"

"Haaahaa! The damned cat."

"Would you believe, that cat is alive to this day?"

"MARVELOUS."

"I'd like to have Metcalf for a son-in-law—he's got a terrible crush on Nellie. But she barely gives him the time of day. It's too bad, too. He's perfect for her." Sadly, I couldn't help but think how few people Nellie would have left in her life to love her when I was gone. Much to my chagrin, a sob escaped me.

Miss Hastings patted my hand. "Don't you worry, dahrrrling, Nellie is nobody's fool. She takes after her mother!"

"You're the only person I know who sees *that* similarity!"

"Just you wait. One day Nellie will wake up and realize what a gem Doctor Bart is."

"I just hope it's not too late." I sniffed, trying to hold back my tears. A second sob followed on the heels of the first.

"Dahrrrling, I hate to see you so discouraged. It's not like you!"

"I know, I know—but I can't seem to help it these days." I began to weep openly. I searched frantically through my pockets for a tissue to stem the tide but once again came up empty handed. Miss Hastings leaned over and pulled open the little drawer in the front of her nightstand. She reached in and withdrew two white ladies handkerchiefs and held them out to me. They were simple white cotton with the letters *ALR* embroidered in purple on one edge. Tremulously, I touched one of the handkerchiefs. "Addie's?"

"The very same! One she gave to Mother—I found it tucked away in Mother's secretary after she died—and the other Addie gave to me. 'Never underestimate the power of a handkerchief,' she used to say, and by golly she was right! I don't know how many times I've used mine over the years and I've always felt better afterwards." She proffered the handkerchiefs again. "Take one, dahrrrling! I don't need them both. I haven't got that many tears left in me."

"But I can't," I protested. "These are family heirlooms."

"Dahrrrling, we're family, aren't we? Besides, who else do I have to leave things to?"

I accepted one of the antique handkerchiefs and dried my eyes. I heaved a sigh of relief, and realized that I did feel better. I re-folded the handkerchief. "You know, I think everyone should have a

Grammie Addie in their lives," I said, tucking the sacred artifact into my shirt pocket.

"Amen to that, dahrrrling!" Miss Hastings lay back in bed and folded her hands across her thin chest. "I think I'll take a little snooze, now. Don't you worry about a thing! Go home and spend some time with that handsome husband of yours. That will cheer you up."

"Now, that's a plan," I said, smiling.

When I stepped out of the darkness of her shed into the bright April sunshine I had to blink to adjust my eyes to the light. The grass was turning green right before my eyes, and yellow daffodils and purple and white crocuses splashed bright color across the yard. It wouldn't be long now before Gray would be here to mow the lawn. I lifted my face to the warm afternoon sun, reveling in its healing rays. I closed my eyes and drew in a deep breath, holding the fresh fragrance in my lungs for as long as I could. This was one of those picture-perfect spring days which we Mainers dream about all winter. I felt grateful to be alive, grateful that I had survived to witness Mother Nature's spring extravaganza once again.

When I opened my eyes, I spotted someone, a man, moving carefully around Miss Hastings' rose garden. It was Doctor Bart. He was wearing jeans, a long-sleeved canvas shirt, and leather gloves, and he appeared to be pruning some of her old-fashioned roses. Metcalf had a reputation as the foremost old-fashioned rose expert in central Maine, and I'd known many a new purchaser of an old homestead who had applied to him for advice. I wasn't surprised to see him there, for Miss Hastings' rose garden was legendary, her mother having started the garden with some celebrated Russian cuttings she had smuggled out of her native country. Helen had transplanted the heirlooms from place to place until she and Andy had settled permanently in Sovereign. Unfortunately, Miss Hastings hadn't inherited her mother's legendary green thumb, and lately Gray had done little to keep the old-fashioned roses in check other than mow around them and occasionally mow over them.

I strolled across the broad expanse of lawn to the rose garden, which was delineated by a white picket fence with a traditional rose trellis arch now overgrown with tangled vines. Metcalf straightened up and watched my approach. He pushed his baseball cap back with the tip of his pruning shears. "Hello, Aunt Maggie."

"Don't stop on my account," I said, ducking under the archway. "And when you get done here, can you come over to my place and prune my azaleas?"

He chuckled, and gestured around the rose garden with a wide, sweeping motion. "I don't think I'll ever be done here. I shouldn't even be doing this now, but somebody once said that the time to prune is when you've got a pair of sharp pruning shears in your hands. Did you ever see such a mess?"

"Now that you mention it … no."

He pointed to a rambling rose that was sprawled along both sides of the paint-flaked fence on the garden's eastern edge. "Look at that—that's Seven Sisters, although it looks more like seventy-seven sisters today."

"Seven Sisters?"

"A grand old multiflora—Redouté painted it back in the nineteenth century. It blooms with seven different colors all the way from cream to crimson. It's one of my favorite old-fashioned roses."

"I never heard of it."

"It's not as common up here as it is in the south. When I spotted the Seven Sisters yesterday, I asked Miss Hastings if I could dig up a piece."

"What did she say?"

"She said I could have the whole plant—imagine me digging up all of that!"

"I'm sure she just wants to give you something in return for what you've done for her, dear. We were just speaking of you, in fact."

His freckled face flushed with embarrassment. "Miss Hastings doesn't need to do that. I'm her doctor."

"A doctor who goes over and above, I'd say. There aren't many who make house calls these days, and even fewer who prune their patient's roses when they get there!"

"Well, I'm glad to know she's satisfied with her care. By the way, how are you feeling, Aunt Maggie?"

I rested my hand on the white picket fence and accidentally collected a thorn in my palm. "Ouch! Well, I was feeling fine."

"Are you taking the capsules exactly as Dr. Grimson directed?"

"Yes, dear. I've had the usual nausea but thank God no vomiting yet."

"Any mouth sores? Skin changes?"

I shook my head. "Nope."

"Good. When is your next follow-up with Dr. Grimson?"

"Wednesday."

"OK, let me know if you need anything before then. You know where to find me." He gestured toward the trellis archway. "My door is always open."

Before heading home, I stopped down to the old Russell homestead to see Rebecca. Nellie's possible future without a mother had been weighing heavily on my mind, and I wanted to ask Rebecca to keep an eye on my daughter if I didn't make it. I was hoping to speak to her in private, without the benefit of Cora's erudition. When I drove in the driveway, I could see someone scootched down in the rich black soil of the freshly-tilled vegetable garden. I popped open the door, shielding my eyes from the blinding sun to see who it was. It was Addie, out planting her peas.

She stood up, and brushed the dirt from her everyday dress. She was wearing her barn boots and a wide-brimmed straw hat over her short gray curls. There was a questioning look in her eyes as I approached. I felt in my pocket for her handkerchief, calculating that this would be a good time to return the handkerchief to her.

"It's a gorgeous day, isn't it?" she said, adjusting the brim of her hat. "You're just in time—I was just about to go in for a glass of iced tea."

At the sound of Rebecca's voice, I stupidly realized I had once again conflated the two worlds. I tried to shake the cobwebs out of my brain, blaming my numbness on the chemotherapy.

"Maggie? Is something wrong?" Rebecca took my arm. "Come— let's go sit on the porch."

She led me to the comfortable cushioned loveseat Wendell had restored a few years ago. After settling me down, Rebecca doffed her straw hat and went into the kitchen. She returned to the porch in a few minutes with two tall glasses of iced herbal tea. "This will make us both feel better," she said. She handed me one of the frosty glasses and joined me on the settee.

I took a big swig of the homemade tea, relishing the delicate herbal flavor. "Where's Cora?" I asked, setting the glass down on the end table. We began rocking gently as we chatted.

"She's gone to help Leland plant his peas."

I chuckled. "By that you mean she's holding the package of seeds for him."

Rebecca laughed. "Exactly!"

"How much longer do you think she'll hang around Sovereign?"

"Oh, I give her until the black flies come out."

"That could be any day now."

Rebecca nodded. "Better sooner rather than later, I think. I'm afraid Leland might do something silly, such as propose to her."

"It'll be awfully hard on Leland when Cora leaves town, though."

"I know! I wish now we hadn't taken her in. But what could I do when she told me there was no one else who cared for her anymore?"

"You're too kind-hearted. If Lila was still here Cora wouldn't have stayed more than one night."

Rebecca sighed. "You're right about that. Let's keep our fingers crossed. Everything usually works out for the best."

"Does it? Hmm, I wonder."

We fell into a pleasurable silence as we rocked. It was restful sitting on the open porch, enjoying the expansive view of the lush verdant field sweeping up the hillside toward Miss Hastings' house. The field was dotted with bright yellow dandelions, their fuzzy faces turned eagerly toward the sun like supplicants. A phoebe fluttered impatiently from branch to branch in the lilac bush, her brown tail bobbing up and down as she waited for us to vacate the premises so she could continue her nest building on top of the porch light. *"Phoebe!"* she screeched in her signature throaty voice, which sounded as though she had swallowed her own name. *"Phoebe!"*

I was about to ask Rebecca to keep an eye on Nellie, when suddenly she broke the silence first. "I'm glad you're here, Maggie. There's something I've wanted to talk with you about."

We stopped rocking. Immediately, I gave her my full attention. "Is something wrong?"

"I haven't been feeling well lately. I'm sad and tired all the time, and I've even been downright grumpy. I raised my voice to Wendell last night, the poor dear!"

"Maybe you're just sick of having Cora underfoot," I suggested. "I know I'd be tearing my hair out if someone imposed on me this long."

"That could be. But then, I've also been having these crazy mood swings. I'm ridiculously happy one moment and the next I'm crying my eyes out! I wondered if you thought it could be menopause? I didn't think I was quite old enough to go through the change yet, but I guess we never know when it will hit us."

I knew that Rebecca was about ten years younger than I, and I tried to remember at what age I'd gone through menopause. But those days seemed like a distant memory to me now, so much had occurred in the past few years. "Sounds like it could be menopause," I agreed. "Have you seen a doctor?"

"I haven't got a Maine doctor yet. I haven't needed one. Do you think Doctor Bart would see me?"

"He's a GP not an OB/GYN. But I'm sure he'd be happy to take you on as your primary care physician and then recommend a specialist, if he thinks you need one."

"It's probably nothing—just the residual effects of the long winter. All I could think about in January was the hundreds of daffodils I was going to plant this spring, but now I'm so tired I can barely get my peas in the ground!"

I put my arm around Rebecca's shoulder and gave her a brief hug. "Don't worry—Doctor Bart will get you straightened out in two shakes of a lamb's tail."

"I hope so! I don't like feeling sad all the time. The other day I was sitting at the kitchen table and I suddenly remembered the first morning Lila and I were in town. We'd driven up to Miss Hastings' house Friday afternoon—after I got fired from Perkins & Gleeful—and we were having a pillow fight in the rose room when all of a sudden we heard her playing Rachmaninoff's arrangement of Mendelssohn's opus 21, *A Midsummer Night's Dream*. It was the most beautiful thing I'd ever heard. I just burst into tears, thinking of that morning again." As she spoke these last few words, Rebecca began to cry openly. "I don't want her to die," she sobbed, "but I know Miss Hastings can't live forever!"

I reached into my shirt pocket and pulled out Addie's handkerchief. "Here, take this," I said. "I have it on very good authority that this is an excellent antidote for what ails you."

Rebecca wordlessly accepted the white handkerchief and pressed it to her eyes. She sobbed for a few more moments, then dried her eyes and blew her nose. "Oh, sorry! I'll wash it and give it back to you tomorrow." She ran her fingers curiously over the purple embroidered initials. "*ALR*—why these aren't your initials, Maggie …?"

"Nope," I replied. "This little handkerchief has finally come home to roost. I know Grammie Addie would have wanted you to have it."

Rebecca's face brightened. "Really? It was hers?"

"Yep. I got the hankie from Miss Hastings, who got it from her mother, who got it from Addie. You know, I think you're right—everything usually does work out in the end."

"I *do* feel much better. Thank you!"

"Never underestimate the power of a handkerchief," I said, sagely.

CHAPTER 25

PROMISES MADE
MAY 1942

Henry was dying. On Thursday he was officially installed in the sanitized back room. When Jana was at first refused entry because Mrs. Baker didn't think it appropriate for a young woman to visit a young man in bed, Jana staged a mutiny. She and her little band of followers declined to eat until she was admitted. When Henry begged that Jana might be allowed to remain with him during his final days, Mrs. Baker threw up her hands and relented. Jana immediately took charge of Henry's care, relegating the attending nurse to little more than an assistant. Even Dr. Ketchum was in full thralldom, confessing to Helen Saturday afternoon that her daughter had powers of persuasion before which he was helpless. Jana enlisted Arthur as her errand boy, running messages and food back and forth from the sickroom to the kitchen. She turned Sammy over to the care of Bobby and Billy, who eagerly built a special pond for the bullfrog in the upstairs bathtub, causing a scene among the nurses. Jana didn't know what to do with Suzanne until the little girl solved the problem by plunking herself down in back of the sickroom, crossing her arms and declaring that she wasn't leaving.

"I've lost control of the place," Mrs. Baker confessed to Mrs. LePage, the cook. "Frogs in the bathtubs and patients nursing each other! Whatever will the parents say?"

"Need they know?" Mrs. LePage quizzed. She wiped her hands on her apron. She was rendering a chicken for a poultry consommé for Henry although she suspected that the rich broth would be consumed by one of the younger children instead, probably Arthur.

Mrs. Baker hesitated.

"It wouldn't be lying, Sylvia," Mrs. LePage continued. "*Not* to tell them."

Both women were thinking that Jana's thralldom would be short-lived for Henry was likely to die any day. But both were soft-hearted and neither wanted to put into words what the other was thinking. "I suppose not," said Mrs. Baker. "Oh, oh!—your stock pot is boiling over, Renée!"

On Tuesday morning, when Jana was reading silently to herself she glanced over and noticed Henry's eyes were open. She leaned over the bed. "How are you feeling, darling?" she asked.

He smiled up at her, his face wan and peaked. "I feel as though I'm all at sea, like I do sometimes when I'm out in the catboat. I wonder if that's what it will feel like when I die, as though a little squall has blown up to push me off the edge of the earth." He paused to catch his breath. His eyes glowed. "I do hope we've made a mistake and I find out that the world isn't round. Maybe that will be my great discovery! Wouldn't that be a good joke?"

As she listened to Henry, Jana was reminded of the Judge's last conversation with her. She understood now how helpless Judge Graham must have felt and why metaphorically he had tried to hold onto the hem of his wife's dress for as long as he could. She herself wanted to grasp hold of Henry's oar so that he wouldn't be able to push his catboat away from shore.

"Then I must learn to sail and come out with you," she replied, smoothing the hair away from his forehead.

"No, no. You'll never make a sailor—you don't have the legs for it. You're a songbird. You need to be free to fly!"

"Then I'll be an albatross and hang around your ship, love," she pronounced. "You won't be able to shake me!"

"I wouldn't want to shake you, dear."

On Wednesday, Henry reached out and took Jana's hand. "I wish I'd known you sooner," he croaked. "I can talk to you about things I never did speak to anyone else about. Now, I've got to go away and leave so many things unsaid!"

"Can't you tell me now, Henry? You can tell me anything, you know."

"There's too much to say—I don't have breath for it all. I'll have to wait until we meet again. I suppose we'll meet in Heaven?"

She squeezed his hand, but said nothing. While she was absolutely certain Henry would go to Heaven—he was so good!—she was not so sure she would meet him there.

"You must promise me one thing, dear," he continued.

"Anything!"

"Promise me not to come too soon. I want you to live a good long life."

Jana thought a moment. "I'll probably live to be seventy-five, at least," she allowed.

"Seventy-five isn't long enough. I want you to live to be eighty-five or ninety."

"Ninety! I'll be so old then you won't recognize me. Why do you want me to live so long, Henry?"

"Because you've got to live my life as well as your own—that's going to take you some extra time. Promise me you'll do that?"

"I'll try, darling. But what if God doesn't want me to live that long?"

"Don't be silly—God wants you to live forever."

Jana duly made the promise. She kissed Henry on the brow, and tucked the covers back around him. Four hours later his breathing became heavy and labored. The light in his eyes grew dim. Soon he didn't know her. He was restless, fading in and out of consciousness. Suddenly, Henry startled her by lurching up in bed. "Oh, oh! I'm going home," he cried. He collapsed back against the sweat-stained sheets, his body shaking with one final paroxysm.

"Henry!" she called to him, clutching one of his hands. But his muscles relaxed and when she let go his hand fell heavily to one side. She placed her ear against his chest. There was no heartbeat. She watched helplessly as the life-force drained away like the outgoing tide, taking Henry with it. She fell onto her knees at his bedside and gave thanks to God for having given her the gift of Henry Graham.

How much he had taught her about love and life! She had become a better person for having met him. She vowed to God that when she left Windmere she would take his spirit and his wisdom back into the world. When she became a teacher, she would share his enthusiasm with her students—their students! Henry had taught her how to be a mentor and she wouldn't forget that valuable lesson. She wasn't going to be just an ordinary music teacher! No, she was going to be an encourager, a supporter. She was going to be the audience for her student's parade. How she would clap and cheer her children from the sidelines, throughout their entire lives!

She would never love anyone as she had loved Henry Graham. But she would be able to love everyone else so much better for having loved and been loved by him.

Jana was still in the sickroom with Henry when the attendants from the funeral home came the next morning to collect the body. Both Dr. Ketchum and Mrs. Baker had tried to persuade the exhausted Jana to return to her bed for some rest overnight, but she refused to leave Henry's side. Instead, she waited for them to come and take him away.

"They're here, dear," Mrs. Baker announced, placing her hand on Jana's shoulder. "You must let him go now."

One of the funeral attendants stepped forward. "Don't feel bad, ma'am—this is just a shell," the young man said, trying to be helpful. "Your friend isn't in there anymore."

"Thank you," she replied. "I know he's gone. I watched him sail away." She rose gracefully and exited the room. She didn't know what she would do next, but she must prepare herself to live a life for the two of them. After all, she had promised Henry!

Her mother came the next day, even though it wasn't Saturday. "I've talked to Dr. Ketchum and told him everything," Helen said. "You must pass one more sputum test, but then, dahrrrling, we'll be able to take you home!"

Jana nodded dumbly. She didn't ask her mother if she would be able to go to Henry's funeral, because she knew she wouldn't be allowed to leave Windmere until it was proven she was no longer contagious. But she had already said her 'goodbye' to him. She was confident now that they would be joined together in eternity one way or another. After she had given him *her* promise she had extracted one from *him*. Henry had scribbled his promise down on a piece of paper, which she had in her pocket. She patted her pocket. Yes, Henry's promise to her was still there.

"Did Father come with you?" she asked her mother.

"Not today, dahrrrling. Mrs. Russell brought me over. You know how busy your father is down at the factory! But he's promised to come collect you when Dr. Ketchum says you can go home." Helen reached out and lovingly rearranged one of her daughter's curls. "I've brought you some mourning clothes. You don't need to wear them, if you don't want to."

Jana threw her arms around her mother's neck and hugged her. "Thank you, Mother! You think of everything. I do want to wear them!"

"I thought you would, dahrrrling. What do we care if others do not go into mourning these days, hmm? We do not mind wearing our hearts on our sleeves." Helen's eyes filled with tears. "So much sadness! Poor

Mrs. Russell had word yesterday that Carroll has already fought his first battle. He's in the Philippines, in Bataan. He joined the Army after the attack on Pearl Harbor, you know."

"Oh, no! Not Carroll. He used to pull my hair. I hope he'll be careful!"

"He was so eager to go to war! Stupid child."

"What about Wesley and George?"

"They've gone off to fight, too. I fear that by the time this horrible war ends there will be no family in America left untouched. You are coming home to a much different world than the one you left, dahrrrling."

Jana thought to herself that she was coming home a much different person, too. But she kept this sentiment to herself.

"Sugar has been rationed, and we have been given stamps for gasoline," her mother continued. "Fortunately for us, your father's job is very important, providing food for the soldiers. He is allowed unlimited amounts of gasoline. Mrs. Russell isn't so lucky, however. They have been given coupon stamps for only seven gallons a week, except during the corn harvest. That means if I cannot get your father to lend me the car I will not be able to see you again until your father and I come to bring you home. I cannot ask Mrs. Russell to use her precious gasoline to drive me here, although I know she would."

"Don't worry, Mother. I'll be home soon," Jana said. "You won't have to drive over anymore."

"What shall you do first when you are home, hmm? If I knew that, I would help make your wish come true, dahrrrling."

Jana paused to contemplate this question. What *would* she do first?

She had given little thought to her immediate future beyond the moment. The last few days had seemed like years as she had focused all her efforts and attention on Henry and his dying needs. She could hardly imagine a world without bedpans, starched towels and sputum cups—or without Arthur, Suzanne, and the Snow Babies!

A little cry escaped her. "Oh, Mother—will *I* be able to visit Windmere? You must teach me how to drive a car!"

"Ah, I see how it will be. Our little songbird will come home, only to fly away." Helen smiled. "I will ask Mrs. Russell if she will teach you to drive during haying season. They will have the extra gasoline then and will likely need the assistance, with the boys gone off to war. She is a very good teacher. Would you like that?"

"Oh, yes! Then I can come back here to visit whenever I please."

"Only if you can get your father to lend you the car. And only on Saturdays from one o'clock to three o'clock. You know the Windmere rules, dahrrrling."

Jana laughed victoriously. She tossed her head. Her black curls bounced. "We'll just see about that!"

Helen leaned forward and kissed her daughter. "I'm afraid you are too much like me. We do like to have our own way, hmm?"

"On ne voit bien qu'avec le cœur," Jana replied. "Perhaps we just see differently than everyone else does, Mother. We see what must be done, and we do it."

"Touché, dahrrrling!"

CHAPTER 26

DOWN IN THE TRENCHES
MAY 2014

On Monday Peter went off to Oaknole Farm to help his nephew prepare the family's haying equipment for the season. Next month, June, marks the commencement of haying in central Maine. Having the day to myself, I decided to organize my notes for the book on Miss Hastings. I was hoping not only to move forward with the book but also to distract myself from the nasty side effects of my third course of chemotherapy. Taking the chemo pill was rather like swallowing prussic acid. Sometimes I wasn't sure if the chemo was going to kill or cure me. Peter had suggested I invite Rebecca to spend the day with me, since the restaurant was closed on Mondays. But I bravely assured him I'd be fine alone. I wasn't quite so stiff upper-lipped when I stood at the kitchen window waving him goodbye, however.

"Get to work, Maggie!" I ordered myself. I sat down at the kitchen table with a pile of yellowed newspaper clippings from the 1940s, reference books, and the legal pads on which I had taken notes during my talks with Miss Hastings. I picked up a fresh bundle of white index cards and a new rolling ball pen. Each "character" in the story would net a three by five card with name, personal history, and relationship to young Jana, giving me an easy way to remember the details.

I reviewed my scribbled notes from my last meeting with Miss Hastings, in which I'd finally discovered the disposition of Addie's three sons. We had been talking about the future of the old Russell homestead—Miss Hastings once again lamenting that Wendell had no progeny—and I'd asked how he had come to inherit the place. During the course of our discussion, Miss Hastings had given me information about each of Addie's children and grandchildren. I prepared an index card for George, Addie's eldest son. GEORGE RUSSELL. BORN 1906.

MARRIED. DRAFTED ARMY. WOUNDED. OMAHA BEACH. LOST ARM AND LEG. DIVORCED. ONE CHILD, EVELYN.

Wesley, Addie's middle son, was taken prisoner of war at the Battle of the Bulge. He and the others from the 422nd and 423rd Infantry Regiments were finally rescued by Soviet forces and turned over to the Allies in May 1945 after the end of the war in Europe. Wesley had married and had two sons, Freeland and Harold. Miss Hastings told me that Wesley came home a different man than when he left, however, and took to drinking to ease his physical and emotional pain, what we now call Post Traumatic Stress Disorder (PTSD). Wesley died an early death from alcoholism, not long after his oldest son, Freeland, was killed in Vietnam.

Carroll, Addie's youngest, who had been so eager to "go kill me some Japs," incredibly managed to survive the Bataan Death March. At the end of the war Carroll came home, got a job in the cornshop, married a local girl, and eventually fathered one child, a son, Wendell Russell. When Carroll's wife died, Wendell was raised at the farm by his Grammie Addie, helping with the egg business. When Wendell graduated high school, he joined the Navy, and sailed off to see the world. Not long after Wendell departed the farm, Addie sold her chickens and went out of the egg business. She was eighty years old at the time. Pappy had died in 1956, a year or so after he and Bud put a new standing-seam metal roof on the place. Bud followed him to the grave about a decade later, as did Carroll.

The metal roof was important to the story because it had kept the old Russell homestead standing through many decades of neglect. When Addie passed away in 1971 at the age of eighty-five, she left the place to her only living child, George, who declined to live at his childhood home. George died without a will, and the farm naturally passed to his daughter Evelyn, who at the time was residing in Boston. Evelyn also avoided the place, and it rapidly became run-down. Cousin Harold (Wesley's youngest son) eventually petitioned his cousin Evelyn to let him move into the empty homestead, and she agreed. But, when Evelyn died, her own son inherited the place and Harold moved out. Unfortunately, Evelyn's son perished in the First Gulf War. Harold was preparing to return to the farm, but was killed in a car accident.

By the time the courts decided that Wendell was the legal heir to the old Russell homestead, he was in his early sixties and was the last of

Addie Russell's descendants still standing. Now Addie's grand dream of keeping the old place going forever would end with Wendell Russell.

I thought how differently this story might have turned out had not so many of Addie's descendants been mowed down by war. Two of her sons, her grandson, and her great-grandson—all had been ruined by what seemed like continuous conflagrations around the globe.

Would it never end? I wondered. When would we foolish humans learn to use some method other than violence to settle our disputes?

I was in the middle of this disheartening train of thought when I was interrupted by a knock at the inner shed door. I had been so wrapped up in my work that I hadn't noticed anyone drive in. When I got up from the kitchen table to answer the door a wave of nausea nearly doubled me over. I took several deep breaths to keep myself from retching. Feeling extremely vulnerable, I limped to the door, and swung it open just as Leland was preparing to rap a second time.

"Hallo, Minister," he greeted me, cap in hand. "I was thinkin' maybe ya warn't home. I see Peter's truck ain't heah?"

"He's gone to Winslow," I replied, swallowing back a bit of bile that had crept up into my throat.

"I ain't heah to see Peter, anyways. Got a moment?"

"Uh, sure." I held the door open wider so he could enter. "Come in. Excuse the mess—little writing project." I shoved the papers and index cards into a pile, clearing one section of the table for him to sit at.

"Want me to leave my boots off? Theah ain't no cow shit on 'em."

Before I could reply in the negative, Leland had slipped out of his boots, revealing rather large, awkward-looking stocking feet. His old gray socks sagged around his ankles and I could see there was a hole in one toe. Leland slithered across the linoleum floor and placed his hands on back of the chair opposite mine. He began to fidget. I felt another wave of nausea rising and regretted answering the door. Stoically, I clamped my lips together.

I decided a cup of tea would help settle my stomach, and put the tea kettle onto the propane stove to boil. "Have a seat."

"I gots a confession to make," Leland blurted out like a five-year-old. He scratched his head; his gray hairs sticking up discordantly like contour feathers on a bird. "Kin ya do thet?"

His question took me off guard. I dropped down into my chair. It felt good to sit down. "Take a confession? You mean, like a priest?" I asked, confused. I rubbed my forehead.

"Yep. I ain't no Cath-o-lick or nuthin'. I jest got sumthin' I wants ta git off'n my chest," he further elucidated, sitting down. He placed his cap on the table in a business-like fashion. "It's about Cor-ree."

I had been going to suggest that Leland return another day when I was feeling better, but as soon I heard Cora's name I stopped myself. For several weeks I'd been expecting Cora to dump Leland, like everyone else in Sovereign. I figured that the soft-hearted woodsman was here to "confess" what failing of his had caused Cora to throw him over. Poor Leland!

The only thing was—he didn't look like "poor Leland." He appeared confident and even-tempered, not sad and lachrymose. Although there was obviously something he wanted to talk about.

"Go ahead—I'm listening," I said, somewhat warily. I felt as though a second shoe might drop at any moment, even though the first shoe had yet to fall. But maybe the chemotherapy was just making me jittery. I tasted more bile in my throat and gritted my teeth.

Leland thumped his elbows on the table, and leaned forward. "Wal, 'twas thet outhouse story 'at dun it fer me," he began. He paused, awaiting encouragement per usual.

"You think your outhouse story might have turned Cora off?" I suggested.

He snorted. "No, she warn't even listenin'—thet's the point. When I got to the paht 'bout Phil Fernald 'n why he dinn't hev no dog with 'im, I see Cor-ree sneak a peek at her cell phone. She puts it back in 'er pocket but I see 'er peek agin when I got to the paht 'bout Arnhilda."

"Maybe she was expecting a call from someone?"

"Wal, thet call nivah come. Aftah thet day, I begun watchin' her more careful like. I see she was all-ways lookin' at thet phone."

"That isn't unusual, Leland. Most kids can't have their phones out of their hands for more than a minute. They're lost without them."

"Cor-ree ain't no kid," Leland retorted, rather cruelly, I thought.

"No, you're right about that."

The tea water started to boil, and I rose up from my seat to make us both some tea. When I stood up, the contents of my stomach came up, too. "Oh, oh, I'm going to be si…" I cried, dashing to the bathroom. Fortunately, the downstairs bath is situated next to the kitchen and I just made it to the toilet in time. I hugged the cold white porcelain base for support and heaved up the contents of my stomach. I flushed the toilet, too miserable to be embarrassed.

Leland stuck his head in the open door. "Kin I help ya, Maggie," he offered. Somewhere in the dim recesses of my sick, confused mind I recognized that this was the first time Leland had called me by my given name. Usually he addressed me rather formally as "Minister."

"Water!" I gasped. My shoulders contorted with dry heaves. "Gaaar!"

Leland selected a glass from the cupboard, poured some water from the faucet, and returned to the bathroom. He scootched down on the floor and carefully tilted the glass so I was able to take some of the water without removing my hands from the toilet bowl, to which I clung for life support. I dimly distinguished a comforting scent emanating from him, like my grandfather's wood shop in winter. He set the glass down on the tank top, searched out a washcloth from the vanity, and ran some warm water over it. "Heah, this 'all make ya feel bettah," he said, leaning over to hand me the damp cloth.

I released my death grip on the toilet bowl and rested back against the side wall. "Thanks," I said, gratefully. I accepted the wet washcloth and mopped my face.

Leland threw open the small window, allowing the fresh April air to fill the room. The obnoxious odor of vomit was replaced by the sweet fragrance of spring. "Go 'head—take 'nothah swig o' watah," he encouraged, swapping the water glass for the dirty washcloth. "Yer gonna feel bettah if ya rinse yer mouth out."

I obediently followed his directives, wondering at the calm, sturdy nature of the man. Leland had obviously done time in a sickroom. I rinsed my mouth and spit into the toilet. After I repeated this process two or three times he took the dirty glass away to the kitchen. I leaned back against the wall and gratefully inhaled the fresh air. My stomach had settled down and the room stopped spinning. I experienced that wonderful sense of relief we all feel when we know we're not going to throw up again—at least not for a while. Leland returned, and leaned back against the door jam, examining me. I offered my male nurse a weak smile. "You've got a hole in your sock," I felt obliged to point out.

He lifted up his right foot to take a gander. "Dang it! Got so busy tryin' to woo Cor-ree I fergot to cut my toenails."

"Geez—TMI," I said. I don't mind talking about the condition of people's souls but I'm not the type that likes to know about the state of their toenails, especially when I'm flat on my ass in my own bathroom. "Uh, maybe we should continue your confession?"

Leland dropped down to the floor and made himself comfortable against the opposite wall, his long legs bent close to his chest. I think we both realized it wouldn't be a good idea for me to travel too far from the toilet. "Wal, whar was I?"

"Cora was checking her phone a lot," I reminded him.

"Ayuh. Thet's right. I figgered out 'at Cor-ree was hankerin' aftah somebody."

"You think it was Dennis?"

He shrugged. "So I supposed."

"Did he ever text or call her?"

"Nope. I could all-ways tell aftah she put her phone back 'twarn't nuthin' theah. She play-acted real good like she doan care, but I know wimmen 'n the more they play-act the more they want what they say they doan want!"

I allowed this slur on my sex to pass. After all, I'd done plenty of play-acting in my time. But I didn't think that pretending was solely the provenance of women. I'd seen many men put on a good show, too, especially Nellie's father. But that was neither here nor there at the moment. "So, you figured Cora was still in love with Dennis?"

"Ayuh."

"Then what?"

"I felt real sorry fer Cor-ree. I see she doan belong heah—she's a city gal born 'n bred."

I thought that was the understatement of the year, but wisely bit my tongue. "Hmm," I ventured, instead.

I found myself thinking how refreshing it was to have a heart-to-heart in the bathroom, a place where we are at our most vulnerable. I compared this tête-à-tête to the conversation I'd had with Cora down at my office. I decided I much preferred sitting here with Leland. He and I had a give and take that had been missing from my meeting with Cora. She had wanted something from me then—advice or validation or just an ear—but I was no more to her than a fortune teller or a palm reader. Perhaps that's how pastoral counselling is supposed to be and I know that's how it is in the Catholic Church where a priest hides himself behind a screen during confession. But in small churches, the so-called "Pastoral Churches," which are my particular passion, we try to follow the model offered by Jesus Christ, who spent most of his time down in the trenches with his flock.

"I jest wanted ta see Cor-ree happy, Maggie," he continued, in a pleading tone of voice. I knew we were getting close to the confession part. "She ain't a bad gal, though I doan think she shud be hankerin' aftah a marriet man. But I ain't one ta judge, now, is I?"

I shook my head. By this time, I figured out that Leland must have done something awful. "OK, what did you do, Leland?"

He hung his head. "I got 'em ta make up—Cor-ree went back to the city this mornin'."

I gasped in surprise. "You're joking!"

He shook his head. "Nope. I jest see her off a leetle while ago down to Wendell's. She give me a big hug 'n kiss goodbye. She was real happy. She ain't comin' back."

"Oh, my God! You must be a miracle worker. How did make *that* happen?"

"Wal, yestiddy she left 'er phone on the kitchen table when she went to the powdah room. I knew she'd be awhile—she all-ways takes 'er time fixin' her hair 'n stuff—so I thought 'twas a good opportunity. I checks her phone 'n finds Dennis' numbah, so I decides to send 'im a text message."

I felt like I'd fallen through the rabbit hole into Wonderland. "You know how to text?!" I asked, astounded.

"Ayuh. Trudy showed me 'n case I need to git holt o' her down to the library. It's gotta be real quiet down theah, ya know. She's got one o' them phones 'at buzzes. So I sends Dennis a text message like I was Cor-ree sayin' 'I miss you,' which warn't really lyin' 'cause I know she did miss 'im. Sure 'nuff he takes the bait quicker 'n a sunfish takes a fat worm. Her phone stahats shakin' 'n flashin' 'is name so I grabs it 'n runs ta the bathroom door. 'Cor-ree, ya gots a phone call!' I yells. She hops out lickety split 'n the next thing I know she's laughin' 'n cryin' at the same time."

During the excitement of this confession, Leland's big toe had escaped the confines of the wool sock. I stared at the thing, transfixed. He certainly did need to trim his toenails!

He leaned over and pulled the dirty sock back over the offending member. "Do ya suppose I'll go ta Hell fer meddlin', Maggie?" he begged.

Leland asked this question with such simple sincerity that I felt if God had heard him confess to a murder in the same tone of voice he'd likely be forgiven that mortal sin, as well. "No, certainly not!" I proclaimed. Seriously, if such a minor transgression was all it took to consign one to the Devil I'd have been in the hot spot a long time ago. "Meddling isn't one of the seven deadly sins," I felt compelled to add. "You'll be fine. But I'm glad you told me what you did—I might have felt sorry for you otherwise, thinking Cora had dumped *you*."

Giant horse tears formed in Leland's eyes. Immediately, I realized my mistake. Leland might have been the one to bring this strange relationship to an end, but that wasn't because he didn't love Cora. It was because he did. He had meddled out of pure disinterested affection solely to try to net Cora the happiness for which she'd been seeking. Leland still loved her, of that I was now sure. I scooted across the floor and put my arms around his square shoulders. "I'm so sorry, Leland! I'm sorry it didn't work out for you and Cora."

He sniveled a bit, and then pulled away. "Oh, I know I ain't no catch," he said. "Not like Dennis." He pulled a faded navy handkerchief from his pants pocket and loudly blew his nose.

"Of course you're a catch—you're a *great* catch!" I assured him. "Much better than Dennis."

"Wal, mebe—mebe not. 'Twas good, though, feelin' young 'n foolish agin," he allowed. "I felt like I did the fust time I seed Rowena, settin' on the swing at the school playground. She hed two leetle brown pigtails 'n a pug nose 'n the most de-termined look I evah seed in a gal's eyes! My heart give a jump 'n I niver hed eyes fer no othah woman since then, 'til I seed Cor-ree, leastways. Likely I made a big fool o' myself with Cor-ree …"

"Oh, no!"

"… but I'druther be a fool as had a hand in the game 'an a fool what makes jokes from the sidelines."

I gathered up both his calloused hands and squeezed them reassuringly. I'd never noticed how strong he was before. Despite his age, Leland Gorse still had a lot of life left in him, I calculated. "Don't give up—someday someone else will come along for you."

"Aw, ain't nobody commin' fore me, Maggie. But thanks fer sayin' thet. Heck, I ain't got nuthin' ta complain 'bout. I've hed the best wife a man kin hev, 'n the best daughtah, 'n son-in-law, too." His face brightened up. "Now I even gots me a purty leetle grandaughtah! Ya seen Alice Rose, lately? She loves ole Grandpa, she do! She doan smile fer nobody but me, not even fer 'er Ma!" He chuckled, proudly.

"I'm going over to see Trudy and Alice Rose tomorrow," I said. "Well, if I feel good enough to go visiting, that is." I started to get up, thinking it was finally safe to relocate to the kitchen table.

The agile woodsman stood up quickly and helped me to my feet. For the first time he appeared to wonder why I had been upchucking. I saw him glance surreptitiously at my midsection. I'd never been slim and I certainly wasn't skinny now. "Ya expectin'?" he inquired, politely.

I burst out laughing. "No! Thank God I'm too old for that."

"I thought … bein' as ya jest got married 'n all …" Leland broke off, lamely.

"Not all newlyweds get pregnant, Leland. Especially us old ones. Look at Wendell and Rebecca—they've been married, what, nearly two years now?"

"Ayuh, Wendell ain't no spring chicken, thet's a fact," he replied thoughtfully. He scratched his head. "Likely thet's what took 'em so long."

"Excuse me—took them so long for what?"

His blue eyes opened wide with surprise. "Ya ain't heared then? Rebecca's expectin'!"

A defibrillating thrill shot through my heart. Rebecca—pregnant?! If Leland hadn't been holding onto me I would have fallen back to the floor.

CHAPTER 27

PROMISES KEPT

MAY 1942

On Thursday Jana's sputum test came back negative and by Friday night she was packed in preparation for her departure from Windmere Saturday morning. Leaving the place that had been her home for nearly a year would be a sweet but sad occasion for her. So much had happened since she had arrived last August wearing her favorite lime-green travelling coat with the onyx buttons and carrying a chip on her shoulder. She had come to the sanatorium a spoiled child, but she would walk out the front door a mature young woman.

Friday evening, Jana said her individual 'goodbyes'. With a mixture of tears, hugs, kisses, charges, and admonishments she parceled out her cherished possessions to the Petite Troupe and staff. Jana bestowed her lime-green coat upon little Suzanne, much to the girl's delight. To Arthur she vouchsafed Henry's beloved copy of *Northwest Passage*, instructing him to care for the book as though it was on loan and would need to be returned to her one day. To Billy and Bobby she consigned Sammy the bullfrog, suggesting that the amphibian was homesick and that it was their responsibility to return the frog to his Mummy and Daddy, with Mrs. Baker's guidance, of course. Jana thanked the attending nurses, awarding each a necklace in gratitude for their care. To Mrs. LePage she gave her favorite French novel and to Mrs. Baker her good-luck charm bracelet, the gift from her father when he had delivered her to Windmere. "Thank you, dear," said the supervisor, as Jana fastened the delicate bracelet around the older woman's wrist. "I might just need this. I don't know how I'll ever keep Arthur and the twins in line without you."

Jana pondered long and hard about what she could possibly do for Dr. Ketchum. She surveyed her collection of books, clothing, and jewelry and found nothing amongst her possessions suitable for the venerable doctor. In the end, she sat down and wrote him a letter thanking him for his kindness and care, not only for herself but also for Eleanor and Henry. Jana rewrote her letter twice until she was satisfied with it, and then she tucked it into an envelope and penned Dr. Ketchum's name on the front. When darkness fell and everyone was asleep, Jana slipped into the doctor's study and placed the missive in his top desk drawer where he would find it after she was gone. As she was closing the drawer, a solitary tear rolled down her cheek and dropped onto the envelope, marring the ink of his name. She hesitated, and then quickly shut the drawer. The teardrop spoke volumes—perhaps more than her words—about how much she loved and admired him.

By ten o'clock the next morning, she and her things were gathered in the front hall, awaiting the imminent arrival of her parents. She sat patiently in the foyer, listening to the wind and rain beat against the tall windows. While sitting there, she couldn't help but remember all the Saturdays she had used to sit and chat with Henry and Eleanor while waiting for her mother. Tears came to her eyes as she thought of her beloved friends, and she struggled in vain not to cry. By eleven o'clock her parents still hadn't arrived; however, Jana wasn't worried. She suspected that a problem had cropped up at the canning factory temporarily claiming her father's attention. She only hoped he wouldn't get so wrapped up in his work that he would forget to come get her!

At lunch Jana looked for Dr. Ketchum and Mrs. Baker to ask if either of them had received any word from her parents. But neither the good doctor nor the supervisor appeared in their places for the mid-day meal.

The rain continued into the afternoon. When Jana retired to the green room after lunch to play one last game of *Flinch* with Arthur, Suzanne and the twins, she heard on the radio that some of the secondary roads were flooded. For the first time she began to worry that her parents might not be able to reach Windmere. Immediately, she berated herself for worrying. "What's the worst that can happen?" she asked herself. "I might have to stay here an extra day or two!"

At three o'clock a nurse came to fetch her to Dr. Ketchum's office. Jana's pulse quickened. She assumed that the doctor had either discovered her letter or had finally received word from her parents. When she entered the room, however, she was surprised to discover not Dr. Ketchum but Mrs. Russell perched awkwardly in one of the two George III chairs in front of the brick fireplace.

"Mrs. Russell!" Jana exclaimed, quickly hiding her disappointment. Once again her father had been too busy to leave the canning factory! "I was beginning to think you wouldn't be able to get here because of the flooding. Is Mother with Mrs. Baker?"

The older woman stood up. She gestured toward the opposite chair. "Sit down, my dear. I have something I need to tell you."

Jana's heart skipped a beat. She noted that Mrs. Russell was wearing black, and immediately surmised that poor Carroll must have been killed in Bataan. She obediently appropriated the matching chair, her senses on the alert. Mrs. Russell resumed her seat, clutching her purse in her lap. Jana could see that the older woman was deeply troubled. Her face was drawn and haggard, and her gray curls hung limply beneath a crushed felt hat. "Has something happened?" Jana asked.

"My dear, I almost don't know where to begin. Mrs. Baker and Dr. Ketchum thought we should wait a few days to tell you, but I thought you'd want to know the truth as soon as possible." She hesitated, appearing to seek direction from Jana.

Something was terribly wrong! Jana leaned forward anxiously. "Please tell me what's happened, Mrs. Russell," she entreated. "Is it Father? You must tell me everything, no matter how bad it is!"

"That's what I thought, my dear." She paused a moment to fumble through her purse—which to Jana seemed a maddeningly long time, but was in actuality only a few seconds—to gather her thoughts and collect a handkerchief. Mrs. Russell set her purse on the side table and drew in a deep breath. Jana saw that the older woman's hands were shaking. "Your parents have had an accident on the way to fetch you. Your father took the corner by the bridge in Burnham a little too fast and the car went off the road into the river. Andy was able to get out, but your mother ... your mother was trapped by the flood waters. Some bystanders saw the whole thing. Unfortunately, they couldn't help because they were on the other side and the water was very high. Your father tried to save your mother, but he failed and ... and they both perished. I'm so sorry, my dear!"

Jana had been listening in abject shock and horror. But when Mrs. Russell got to the part about her father failing to save her mother she let out a shriek and leaped up wildly. "No! Not Mother! My mother *can't* be dead!"

"I'm so sorry, my dear. I'm so, so sorry!" Mrs. Russell stood up and opened her arms to Jana. "Come here, my dear. Let me comfort you."

"I don't believe you. I don't!"

"My dear, what can I say?"

Jana whirled around, giving her back to the older woman. She rushed to the window and whisked aside the two panels of cotton sheers. She spotted the Russells' old Ford pickup parked in front of the granite steps. The rain had slowed and giant raindrops splattered against the hood of the truck. She saw Bud loading something into the bed and realized it was her travelling trunk wrapped in khaki-colored canvas.

Dear God ... her parents were—dead?!

"I'm so sorry, my dear. So, so sorry," Mrs. Russell repeated. She advanced two or three steps toward Jana, and then stopped.

Jana sagged against the windowsill for support. She pressed the side of her forehead against the cold windowpane. An excruciating pain pierced the center of her being. "Oh, oh!" she cried, clutching her midsection. From a disembodied distance she felt the touch of a hand on her shoulder, and instinctively turned toward the human contact. She allowed herself to be gathered into Mrs. Russell's grandmotherly embrace. "I can't live without my mother!" she sobbed, burying her face into the older woman's soft bosom.

Mrs. Russell patted her on the back. "There, there, my dear. Let it out—get that poison out of you. It's a *horrible* thing, just too horrible to contemplate!"

"Arrrnn-ah-ah! Why did God have to take my mother?"

"I don't know my dear. I surely don't know."

As Jana gave full vent to her grief, Mrs. Russell continued to hold her and whisper words of comfort into her ear. After five or six minutes, Jana pulled away. "It's not fair!" she protested, angrily brushing the tears from her cheek. "I wish I'd never come here—then Mother and Father would still be alive!"

"But you might have perished without treatment, my dear!"

"Better me than Mother. Mother never hurt anyone—she was the nicest person on earth. How could God have allowed such a thing to happen?!"

At this question, the stolid matron's shoulders sagged. To Jana's surprise, she noted that Mrs. Russell's knees were shaking. The soft bosom upon which she had been comforted now heaved with emotion. The older woman groped for her chair, clutching the arm for support. "Oh, oh! I loved her too, my dear," she cried. "I would have tried to save her, too! I never honored your father so much as I did today. The poor man! In that water all by himself trying to save her. Oh, oh!"

Mrs. Russell sank into the chair and pressed her white cotton handkerchief to her face. She wept freely. Embarrassed, Jana averted her eyes. She was surprised by the depth of feeling evinced by her neighbor. For the first time it occurred to her how difficult it must have been for her mother's best friend to give her the awful news. Her heart swelled with feelings of gratitude toward the older woman and she thoughtfully reclaimed her seat.

After a minute or two, Mrs. Russell unabashedly dried her tears and readjusted her suit and hat. "Well, my dear," she said. "Here we are—the two of us together."

"Thank you for telling me the truth, Mrs. Russell."

The older woman sighed. "Sometimes it's best to meet our troubles straight on, like a sailing ship on the ocean," she replied. "Nothing makes for fewer headwinds in the long run than facing the truth at the start. Oh, there might be a bit of choppiness in the beginning, but we'll avoid those storms that would sink us if we put off the bad news for another day."

Jana considered her words. "I do feel better knowing that Mother wasn't alone," she admitted. "That they died together."

"You're very brave, my dear."

"But what shall I do now, Mrs. Russell?"

"Well, Jana, your mother told me you were planning to become a music teacher. There's no reason why you can't pursue that career, if that's what you want to do."

Jana glanced down at her hands. She wasn't sure she would ever feel joyful enough to play the piano again, much less teach music to others. She wished that Henry was here to tell her what to do.

"But there's no need to make any decisions right away," Mrs. Russell continued, kindly. "Take some time to grieve, my dear." A heartfelt pause ensued, as neither woman felt capable of further speech.

The matron broke the silence first. "I always envied your mother, you know," she said, wistfully. "Helen was so lovely, and she had so much life in her! Whenever we went someplace together, everyone wanted to speak with Helen. No one even noticed I was alive."

Jana started to protest, but Mrs. Russell stopped her. "No, no. It's true. But I didn't mind—I was always content just to be with her. No, what I envied most about Helen was her daughter—you. I always wanted a girl to help balance out those three boys of mine. But God never granted my prayers. Years ago, when you were six or seven – not long after your parents moved to town – I promised your mother that if anything ever happened to her and Andy I'd look after you. Of course I thought that day would never come. I know I can never replace your mother. Nobody could ever replace Helen! But I'd like it very much if you would come and live with us, with me and Pappy and Bud, at least for a little while. What do you say to that, my dear?"

The matron's words had been spoken with such earnestness that Jana knew the older woman was speaking from the heart. She recalled how fiercely her mother had always defended Mrs. Russell, even from Jana's own disparagement, and Jana admitted to herself that, until today, she had been blind to the true value of the older woman's character. Now, she understood why her mother had once said to her: "The beauty that Mrs. Russell possesses is of a more permanent nature, like granite."

"I'll even let you collect the eggs," the matron added, in a half-pleading, half-jesting tone.

Jana was deeply touched. "I'd like that. I'd like that very much."

The next thing Jana knew the two women were crying and hugging each other. After a few moments, Mrs. Russell pressed a clean handkerchief into her hand. "Take this, my dear—you might need it. Never underestimate the power of a handkerchief!"

Jana accepted the cotton talisman. "But I've already lost everyone I've ever loved," she said, sadly. "Eleanor, Henry, my parents. Who else do I have to cry for?"

"My dear, is there no one else in the world? Your mother taught me that you need never look far for someone to love. Why, Helen never met anyone she didn't love! When you walk out the door today look around you at the faces you're leaving behind and then tell me if you still feel the same way. You're going to live a good long life, my dear. Just think of all the wonderful new friends that you've yet to meet! Think of all the children who'll need your love."

As Mrs. Russell spoke, the matron unconsciously lifted her hand in an attempt to express the expansiveness of opportunities for unconditional love. Jana followed the older woman's arm with her eyes, gazing beyond the arthritic hand to a shard of May sunlight that had broken through the storm clouds and streamed into the study. She envisioned herself following that beam of light, soaring like a bird out through the open oriel, away from Windmere. But she was no longer a colorful song-bird liberated from a gilded cage—no! She was a little blue barn swallow shooting up into the sky, up, up and away from the dusky depths of the Russells' cavernous barn.

She was free to fly!

Suddenly, a knock at the door interrupted them. Mrs. Russell immediately reverted to her practical, pragmatic self. "Come in!" she called, glancing at her wristwatch.

The door swung inward and Bud stepped carefully into the study. "I gots the truck all loaded, ma'am," he said, shuffling his feet awkwardly. "Nuthin' got wet, neither."

"Thank you, Bud." Mrs. Russell stood up and retrieved her purse. She smiled encouragingly at Jana. "Let's go get your coat and hat, my dear."

Bud approached Jana with hesitant steps. He doffed his red cap. "I'm real sorry fore yore loss, young ma'am. I surely am."

"Thank you, Mr. Suomela."

"Yore Ma was the best wommin I evah met." A sob escaped the hired hand's throat. "Thar ain't no one else like 'er, thet's fore sartin." Bud turned quickly on his heel and exited the study. Jana heard him weeping out in the hall.

Mrs. Russell held out her hand. "Shall we go, my dear?"

When they reached the foyer, Jana saw that the front door was open. Mrs. Baker had assembled all the children out on the front steps. She glanced around the familiar hallway one last time—how she would re-member every detail, every moment, every cherished face at Windmere! Jana took a deep breath, preparing herself as she used to do before step-ping out onto stage. "I'm ready," she declared.

Dr. Ketchum suddenly appeared around the corner, just in time. "Be well, my dear," he said, kissing Jana on the forehead. "Let me know if you need anything. You know where to find me."

Outside in the fresh, rain-washed air, Jana shook hands with the cook and hugged Mrs. Baker, who didn't even attempt to hide her tears. She admonished the Snow Babies to be good, and told Arthur and Suzanne that she expected them to write at least once a week. Then she allowed Bud to help her up into the old Ford pickup. The dark green truck be-gan to roll down the puddled drive, water plashing against the tires and undercarriage. Jana turned around on her knees and waved vigorously at her friends through the back window. She waved until the children and the granite steps and the stately white mansion disappeared from sight. She sighed, and dropped back down into her seat. She surveyed the sunny vista opening up before her eyes. Her old life had ended, but a new life was just beginning.

Chapter 28

The Songbird of Sovereign

May 2014

"Oh, good God—what a terrible tragedy!" I exclaimed. "Your parents were killed in a car accident on the way to bringing you home from Windmere?"

Miss Hastings bowed her head and folded her hands. She was very weak these days, and rarely got out of bed. "God BLESS them! Poor Mother. And poor Father! I never saw him again after he delivered me to Windmere in August of 1941." A tear slipped out from under her translucent eyelids and fell onto the stiff, clothesline-dried sheets.

Her poignant words reminded me of the importance of kindness, forgiveness, and grace. We never know when our 'au revoir' to someone we love will turn out to be an 'adieu'. How easily we forget that death dogs our heels every hour of the day! I made a silent vow to go home and tell Peter that I loved him, and repeat that important declaration daily.

"How long did you live with Grammie Addie?" I asked.

"About four months. In September I started my classes at Plymouth Teachers College. Bud and Pappy took care of the house and my mother's roses until I was graduated, and Addie wrote to me twice a week, just like Mother. I came back here to teach music, and I've been here ever since. Now you know the REST of my story, dahrrrling!"

"It's a remarkable story. I only hope I can do it justice in my book."

She patted my hand. "You'll do a MARVELOUS job, dahrrrling. I have every confidence in you."

I hesitated, not wanting to cause Miss Hastings additional pain but still having a few more questions. "How were you able to carry on? I mean—all those losses!"

She offered a mystical, mysterious smile. "Sometimes the years pass without any losses in our lives, but other times the losses come rushing at us like a freight train. We feel as though we've got no choice but to let the train run us over. But after we get dragged along the tracks for a while we realize that we have the power to stand up, to step off the tracks—to go in the opposite direction, even. Eventually we learn to hope again, to laugh again, and, most importantly, to love again."

"Addie?"

She nodded, misty-eyed. "Mother was my role model; Henry was my inspiration; but Addie was my rock! We carry on because we must carry on, not only for those we love today but also for those we will come to love in the future. By the way, have you heard the WONDERFUL news, dahrrrling?"

"About Wendell and Rebecca expecting? When Leland told me you could have knocked me over with a feather."

"I just knew that Mr. Wendell Emerson Russell had it in him!" she declared. "Although Wendell always *was* a little slow to get started—haaa-haa! I can't wait to tell Addie the GOOD NEWS."

"It looks as though her dream to keep the old place in the family is going to come true. At least for another generation."

"One baby at a time is all it takes! Although it never hurts to have a back-up." As Miss Hastings had been speaking, her frail hands fluttered tremulously like a butterfly's wings. Now she clasped them to her chest and sighed fervently. I knew she needed to rest. Doctor Bart had specifically cautioned me against overexciting her. Still, I had one last important question.

"Did you ever sing again?" I didn't realize until I spoke the words aloud how much I wanted to hear an affirmative answer to that question.

"Well, strictly speaking, no—not professionally, certainly. My vocal chords were horribly scarred by the TB. When I left Windmere I sounded like a cranky frog. But the children never cared about that, and so I always played and sang to them. And every now and then over the years I'd sing one of Mother's favorite tunes, just to remember, you know. Don't tell Doctor Bart," she continued, her voice dropping conspiratorially, "but sometimes I creep into the studio at night—with the lights out so that no one will see me—and I sing a few stanzas of *After the Ball*. That was always my favorite."

"Oh, I'm so glad!" I leaned over and kissed her cheek, which felt dry and cool to my lips.

She fondly patted my hand again. "Goodbye, DAHRRRLING," she whispered. Her eyelids fluttered shut. "Now, go home and give your handsome husband a GREAT BIG hug for me."

"I definitely will," I promised. There was no mistaking the significance of her parting words—I knew they were her final farewell to Peter and me.

Miss Hastings died in her sleep two days later. Lila was with her when she passed. Having sensed that the end was near, Lila had left Claire with Mike and her father-in-law and drove the five hours down from Aroostook County to be with the woman who had made such a difference in her young life. I was glad to hear that Lila was the one who was with Miss Hastings at the end, not only for Miss Hastings' sake but for Lila's sake as well. It was the passing of the baton, of sorts, for Lila encompassed the same effervescent, loving, and fun-loving qualities as Miss Hastings.

Lila called me on my cell just as the sun was rising in the east, splashing liquid gold across the hayfield next to my house. "She's gone, Maggie," she announced sadly. In twenty minutes I was standing with her at Miss Hastings' bedside. As I comforted the younger woman, I glanced over her tall shoulder at the heart-rending sight of Miss Hastings' corpse. We never realize how much the spirit of a person animates her until we see the stiff empty shell left behind when the spirit has flown.

"Omigod, what are we going to do without her?" Lila wailed, tears running down her cheeks.

"We're going to carry on," I pronounced. "Just like she did."

Ryan was the administrator of Miss Hastings' estate, and he immediately took charge of all the details. Miss Hastings had left grateful tokens of affection to all of us who had helped care for her in her final days. In addition, she left her mother's grand piano to the Sovereign Union Church, along with a substantial legacy. She gifted me the beautiful Russian shawl that had been draped over the piano at her birthday bash, and the travelling trunk containing the framed photos of Henry, Helen, Addie and all the rest. As I sifted through the black-and-white photos of the faces with whom I was now so familiar, it occurred to me that Miss Hastings gave away all her worldly goods, but it was her other-worldly goods she also gave away that were most valuable: hope, faith, and love, and the greatest of these was love.

To the surprise of everyone, except Ryan of course, Miss Hastings had bequeathed her house and real estate to Doctor Bart.

"You're joking," I said, when Metcalf told me the news on the Thursday after Miss Hastings died. I was in his office at the clinic in Unity for a follow-up visit, and Ryan had just been down to see him.

"I'd never joke about something like that, Aunt Maggie."

"I guess she wasn't kidding when she said you could have her Seven Sisters rose. She never meant for you to dig it up—she meant for you to have the whole dang garden!"

"I can hardly believe it," he said, shaking his head. I'd never seen Doctor Bart so befuddled. It was a refreshing sight. Maybe there was hope for him yet!

"Did Ryan tell you why she left the place to you? Although it's perfectly understandable," I added, hastily. "Miss Hastings was very grateful for your care. She wouldn't have been able to die at home without you."

"That sounds a bit nefarious, the way you said that."

"I mean, she would have had to go to a nursing home if it hadn't been for you. She never mentioned anything about the place?"

"Not a word. Ryan told me Miss Hastings was worried about my student loans. I remember now that I complained to her once about all the money I owed for my education. We were talking about home ownership, and I told her my generation would never be able to afford our own homes because by the time we got done paying off our student loans the last thing we'd want was to be shackled with the debt of home ownership."

"Be careful what you wish for," I advised. "You might just get it." I tried not to think of Addie's succinct warning about pining unrealistically: "If wishes were horses then beggars would ride."

"Speaking of wishes—have you heard from Nellie, lately?" he asked. His freckled face turned the color of his hair.

Alas, I wished I had better news to tell my hoped-for son-in-law. "She called a week or so ago, just before she left for Argentina," I replied. "She's helping some NGO implement a clean drinking water initiative down there."

Doctor Bart's face fell. "She won't be coming home for Miss Hastings' funeral, then?"

"I'm afraid not, dear. I'm sorry."

He stared out the exam room window. I could tell he was processing this latest disappointment. Metcalf had always been slow, methodical, and thorough. That's one of the reasons I thought he'd make such a good husband for my daughter, who was often blown hither and thither by the latest environmental scare or social movement of the month. Nellie needed an anchor and Doctor Bart could give her plenty of security.

He turned his beseeching hazel gaze back to me. "Do you think she'll ever come home again, Aunt Maggie?"

This question was one I'd asked myself a thousand times since Nellie had left for boarding school. Would my daughter ever come back to Sovereign, Maine? "I don't know—I'm not even sure that she considers this place her home. Maybe she needs someone to show her how much Sovereign means to her?"

"Maybe," he replied, thoughtfully.

Miss Hastings' funeral was held at the Sovereign Union Church on Saturday afternoon. The little white church was filled to capacity with mourners, who crammed into every inch of the pews and spilled down the red carpeted aisle onto the front steps. I kept my remarks to a minimum, touching briefly on her happy childhood, the year at Windmere, and her many decades teaching music in the local schools. I also mentioned how much she had meant to me personally, before opening up the microphone to those who wanted to share their own memories of this Sovereign icon. It was nearly three hours later before I was able to offer the closing prayer.

As I was preparing to depart for the cemetery where Miss Hastings would be laid to rest next to her parents, I was waylaid by an elderly couple. The gentleman's blue eyes twinkled as he introduced himself and his pretty, petite wife. It was Arthur and Suzanne! Miss Hastings had neglected to tell me that the youth with the blond Dutch-boy haircut and sailor collar on his blouse had married the bold-faced little girl who reminded Miss Hastings of her younger self!

"That was a fine job you did, Reverend," Arthur said, enthusiastically shaking my hand. "Jana would have been so pleased."

"Don't be a goose, Arthur," said Suzanne. "She's a minister—she does these things all the time."

"No, this was different, honey, I could tell. You really loved Jana, didn't you, Reverend?"

It was refreshing to hear Miss Hastings spoken of by her given name. "Did anyone who ever knew her *not* love her?" I replied. "By the way, do you know if the Snow Babies came today?"

Arthur and Suzanne exchanged puzzled looks. "The Snow Babies?" Arthur repeated.

Then I realized that the couple had likely not known Miss Hastings' fanciful nickname for the twins. "Bobby and Billy," I said.

"Oh, the twins! They wanted to be here but Bobby just had open-heart surgery. They all knew that Jana would understand their staying together."

"All?"

"Bobby and Billy married sisters," Suzanne clarified. "We're very good friends. They own a hardware store in Manchester. We see them all the time."

Peter approached and took me by the arm. "Excuse me—Maggie, we need to go to the cemetery. The hearse has already left."

I shook hands with Arthur and Suzanne again. "Be sure and come back to the church for the gathering after the committal," I entreated them. "There will be plenty of food and drinks, and I've got a few more questions for you, too."

Departing the church, I spotted Wendell helping an elderly lady into a waiting vehicle. When he closed the car door and turned around, I accosted him. For one reason or another, I hadn't seen Wendell since Leland had sprung the news on me about Rebecca's pregnancy. "So, you're going to join the ranks of all the rest of us tearing our hair out over our kids!" I said, giving him a congratulatory hug. "I'm so happy for you both."

"Wal, you know, I figgered twarn't no worse 'an herdin' chickens."

"Ha, ha! That's *exactly* what raising kids is like—trying to herd chickens!"

Rebecca, who had joined her husband as we were talking, spoke up. "We never gave much thought to birth control," she admitted. "Who knew I could get pregnant at *this* time of life!"

I gave Rebecca a kiss and a hug. "It was meant to be. Grammie Addie would be so pleased."

"Wal, you know, when I come to live with her, Grammie Addie told me I was her ace in the hole," Wendell continued, bashfully. "Mother had jest died, you know, and I thought Grammie Addie was tryin' to make me feel bettah. But I guess she knew what she was talkin' 'bout all along!"

"Maggie, we've really got to go," Peter whispered in my ear, more urgently now.

"Don't worry—they won't start the committal service without me," I said, brushing him off. I had seen a suited up Gray Gilpin and I wanted a word with him. Miss Hastings had left Grayden a substantial contribution to his college fund. I caught up with the gangly youth and congratulated him.

"Only two more months afore I staht school," Gray informed me, wrestling his tie uncomfortably. "I wish she coulda lived long 'nuff to see me graduate."

"She'd be ninety-three by then!"

"My great-granddad was in his nineties when he went off. I thought old people was, like, livin' longah nowadays?"

I sensed that Gray was worried about his grandfather, Ralph Gilpin, with whom he was very close. I gave Gray a reassuring hug. "Don't you worry—your grandfather will live to be a hundred. Your grandmother will see to that! Oh, look! There's Ryan and Trudy, and little Alice Rose. Isn't she adorable?"

"She smells like a baby," Gray sniffed, unimpressed.

I hugged Gray again, and left him to go over and greet the Gorse contingent. I kissed Alice Rose and made a fuss over how much she'd grown since I'd last seen her, which was only about five days ago. "Where's Leland?" I asked, anxiously, seeking my new best buddy's reassuring weathered face amongst the crush of mourners.

"Rite heah," the woodsman replied, popping up from out of nowhere. Leland tugged on the ends of the colorful silk scarf that was keeping the few remaining tufts of hair on my head. He grinned with familiarity bred by mutual approbation. "What's heppened to yer hair, Rapunzel?"

"Careful or I'll come back and haunt you after I'm gone," I admonished him.

"I ain't scairt. I'll be pushing up daisies long afore ya gits theah, Maggie."

This time Peter interrupted us much more forcibly. "Maggie, we've really got to go," he declared, grasping my hand with a grip that I knew wouldn't take "no" for an answer. He pulled me aside, around the corner of the church. "Honey, what's the matter? I know something's wrong."

I burst into tears. "I don't want to say 'goodbye' to her!" I cried. Peter held me while I released my pent-up grief. He patted me on the back, whispering little reassurances in my ear.

As my husband comforted me, I prayed silently to myself. *Dear God, thank you for Miss Hastings! And thank you for allowing me to see the light with Peter!*

An idea about Nellie and Doctor Bart suddenly occurred to me. If I wanted some red-headed grandchildren, I might have to make a bold move to open Nellie's eyes. But this was a convoluted scheme that would require serious contemplation another day. In the meantime, I had a committal service to lead. I searched my purse for a handkerchief or tissue to dry my eyes. "Dang it," I muttered, coming up short.

Rebecca sidled up to me. "Take mine," she said, slipping me Addie's hankie. "Sorry it's a little damp."

We looked at each other. "Never underestimate the power of a handkerchief!" we both proclaimed at the same time.

Peter helped me into the car and we drove the short distance up to the Russell Hill Cemetery where the mourners had regrouped a scant half mile from Miss Hastings' home. From that vantage point on the hill there's a lovely panoramic view of the sprawling settlement that became known as Sovereign, Maine. It was an enchanting May afternoon, the kind of day where one feels grateful to be on this side of the ground. Peter turned into the open gate at the cemetery entrance and drove carefully up the narrow grass lane past a few stragglers. The solemn-looking weathered gray gravestones seemed to salute us as we passed by on the way to the Yaroslavsky plot. When we stepped out of the vehicle, the milling crowd parted and allowed us to pass directly to the open grave. The pall bearers had just lowered the plain wooden coffin into the earthen void, which now awaited only a few words from me before swallowing Miss Hastings forever. I moved to the head of the grave, taking my place in front of her pre-set stone. I reverently faced the crowd, bowing my head, signaling that the committal service was about to begin. I clutched my Minister's Service Book and inhaled deeply. I made another silent prayer asking God to give me the strength to commit Miss Hastings' mortal remains without weeping uncontrollably.

The murmurings died down, and it became so quiet that I could hear the flutter of a bird in a nearby lilac bush. I caught a whiff of the old-fashioned lilacs carried by the light, tantalizing breeze. A sensation of peace stole over my being. I opened my little service book, found the marked passage and glanced up. My eyes rested on the face of a distinguished looking older gentleman who, for some reason, reminded me of Dr. Ketchum, although the good doctor would have been long ago gathered to his ancestors. I made a mental note to ask Arthur and Suzanne what had become of Dr. Ketchum and also Mrs. Baker.

"Dearly beloved," I began. My eyes continued to roam through the sea of mourners, which suddenly separated into smaller waves of faces: Arthur and Suzanne; Doctor Bart; Gray Gilpin and his parents; Wendell and Rebecca; Leland, Ryan and Trudy; and Mike and Lila. Miss Hastings had loved each and every one of these people gathered here today and they had loved her in return. She had been the embodiment of unconditional love. Surely goodness and mercy would follow her for the rest of her life, and she would dwell in the house of the Lord forever!

I concluded the service with the customary and comforting 23rd Psalm, inviting everyone to join in with me. I closed my book and began to recite the well-known words: "The LORD is my shepherd; I shall not want. He maketh me to lie down in green pastures: He leadeth me beside the still waters." I glanced out into the crowd once again and spotted another familiar face, an older woman with short gray curls, wearing a rose-figured apron over her everyday dress.

Addie!

She lifted her hand in a neighborly wave, and glanced down at her wristwatch. It was time for Miss Hastings to go home. I blinked, and Addie was gone.

I bent down, grasped a moist handful of rich Sovereign soil and tossed it into the open grave, formally marking the end of the committal service. Mourners began to file past, paying Miss Hastings their last respects, tossing an assortment of wildflowers on top of her small plain coffin. The line paused briefly as Arthur and Suzanne hesitated at the foot of the retired music teacher's final resting place, whispering to themselves. Suzanne pointed to a matching headstone next to us and whispered once more to Arthur. Curious, I looked over to see what had claimed their attention. A solitary gravestone sprouted up from the burial plot next to Miss Hastings' and when I read the inscription I kicked myself for not having noticed the stone before:

Here lies Henry Graham, born 1920 ~ died 1942, awaiting his eternal love, the Songbird of Sovereign.

Instantly, I knew that the hastily scribbled note on Henry's deathbed had been a request to his father that he be buried in the Russell Hill Cemetery. Judge Graham had kept Henry's promise to Jana and now she had fulfilled her promise to him. She had lived a good long life—a life lived for both of them.

I turned around and for the first time read the inscription on Miss Hastings' matching tombstone. She had written the epitaph herself and it was plain yet powerful:

Here lies the Songbird of Sovereign ~ free at last.

THE END

End Notes

1. p. 21, *"When all the world looks dark and gray..."*, part of an optimistic poem popular in the first half of the twentieth century. The poem was framed and hung over the kitchen sink in the author's home when she was a child. When Jennifer was a teenager, she put the poem to music and sang the little ditty while doing up the supper dishes.

2. p. 111, *"GATHER ye rosebuds while ye may ..."*, from the poem *To the Virgins, to Make Much of Time*, by Robert Herrick (*Hesperides*, 1648)

3. p. 117, "On ne voit bien qu'avec le cœur." (Translation: "One sees clearly only with the heart."), from the book *Le Petit Prince* by Antoine de Saint Exupéry. The book, known in America by its English title, *The Little Prince*, was published in 1943 *after* Helen Hastings' death in 1942 (thus she would not have had a chance to become familiar with this expression which she uses in *The Songbird of Sovereign*).

4. p. 179, *Ha'nts of the Kingdom of Spruce*, one of Holman F. Day's popular poems published in 1900 in his anthology, *Up In Maine*.

Bess Klain – Music Teacher and Inspiration Extraordinaire.
Photo courtesy of the Klain Family.

THE INSPIRATION
BEHIND *THE SONGBIRD*
OF *SOVEREIGN*
– BESS KLAIN

When I was seven years old my grandfather, who was my favorite person in the whole wide world, was diagnosed with colon cancer. Our tight-knit, multi-generational farming family was shocked and our little household was broken up for several months as my mother helped care for him in his final days. My older sister and I were shunted off to Norway (Maine) to live with "Nonie," our other grandmother, with whom we would be attending school. This grandmother was Supervisor of Elementary Education in the Oxford Hills and also a bit of a tartar. We always had to call her "Mrs. Palmer" at school. Upon serious reflection, I calculated that I'd never be happy again. But one day at school when I was moping at my wooden desk feeling sorry for myself the door to our second grade classroom was thrown open and in whirled a dynamo of a woman, no bigger than the biggest boy in our class. It was the music teacher Miss Klain. She had wild black hair, a short skirt, high heels, and the most gleeful unreserved cackle of a laugh that I'd ever heard in New England. The next thing I knew we lethargic kids were whipped into shape, lined up in no particular order, and begun to march around the room behind her—legs flying, arms flailing—singing at the top of our lungs in a musical parade. Ten minutes after Bess Klain stepped into the room I was not only happy but also filled with the joy of being alive.

Later, as a young adult, I had the great good fortune to get to know Bess Klain as a friend, not just as a teacher. When I was twenty-one, I moved in with Nonie (who turned out to be not such a tartar after all), and, sharing my grandmother's daily life, I often felt as though I'd walked into the teacher's lounge at school and caught them all smoking. I chauffeured Nonie and Bess around, taking day trips in the area, often stopping for lunch at Cole Farms in Gray or Goodwin's at the railroad tracks in South Paris. When Bess and some mutual teacher friends came to the house to visit, Nonie broke out her hidden bottle of apricot brandy and served us all aperitifs. I noticed that my grandmother laughed more in Bess' presence than she did with anyone else. Bess had that effervescent effect on everyone. She bubbled over with good humor and cheer. Although she was the eldest of the little group of educators, she pranced through life one step ahead of everyone, one step closer to Heaven, I always thought.

Unfortunately, I was never very musical—I could throw a softball a lot further than I could carry a tune—but Bess discovered early on that I liked to write poetry and short stories. She had the effrontery to ask to read some of the things I'd written, and after she did she pronounced in her "There-can-be-no-other-judgment-about-it!" teacher tone of voice that I was an excellent writer. One day Bess and Nonie put their heads together, and these two little old ladies determined that I was going to be a Great Writer. Since this was my own goal, I was pleased to hear their pronouncement. But the years went by and the rejection slips kept piling up on my wooden desk (albeit a bit bigger desk than the one I had in second grade), yet Bess wouldn't hear of me quitting. "Keep writing, Jennie!" she urged me. "Practice, practice, dahrrrling! You're going to do GREAT THINGS one day. I just know it!"

I did keep going, despite rejections, despite failure, frustration, fear, and all sorts of tear-your-hair-out personal crises. One day, a decade or more after Bess and my grandmother had both gone to claim their Great Reward I asked myself why I didn't just give up writing and get a "real job." My answer? I couldn't quit because, well, because I had begun to believe them! I *was* going to do great things with my writing one day.

When I conceived of the town of Sovereign, Maine as the setting for my novel *Hens & Chickens*, I wondered who would live in this town. I wanted the local folk to be kind and thoughtful, fun-loving and good-humored. I scanned my memory banks for people I'd known in the real world who might belong in Sovereign and naturally Bess Klain sprang to mind. Every town needs a music teacher like her, I decided, and so the character of Miss Hastings was born. I included the musical parade in *Hens & Chickens* because it was such a wonderful memory from my childhood. In addition, Bess had a favorite pet, a canary that my grandmother had raised for her. She named the canary "Socrates" and spoiled it to death. Socrates was sort of Bess' familiar. Instead of a canary, however, I decided to give Miss Hastings a pet chicken, Matilda.

Like Bess Klain, Miss Hastings has turned out to be an extremely popular character. Some of my earliest fans of the series fell in love with her and begged me to write a book about her. Not wanting to disoblige these few loyal fans, I created *The Songbird of Sovereign*.

Jana Hastings and Elizabeth Mae Klain have a lot in common. Both are beloved music teachers who share the same inspiring, joy-filled nature. In addition, the parents of both women did escape persecution in the Old Country and ended up settling their families in small Maine towns where they were warmly welcomed into the community. But after that, their personal histories part ways. Those who knew Bess Klain will instantly realize that this book is not a biography of her life. Bess did not have TB as a child nor did she spend time in a sanatorium. As far as I know, she had a normal, fabulous childhood. (See, *A Niece Remembers*.)

Upon serious reflection now, I think that Bess would be proud of *The Sovereign Series*, and even pleased that I created a character in her image. But if what Plato says is true (or was it Socrates?) that the past is only prologue, I know that I can't rest on my laurels yet. Because Bess and Nonie are probably putting their heads together right now somewhere deciding what I'm going to write next when I finish the final installment of *The Sovereign Series* in 2015. Heaven only knows what that will be! But I'm ready for my next challenge because, after all, I *am* going to do Great Things.

Jennifer Wixson
May 19, 2014
Troy, Maine

p.s. Bess, like Miss Hastings in *The Songbird of Sovereign*, willed upon her death that her grand piano be given to her local church, the First Universalist Church of Norway, Maine.

A NIECE REMEMBERS

BY JOYCE KLAIN WILSON

Elizabeth Mae Klain, born in March of 1902, was the last of the eleven children born to Morris and Rebecca Rose Harkin Klain. Unexpected, she arrived four years after her closest sibling, my father, David Aaron.

When she was in her eighties, Bess told me that my grandmother was not happy when she discovered she was pregnant again. "But now, what would I do without you?" Grandmother said to her. In such a large family the older brothers and sisters were already in their teens and twenties when Bess arrived, some of them married and starting their own families. The day Bess was born in the front room of the upstairs bedroom in the farmhouse on lower Main Street several of her brothers were in bed with the measles in the middle bedroom. They cried to see the new baby, so Grandmother tucked Bess in with them. Bess lived nearly ninety-one years and spent almost four decades with infectious small children during her career as a music teacher in the Norway Public Schools and yet she never caught the measles!

Grandfather was a prosperous farmer who raised horses, cattle, hens, and also grew the hay and grains to feed them. He raised all the family vegetables and fruits as well. Somewhere there is a tiny picture of Bess, maybe five or six years old, holding a hen and grinning mischievously. My father told stories of going berry-picking when they were young, and reported that Grandmother knew all the mushrooms good to eat, often gathering them and making a fine mushroom soup.

In those early years of the 20th century there was no public high school in Norway, just the old three-story yellow building (long gone), known as The Academy. High school diplomas counted about as much as a four year college degree does now. A young man didn't really need high school because the mills and shoe factories promised good steady

261

employment and a far shorter work week than farming did. But our family valued education and when the town bought The Academy and opened its doors for a public high school, the Klain brothers and sisters all enrolled

David, who was the last baby until Bess appeared on the scene, and Bess, both seemed to be treasured by their older brothers and sisters. Ruth Wiles [a friend and fellow teacher] commented to me that Bess was the family princess. She grew up surrounded by love, and that probably affected her character all the rest of her life. She met life with love, joy and laughter, and boundless energy all of her ninety-plus years.

The older brothers and sisters who left home to pursue their lives all came back [to visit]. It seems that they had a strong interest in Bess' development. One sibling purchased an upright piano and another paid for Bess' lessons. Of course there weren't any electronic or even wind up musical players then, and everybody sang. The boys made wonderful harmony, too. As her studies progressed, Bess accompanied her brothers with great verve.

When Bess was a young teen, "The Great War" came along and a flush of patriotism was felt strongly by this first generation American family. Of the eleven children [in the Klain family], seven wore the uniform, including Bess' adored older sister, Esther, a trained nurse who enlisted, became a second lieutenant, and served in combat in France. One brother died, another served as a medic, also in France, and Jack was gassed and wounded by shrapnel in the war.

After the war when she was graduated from Norway High School, Bess was supported by her music teacher who believed in her talent and love of work. Under this teacher's urging, my grandparents decided to send Bess to Boston where an older sister was working. In Boston, Bess attended the Faelton Pianoforte School. She remembered Grandfather driving her in the wagon with her trunk over to the train station in South Paris when it was time for her to catch the train [to Boston]. She told me he wept all the way because he was already missing her so!

After graduating from Faelton—where her graduation recital was a performance of the newly published Rachmaninoff Second Piano Concerto—the family welcomed Bess home. Now all the brothers and sisters were very busy with their own lives, and the parents were coming to the time when they needed care. (One cousin, Uncle Abe's son, assured me that Aunt Bess was "good enough" to pursue a professional career at that time.) Grandfather had the Studio built for her, across the shared driveway, and there she had her own place. I've seen notes that said she valued her privacy, but there never was a hint that she regretted coming home to care for her beloved parents. She offered piano lessons at her Studio and many townspeople remembered the recitals of the students that she produced.

Grandmother Rebecca died in 1940, and Grandfather died in 1941 (from a broken heart, Bess told me, because he missed her so). Now Bess' older brother, Zora, a professor and Dean of Education at Douglas College for Women (part of Rutgers) needed Bess. He was one of the older siblings who had promoted Bess' music lessons. Widowed, Zora had three young children, and they needed care. So Bess packed up and moved to Stelton, NJ where she helped raise these nieces and nephew. She was the church organist there as well.

After World War II, the Zora Klain children became independent, and Bess came home again. She moved furniture into her Studio and took up residence there. Now comes a little conspiracy in which my own Mother, Adeline, Bess' sister-in-law, participated. It was known that the Norway schools planned to hire a music teacher. Bess felt awkward about putting herself forward, so Adeline called the State Superintendent of Schools, saying she was Elizabeth Klain and wanted to apply. Bess had her certificate from Faelton but no college or normal school diploma. They agreed upon an interview date in Augusta, and Bess went to meet this official. He told her it seemed strange to him that her voice was so different in person than it sounded over the telephone! But he certified that she was competent to teach in the public schools, and the rest is the glorious history of Bess' thirty-eight-year career delighting all the children in our Norway schools, laughing with them, singing with them, conducting the choruses, making each one feel special. She knew such fulfillment giving all that love and joy!

Joyce Klain Wilson
Nov. 28, 2013
Bloomington, IN

TB Treatment
in Maine

In the early years of the 20th century, before the advent of antibiotics, Mainers who contracted *Tubercule bacillus* were treated at sanatoriums much like Windmere in *The Songbird of Sovereign*. From 1915 to 1969 the state of Maine operated three public institutions for the treatment of TB: the Western Maine Sanatorium in Hebron, the Central Maine Sanatorium in Fairfield, and the Northern Maine Sanatorium in Presque Isle. The goal of these sanatoriums was two-fold. First and foremost their mission was to segregate the infected from the rest of the general population in order to stem the spread of this communicable "wasting disease." Secondly, the objective was to (hopefully) cure the patient via the "fresh air and rest" approach to treatment, bringing the patient to the point where the disease was in remission. Patients were given regular sputum tests and when they had received two "clean" tests in a row they were declared "sputum free" (although the disease could return, as in the case of both Eleanor Luce and Henry Graham in *Songbird*).

Windmere Sanatorium is a fictitious place loosely based upon the Western Maine Sanatorium in Hebron, which, when it opened in 1904, was only the fourth sanatorium in the United States. The facility was the brainchild of Dr. Estes Nichols, who was said to have visited all the sanatoriums in North America at the time, and from those visits envisioned this sprawling stick-built, farm-based compound on the top of Greenwood Mountain. Originally known as the Maine State Sanatorium, the facility in Hebron accepted only those patients whose prognosis looked promising. Those who were likely to die had to seek other means of treatment. At the Western Maine Sanatorium, patients slept in open-air "sleeping cottages" where they were exposed year-round to the clean, dry (and often cold) Maine air. The Western Maine Sanatorium seems

Western Maine Sanatorium – Hebron, Maine

The Children's Cottage, Western Maine Sanatorium, 1928.
Photo taken by Merle Wadleigh, who was a tuberculosis patient
at the sanatorium 1928-1929. (From the collections of the Maine
Historical Society, courtesy of *www.VintageMaineImages.com.*)

July 4th Parade, an annual event at the Western Maine
Sanatorium. Photo taken by Merle Wadleigh in 1929.
(From the collections of the Maine Historical Society,
courtesy of *www.VintageMaineImages.com.*)

to have been a much more casually run facility than its sister sanatorium in Fairfield, a brick and mortar institution-type sanatorium where the sick were later sent to die. Patients at the farm setting in Hebron were physically healthier than their counterparts in Fairfield, and were able to help produce their own food, including fresh vegetables, eggs, and butter. They also participated in events such as the annual 4th of July parade, which members of the local community often turned out to see. (Some of the "color" for Windmere also comes from the Wallum Lake House, a sanatorium in Burrillville, R.I. When Wallum Lake House opened in 1905, TB was the leading cause of death in Rhode Island.)

Patients often spent a year or more recovering at sanatoriums, and during this time they naturally formed personal attachments with one another. It wasn't uncommon for romantic relationships to bud and then develop, such as what occurred between Jana Hastings and Henry Graham in *Songbird*. In fact, the author's great uncle met his wife at the Central Maine Sanatorium in Fairfield.

With the arrival of antibiotics, however, sanatoriums and their "fresh air" approach to TB treatment became outdated. One by one Maine's three sanatoriums closed their doors (the Central Maine Sanatorium was the last to close in 1969), bringing an end to this unique and remarkable era in Maine history.

For more information visit Maine History Online—the Maine Memory Network, *www.mainememory.net* and check out "Among the Lungers: Treating TB," "San Life: the Western Maine Sanatorium, 1928-1929," and "Estes Nichols' Sanatorium," from which much of this information was taken.

THE SOVEREIGN SERIES
TRADE MARK
I went to Heaven—'twas a small Town—Emily Dickinson

The Sovereign Series is a four-volume work of fiction by Maine farmer, author, and itinerant Quaker minister Jennifer Wixson. The books are set in the mythical town of Sovereign, Maine (pop. 1,048) a rural farming community where "the killing frost comes just in time to quench all budding attempts at small-mindedness and mean-spiritedness." Good-hearted and lovable characters, such as the old chicken farmer Wendell Russell and the town's retired music teacher Miss Hastings, weave in and out of the four novels like beloved friends dropping in for a cup of tea.

Visitors to Sovereign partake in the felicity that abounds in the picturesque hamlet of rolling pastures and woodlots, whether while sharing a picnic at the Millett Rock or wandering with a lover beside Black Brook. Readers, like the residents of Sovereign, become imbued with a sensation much like that described by Ralph Waldo Emerson, a "certain cordial exhilaration ... the effect of the indulgence of this human affection."

Book 1, *Hens & Chickens* (White Wave, August 2012) – Two women downsized from corporate America (Lila Woodsum, 27, and Rebecca Johnson, 48) move to Maine to raise chickens and sell organic eggs, and discover more than they bargained for—including love! *Hens & Chickens* opens the book on Sovereign and introduces us to the local characters, including Wendell Russell, Miss Hastings, the handsome carpenter Mike Hobart, and the Gilpin clan. A little tale of hens and chickens, pips and peepers, love and friendship, *Hens & Chickens* lays the foundation for the next three titles in the series.

Book 2, *Peas, Beans & Corn* (White Wave, June 2013) – The romance of a bygone era infuses Book 2 in *The Sovereign Series* when Maine Army

Guardsman Bruce Gilpin, 35, returns to Sovereign with the secret dream of restarting the town's old sweet corn canning factory. He's aided in his new mission by the passionate young organic foodie Amber Johnson, 21, who reawakens his youthful heart. The course of their true love is muddied by their well-meaning mothers, however, and by the arrival of Bruce's ex-wife Sheila and the handsome corporate attorney Ryan MacDonald, who hits town to rusticate. History pervades this little tale of hummingbird moths and morning mists, horse-drawn sleighs and corn desilkers, and the words of the poet Emily Dickinson, who could have been describing Sovereign when she once wrote: "I went to Heaven – 'Twas a small Town."

Book 3, *The Songbird of Sovereign* (White Wave, July 2014) -- She's the most popular resident of Sovereign, Maine yet no one in this rural farming community of 1,048 souls has ever known the story behind Miss Hastings' seven decades of dedication to schoolchildren. In Book 3 of *The Sovereign Series*, Maggie the town's minister sets out on a quest to plumb the mystery of Miss Hastings' past before the retired music teacher – nearing her 89th birthday and in failing health – departs this world forever. But Maggie has a mystery of her own, a conundrum that might upset the apple cart before she can uncover the rest of Miss Hastings' story! *The Songbird of Sovereign* moves effortlessly back and forth through time, from a poignant first love at a central Maine sanatorium in the 1940s to a merry winter picnic in the present day Maine woods. Two intertwining story lines come together in a stunning and inspiring conclusion.

Book 4, *The Minister's Daughter* (White Wave, August 2015) – Although she is tall, blonde and lovely, Nellie Walker, 22, the daughter of Maggie Walker, minister of the Sovereign Union Church, is also selfish, snobby and vain. When a tragic event leaves Nellie alone in the world, she returns to Sovereign and initiates a desperate search for the father whose identity her mother has never revealed. Helping Nellie through this dark time is the compassionate country doctor, Metcalf Bartholomew Lawson, 29, known locally as "Doctor Bart." Doctor Bart's love for Nellie has long been suspected by her mother, although to date Nellie has exhibited little use for her pedantic suitor, a man more at home among herbs and rose bushes than cityscapes and boardwalks. In this fourth and final install-ment of *The Sovereign Series* Nellie is forced to face and overcome some long-held prejudices and erroneous beliefs. While we sit with Nellie

Walker watching the sun set in Sovereign for the last time, we know that the sun is rising elsewhere with new hope.

The Sovereign Series Cookbook (also coming from White Wave in 2015) – A companion to the novels of *The Sovereign Series*, the cookbook contains recipes for all the mouth-watering foods described in the four books. Included are recipes for Euna's Hot Water Gingerbread, Maude's Rose Petal and Caraway Shortbread Cookies, Miss Hastings' Raisin-Filled Cookies and much, much more. The cookbook also includes tidbits of Maine history and little-known facts about the making of *The Sovereign Series*. The cookbook is compiled by Laurel Wixson McFarland, niece to *Sovereign Series* author Jennifer Wixson.

JENNIFER WIXSON

Maine farmer, author, and itinerant Quaker minister, Jennifer Wixson writes from her home in Troy, where she and her husband raise Scottish Highland cattle. A Maine native, Jennifer was educated at the School of Hard Knocks, and also admits to a Master's degree in Divinity from Bangor Theological Seminary.

You can follow Jennifer's adventures on Twitter @ChickenJen and visit her Facebook author's page for the latest on her writing: *www.facebook.com/Jennifer.Wixson.author.*

For more information on *The Sovereign Series* please visit: *www.TheSovereignSeries.com*

ADVANCE PRAISE FOR THE SONGBIRD OF SOVEREIGN

I read *The Songbird of Sovereign* in one afternoon. I did. I loved it. My plan was to read a few chapters, go on with my day, read a few more chapters later that evening, and so on over the course of a few days. But I could not put the book down!
— *Michelle H., Morganton, GA*

The Songbird of Sovereign is Jennifer Wixson's best effort yet. Weaving like a fine tapestry from the past to the present we discover the incredible life of Jana Hastings, a remarkable soul who could have become bitter due to personal losses she suffers early in life but who chooses instead to rise above her grief and share unconditional love with those around her. This is not only a touching love story, but also a tale of faith, community, and fellowship.
— *Adeline W., Dover, NH*

I loved the book's poetry, the descriptions of the "real" farm-to-table food, the quiet determination and loyalty of friends and family that we all crave. As a novel, *The Songbird of Sovereign* stands on its own, although having read the two prior books added to my depth of understanding of the characters.
— *Lucinda H., Longboat Key, FL*

ADVANCE PRAISE FOR
THE SONGBIRD
OF *SOVEREIGN*

Miss Hastings' mysterious past comes to life in this story of love and devotion, in a beautiful tribute to teachers ... My only complaint with *The Songbird of Sovereign* is that now I'll have to find another book to read on the beach this summer since I've already read the one that everyone else will be reading!
– *Sue S., Wells, ME*

Not many books move me to tears ... but this one did!
– *Carrol P., Fairport, NY*

Wonderfully written, *The Songbird of Sovereign* captures the past and present life of the town's matriarch with such compassion, love and humor that you automatically fall in love with Miss Hastings ... Jennifer Wixson pulls you into the story to the point where you cry when the characters cry, and laugh when they laugh. This book is a charming piece of Maine history. I had a hard time putting it down and can't wait for the next book in the series.
– *Tanji S., Hooksett, NH*

Reading *The Songbird of Sovereign* is like spending time with old friends ... The descriptions are so vivid I can almost hear the chickens and smell the fresh baked bread."
– *Carolyn M., Bangor, ME*